Alaska Blaze

The Blazing Hearts Wildfire Series

LoLo Paige

Dedicated to the memory of all wildland firefighters who have paid the ultimate sacrifice, and to those who continue to risk their lives to protect people, property, and natural resources from the destructive force of wildfire in North America and around the world.

And to Marc Simenson, the love of my life, also a former wildland firefighter, who encouraged me to keep writing and helped me create this story.

Praise for the novels of LoLo Paige

"The strong women and smoking hot men who fight wildland fire, written by a lady who knows from personal experience. The books in this series are fiery page-turning reads."

—*Kat Martin, New York Times bestselling author*

"This series is cinematically plotted in spectacular, dangerous settings with a smoldering passion where fire isn't the only heat!"

—*Cherry Adair, New York Times bestselling author*

"*Alaska Spark* is a feel-good love story, adventurous setting, and invigorating action combine to create a fresh romance novel that features a strong-willed yet troubled heroine, who the reader can't help but root for." —*Publishers Weekly Booklife Prize*

"*Alaska Inferno's* many storylines create a maelstrom of excitement. The poems bookending the narrative show its literary foundation. With a hopeful and happy conclusion, Paige successfully crafts a romance replete with adventure, whodunit intrigue, and art to suit many tastes. Paige's *Alaska Spark* was a 2021 Eric Hoffer Book Awards as an ebook fiction honorable mention."

—*U.S. Review of Books*

"Lolo Paige writes very satisfying romances while incorporating details that bring alive the challenges of fighting forest fires in the remote Alaskan wilderness as only someone who has been there, done that could write. —*U.S. Amazon Review*

Alaska Blaze

Blazing Hearts Wildfire Series, Book Three

USA Copyright © 2023 by LoLo Paige

U.S. Copyright Registration No. TX 9-289-823

First published by Avoca Press Publishing 2023

ISBN 978-1736095133

This is a work of fiction. Though based on actual events in an actual setting, it is an imaginary story. The author has taken artistic license with details regarding locations and wildland firefighting activities for the story to flow smoothly and has made every attempt to make the technical aspects of the story as accurate as possible. Any resemblance to actual persons, living or dead, is entirely coincidental.

Cover Design by Bookbrander

Edited by The Word Slayers and S. R. Cyres

Poem, "Side By Side" by former Alaskan S. R. Cyres, with permission of S. R. Cyres

Wildland Fire Terms

AFS: Alaska Fire Service, located at Fort Wainwright, in Fairbanks, Alaska. The Alaska Fire Service is a branch of the U.S. Bureau of Land Management that takes the lead on wildland fire suppression for the northern half of Alaska.

After Action Review: A discussion of what went right and wrong while fighting a fire, resulting in lessons learned and how they'll be applied in the future.

Alphalicious: One who takes charge with a confidence that others admire and find attractive.

Anchor point: The point where firefighters begin fireline construction.

BLM: U.S. Bureau of Land Management, in the U.S. Department of the Interior, who employs federal firefighters in several states.

BOLO: Be on the Look-Out. A term mostly used in law enforcement but also used in fire.

Brown bear vs. grizzly: Though classified as the same species, in Alaska, brown bears are mainly coastal, while grizzlies occur mostly in Alaska's Interior.

Containment: A fire is contained when it's surrounded by a fireline, where trees and brush are removed, robbing the flames of fuel. Fires can jump containment if wind-driven.

DOF: State of Alaska, Division of Forestry. Lead agency for wildland fire suppression for the southern half of Alaska.

Demobe: Short for demobilization when crews and individuals are released from a fire.

Flank: The two side boundaries of a fire roughly parallel to the main direction of spread.

Head: The leading edge and most rapidly spreading part of a fire.

Incident Command System: A standardized on-scene emergency management system all entities use without jurisdictional boundaries. The IC, or Incident Commander oversees all of it.

JBER: (pronounced J-Bear) Joint Base Elmendorf–Richardson is a United States military facility in Anchorage, Alaska. It's a consolidation of the United States Air Force's Elmendorf Air Force Base and the United States Army's Fort Richardson.

LCES: Four critical things a wildland firefighter must always have while fighting an active fire: Lookouts, communication, escape routes, and safety zones.

Mop-up: The process firefighters use to extinguish and remove burning debris after an area has burned. Firefighters often cold-trail soil, feeling for still burning hot spots.

NIFC: The National Interagency Fire Center in Boise, Idaho, consists of nine federal and state agencies who establish wildland fire policy. They also provide nationwide logistical support with people and equipment for wildland firefighting.

Pulaski: A long-handled chopping and trenching tool used in fireline construction. The tool has an axe blade on one side, and a hoe-like blade on the other.

SIDE BY SIDE

Hoping daylight will breathe
new life where greed betrays
and burning hunger feeds,
run through the night and day.
Adventure by your side
fired by love and pride,
gives me a second wind to
run through the night and day.
Flee from a smoking fate;
save me before it's too late.
Flee burning bush and tree
side by side; don't betray me.
– S. R. Cyres, 2021

Chapter 1

Eagle River, Alaska

The last thing Raynie Atwood expected while fighting a vicious wildfire on Hiland Mountain was a brown bear barreling straight at her on a dead run.

Unfortunately, she didn't have time to negotiate with deadly claws and teeth. Her options were to drop and play dead or swing the hoe-end of her long-handled tool at the bear's broad head, hoping to buy time to get away.

Adrenaline pulsed through Raynie's neck as she chose to whack the bear.

Head down, ears back, the massive bruin snarled as she raised her Pulaski high to knock out the bruin's lights. But the bear unexpectedly veered to the right and bulldozed through the dry foliage like it wasn't there.

Two bawling bear cubs followed. Great, a sow and cubs.

Her throbbing pulse beat like a bass drum on the back of her skull. It wasn't uncommon to see panicked animals fleeing from a fire, but a mother bear with cubs was a definite pucker factor. Huffing into smoke-filled air, she slowed her racing pulse and willed her heart to stop knocking around.

She'd live to fight fire another day.

A shower of sparks and ash gusted up at her. Tall flames erupted like lava a short distance away, devouring a mature stand of beetle-killed spruce—dining on it like an enraged dragon with an insatiable appetite.

This was her first time as an incident commander in charge of containing the Hiland Mountain Fire—and by God, she was going to succeed. Two twenty-person crews under her command depended on it.

Convective heat rushed at her like a blast furnace. She pulled the hand-held radio from her chest harness. "Twin Peaks and Eagle River Hotshots, this is Atwood. Change position. Retreat to Hiland Road," she instructed into her radio.

"Copy that," an unfamiliar voice replied.

Raynie wondered who that was—she knew everyone on her state hotshot crew. Sounded like that federal crew supervisor who'd countered every word she'd said about fire suppression strategy in this morning's briefing.

Shouts hit her ears as she scrutinized the flames racing up the timbered mountain. She shot a nervous glance down the glacial river valley, wild and dramatic as any in Alaska, yet close to the town of Eagle River and city of Anchorage.

Houses dotted both sides of the road in this Eagle River subdivision, and it wouldn't be long before the flames hurtled up to meet them. Even knowing the fire danger, people loved living at the edge of wilderness. Hiland Road led to spacious homes above the timberline, and one prominent house at a high elevation drew her attention.

"We'll lose that home up there if the retardant ship doesn't get here soon," she grumbled, eyeballing a sprawling home surrounded by dried out spruce and thirsty birch. She anxiously scanned the sky for planes.

It seemed like hours before her radio crackled. "Atwood, this is Air Attack from the State DOF, Department of Forestry. The mud drops you ordered are on their way. The first retardant ship is wheels-up and on its way from Palmer. ETA in five minutes."

Good. I can always count on the State of Alaska, Department of Forestry, to help save the day.

"Copy that. Standing by."

Relieved, she sprinted uphill to the paved road with fire engines strewn along it. The state and federal fire crews had gathered, waiting for her direction. "I've ordered mud drops," she called out. "Move the vehicles further up the road so they don't get blitzed with slurry."

The city engines were already rolling uphill, out of harm's way as firefighters piled into the rest of the fire engines.

A tall, blond firefighter in a blue hardhat stepped forward. He lifted his goggles up onto his hat.

"If we move the vehicles further up, we won't be able to access them once the fire jumps this road."

Raynie lifted her goggles and noted the name on the left side of his yellow Nomex shirt. *Cohen Tremblay, Crew Supervisor.* Above the pocket was the blue-green triangle logo for his federal agency.

Typical for the feds to question a state directive, she thought to herself.

The guy stood, hands on hips, drilling her with a displeased stare.

Here we go. Another fire boss who thinks I'm an incapable airhead.

"If we take them *down* the road, we won't get hoses to the flames," she said, with an air of authority.

He tilted his head to the side, squinting at the flames racing up the slope. "Hose won't reach from up there either."

"We'll have gravity on our side," countered Raynie, lowering her goggles over her eyes. She called out to the fire crews. "Vehicles are to move up, not down. Everyone go!" She gave the blond dude a *so there* look, then about-faced and stepped back to her vantage point.

"You're making a tactical mistake," he called after her, then headed to his U.S. Bureau of Land Management truck.

Raynie glanced at the hung jaws of the firefighters within earshot, irritated they'd witnessed this exchange. And because she had to have the last word, Raynie strode over and leveled her gaze at the federal firefighter sitting in his truck.

"I know this area. I've predicted this fire's behavior. And need I remind you, this isn't a federal show." She flashed him a sardonic smile.

"They warned me about you state people," he drawled, his elbow hanging out the window. He said "aboot" instead of "about"—a dead giveaway he was from the country next door.

"You feds are the worst—you always waltz into a state-run fire telling us what to do!" This guy was something else. It was hard to remain professional when all she wanted to do was cuss him out for obstruction.

"That's not altogether true. Not always." A corner of his mouth twitched.

He thinks this is funny?

She pivoted and stormed off. No way would she give him the satisfaction of turning around to watch him peel off, despite his leaving a cloud of dust for her to choke on.

Ben, a crewmate on her hotshot crew, sidled over. "A fed *and* someone from Outside."

"Figures. The ones from outside of Alaska think they're the experts. Damn the feds anyway!" she sneered. "You'd think they'd know how we handle wildland fire suppression in southcentral Alaska by now."

"Canadian accent," said Ben. "He's a cheechako."

"Yeah, I got that," seethed Raynie, wishing she could shove his federal logo where it would never be seen again.

The familiar drone of a Twin Aero Commander engine grew louder.

"Here comes the drop!" she warned. "Everyone, get clear." She moved to a rocky outcrop and lifted her radio. "DOF Air Attack, hit the fire's leading edge below Hiland Road. Hit that first. Then aim a load on the left flank to prevent it from reaching our vehicles."

"Copy that. Thanks for clearing vehicles and firefighters," said the pilot of *Bird Dog*, the lead spotter plane, who ensured all was safe for the air tanker to drop the load.

"We've got this." He dipped a wing, then banked, circling back to the lower valley to lead the Dash 8-400AT air tanker to the drop site.

"Let her rip, boys!" Raynie studied the billowing yellow smoke on Hiland Road to ensure all the fire traffic had cleared.

A figure emerged from the smoke, like something out of a disaster movie.

She groaned. *Well, if it isn't Mr. Congeniality.*

"Need any help?" Tremblay moved to her position, radio in hand.

"Do I look like I need help?" she challenged him.

"Heard you on the radio." He pointed up Hiland Road. "There's a better overlook up there where you'll have a better visual on the drops."

She glanced up to where he pointed. "You don't say. Okay," she said primly, refusing to thank him. She didn't reward arrogance.

Tremblay stepped off the road, parting alder bushes to cut through the brush. He led the way to a bluff, thick with fireweed buds.

She twisted foam plugs into her ears as the roar of the turboprop engines signaled delivery of the scarlet mixture of phosphates, sulfates, and water. Firefighters called it mud, slurry, or Phos-chek, depending on who was talking.

Tremblay grinned in wonder and admiration as the air tanker approached. "This part never gets old. We use these same airships in Canada."

"Where in Canada?" She stayed guarded, eyes glued to the long sleek red and white aircraft, slowing to one hundred twenty-five knots to make the drop.

"The British Columbia Wildfire Service. Kamloops Fire Center."

"Oh." She was familiar with the B.C. Wildfire Service. Alaskan firefighters held them in high regard after working with them on some nasty fires. But no way would she tell *him* that.

The Dash 8-400 aimed for a center drop on the leading edge of the fire. The incoming retardant ship slid its door open. A billowy red cloud cascaded, settling on the burning spruce like a cerise quilt. Her take on the whole thing...when Phos-Chek gel met with flame, it sounded like cheese crisps frying in oil.

Tremblay stood wide-eyed, as if seeing this for the first time.

"I've always thought of slurry drops as performance art in the sky. It's a pyrotechnic aerial painting, the way the plane paints the sky crimson...then wafts down to smite the orange monster."

She did a double take and snorted. "Never thought of it that way."

This walking Wikipedia reminded her of a coffeehouse poet. She sized him up...early thirties. Educated. Arrogant. Probably from a moneyed family.

He pointed. "Watch when he cuts loose the second load—like a chemical ballet that pirouettes gracefully to the ground. Tell me that isn't Monet in the sky."

She pulled back and gaped at him, as if he'd flown from Uranus on a unicorn. *Works of art?* To her, mud drops were just another tool in the wildland firefighting arsenal.

"Yeah, right." She turned away and crossed her eyes at the trees.

This guy's plane isn't firing on all cylinders.

The flames slowed their advance toward Hiland Road, just as she'd expected. She radioed the firefighters to keep a steady stream of water on the flames to prevent them from reaching the homes.

"What's your Plan B if the mud doesn't work?" Tremblay crossed his arms as he leaned against a birch, tilting his head to stare down at her—still with the same air of superiority as he had in that morning's fire briefing.

Irritated, she pointed at the obvious. "Don't need a Plan B. Obviously, this worked." She said it with pride. In her view, the state aerial firefighting fleet was one of the best in Alaska.

"So, no Plan B *or* Plan C?" Tremblay said in a condescending tone she didn't appreciate. His eyebrows climbed higher with every question.

"Think I've never done this before?" It annoyed her that he was treating her like she didn't know what she was doing. *Egotistical jerk.*

The retardant ship returned, engines vibrating her chest as the plane lined up for a second drop. When the tanker cut loose with its second load, the slurry looked more like a reverse firework display—not a Monet. Frankly, all she cared about was that the Phos-chek gel slowed the flames.

"Atwood, this is Air Attack. Me and the *Bird Dog* are returning to base for a refill. Holler if you want more," radioed the tanker pilot in his deep, throaty voice. "You know where to find me."

"Thanks, Kipp." She wondered if this was a subtle invitation. Her lips curved into a smile. "We could use a couple more drops to ensure these homes don't burn. I enjoy watching you paint the sky crimson," she gushed.

"Copy that," Kipp rumbled back, his voice tingling her.

Tremblay's intent look pierced the distance between them. "Hey, you stole my line! You always flirt with Air Attack?" There was a critical tone in his voice, his words prickling her like a thousand spruce needles.

Raynie recoiled. "I did no such thing! Kipp and I are good friends. Everyone knows that." She'd appreciated Kipp helping her after her fiancé died, by offering her a place to live in exchange for taking care of his brother's sled dog kennel. But this guy didn't need to know that.

"Oh. I get it. That thing about Alaska being a small town," said Tremblay, adjusting his hardhat and goggles.

"And Canada's not? We like our cozy isolated world," she fired back, eyeing the fire behavior below them.

"More like a fishbowl here, if you ask me." His condescending tone was getting old.

"Well." She shot him an icy glare that could freeze the sun. "I didn't ask you, now did I?"

"Why do I have this feeling I rub you the wrong way?"

"Hmm...let me think..." Raynie pressed her lips together to emphasize her point. "Could it be you questioned my directive in front of my crews?" she challenged him, one eye on the flames below where they stood.

"That bothered you?"

She stiffened. "Hell yes, it bothered me. It was bad form. How would you feel if I questioned your decisions in front of your crews while fighting a fire?"

"I didn't counter your directive. I merely pointed out the obvious." His patronizing tone was now front and center on her nerves.

Raynie tamped back her inner lioness wanting to claw out this guy's eyeballs.

"You could have pulled me aside to talk to me privately."

His eyes gleamed with self-assurance. He seemed to enjoy her derision. "People might talk."

Was this interloper full of himself or what?

"Oh, please. Has anyone told you how vain you are? Yeah, just like the song." She blew out air. "I could interpret your remark as sexist. Which, as you *should* know, is inappropriate." She crossed her arms. "But I'm in a good mood today, so I won't."

His hands flew up in a stop motion. "I was joking. Don't jump to conclusions."

They stood, exchanging intense glares until wisps of smoke drifted up to them.

The sooner she got away from this clown, the better.

Chapter 2

Tremblay's piercing blue gaze resembled the crystalline hue of a glacier, tossing Raynie's equilibrium off balance.

Why do the jerks of the world have the loveliest eyes?

Raynie looked away and straightened. "I have a fire to contain." She pushed off from the massive boulder she'd been leaning on.

"Whatever you say, Incident Commander." A corner of Tremblay's mouth lifted. *Was that a smirk?*

She narrowed her gaze. "Don't patronize me."

He gave her an innocent look. "I wouldn't do that. Especially on a fire."

"Well, see that you don't." She issued him a haughty look, then strode toward Hiland Road, talking on her radio. "This is the IC. Bring the vehicles back and start hose-lays ASAP." It pleased her that the mud drops had calmed the flames enough for crews to construct a line around the fire.

"Copy that. On our way," responded the Twin Peaks crew boss.

"Nice working with you, Raynie." Tremblay tapped a farewell on his hardhat and set off to retrieve his truck.

"Wish I could say the same." His presumptuous use of her first name in the guise of being friendly further irritated her. She insisted on Atwood when she worked fires, to evade the merciless jokes that she was the daily weather forecast.

She studied his easy gait and brawny backside in his yellow shirt and forest green pants. Some guys rocked their yellow and green Nomex, and she infuriated herself in thinking this one did.

He's still a jerk, she thought stubbornly.

He'd questioned her decision in front of the crews, and it still irked her. Was she overly sensitive as a petite woman in a mostly male work environment? *Or am I tense around all men in general because each one reminds me of Taydon?*

A sudden crash in the alder stuttered her heart. This time, a young moose burst through the brush. The gangly male trotted across the dirt road, ignoring her, then leaped into the woods.

How many more jolts could her heart withstand today? It was one thing to face a charging bear, but a terrified moose could stomp her to death. Yet that was the world of wildland fire. Expect the unexpected when fighting wildfires in Alaska. Her goal was to work her way up to a chief of operations job. She preferred having her own country to rule, but for now, she'd settle for inching her way up the wildland fire ladder—glass ceiling be damned.

She stepped back to observe the well-trained crews do their level best to contain this blaze by streaming water down from the road, to prevent families from becoming potentially homeless.

This was her mission, her game. And she loved it. Her gaze rested on the tall blond Canadian as he supervised his federal Aurora Crew with their hose-lay operation. She grudgingly had to admit he'd trained them well. Not a slacker on the crew.

Maybe I was too hard on him. But I can't have him questioning my authority.

Fire bosses encouraged firefighters to question decisions regarding safety. As the state IC on this fire, it was her decision to move the fire trucks up the mountain, not Tremblay's. It wasn't her nature to make reckless decisions. Her bosses knew that, and it was why they made her the incident commander of this fire.

Cohen Tremblay might have one of the more fetching derrieres on this mountain, but she'd likely not run into him again this fire season. He and his Aurora Crew were based at the Alaska Fire Service in Fairbanks, and that was fine by her.

Just as the flames settled lower, Raynie noticed clouds slide over the valley. The predicted rain was late to the party, but she hoped it would kill the fire.

A high-pitched whine from the alders below caught her attention. Sounded like a whimpering dog. She crept toward the sound and parted the alder bushes. Two of the most adorable coyote pups huddled inside the alder bush, staring up at her. One was yipping for all it was worth. They didn't seem old enough to be weaned. Mother coyote was nowhere around.

Raynie eased toward the pups. She didn't want them to run, though they were small and likely wouldn't get far.

"I'll create a distraction so you can grab them," said a quiet male voice behind her. Tremblay had popped up right when she needed help.

She nodded. "Sure. Thanks."

He stepped around her and made a sound like a whimpering puppy. The pups homed in on it, and Raynie scooped them up with her leather-gloved hand in case they chomped on a finger.

"I have a cardboard box in the back of my pickup. We'll put them in it, and I'll take them to Wildlife Rescue," he volunteered.

"I'll deliver them," she assured him.

"I can drop them off," he insisted.

This was *her* fire, *her* responsibility. "Nope. I'll do it," she said stubbornly.

He studied her for a moment, tilting his head, irritating her. *Taydon used to do that.* "You should learn to delegate."

"I know how to delegate." She flicked her eyes at him, then turned her attention back to the pups, checking each one for injuries. "Our crews contained the fire and are mopping up. The trucks aren't painted red with slurry because I delegated."

"You're right." He paused, studying her.

She lifted her chin in surprise. "Excuse me, did I hear you correctly? Now I'm right?"

"You made a gutsy decision." His manner was business-like, and she welcomed his admission, but now he confused her. *He thinks I did the right thing?*

"Then why did you question it?"

"Wanted to see if you trusted yourself enough to stick to your decision." She gauged him to see if he was serious. He was.

"Who are you, the wildfire CIA? Do you slink around doing secret performance evaluations?" She regarded him with a cool look. "Let me lay it out, crystal clear for you. In the future, if we ever meet up on a fire, don't question my orders in front of my crews." She said it in a non-threatening, casual tone.

His brows shot up. "Copy that, loud and clear." To his credit, he didn't return fire. "Now let me get you that box."

She'd expected push-back and was somewhat surprised when he didn't give her any.

Tremblay hauled the empty box to her state rig. He tossed a scruffy hand towel into the box and helped her lower in the pups. One whimpered, while the other gave them a wide-eyed stare.

Raynie lifted the box onto the passenger seat, and then turned to him. "Thanks."

He gave her a plaintive look. "Do you believe I undermined your authority on this fire?"

She shrugged. "Didn't you?"

"I was only pointing out the obvious."

"Which was?" She furrowed her brow.

"Where to position our fire vehicles."

"Why are you dogging me about this?"

"Because you'll have to list the basis for your decision in your after-action report," he said matter-of-factly.

"I'm more than prepared to do that." She lifted her chin. "So, Grasshopper, what other words of wisdom wilt thou bestow on me today?"

He tilted his head, upping the ante on her annoyance. "You have a combative nature, you know that?"

"Pot. Kettle. Black. What's your point?"

"You always answer a question with a question? You just asked four questions in a row." He crossed his arms. "Good avoidance tactic. They teach you that in state fire training?"

"Bite me!" she flipped back at him. "I don't avoid anything." Enough of this shit. She was dog-tired and wanted to flop on her couch with the remote. "I have to get these pups to an animal rescue facility."

He gave her a slow smile. "Then have a safe fire season." He strolled off and called over his shoulder, "Make good choices, Raynie Atwood."

"Thanks for the brilliant advice. And...for your help," she forced out, the words stinging like sour lemons on her tongue.

Raynie stared after him, her blood on a low simmer. *Why did these irritating men have the most fabulous asses?* She scolded herself for even thinking it.

Yawning, she climbed into her vehicle, spiraling down from the adrenaline-fueled fire fight. It was 10:30 p.m. by the time she pulled onto the Glenn Highway toward Palmer. The sun teased the mountaintops like a jokester, deceiving everyone below into thinking it was earlier than it was. She loved this time of year in Alaska: there was no such thing as "get there by dark."

She shrugged her shoulders in relief. She'd commanded her first fire, and her state agency declared it a success. Her boss, Elmore Perry—everyone called him Morrey—texted congratulations for a job well done.

A good day by fire standards.

But her grief at losing Taydon was still fresh. Raynie couldn't drive this road without tears. She'd been robbed of the love of her life five months ago on this same highway. When the Alaska State Troopers had appeared on her doorstep in Anchorage, her world had collapsed. Taydon had disappeared forever, in a matter of seconds. The blink of an eye.

Just. Gone.

She swiped at her cheeks and glanced sideways at the box in the passenger seat. Both coyote pups were sound asleep. She reached inside her fire shirt and lifted the necklace with the silver heart she wore next to her own. Her thumb traced the curve of a flame with "R+T" engraved on one side.

More tears fell. The highway blurred.

She pulled over onto the shoulder and shifted into park. Sobs burst out in a torrent, waking the sleeping pups. They sat up and stared, as if understanding. She wished they did. She could use a shoulder to cry on right now.

"Sorry, guys," she choked out, wiping her ash-smeared cheeks with the sleeve of her sooty fire shirt. "Get a grip, Atwood," she muttered to calm herself, although the crying jags had control of her.

"Taydon, why did you leave me?!" she yelled at the windshield, her fist hitting the steering wheel, inadvertently honking the horn. They'd gone to high school together, planned their futures together. Raynie was in Alaska because of him.

He was my best friend and soulmate, dammit. You don't get two in a lifetime.

A pup whimpered, and she glanced over. "It's okay, little ones. I'm getting you to your new home."

When her sobs calmed, she sucked in a deep breath and pulled onto the Glenn Highway to the Wildlife Rescue Center outside of Palmer. After delivering the coyote pups, she drove to the cabin she was taking care of for the sled dog musher.

Her phone pinged a text notification from her boss, Morrey: *Have a new temporary duty assignment for you at the new state wildfire base in Talkeetna...to help organize the new fire base. A positive change of pace?*

Her brows raised. It would be closer to home, and she'd get to meet more state fire people. She texted back: *Sure, if it's temporary, I'll do it. Still want to get out with my state fire crew, though.*

Morrey responded: *In that case, report to Dave Doss at the Talkeetna Wildfire Base first thing tomorrow morning.*

Well, how about that? *Didn't see this one coming. Who knows, it might turn out to be fun.*

Raynie blew out a lungful of air, shifted the truck into gear, and pulled out onto the Parks Highway toward Sleeping Lady Kennel, near Talkeetna.

Chapter 3

Cohen mulled over Raynie's behavior as her truck disappeared down Hiland Road. Despite her beauty, she seemed temperamental and defensive. Was that her usual behavior? He'd never know, since the chances of him ever seeing her again were slim. Too bad, too. Despite her fiery personality, she seemed like a person to know.

He'd worked with lots of women in wildland fire, including training and supervising an all-woman crew in Canada. He prided himself on his ability to get along with people, regardless of gender. He'd dated a few women in wildland fire, but no genuine relationships ever came of it—except for Deanna, a smokejumper from Missoula he met on a fire the season before last.

He'd tried dating Liz last year when they crewed together, but that fizzled, so he wasn't interested in mixing work and romance again.

"Hey, Tremblay," Nick Rego called out, after the rest of the Aurora Crew had stowed their firefighting equipment in the vehicles. "Are we officially demob'ing?" Rego rolled his toothpick to the other side of his mouth.

"Yep. The state incident commander has assigned mop-up crews to finish up now that we contained the fire," he responded, accepting the stick of gum Rego offered.

Cohen's phone pinged a notification, and he glanced at a text from Tara Waters, the Aurora Crew supervisor. He'd filled in for her on this fire, because she'd caught a flu bug a few days ago and couldn't be dispatched to the Hiland Mountain Fire with her crew.

"Good," said Rego. "We should get started on our six-hour drive up to Fairbanks."

Cohen raised his phone. "We're only driving an hour and a half...to Talkeetna."

"What? Why there?" asked Rego as the rest of the Aurora Crew gathered around. "There's no federal fire base there."

"Dave Doss has reassigned us to the newly constructed State of Alaska Talkeetna Wildfire Base, to help the state folks finish things and prepare for the fire season," explained Cohen.

"I like our federal fire boss. He dishes out sweet assignments," McKenzie Quinn chimed in. "I've not been to Talkeetna." The tall, lean Aussie had joined the Aurora Crew in Fairbanks last fire season in a firefighter exchange with Canberra, Australia. Cohen admired her solid capability as a firefighter.

He glanced around the crew. "Good. Glad you're open to this. Not that we have a choice. Doss is returning the favor to the state for helping us with our fire fights near Denali Park last season. Tara will meet us in Talkeetna. She's driving down from Fairbanks to help us get situated."

Liz Harrington spoke up. "We should get something to eat before we hit the road. We're all famished. There's a good Mexican restaurant in Eagle River."

"Great idea. It's enchilada o'clock!" shouted Rego, rubbing his belly. "Lead the way."

Stomachs growling, the Aurora Crew climbed into their vehicles to drive down Hiland Road towards town.

WHEN COHEN ARRIVED at the Talkeetna Wildfire Base the next morning, he opened the screen door and inhaled the aroma of fresh-brewed coffee, sawdust, and newly painted walls.

"Hey stranger, good to see you!" Tara greeted him, her auburn hair smoothly pulled back in its usual, long ponytail. "Thanks for coming in an hour early before the crew reports to work."

He nodded, grinning. "Sure. Feeling better?"

"I finally got over the virus." Tara pointed to one end of the rectangular building. "Come on back to the conference room. Dave Doss has a proposal for a new assignment." Tara led him to a spacious room where a silver-haired man scribbled in a notebook.

Cohen's curiosity increased with every step. He'd enjoyed supervising the Aurora Crew on the Hiland fire. Now, what did they have in mind for him?

Doss peered over his cheaters. "Hey, Cohen. Thanks for coming today."

He took a seat across from Doss, and Tara sat next to him. "Good to see you, Dave."

Doss leaned forward with folded hands on his notebook. "As you know, our fire seasons have been intensifying in recent years in Southcentral Alaska, where much of our population lives. It's a growing concern."

Cohen cleared his throat. "The NIFC prediction center says Alaska is hotter and drier than usual. We're in for another active fire season after last year's record number of lightning strikes."

Doss scratched his nose. "Both the State of Alaska and the federal fire suppression agencies need to bolster our specialized ground resources. The Alaska Fire Service wants to qualify the Aurora Crew as a hotshot crew. That's where you come in. We want you to help us do it."

"Yes, but with all due respect, why me?" Cohen shot a glance at Tara, who nodded.

"Because of your leadership and training crews on fire," said Doss. "We've talked to your former employer in Kamloops at the B.C. Wildfire Service."

Cohen stiffened. He'd had a run-in with a misogynistic fire boss there. "And?"

"They said you did the Canadian equivalent of hotshot firefighting and leading crews on major project fires." Doss smiled. "And you're good with people, having trained firefighters in Canada."

"They said that, huh? That I'm good with people?" This amused Cohen.

Doss sat back in his chair. "They also said you put your crew ahead of yourself, although you're opinionated. But you listen, weigh decisions, and know how to compromise."

Tara chimed in. "Not to mention your stellar evaluation from the last fire season."

Cohen's cheeks warmed at their accolades.

"We'll raise your pay grade and make sure you have the support you need," said Doss. "Tara will remain the Aurora Crew supervisor. You'll take charge of training the crew to be an interagency hotshot crew."

"The Delta Force of firefighting. That's why I came to the States—to get on a hotshot crew." Cohen was blown away by this. "I'm honored you're asking me to do this. What's the plan?"

"Normally, it's a three-year process to qualify firefighters for a hotshot crew," explained Doss. "But our need is immediate. With your help and expertise, I think we can fast track this. We want everyone red-carded as hotshot-qualified by Alaska's next fire season."

As all this sank in, the magnitude of the responsibility for what they wanted him to do ached Cohen's brain. How would he pull it off in this short amount of time? *I'll find a way.* "Then let's get this party started."

"Good man." Doss stood. "It's settled, then. We'll file the paperwork with immigration to extend your temporary work visa." He offered his hand.

Cohen stood and shook it from across the table. "Thank you, sir."

"Sorry to rush off, but I have a meeting at the Alaska Fire Service up in Fairbanks." Doss grabbed his notebook and pulled on a worn baseball cap with the AFS logo on it. "Congratulations on your new role. Good luck." He breezed out of the room.

"It's official, then. Don't worry, I'll help you." Tara reached for his hand and shook it. "We have an excellent crew. You just need to tell them your expectations, then consider it done."

"Thanks for this opportunity. I won't let you down." Cohen got to his feet.

"You'll be my right hand from now on. I'll still have crew supervisor authority, but you'll oversee the fitness tests and develop a training plan to turn us into a crack hotshot crew." Tara started out the door and paused. "Have you talked to Liz?"

He hesitated, knowing Tara was referring to his unsuccessful pursuit of Liz Harrington last fire season. "Nah, we've all been too busy," he said dismissively. "I've moved on from last year," he added.

Tara gave him an understanding smile. "Sorry things didn't work out for you and Liz. I truly believe there's someone out there for each of us. Usually someone we least expect."

"Like with you and Ryan?"

Tara laughed. "Well, that was all kinds of destiny. I told you how we met on that fire outside of Butte, Montana, when I was on the Missoula Ranger District fire crew the season before last."

"I appreciate you recommending me for this," he said.

"I know a good firefighter when I see one. Thanks for agreeing to do this." Tara glanced at her wristwatch. "Time for lunch. Oh, I forgot to mention...Alaska DOF is sending one of their hotshots here for a few weeks, to give us a hand in training the crew."

"That's nice of them. What prompted that?"

"Part of Doss's let's-be-buddies-with-the-state plan." Tara grinned. "You know how state and federal managers like to keep peace in the valley. In the spirit of agency cooperation and all that fluff."

"Reaching across the aisle...what America does best." He gave her a wry smile. "Collaboration is what I do best."

"Good. I knew you'd be cool with it. See you at this afternoon's staff meeting." Tara *tap-tapped* the table and left the conference room.

He stood immobilized, his brain somersaulting. His role in the Aurora Crew would change. Supervising the crew on the Hiland Mountain Fire was one thing but training them for hotshot qualification was a moose of a different color. He hoped the bond with his crewmates wouldn't go south with the Canadian telling the Americans what to do—and how to do it.

Cohen's stomach twisted. Nothing like jumping from the frying pan into the fire. But what an opportunity! He came to the U.S. for the sole purpose of joining a hotshot crew. While this excited him, he wondered how he'd deal with the pressure of fast-tracking the training. He hoped to live up to expectations.

His thoughts turned to who the State of Alaska would send to assist him. He looked forward to finding out who it would be.

Chapter 4

"Raynie, time to get up!" Kira hollered from the kitchen of the modest, one-story cabin.

A lump of golden fur plopped on top of Raynie, followed by enthusiastic barking outside her bedroom window.

"Rooby, get off me!" She pushed her golden retriever to the side as she dragged herself to full consciousness. Turning sideways, she caught sight of an airborne Alaskan husky, tail waving madly as he repeatedly leaped from the ground to snatch glimpses inside her bedroom window, like a goofy peeping tom.

The sled dog jumped so high, he reminded Raynie of the gravity-defying dogs in cartoons she'd watched as a kid. She swore rocket boosters powered his launches. Wacko thought he could fly like an eagle. At least he was graceful.

Raynie's mouth curled into a lazy smile. "Morning, Wacko," she said, waving at the bouncy dog.

Remembering today's commitment, she jerked to sit up. "Oh no, am I late?" She groped for her phone to check the time. Tossing her long dark ponytail over her shoulder, Raynie sprang from her bedroom to the kitchen, where seventeen-year-old Kira stood, buttering toast.

Kira handed her a slice of cinnamon toast. "About time you got up."

Raynie rubbed her eyes. "Morrey reassigned me to the new Talkeetna Wildfire Base. We'll take turns feeding the dogs before work."

"How long?" asked Kira.

"Only two weeks. If you feed the dogs today, I'll do it tomorrow." Kira chomped on her toast. "So, what's the new job?"

"To help train a federal fire crew to be an interagency hotshot crew."

"Like yours with the State?"

"Yeah." Raynie pulled her head back and gave Kira a once over, noting her sister's perfectly spiral-curled hair. "How do you manage to look so glamorous at this ungodly hour?"

Kira tossed her dark curls. "I've always gotten up early to put on my face and do my hair." She tugged her older sister's long, dark ponytail. "You have split ends. And circles under your eyes."

"I don't have time to Barbie myself," sniffed Raynie. "No reason to anymore."

Kira shot her a look. "Don't talk like that. You should always look your best."

"I don't have time," grumbled Raynie. "Not when I fight fire and keep this bakery business going. Plus, taking care of these sled dogs for Kam."

"Have you noticed how pregnant his lead dog, Madonna, is? She'll be having puppies in a few weeks."

"I thought she was just getting fat. We better increase her food and get her checked out at the vet," said Raynie, scribbling a note to herself on a sticky.

"So, back to looking your best." Kira set the butter knife on the counter and turned to her sister. "Taydon is gone, Big

Sister. When someone leaves our world, others enter it. There's still someone out there for you." Kira was born older, with intelligence beyond her years—something Raynie had always admired.

"Thanks for the motivational speech but finding someone new is the last thing on my mind." Guilt jabbed Raynie as soon as she said it. "Oh, Kira, sorry I snarled at you. Thanks for flying up here to stay with me for the summer. I really do appreciate you being here."

"That's okay, I know you're still hurting." Kira gave her sister a playful stare. "But seriously. Stop moping around. Get out and meet people."

"I'll try. Thanks for your concern." Raynie smiled at her sister. "After work today, I'll take Madonna to the vet. I don't know anything about whelping puppies."

"Dogs do it on their own, don't worry." Kira smiled and tossed back a glass of milk like a barfly tossing back a tequila shot. "Hurry up. Don't forget, you have to drop me off at Denali Roadhouse. I need to finish getting ready."

Kira dashed to her bedroom and soon, loud music played on her laptop. "Fever," by Peggy Lee, wafted out of the bedroom. This was the song they listened to when she and Kira did their baking.

"It's too early for baking music," yelled Raynie.

Kira responded by cranking up the volume.

"Rooby, let's feed you first." Raynie measured kibble into the golden's dog dish. Rooby wagged appreciatively; her feathered tail curved over her back in a perfect arc.

This was when her mind invariably drifted to Taydon. He'd given the golden puppy to her as an early Christmas present. She still pictured his handsome smile and gleaming chocolate eyes when he'd given her the wriggling puppy to hold for the first time.

Taydon had asked her to marry him, then died a few weeks later. She wasn't a widow. So, what was she, then? Surviving fiancée? Kira was right. She had to stop grieving and get on with her life. Whenever she inched forward, memories wriggled in, plummeting her back to the bottom of an ocean trench without the will to climb out.

Easier said than done.

Outside, the sled dogs howled and barked, snapping Raynie back to the present. She opened the door for Rooby and followed her golden outside to feed the dogs. Alaskan huskies needed a ton of protein, and she had to make a special mix that Kam had prescribed before he left. The dogs yipped until she distributed dishes to each one.

After they'd gobbled their food in an insta-snarf, Raynie walked around to each dog, tethered to their doghouses. They'd ramped up their usual howling and barking again.

"Hey, you guys, simmer down!" she hollered, arms spread wide.

Yeah, that was effective. They continued yipping and howling.

Raynie pinched her thumb and forefinger together and pressed them firmly against the tip of her tongue and whistled. The barking stopped, except for a few whimpers. She stepped toward the huskies, taking advantage of the split-second silence. "I can't run you today. I have things to do. Kira will run you when she gets home from work," she said, expecting to reason with eight crazed Alaskan huskies, who lived to run.

They wagged their tails, then Wacko the Weird led the cacophony of the howl-a-thon again. Sleeping Lady Kennel was a mile from town, so she let them howl and carry on.

"You're impossible, Wacko. Goodnight," she said to the goofy sled dog. She went inside the cabin, letting the door slam behind her.

RAYNIE LURCHED TO A stop at the Talkeetna Wildfire Base and glanced up at the Alaska state flag, waving in a slight breeze—eight stars of gold on a field of blue, just like the state song. She opened her truck door with the State DOF logo on the outside, noting several federal rigs parked in the lot. People were busy erecting a low rail fence around the front of the main building, and others stood on ladders, painting the exterior plywood siding.

She hurried up the four wide steps to the main office and opened the screen door. Instead of stepping inside, she smacked into a solid chest and stumbled back. Raynie's jaw dropped in stunned amazement when her eyes fell upon Cohen Tremblay in all his yellow-shirted, tall blond glory.

After they recovered from bouncing off one another, each stood back, gaping in disbelief.

"Oh, it's *you!*" It rolled out of Raynie's mouth like a sour Skittle. She swallowed back an *oh shit.*

"Well, hello, Incident Commander Atwood." Tremblay didn't seem as surprised as she was—in fact, he appeared to be enjoying this heinous moment. With a twinkle in his eyes, he said, "Sorry, didn't see you. What are you doing here?"

He looked different, all cleaned up in his clean Nomex shirt, unlike the sooty, ash-stained one from the Hiland Mountain Fire.

"I might ask you the same thing." Tremblay's sudden presence was a shock to Raynie's system. Sharing the same air with him made it hard for her to breathe, like he was a walking wildfire oozing smoke.

"The Alaska Fire Service sent our crew here to help get the state fire base up and running," he said casually, with a sweep of his long arm.

"Is that a...is that a...fact?" Raynie swallowed. She'd counted on never seeing this guy again. Gobsmacked didn't begin to cover this numbing reality.

"What about you?" His bright blue gaze penetrated her.

Her eyes darted to the rolled-up sleeves, revealing muscled forearms with a small tattoo of a red maple leaf on the underside of one wrist. She glanced away as dread snaked through her chest.

"I'm assigned here to help train a federal BLM hotshot crew."

Tremblay stepped back and folded his arms. "That would be the Aurora Crew. I'm also training them to be hotshots." He gave her a broad smile. "Looks like we'll be working together."

No, no! Not this guy. Anyone but him. Is this a cruel joke? Raynie's heart fell out of her and inched along the floor.

"There must be some mistake." Her brain exploded. "Morrey didn't mention which crew I'd be training," she said, scrambling to make sense of this.

"Yep. It's the Aurora Crew."

Why did he sound so damn happy about it?

Raynie wanted to snatch that silly grin off his face. She had a sudden urge to run when a woman with dark curly hair appeared on the porch.

"Are you Raynie? Hi, I'm Angela Alexanderson. I'm the office admin until the permanent one comes on board," she said with a Southern drawl, glancing from Raynie to Tremblay. "So, you two will work together to train our hotshot crew. Have you two met before?"

"We met on the Hiland Fire." Tremblay stood there with a smug expression, cocking his head in that conceited way of his, as if they'd been friends since their sandbox days.

Dammit, why him, of all people?

"Honey, fires are like social events," gushed Angela. "Where else do we meet people? Come in, Raynie. We'll get you squared away."

"Sounds good." As she followed Angela inside, Raynie did her best to disguise her shock at having to work with Cohen Tremblay.

"See you later, eh?" He emphasized *eh*, which she took as his subtle way of irritating her. Tremblay tapped down the porch steps, and she watched his brawny backside as he moved across the lawn.

"Not if I can help it. Eh!" she muttered under her breath.

"Y'all can follow me." Angela crooked her finger, and Raynie followed her to one end of the rectangular building and into a conference room. "Take a load off," she said, pointing to a chair.

"Good morning!" An auburn-haired woman in yellow Nomex breezed into the room. "I'm Tara Waters."

"Morning." Raynie extended her hand, and Tara shook it warmly. "Raynie Atwood, with the State of Alaska DOF."

"Welcome. We're so glad you're here," said the tall, slender woman with a toothy smile.

Raynie sat as a gray-haired man in a yellow shirt and olive green pants entered the room, pulled out the chair across from her, and folded himself into it.

"Miss Atwood, my name is Dave Doss. I'm a fire management officer with the Alaska Fire Service. Thanks for helping us out with our hotshot training." His phone lit up and vibrated. After a glance, he turned it face down on the table.

Doss smiled at her. "Tell me about yourself."

She took a deep breath. "I fought fire with a Type One hotshot crew in Arizona for four seasons before coming to Alaska. Got on with the Twin Peaks Interagency Hotshot Crew with the Alaska State Division of Forestry for a couple of seasons, and most recently I was the incident commander on the Hiland Fire near Eagle River."

"Impressive," said Doss. "What brought you to Alaska?"

She hesitated. Speaking candidly without emotion was still difficult. "My fiancé got a job in Anchorage, and I came up to be with him."

"Congratulations. You're to be married?"

"No. He died in a car accident just before last Christmas. On the Parks Highway, in fact." She maintained a neutral demeanor.

"I'm sorry to hear that," said Doss.

She was quick to explain. "I stay focused on my fire responsibilities, though."

"I've heard good things about you," Angela added, as she leaned back in her chair. With her yellow shirt unbuttoned a little, she revealed serious cleavage. One side of her ample chest was wet.

Raynie must have been staring because Angela glanced down.

"Oh shoot, excuse me, y'all, I have a ten-month-old. Dave will get you lined out. I'll be right back." She nodded at the fire boss and hurried from the room.

Doss smiled. "Angela is a new mother." He leaned back in his chair. "Your supervisor, Morrey, said you were a good fire crew trainer and quick to rise to a leadership capacity. Again, thanks for helping us out. You'll be working hand in hand with Cohen Tremblay, your federal counterpart."

Here it was, officially. Wonderful.

Raynie swallowed her words back before saying, *Oh gee, I can't wait.* Instead, she dipped a nod.

"Yes, I've met him."

"Good. There's a glitch in state hiring until the new fiscal year. The Alaska Fire Service reached out to help get this wildfire base up and running until it's fully staffed."

"Glad to help," she said, in a hopefully convincing tone.

"Are you familiar with this area? Morrey sent your resume, and I noted you mostly worked in Anchorage, then at the Palmer hotshot base.

"Yes, I'm familiar with the area around Talkeetna. A musher friend asked me to watch his sled dog kennel for the summer while he's in the lower forty-eight," she explained. "I've been living in Talkeetna for a few months."

"What do you do in the off season, when you aren't fighting fire?"

"I have a small bakery business. I make muffins and cookies for local businesses, mainly the Denali Roadhouse. My sister helps me," she added.

Doss smiled. "We wouldn't complain if you wanted to bring some in. We'll pay you for them. What's the name of your business?"

"The Tufted Muffin." She kept the name Taydon had given her business when he'd thumbed through a wildlife magazine and found a tufted puffin. Her heart pinched, loving that memory.

Dave's phone vibrated. "Outstanding. Angela will get you settled in. You'll report to Tara Waters and me." He tapped his phone and talked into it as he exited the room.

I must work with Cohen freaking Tremblay. Are you kidding me?

Raynie gulped as she followed Doss out. She headed over to Tara, who pointed to a new desk in one corner of the main office.

"You and Cohen will share that workstation over there. Make yourself at home. We don't get hung up on the state and federal thing. We all work interchangeably for the common good." Tara smiled at her.

Angela spoke up with her southern drawl. "I'm the temporary office admin, handling dispatch and logistics. Basically, I run the office shit show." She grinned and answered her phone.

"Sounds good." Raynie noticed the sparkling rock on Angela's finger as she talked on the phone.

The door opened, and Tremblay entered, carrying a large box. "This is the dispatcher's computer. Where do you want this?" He glanced around, his gaze settling on Raynie.

She looked away. Why *this* guy? Why not the guy with the sorcerer eyebrows who rolled toothpicks around his mouth and talked like a mafia hit man? Or the huge Pacific Islander everyone called Tupa, with the Māori tats on both sides of his redwood tree neck? Despite his constant scowl, he'd still be the preferred choice.

"Put it on that center desk." Tara pointed.

Tremblay gave Raynie a tentative smile. "There's another desktop I'm bringing in. I guess you and I will share."

"I have my state issued laptop," she said coolly.

I'm not sharing squat with this guy.

"This is the state-issued desktop for the main office." He gave her a sage look and set the second box on the desk in the corner.

She pasted on her resting snooty face and stepped over to open it.

"I've got it." Tremblay pulled a pocket knife from his pants and snapped it open.

"Nope. I've got it." Raynie fished a compact knife from her own pocket and flipped it open with her thumb. Suddenly the air felt heavy, as if their animosity inhabited every air particle.

"Ha, beat you to it," he said triumphantly.

So, Tremblay is the competitive type. Doesn't like a woman besting him. Okay buddy, you want a competition? You've got it.

"I'd say it was a draw." She narrowed her eyes in an unblinking stare.

They stood with open knives in a showdown, like they were at the O.K. Corral, in Tombstone.

The door slammed, and Nick Rego sauntered in. "You two came to blows already?" His Bronx accent went into overdrive, and he spread his arms as if separating heavyweights inside a boxing ring.

"Ha, the state and feds are already going at it."

Tremblay snorted and shot Rego a dour look. "We're opening a box."

"I see." Rego cocked a brow. "Gee, I can't wait to see you two out on a fire."

Raynie used Rego's distraction to slide her knife through the tape seals. She lifted the cardboard lids.

"I'll set it up." Tremblay flickered his eyes at her, then reached inside the box.

"Nope. I'll do it!" The way she said it caused Tremblay to back away.

With raised brows, he swept his hand in a grand gesture.

"By all means. Have at it."

Raynie caught Angela and Tara's amused looks out of the corner of her eye. They appeared to be enjoying this battle of wills.

"I'm thinking this woman has things under control." Angela patted Tremblay's shoulder. "Come on, Cohen, let's bring in the rest of the boxes."

He flicked his eyes at Raynie and followed Angela out the door.

Tara smiled. "Cohen can be intense sometimes, but he means well."

"Uh-huh. Whatever," muttered Raynie.

"No, seriously." Tara winked at her. "You'll have fun working with him. He comes on strong sometimes, but he's a pussycat."

"If you say so." Raynie bit her tongue to stop herself from adding, "With fangs and claws."

Later, as she climbed into her rig to head home, her phone sounded, "Hot Hot Hot," by Buster Poindexter and His

Banshees of Blue. She glanced at the Caller ID. Her boss, Morrey.

She tapped it and skipped saying hello. "Morrey, I want to be reassigned. Can you get someone else to do this hotshot crew training duty in Talkeetna?"

He paused, then let out a sigh. "Raynie, this will do you good. It'll be a pleasant change of pace. Also, the feds can use your expertise."

Pleasant? Yeah, right.

She rolled her eyes. "But what about incident commanding more state fires?"

"You did an excellent job containing the Hiland Fire, but you're also an excellent trainer. Dave Doss asked us for the best person we could spare to help train their crew. Naturally, I thought of you. It's only for a few weeks."

"But what if fires blow up?" she interjected.

"We'll pull you back if we need you. Aren't the feds treating you well?" he teased.

"Yes, it's just—there's this person who's a pain in the—oh, never mind." She let out an impatient sigh.

"There's always a pain-in-the-butt in wildland fire. Goes without saying." He hesitated. "You know, it takes time to get over the loss of someone you planned to marry."

She let his words hang for a few seconds.

"There is no getting over it. The time heals all wounds thing is a bunch of malarkey. Wounds don't heal, they only deepen until the hole in your heart becomes a bottomless crater, devoid of all joy."

Silence. Raynie squeezed her eyes closed. *Oh God, why did I say that?*

Finally, Morrey spoke. "And on that uplifting note—all the more reason why you should do this assignment. Show the feds how we do things downtown. Look, I have to go. You've got this, Raynie. Stiff upper lip and all that. See you later."

"Thanks, Morrey."

Raynie ended the call and leaned back in the driver's seat, watching people leave for the day.

Tremblay sauntered out with his usual determined gait.

What made him so driven and focused? What did he do outside of the job?

He glanced at her truck.

She scooched down in her seat. He was the last person she wanted to talk to. Avoiding him was immature, but she lacked the energy to deal with him right now. She stretched her neck to peek out the windshield, craning it like a curious turtle.

Whew, he was gone. She blew out resolute air.

I'll do my time here, then go back to my state hotshot crew where people don't question every move I make.

She reassured herself that if wildfire erupts in Southcentral Alaska as it did last year, she'd be called back to action with her own crew. She would train this Type Two crew to be a Type One hotshot fire crew, the kickass Delta Force of American fire suppression.

If nothing else, she'd show this Canadian dude how Alaskans get things done downtown. She prided herself on her willingness to stick this out.

Challenge. Accepted.

Chapter 5

Early the next morning, Cohen filed into the conference room with the rest of the Aurora Crew for the daily fire briefing.

Tara breezed in and stood at the head of the long table.

"You may have heard the rumor about the Aurora Crew converting to a Type One hotshot crew. This isn't a rumor." She smiled as whoops and hollers erupted around the room.

"I figured you'd like that."

"Damn straight!" piped up Rego as heads nodded around the room.

"Director Martelle and Dave Doss decided we must increase our Alaskan hotshot crew resources. They selected this crew because of the exemplary way you've worked these past few seasons," explained Tara.

Cohen glanced at Raynie, standing off to the side. He noticed other guys also glancing in her direction. Now that he could study her features unmarred from sweat or fire soot, she was incredibly pretty.

She glanced his way and caught him staring at her. He snapped his focus back to the front of the room.

Tara continued. "We'll have a year to get you all qualified as hotshots. Normally it takes a couple years to qualify a crew, but we're fast-tracking it because of immediate need, and we know each of you is capable." Tara hesitated. "If you aren't on board with this decision, I need to know right away. Don't feel bad if you choose not to take part. Hotshot work isn't for everyone."

Tara glanced around the room. "See me if you have concerns or questions. All crew members must fill out an application, so we know who wants to commit. Cohen will be your fearless leader for hotshot training." She motioned at him. "Want to say a few words?"

His chest tightened. He'd been anxious about this moment, not knowing how his crewmates would react.

"I'll be the one brutalizing each of you along the way. Tara will remain the crew supervisor."

Tara jumped in. "Cohen's expertise at training the equivalent of hotshot crews in Canada is a perfect fit, and he comes highly recommended."

The room quieted, and Cohen's stomach dropped to his boots. He could have heard a spruce needle drop during the awkward silence.

A shout erupted from the other end of the table, and Tupa raised his fist in the air.

"Yeah, brah! Excellent choice."

Many echoed his sentiment, clapping at the news.

Cohen heaved out a sigh of relief as Rego gave him a guy slap on the back.

"Way to go, Maple Leaf!" He liked Rego's rough-around-the-edges personality. Rego had regaled the crew last year with enough Marine stories to last a lifetime.

"Thanks, everybody. It's an honor to be chosen for this." Cohen glanced around the room, catching Raynie's eye. He motioned to her. "I'm sure you remember Raynie Atwood, the incident commander of the Hiland Mountain Fire. The Alaska

Division of Forestry has generously loaned her to us for her hotshot training expertise. She'll be assisting me to get you started."

Several voices chorused. "Hi Raynie, welcome!"

"Thank you, it's good to be here," lied Raynie, feigning a polite smile.

"We appreciate you being here, Raynie," said Tara. She briefed the crew on fire weather expectations and laid out the crew's work plan for the day. "All right, people, back to work. We're trying to get everything situated before fires ramp up."

Several crew members shook Cohen's hand and gave him a thumbs-up on their way out. He was thankful most seemed positive about the Canadian telling the Americans what to do. After being the newcomer last year, he wasn't sure how they'd receive the news. But they seemed to respect his experience.

Cohen waited for the room to empty so he could talk to Raynie. "Want to get together to organize a training plan?"

She gave him a dubious look. "What do you have in mind?"

"Eat dinner with us in the mess hall. We'll do it after we eat."

"All right." She didn't seem overly enthusiastic.

He dipped a friendly nod. "See you after dinner."

Tara raced back into the conference room. "Fire call! Trapper Creek. Get your fire packs and let's go!"

"So much for planning, eh?" quipped Cohen as he and Raynie rushed to gather their gear and head to the fire engines.

To his disappointment, Raynie headed to another vehicle. He'd wanted to discuss the training on the way to the fire. At least, that's what he told himself.

COHEN CLIMBED OUT OF his vehicle upon arriving at the Trapper Creek Fire. He waited for Tara to get the Aurora Crew lined out on their direct attack. This was a slow-moving fire with flames staying in the understory. They aimed to contain the fire before it reached the beetle-killed spruce a quarter mile away.

"Let's get these hoses laid, pumps started, and water flowing from the river," Tara called out, flipping her auburn ponytail behind her. "Squad bosses, let's get this blaze contained. Raynie, you go with Tupa's squad. Cohen, stay with me."

All heads nodded in affirmation.

Squad boss Nick Rego spoke up. "Make sure each of you knows how the fire's behaving at all times." He sounded more like a New York forester than an Alaskan firefighter.

"Afi Slayers Squad, to the hoses," rumbled Tupa in his deep voice. "Kenzie, help me get situated." His shy fondness for the even-keeled Aussie and her laid-back manner were obvious to members of the Aurora Crew.

"Raynie, get the other hose and unspool it, if you would," ordered Tupa.

Kenzie unfastened a hose clamp and unreeled it from their largest fire engine.

"Tupa, why haven't you ever told us your last name?"

Cohen glanced up, enjoying how Kenzie had a knack for putting the refrigerator-sized Samoan on the spot. "Or are you a one-name guy, like Sting or Bono?" he joked.

Tupa opened a compartment to unload the water pump equipment to extract water from nearby Foraker Creek.

"No one can pronounce it."

"*You underestimate me, friend,*" said Kenzie in Samoan, shocking the pants off her crewmates. She reverted to English. "I'm from Down Under, remember mate?"

"You've been holding out on me! Where did you learn to speak Samoan?" Tupa charged forward with his hose as if it were crepe paper, with his pitch-black man bun and Māori tattoos that wound around his neck and forearms.

"I taught English at a school in Samoa a few years ago," said Kenzie.

"Tamailelagi." Tupa squatted to situate the water pump next to the rushing stream. This was the most he'd shared after two seasons of fighting fire.

"Ta-mall-a-LOGGY," Kenzie hollered back. "I knew a family named Tamailelagi in Asau."

"My cousins," said Tupa, with a hint of a smile as adoration crossed his face.

Kenzie squatted to connect her hose to the pump. "Why do you have Māori tattoos, then?"

"My mother is from Aotearoa—what Maoris call New Zealand. Father is Samoan." He lifted a bushy brow with a brown-eyed, menacing stare at his crewmates.

"Anything else you want to know?"

Tara interjected. "Thanks for the geography lesson. Now it's time to fight fire. Cohen, you, and Liz scope out our safety zones."

Liz traced his gaze to the new dark-haired firefighter with the DOF logo on her shoulder. Smiling, she nudged him.

"Get a move on, Tremblay."

"Hey, I'm all over this," he shrugged, as they hiked down the gravel road to scope out a safety zone if the fire were to take a run.

"I've noticed you scoping out the state firefighter," teased Liz.

"What? No," he said defensively.

"Oh, sweetie, I know you better than you know yourself." Liz gave him a sisterly pat on the arm. Liz was Cohen's squad boss last year when he'd tried unsuccessfully to win her affections.

"You should follow your heart on this one."

"What do you mean?" Cohen glanced around at the surrounding terrain to see where the fire might burn.

"You know how working fire makes having relationships next to impossible. Take a risk—have yourself a little romance." She elbowed him.

He pulled away to look at her. "Not with anyone I work with. You know things never end well. Besides, Atwood hates me."

"No, she doesn't. You and Raynie got off on the wrong foot, that's all." Liz paused. "Last year was, well...my lack of interest had nothing to do with you. I was in love with someone else."

He shrugged. "How can I get her to un-hate me?"

"Look at me, Cohen." Liz stopped walking. "Just be yourself. You charmed the rest of us with your badass personality."

He let out a drawn-out sigh. "Yeah, well, I'll think about it."

With Liz's encouragement and her green light, he would absolutely do more than think about it.

Chapter 6

Raynie noticed Tremblay move off with the perky petite firefighter, and she could tell they knew each other well. Her arm slipped around his waist, and she tugged him to her and gave him a sideways squeeze.

Do they have a thing going on? Everyone seemed to like this guy but Raynie.

She tore her gaze away from the two Aurora Crew members as they disappeared down the road. She focused on getting the hose-lays in place, then helped Tupa set up the pump operation next to the swift water stream.

Raynie finished connecting the hoses and squinted. "The flames aren't tall, but they're eating steadily through willow and alder in the understory. We don't want these flames to reach the beetle kill up there." She pointed at a slope of dead spruce.

Tupa surveyed the gentle slopes, mostly covered with dead spruce. "The sooner we get water on this foliage, the better. Ready for a swim?" He waded into the stream, which hit him mid-thigh.

"Sure, why not?" The water came to Raynie's waist, but the current wasn't strong enough to throw her off balance. She hated getting her boots wet, but one thing she'd learned when fighting fire in Alaska was to get a second, and even a third pair of boots. When she first fought fire in Alaska, she'd been surprised to learn that wildfires still burned through boggy wetlands.

Tupa, Kenzie, and Raynie, with two other crew, crossed the icy stream, gray with glacial silt. They clambered up the opposite bank, with their one and one-half inch, flat booster hoses, then took turns waiting for the pump to pressurize each hose with water.

Raynie had three hundred feet of hose to work with and moved cautiously toward the flames. Pausing, she widened her stance to balance herself before opening the nozzle to spray water on the blaze. Gripping the nozzle, her mind circled back to Cohen Tremblay, and his uncanny ability to push her buttons.

She'd worked with his kind before—guys that showered women with compliments in the guise of being helpful.

When what they really wanted was to help themselves into your pants.

She noticed a colorful rainbow inside her spray as she saturated the vegetation to slow down the flames.

"Look at that, mate!" Kenzie pointed at their three hose sprays. "They all have rainbows! It's a good omen."

"You're right. It is!" Raynie laughed. It felt good to laugh. She hadn't done much of it since Taydon died. He'd always been the one to make her laugh.

The crew made progress, dousing the flames, and drenching the vegetation, filling the air with smoke instead of fire. Raynie coughed when she inhaled some that drifted back at her. She welcomed this opportunity to get to know the Aurora Crew and work with them first before putting them through their fitness paces, then yelling at them like a drill sergeant once they got into the intense part of their training.

One thing she knew about being a Type One hotshot: It was brutal work. They weren't considered the Delta Force of firefighting for nothing. Often, it was the hotshots working with smokejumpers to get fires contained fast and efficiently, to protect lives and properties.

"Okay, folks, step to the south," yelled Tupa, and they dragged their hoses down to do the same for another couple hundred feet.

A familiar male voice called out across the stream behind them. "Good job, squabs!"

Raynie turned to see Tremblay standing in that arrogant hands-on-hips stance of his, head tilted, with one hip canted out. If she didn't detest him, she might consider him almost handsome. *Almost*. She scolded herself for even thinking about it.

One thing that annoyed her to tears was his incessant head tilting—the same way Taydon used to, when she'd give him a hard time or when he'd seduce her. It felt like Tremblay had copied a page from Taydon's playbook.

The Aurora Crew soon had the flames tamed like a docile lion, with a fuel break around the fire.

Ah, the sweet smell of containment.

"Okay, sports fans, we're demob'ing. A DOF crew is on their way to do mop-up," called out Tara, who then spoke into her radio. "Doss, Aurora Crew here. Do we have drones to fly over the fire?"

Radio static, then Doss's voice. "Nope. I dispatched Mel Faraday instead to fly N-74 Juliet down to help with water drops. He can do a flyover. His ETA is in thirty."

"Copy that." Tara shoved the radio into her shoulder holster.

The crew loaded the last of their equipment into the fire engines, and people climbed in. Raynie landed in the back seat of the crew-cab pickup, sitting next to none other than Mister Hot Stuff. She stifled a groan.

Tremblay's lips curled up. "So, you were a hose jockey today. I love squirting flames. Makes me feel like I've accomplished something."

"Yes, it does." She considered tossing back a smartass remark. Instead, she crossed her arms and leaned back, like she did on planes, to keep passengers from bugging her. Except this passenger didn't take the hint.

"We still have to organize a training plan." He elbowed her. "How about this evening?"

Tremblay reminded her of an energizer bunny amped up on caffeine.

Raynie leaned away from him, opening one eye. "Nope. Tomorrow morning. Can't do it this evening. I have things to do."

"Then tomorrow it is." He said it with an annoying, self-assured finality.

She pretended to sleep on the way back to the fire base. She was glad she took Madonna to the vet yesterday. Today she was too exhausted and would have had to postpone the vet appointment. She felt guilty for not exercising Kam's dogs.

I'll run them tomorrow.

AFTER ANOTHER DAY OF battling the flames alongside the Aurora Crew, Raynie was drained. She enjoyed working with Tara Waters, but she'd kept her distance from Cohen, if for no other reason than she didn't want to be around him. Her first impression of him still left her with sour grapes.

All she could think of was to chill in the cabin and rest from the day. She closed the door, sunk onto the couch with a glass of iced tea, and closed her eyes. Kira had texted she'd be working late at the Roadhouse.

A forceful banging on the front door made her jump. She pushed up from the worn couch and swung open the door. Fear clamped down on her at the man standing on her doorstep.

"Thought you were in jail?" Raynie couldn't believe Avery Maddox was in Alaska.

"What a way to greet an old friend. Not going to invite me in?" He pushed past her and stood in the middle of her tiny living room, glancing around.

Heart pounding, she didn't want to close the door. The sled dogs barked up a storm, and Rooby barked her confusion at this stranger in her house.

"Rooby, stop," she instructed. She moved to her mostly grown puppy, motioning her to lie down. Rooby reluctantly obeyed with a low growl.

Maddox leered at her, then at the golden. "Is that the puppy your lover boy Taydon got you last summer?" He sauntered to the fridge and opened it. "Where's the beer?"

"I haven't had beer in the house since Taydon's been gone." She kept her voice steady, to hide the fear from her tone. "You can't mooch off me like you used to. What are you doing here?" Her stomach twisted into a sickening knot.

Maddox helped himself to a half-gallon container of milk and guzzled it. He wiped his mouth with the back of his hand

and put the milk back in the fridge. He closed the door and leaned against it, his eyes roving over her.

"You haven't changed. You're still a little hottie." His eyes became heavy-lidded, and Raynie's unease grew. She'd gone down this road with him years ago in Arizona, and it hadn't ended well.

"What do you want?" She moved to where Rooby lay, growling. The golden's brown eyes fixed on the red-headed stranger with the dark sleeve tattoos and green eyes that would have been attractive on anyone's face but Maddox's.

"I'm here for my money."

"I haven't a clue what you're talking about." She lifted her chin. "You were Taydon's best friend, and you never even came to his funeral."

"Had business that day. Then ran into a state trooper who decided I should hang out at the Spring Creek Correctional Center for a while." He sat on her couch and swung his muddy boots up onto her coffee table. He popped a piece of gum in his mouth and took his time chewing, not taking his eyes off her.

"Busted for drugs, I heard. Didn't you learn your lesson after doing time in Winslow?" Raynie crossed her arms and glared down at him.

"You helped slam my ass into Winslow Prison, as I recall." His eyes became dark ice.

She knew that murderous look, and her heart thundered. "I did what I had to do after you raped my best friend," she said in a measured tone, her stomach squeezing.

"Good thing I'm not the vengeful sort." A sickening, lusty expression crossed his face. His eyes hardened, and he swung his feet to the floor.

"Me and Taydon did a business deal before the crash. He agreed to hang onto the cash until I got out. Now here I am." His smile caused a shiver to work up her spine.

"Taydon never told me about any money. I don't have any money. Even if I did, you're the last person I'd give it to. Not only that, he also didn't deal in Alaska. Taydon left all that behind in Arizona."

"Oh, you think so?" he sniggered.

"I know so." She folded her arms and glared down at him.

"I've always liked that about you—your cluelessness. You believed anything he ever told you." Maddox stood and stepped toward her, his nasty stench nearly gagging her.

She backed up, while Rooby bared her teeth and growled.

"Control your damn dog."

"Rooby, lie down." Raynie snapped her fingers, and the golden lowered herself at stiff attention.

"You're in no position to play games." Without warning, he reached out and grabbed her by the back of her neck, then forced his revolting mouth onto hers, driving his disgusting tongue inside her mouth.

Rooby was on all fours, baring her teeth and barking.

Raynie pressed her hands on Maddox's chest and shoved him hard enough that he stumbled backward.

"Get your sickening mouth off me," she sputtered through gritted teeth.

"You of all people know I always get what I want," he said in a guttural, threatening tone.

She backed away. "Get out! Now!"

"Or you'll what?" he taunted her. "Your precious Taydon can't protect you anymore. I can tear your clothes off and take you right now if I want." He glanced at her open bedroom door, then took a menacing step toward her, eyes drifting down her body.

She braced for an assault, her mind racing.

How fast can I get to Taydon's nine-millimeter in the end table drawer?

Maddox straightened, and he brushed his unwashed hair back with his fingers. "I have business in Fairbanks. When I come back, you'd better have my money. Or..." He cocked his head and flashed her a sardonic smile. "You know I'm a peace lover. Don't make me mad."

"If you lay a finger on me, I'll make damn sure you wind up in prison again," she shot back, hoping he wouldn't notice her knees shake.

"Get out of my house!" she hissed.

He opened the front door, then turned around. "Me and you would be together if Taydon hadn't screwed that up back in Arizona. Now that he's gone there's no one to stop me now, is there?" He stepped to her and lifted her chin.

"Is there, Raynie?" He smirked, brushing a palm across her breast.

Raynie tossed off his hand. "I said get out!"

Rooby charged at Maddox, but he slammed the door before the dog reached it. She stood barking and growling at the closed door.

"Come here, girl." Trembling, Raynie scratched Rooby's head, waiting for the vehicle to start up. It felt like an eternity before Maddox drove away. When he did, Raynie beelined for the toilet and vomited. She wiped her mouth and let out a shaky breath.

She hadn't a clue about the money Maddox was talking about. She and Taydon never had enough to even open a savings account.

Thank God Kira wasn't home when Maddox showed up. He preyed on women like the scum that he was—as he'd done to her best friend, Vicky, back in Arizona when he sexually assaulted her. Raynie was the one who'd taken Vicky to the hospital and encouraged her friend to report it—and testified against Maddox during his trial.

Why couldn't it have been Maddox in the crash instead of Taydon?

She moved to the end table and dragged the drawer open. The pistol rested on its side with a loaded magazine next to it Taydon had kept for bears. She hated keeping a weapon lying around. But if Maddox tried anything, she'd be ready—Raynie had her younger sister to protect.

God help Maddox if he tries to harm Kira.

Chapter 7

After helping to unload firefighting equipment from the vehicles, Cohen humped his gear to the crew bunkhouse. Grabbing his civvies, jeans, and a T-shirt, he headed for the men's shower.

He finished, dressed, and slid on his flip-flops. When he stepped outside, his gaze drifted up to Denali. The massif was out and at her best in an alpenglow splendor, stark against streaks of orange and red in a lava-flow sunset. The May evenings stayed lighter as Alaska moved toward the summer solstice.

Tupa walked out behind him. "There she is, in all her glory."

"Spectacular, isn't she?" Cohen gaped at the monolith, when a brown and white dog came out of nowhere and rushed at him.

He jumped back as the dog stopped and wagged his tail.

"Hey buddy, where'd you come from?" Tupa held out his hand, and the dog sniffed but stayed still, wagging like mad.

Cohen took a step toward the dog, who skittishly backed up and barked.

"Best not to do that," said Tupa. "Alaskan huskies aren't always friendly."

"Looks like someone's sled dog got loose." Cohen whistled, and the dog cocked his head, staring with bright glacial eyes.

"He has a collar with a tag. Come here, boy. Let me read your info."

Cohen held out his hand, and the dog sat, staring at him. When he approached the husky, the dog flipped around in circles, then stopped and pawed the ground.

"He wants to play." Tupa pulled the towel from around his neck and dragged it along the freshly cut grass. The dog pounced on it and tugged it with his mouth. Tupa let him shake it a few times, then he petted the dog.

The husky stayed still long enough for Cohen to get a good look at the ID tag.

"Wacko," he read out loud. "Sleeping Lady Kennel. Here's the phone number. Cohen retrieved his cell from a shirt pocket and tapped it.

A young woman answered. "Hello?"

"I'm a firefighter at the Talkeetna Wildfire Base. Do you have an Alaskan husky named Wacko?"

A heavy sigh. "Oh no, did he escape again?"

"He's here at the fire base."

"That darn dog!" She sounded exasperated. "Hold on a sec."

Cohen waited until she got back on the phone.

"Is there a way you can bring him here? My sister went to bed, and she doesn't want me driving—"

"Sure, I can deliver him. Where do you live?"

"A mile and a half down Whispering Spruce Road. Number seven-oh-nine."

Be there in a minute." Cohen ended the call and tapped the maps app on his phone. He found the address and fished the truck keys from his jeans.

"Help me get this dog in my pickup."

"Come here, Wacko." Tupa squatted next to the husky and scratched him behind the ears. Then he stood and whistled for the dog to follow.

The two men walked to the parking lot, followed by the husky. Cohen opened the rear door of the crew cab, and Tupa hefted the dog inside. Wacko appeared miniature next to Tupa's oversized frame.

"Thanks," said Cohen, climbing into the driver's seat.

"See you later, brah." Tupa slammed the rear door, and Cohen fired up the engine.

He tapped the GPS app on his phone. The address was a straight shot down Birch Spur Road, then left onto Whispering Spruce.

Wacko's loud sharp barks slammed into his ears like a shattered sound barrier.

"Hey, quiet down there, buddy!" shouted Cohen over the incessant barking.

The dog kept it up, relentlessly.

"Wacko! Stop!" he yelled, stepping on the gas. Didn't do any good. *Crazy dog.*

Cohen slammed on the brakes and checked the glove box for ear plugs. He found aviation headphones instead. Perfect. He put them on, then spotted Whispering Spruce Road and turned left. He drove a short distance and spotted a painted sign sticking up from a mailbox, *Sleeping Lady Kennel.* He stopped in front of a modest log home with a dog lot next to it.

He climbed out and opened the rear door for the husky to jump out. Graceful as a gazelle, the sled dog caught air and sailed out to join his buddies, who yapped welcomes and wagged tails.

A door opened to the house, and Raynie Atwood stepped out in a short blue bathrobe, tied at the waist. A mass of thick wavy hair pulled to one side hung to her chest.

"You're the one who found Wacko? So, what's with the headphones?"

Cohen laughed, remembering he had on the green headphones. He took them off and tossed them onto the driver's seat.

"Your husky killed my ears on the way here. That dog has a loud bark."

"He breaks the sound barrier when he barks." She pointed at the husky with one ear flopped over. "Bad dog, Wacko! You're a pain in the butt."

"He's a handful, for sure." Cohen kept his eyes trained on her face.

"Where did you find him?" She pulled her bathrobe together to hide her generous cleavage—which his gaze had snagged on for the first few seconds upon seeing her.

"Wandering around the fire base. You own this sled dog kennel?" He nodded his head toward the dog yard.

"I'm the temporary caretaker for the musher who owns it."

"Do you mush?"

Raynie shook her head. "I've tried hooking them up, but unless someone helps me get the dogs attached to the sled with the gangline, I have a hard time."

"I used to mush dogs with my cousin," he said casually, trying not to sound like a braggart.

"In Canada?" She flicked her eyes up at him.

He nodded. "I've done a few sprint races. Not long distances. Not like the Iditarod."

"That race takes serious training all year. Thanks for dropping off Crazy Dog. Morning comes early around here, so we'd better go to bed." Her cheeks turned red. "I mean, each of us needs to get some sleep."

Her go-to-bed reference clung to his male psyche and rolled around for a few seconds.

"See you in the morning, then. I'll be the one with a coffee in each fist." He hesitated, as something tugged at him not to be in a hurry to leave.

Raynie didn't smile, but her face softened. "Thanks for returning Wacko."

Cohen grinned. "Glad he's back with his homies, eh?"

Raynie gave him a blank stare.

"That was a joke. You Americans expect us to say 'eh' all the time."

"Oh, right. Well, I don't expect that, but whatever." She shrugged.

"I'll see you in the morning." He smiled, fiddling with his keys.

"Yep. In the morning." She raised her hand for a quick wave, then ducked inside the cabin.

He stared at the closed door, hoping this woman wouldn't be a pain to work with. She knew her stuff, but her aloof and snippy attitude could prove to be a challenge.

Cohen glanced at Wacko, wagging his tail on top of his doghouse.

"See you later, Bark Machine."

Wacko responded with a sharp bark and wag of his tail. Happy little sled dog.

On the way back to the fire base, Cohen wondered what Raynie's story was. Maybe in time he'd find out, but he wouldn't intrude on her personal life. They were coworkers. And certainly not friends.

Hell, she doesn't even like me.

Raynie was one of those women who built a fortress around herself. No ring on her finger. Not that he was interested, but he'd noticed. She was pretty when she wasn't being difficult—and even when she was.

He'd sensed sadness in her eyes on that first day at the Hiland Fire. That must have been what compelled him to offer his help. Only she'd taken it as an insult. He wasn't a misogynist and hoped he hadn't come across as one when he'd questioned her decision-making on the fire.

For whatever reason, he'd rubbed Raynie Atwood the wrong way.

Now he had to figure out how to get along with her.

Chapter 8

The next morning, Raynie's phone tinkled an alarm of soft chimes. She heard it increase in volume, but she couldn't budge. Instead she remained still as a slug—willing the alarm to stop on its own.

Her bedroom door burst open. "Don't you hear that? It's time to get up." Kira stood, scowling at her.

Raynie sat up, bleary-eyed and blinking. "I have to deliver muffins to Trish at the Roadhouse before I go to work. Kira, later on I'll need your help with the baking." She rubbed her eyes. "Geez, this new job stresses me out."

"Why are you stressed? Thought you loved your fire job?"

"There's this guy..." She trailed off, shaking her head.

"A good guy or a bad guy?" asked Kira. "Is he cute?"

Raynie let out an exasperated sigh. "Not bad. Just a pain. Can you feed the dogs while I get the muffins for Trish?"

"I'll take care of it," said Kira. "And I'll exercise them today when I get off work." She headed out the back door to feed the pack of sled dogs, already howling for breakfast.

"Thanks. We'll take turns feeding them. Need to bake more muffins tonight." Raynie wasn't sure how long she could keep up this schedule, but she needed the cash from her bakery business.

She sped through her morning routine and loaded her trays with pre-made muffins, cinnamon rolls, and cookies into the back seat of her extended cab pickup. Raynie slammed the door shut, sighing as she read the custom magnetic sign Taydon had made: *Tufted Muffin Bakery. We bake 'em, you take 'em.*

When Kira finished feeding the dogs, the sisters climbed into the pickup and drove to the Denali Roadhouse.

"Hey Trish, sorry I'm late." Raynie breezed in to find the morning customers already waiting. She set her trays on the counter.

Raynie smiled at the nice-looking curly-haired guy who mushed sled dogs. "Hi, Donny."

"I can't run my dogs until I've had one of your cinnamon rolls." The older musher's welcoming eyes roved over her as they did every day when she delivered. He was a nice person, but she wasn't interested in returning his flirtations.

"Glad you like them." Raynie turned her attention back to the owner of the Roadhouse.

"How are things going at the new fire base?" asked Trish, as she arranged the muffins and rolls inside a large display case.

"Great. I'm helping to train a new hotshot crew," replied Raynie.

Trish lifted her head from the display case. "That federal fire crew from Fairbanks was in here talking about the Trapper Creek Fire they contained yesterday. Glad they caught it before it tore into all that doggone beetle kill."

"I helped the Aurora Crew on that fire yesterday. It burned next to the river, so was easier to contain," said Raynie.

"We can't afford fires around here with all these dead spruce trees," said Trish, her long red hair pulled back into a messy bun.

Donny piped up. "It's super dry this season and spring breakup was early this year. Ice jams didn't stick as long." He pointed at the display case. "I'll take two cinnamon rolls."

Kira bagged two rolls for him. "Here you go. Eight bucks."

"Thanks. Keep the change." Donny handed Kira a ten and winked at her, which quickened Raynie's pulse. And not in a good way.

"See you later, ladies." Donny's eyes rested on Raynie. "Anytime you need help running Kam's sled dogs, you know where to find me." He touched his Sled Dog Association baseball hat and headed out the door.

"Bye, Donny," the women chorused, watching him climb into his pickup through the wall of windows.

Kira set to work taking breakfast orders from table customers, while Raynie helped Trish finish arranging muffins and rolls inside the display case.

Trish straightened with her hands on her hips. "You do realize he likes you."

"Donny likes everybody." Raynie shook her head impatiently. "Besides, I don't have time for guys in my life." She appreciated her work relationship and friendship with Trish. Never hurts to know an Alaska State Trooper's wife.

"That might be exactly what you need."

"Too busy. Fire, muffins, sled dogs. No time." Raynie waved her hand dismissively. "I have to get going."

"So, you're training all those good-looking fire guys?" Raynie adored Trish, but she was a tad on the nosy side. Her gossip moved faster than lightning.

If you want the whole town to know something, just tell Trish.

"I'm training *everyone* on the crew," said Raynie.

"Some of the guys are quite the lookers. Especially that Canadian."

Raynie did a double take. "You've met Cohen Tremblay?"

"Oh! You know him? He likes your macadamia nut cookies." Trish smiled sweetly. "Such a polite man."

Yeah, he's polite all right. A wolf dressed in Nomex sheep's wool.

Raynie ignored the polite man comment. "Heading out now. Can we settle up tomorrow morning?"

"Sure." Trish wrinkled her nose. "Make sure you give me plenty for tomorrow morning. Three dozen muffins, at least. Next to the cinnamon rolls, they go the fastest. And don't forget the cookies."

"Kira and I are baking tonight." Raynie eyed her younger sister, busy behind the counter, wiping things clean. "Bye, Kira. Holler if you need a ride after work." She grabbed her empty trays and hustled out the door.

How will I manage all these commitments?

As she drove toward the fire base and crossed the railroad tracks on the other side of town, unease tightened her chest. Then she remembered...Cohen Tremblay. Could they possibly get through the day without throttling each other?

Tara spotted her as soon as she entered the office.

"Raynie! Glad you're here. Can you keep an eye on the dispatch desk until Angela gets here? She's running late with Baby Gunnar." Tara waved at the three computer monitors on the dispatch desk, and a sizable black desk phone with way too many buttons. "I have to run some errands and pick up equipment. What do you know about dispatch?"

Raynie shrugged. "Not a lot. I've always worked in the field."

"You can manage until Angela gets here. Cohen is acting as fire ops chief in Doss's absence. He and the crew are in the conference room doing the daily fire briefing. All you have to do is answer the phone and respond on the radio. If there's a fire, jot down the info. Be back in a flash." Tara dashed out the front door.

"Okay." Raynie stared at the three monitors on the dispatch desk. One showed the weather forecast for Southcentral Alaska and the Interior; another had lists of fire crews and equipment; the third displayed available state and federal aviation fleets.

She leaned in to study them when the dispatch radio sprang to life. "Smokejumper recon to Talkeetna Base," a deep voice rumbled.

"Talkeetna Base. Go ahead," she responded into the stand-up radio mic.

"This is Ryan O'Connor. We have a fire northeast of town, at the Willow Creek Campground. About five acres. Emailing the coordinates. Stand by."

Raynie's pulse kicked up a notch, but she spoke calmly. "Copy that."

She studied the computer monitor, waiting for the email. A message from Ryan O'Connor appeared with the GPS coordinates and a photo of the fire.

"Now what?" she muttered, scanning the monitors. She saw an icon for the Interagency Dispatch Ops and clicked it. Images popped up on two screens. One had an area map, and the other a PDF of a form with a handwritten scrawl.

She pressed the button on the radio mic. "Location received."

"Is Aurora Crew available to respond?" Ryan radioed.

She glanced at the closed conference door with voices talking on the other side. "I'll have to get back to you on that."

"Are Tara or Angela available?" asked Ryan.

"No, just me, Raynie Atwood. I'm helping dispatch at the moment. Stand by." She stood and took a step toward the conference room when the door flew open.

Tremblay filled the doorway. "Heard O'Connor on my radio. Tell him you're dispatching Aurora Crew."

"Am I authorized to do that? I'm not a trained dispatcher."

"I'm authorizing you," Tremblay said firmly. "Tell him Aurora is on the way." He brushed past her to peer at the monitors.

Raynie pressed the mic. "Talkeetna Base is dispatching Aurora Crew to the GPS coordinates. The point of origin on the map says it's next to Willow Creek Campground. Is that the fire name?"

"Affirmative. That's the one. Willow Creek Fire it is. Number fifty-seven. Thanks—Raynie, is it? As in, a rainy day?" The smokejumper sounded nice.

She chuckled. "Yes, but everyone on fire calls me Atwood. And you're welcome."

"Copy that. Smokejumper recon, clear."

Raynie radioed back. "Talkeetna clear."

Tremblay moved to study the dispatch monitors. "Ryan O'Connor is spoken for. Don't get any ideas."

"Why would I get ideas?" Her brows shot up. "About what?"

He eased the mouse from under her hand and clicked on the weather report. "You had that flirtatious tone, like on the Hiland Fire, with your retardant pilot," he said casually, eyes steady on the screen.

"Flirtatious tone? Are you serious? Kipp is not *my* retardant pilot!" Her voice rose as people rushed from the conference room. Heat sped up her neck as she prepared to give this cocksure mess of testosterone a piece of her mind.

"Fire call!" called out Tara as she breezed over. "Raynie, do you mind handling the dispatch desk until Angela gets in? Someone must stay with the phone and radios."

"Sure." Raynie wanted to get out on the fireline, but if she stayed behind, she wouldn't be tempted to toss Tremblay into the flames and roast him like a marshmallow for his inflammatory insinuations.

The audacity of this guy.

The room emptied into the parking lot as the Aurora Crew piled into the fire vehicles with their gear. Raynie watched Tremblay climb into the driver's seat of a fire engine and pull out, leading the Aurora Crew to the Willow Creek Fire.

He'd escaped before she could chew him out for his rude assumption that she'd hit on the smokejumper—not to mention the air tanker pilot when they were on the Hiland Fire in Eagle River.

"Calm down," she ordered herself, glancing around for something, anything, to occupy her mind. Angela had stacked the large counter inbox with incoming mail.

Raynie grabbed the pile of envelopes, her residual anger causing her to flip through them at warp speed. Most were cards and letters forwarded to Aurora Crew firefighters from the Alaska Fire Service in Fairbanks.

A pink sweet-smelling envelope with pretty handwriting made her stop thumbing through the envelopes. Some cute little sweetie had written, "Coey Tremblay" in a fancy cursive with artsy-fartsy curlicues. How sweet. No doubt this was from one of his many Canadian girlfriends. Raynie stared at the return address from Vancouver, B.C.

She eyed the waste container under her desk, tempted to toss the letter in.

Don't be vindictive.

With a resigned sigh, she tossed the sweet-scented envelope back into the crew inbox on the counter.

"Whoever she is, you don't deserve her," she muttered, sticking her tongue out at the door, as if Tremblay still stood there.

Out of spite, she grabbed the envelope and shoved it under the stack on the bottom.

Chapter 9

Later in the afternoon, Angela arrived to relieve Raynie. She'd kept Ryan the smokejumper informed and recorded the fire information for Angela to input into the computer system.

And she certainly did not flirt with him. She couldn't figure out why Tremblay would say something like that. She prided herself on her professionalism with her colleagues.

Angela plopped herself into the chair next to Raynie. "I'm so sorry to have left you hanging," she said. "Baby Gunnar ran a fever and went on a nursing strike. I had to figure out what to do with all the milk. Thought I was going to explode, so I skedaddled to Wasilla to get a breast pump."

"I can imagine," was all Raynie could muster. She didn't know much about babies, though she'd wished for them when she and Taydon planned to marry.

So much for that.

Angela sat back in the chair and looked down at her inflated chest.

"These hummers get full, let me tell you." Angela leaned toward her monitors. "Okay, we need to get all this fire information into the system. Thank you for getting Aurora Crew dispatched."

Raynie showed her the tablet where she'd jotted down the fire information.

Angela read through it. "Good job. You jotted down the exact time Ryan reported the fire and when we dispatched the Aurora Crew. I'll enter the data. Oh, I see you emailed the AFS Situations Unit in Fairbanks. Are you sure you don't want to work dispatch?"

"I'm a firefighter. Not cut out to work in an office." Raynie gave her a lopsided smile.

"Sorry you couldn't go with Aurora Crew this morning. You'll be out on the fireline tomorrow for sure. I fought fire with Aurora Crew until I got pregnant." Angela patted her belly.

"How many seasons?"

"Just one. That was enough for me. I wasn't cut out for firefighting." Angela broke out in a wide smile. "Dang smokejumpers. They're all about safety and preparedness, but Gunnar's protection apparently had a hole in it."

"Oh," chuckled Raynie. "Hope it all worked out for the best."

"It truly has. We've been married for almost a year." Angela switched gears. "Have you and Cohen coordinated on the hotshot training?"

"Not yet. He's—exasperating. And such a know-it-all..." Raynie trailed off.

"Why do you say that?" Angela gave her a surprised look. "You two aren't hitting if off? Cohen is one of the easiest guys to get along with on the Aurora Crew."

"He thinks I flirt with people. First the air tanker pilot, then the smokejumper who called in the fire. I don't flirt with people on the job. I'm a professional."

Angela gave her a thoughtful look. "Sounds like Cohen likes you."

"Funny way of showing it," muttered Raynie. "Why do guys think that when a woman is friendly, she's flirting?"

"That's how some guys are. Like there was this kid back in school who called me names, threw stuff at me, and always made me cry. A few weeks later, I got a love note from him." Angela grinned. "You never can tell."

Raynie didn't feel like talking about Cohen Tremblay. She pointed to a tray of leftover rolls and muffins. "I brought these this morning. My sister and I have a bakery business."

"You made these?" Angela's eyes grew wide as she lifted the plastic wrap and peeked. She pounced on a cinnamon roll like a brown bear after a leaping salmon.

"We'd pay you to make these for us. That is, if y'all are willing." Angela quickly added. "I can arrange it with the kitchen staff."

"I'll see what I can do." The last thing Raynie wanted was more on her plate. She had enough, having to deal with Tremblay.

RAYNIE WAS PREPARING to go at the end of the workday when the screen door slammed. A few of the Aurora Crew shuffled in to get mail and check in with dispatch. The smell of smoke lingered after they left to shower and eat dinner.

Tremblay trudged in and ambled to the counter. "How did things go here today?"

"Fine." Raynie focused on the desktop monitor. "How did things go on the fire?" she asked in a flat tone.

"We contained it before the wind could take it." He spotted the muffin tray at the end of the counter. "Where'd these come from?"

"Made them," she said, staring at her monitor, fingers tapping the keyboard.

"Can I have this last one?" he asked cautiously, lifting a chocolate muffin.

"Well. I don't know. Can you?" Eyes still locked on her monitor, she sensed he tiptoed on eggshells. *Good.* If she would've had an egg handy, she might have bonked him with it.

When Tremblay didn't respond, she stopped typing and swiveled her head toward him. If looks could kill, he wouldn't be six feet under—he'd be in a blazing inferno, far worse than the one he'd fought today.

Tremblay froze, with the muffin halfway to his wide open mouth. He flicked his eyes at her, back to the muffin, then set it down. He stepped over to the center of the counter and folded his hands on it.

"Something tells me you're angry. What was it this time? Something I did or something I said?"

She avoided looking at him, hoping he wouldn't notice she'd typed the same paragraph three times.

"If you can't figure that out, then there's no hope for you."

"Well, I guess there's no hope for me, since I'm not a mind reader." He moved to the crew inbox and thumbed through the mail.

She stole glances at him while he rummaged through the stack.

A somber expression crossed his face as he stopped and stared at a pink envelope. He tore it open and read the contents, wincing as he read.

Apparently not good news, and Raynie couldn't resist being snarky.

"What's the matter? Girlfriend dump you?" She hadn't intended to sound snarky, but it leaked out anyway.

Tremblay shook his head, his mouth in a straight line. "I'm going to need that muffin." He stepped over and lifted it.

"Thanks for this. See you tomorrow." A frown pleated his forehead as he jammed the letter and envelope into his sooty shirt pocket. He pushed the screen door open with such force, it slammed shut behind him.

"Yeah. Sure. Bye." Shame flooded her after behaving like Miss Snarky Face.

Angela entered the room and waved her hand in front of her face.

"Woo! Firefighters fresh off a fire are as stinky as a box of armpits." She took her seat at the dispatch desk. "Looks like Cohen received unwelcome news."

"Must be from his girlfriend back in Canada," said Raynie. "A person could smell that envelope from Antarctica."

"Was it addressed to 'Coey'?"

"How'd you know?"

Angela laughed. "Oh hon, that's no girlfriend. That's from Cohen's little sister back home. He always talks about her."

Now it was Raynie's turn to feel like an idiot for making assumptions. "Judging from the look on his face, he didn't like what was in the letter."

"Hope everything is okay," said Angela, staring out the door.

Raynie's curiosity got the best of her. "How long has Tremblay worked with the Aurora Crew? He seems chummy with the women. Is he a player, a womanizer?"

Angela laughed. "Oh goodness, no. He appointed himself crew protector for the women from day one, when he first joined Aurora last fire season. No one gets hyper about it. It's just who he is."

"What do you mean by crew protector? The women I know who fight fire can handle themselves just fine." Raynie stood to gather her day pack and the empty muffin tray.

"Cohen appointed himself as a protector because that's his nature. He said his mama drilled it into him. He's trained all-female fire crews in Canada, so the guys tease him about being too much in touch with his feminine side." Angela grinned. "I think it's cool."

Raynie's brows shot up. "No kidding? That's interesting."

"Cohen is direct and uses big words, but he means well. Not a vindictive bone in his body. Everyone likes him, except Liz's boyfriend." Angela leaned toward her and whispered. "They had fisticuffs last fire season, when Cohen made a play for Liz."

"Liz? The one with the light brown hair who looks like a runway model?"

Angela laughed. "Actually, she was an exotic dancer in Vegas, but she busted his little pussycat heart when she hooked up with our former crew boss."

"They seemed awfully chummy on yesterday's fire," Raynie commented.

Angela's brown eyes twinkled. "Are you interested in our Canada boy?"

"Oh, heck no." Raynie's face heated, and she waved away the notion. "Just curious. Since I have to work with him and all."

Angela leaned forward on her elbows. "I know one thing. Whomever snags Cohen's heart will outdo any record catch of king salmon in Alaska. He's one of the good ones. Trust me on that."

"Good to know."

Despite Angela's best efforts, Raynie remained unconvinced. He may have star-studded looks, but a ripped body wasn't the be-all and end-all. She liked men with substance, who respected women working in wildland fire.

She rose and headed for the door. "I'll see you tomorrow."

As Raynie stepped up into her truck, it occurred to her she may have misjudged Tremblay. If the Aurora Crew women held him in high regard, maybe he wasn't so bad. She'd talk herself into giving him a fairer shake. Hard to do when they resisted each other like crude oil and glacial water.

She heaved out a sigh. Tomorrow was another day. Once she and Tremblay both got organized with the hotshot crew training, maybe they'd get along.

After all, it was only for a few weeks.

I can stand on my head for a few weeks.

Chapter 10

By the time Cohen reached the bunkhouse he shared with Rego, Tupa, and the others, his nose was so far out of joint, it was barely on his face. He headed straight for his locker, got his towels, and beelined for the showers so he wouldn't have to talk to anyone.

His sister Rochelle had written that his parents were getting divorced. It sucked more for her as a sixteen-year-old living at home than it did for him. His parents' constant battles had driven him away, and he wished Shelly was old enough to escape as well. He wanted to talk to his little sister and maybe convince her and his parents to let her live with him. Maybe he'd get a house in Fairbanks and move off the fire base at Fort Wainwright.

He dried off and scowled at himself in the mirror. He'd let his blond hair grow longer in silent protest aimed at his father. Maybe he'd wear a man bun, like Tupa, and start a beard to spite his father's clean-cut corporate image.

Screw the image.

He tramped back to the bunkhouse and flopped onto his bed. The other guys were already sawing logs. He set his phone alarm, stripped down, and crawled between the sheets.

Before he drifted off, Raynie's shocked face played in his mind. Why did he say that asslick remark about Ryan O'Connor and that tanker pilot? Wasn't the first time his off-the-cuff remarks had gotten him into trouble. Words often tumbled from his mouth before he could stop them.

He'd make it right and apologize. They had to work together. He'd offer her an olive branch. Maybe it would help to get her away from the office, go have coffee or something. Clocks were ticking, and soon Raynie would return to her state job in Palmer.

He liked to take walks. Maybe Raynie would like to walk along the Susitna River with Denali Mountain in the distance, set them both at ease and on neutral ground.

Then he wouldn't have to go alone.

EARLY THE NEXT MORNING, Cohen stepped out for a run and spotted Raynie getting out of her pickup in the fire base parking lot. She wore running gear, shorts, and a tank top that revealed a lean build and legs that wouldn't quit. As she stuck earbuds in, he jogged over.

"Care to join me for a run along the Susitna River?" he asked. Maybe they could get along better doing something non-work related.

She glanced up in surprise, giving him an unsmiling once-over in his shorts and muscle tee.

He sensed her hesitation. "Don't feel obligated or anything," he said offhandedly. He waited while she chewed on his invitation.

"Just thought I'd ask."

"Sure. Why not?" She tucked her keys into one pocket, then yanked the buds from her ears and stuffed them in another pocket, along with her phone.

Good. She took my olive branch.

The sun was already high after partying all night like a happy drunk with a hangover.

"I always stretch first," she sniffed, lifting a foot onto the cedar fence railing. Her eyes still held a hint of the hollow sadness he'd observed the first time he met her.

He pointed. "Be careful. We just stained that."

"Now you tell me?" She yanked her foot off and folded herself at the waist, arms stretched around those never-ending legs.

He lifted his shoulder in a partial shrug. "Just did."

She stood tall and turned her face away, but he still caught her eye roll. She swiveled her head back to him.

"Have you started the crew on their one-point-five-mile run, sit-ups, push-ups, and chin-ups?"

Cohen raised his foot behind him and grabbed it to stretch his thigh muscle.

"Started them the day Tara announced we would train the crew as hotshots."

"At least you've done that much."

He didn't appreciate her condescending tone. But instead of reacting like a jerk as he was tempted, he held himself in check, and inhaled a deep, quiet breath.

Patience. She has things going on you know nothing about.

"Have you determined who'll be sawyers, saw boss, and scout captains?" she asked.

"This crew has worked together for several fire seasons, so they already have that figured out."

"First, I want to spend time with the crew and gauge their skill sets." She clasped her hands behind her and stretched, causing her chest to stick out.

Cohen glimpsed the outline of her breasts and jerked his head up toward the dark clouds in the west.

"I'm betting there'll be lightning. We'd better get a move on. Don't want to miss breastfast."

Raynie jerked her head toward him. "*Breast*fast? Are you serious?"

"Whoops!" Heat flooded him, and he squeezed his eyes closed. What a loser thing to say.

Great, not only does she despise me, she also thinks I'm a wolf.

Raynie broke into a jog and called over her shoulder, "I brought muffins today for *break*-fast."

Cohen slammed his lame Freudian slip to the ground so he could stomp on it. He caught up to Raynie as they reached the river. He wanted to get them on a better track.

"I understand you have a bakery business?"

"Yep." She wasn't talkative, and it was his fault. *Way to go, slick,* he berated himself.

An eagle pair caught updrafts and circled above the river, commanding air. He watched them as he continued his run. The trail became uneven, with dips, divots, and fist-sized rocks lying in wait to twist an ankle. He spotted a moose up ahead, munching on willow.

"Let's rest a minute. Give that bull some wiggle room."

"No argument from me," Raynie exhaled and joined Cohen walking in circles to reduce their heart rates. Her cheeks flushed pink, reminding him of apples.

Denali appeared in all her glory. He pointed. "Check out the mountain. It's clear. No haze."

"Beautiful." She feasted her eyes on the spellbinding blue and white monolith that seemed like she could reach out and grab it.

Cohen sucked in a breath. "I need to say...that is, I...well, I'm sorry about yesterday."

"Which part of yesterday?"

"What I said about Ryan O'Connor. It was out of line."

"You bet it was." She fixed her eyes on Denali. "Why did you say it?"

"Don't know. Just had an off day, I guess." But he knew. The engaging way she talked to everyone else and not him bothered him immensely. Questioning her decision that day on the Hiland Fire must have really annoyed her—more than he thought.

"Couldn't help noticing you seemed upset yesterday after reading your letter." She said this out of nowhere, and it caught him off guard.

He stared at the ground, kicking a tree root. "Parents are divorcing. Wasn't completely unexpected, but still hard to hear my mother had filed. The letter was from my sixteen-year-old sister. This is difficult for her. I'm her only brother, and I'm gone." He wiped his brow and took a pull on his water bottle.

"What's her name?"

"Rochelle. We call her Shelly."

"As you know, I have a younger sister as well. Her name is Kira. She's seventeen. My folks live in Globe, Arizona, and sent her up to live with me."

"Because she wanted to experience Alaska?"

Raynie shook her head. "To get her away from the drug culture she was in. She got involved with some not-so-desirable friends, so my mother sent her to stay with me."

"Is she still doing drugs?" he asked.

"Not since she's been here. I've kept her busy with our bakery business and got her a job with Trish at the Roadhouse."

"That's good."

"Yeah. She's met kids her age who are into hiking, fishing, and running dogs."

"I feel bad that I'm not able to help Shelly navigate this divorce." He shook his head. "But I can't leave right when fire season is ramping up. Called her when I got up this morning. She cried on the phone."

"That's a tough one."

Do I detect empathy in Raynie's tone?

He checked his watch. "We should head back."

"Think it's okay to use the ladies' shower at the fire base?" she asked.

"Of course, you work there. Let's meet with the crew to get them started on training soon as we're cleaned up. We can do it over breakfast in the mess hall." He was careful to pronounce "breakfast" correctly.

"Okay," said Raynie.

Good. They'd found something in common. Younger teen sisters they both felt responsible for. Raynie had accepted his first olive branch. It was a start. He was tired of all their discord.

Maybe she'd accept another.

Chapter 11

At the end of Raynie's second week, Tremblay walked into the office late Friday afternoon and leaned on the counter in front of the dispatcher's desk.

"I say we call a truce."

"A truce? Didn't know we were at war."

Raynie cocked a brow at the rolled-up sleeves of his denim jacket, exposing the defined muscles and solid veins in his slightly hairy forearms.

"We aren't as far as I'm concerned. But you seem to think we are." He straightened. "Care to run into Anchorage with me tomorrow? Have to get some equipment. We could do something fun afterwards."

She stopped typing. "Define 'fun.'"

He studied the ceiling. "Well, we could go to the Anchorage Museum or to the Alaska Zoo. I haven't been to either. It would be a change of pace from all things fire."

She folded her arms and gave him a quick up-and-down assessment. He was a whole different person without his constant yellow Nomex. Faded denim suited him well, and so did the red T-shirt that hugged his chest. A virtual arrow pinged at her, but she mentally blocked it.

Raynie jerked a breath into her lungs. "I told Angela I'd fill in so she could spend time with her baby."

"Too bad. We could have worked out terms for a peace treaty."

"I highly doubt it." She recalled their roller coaster of a week. "We didn't agree on a single thing at work all week long. You picked arguments with me over everything—how fast to deploy a fire shelter, the proper way to carry a chainsaw—even how to swing a Pulaski. The last thing I'm up for is to be trapped inside a vehicle with a perfectionist, arguing over the speed limit on the Glenn Highway to Anchorage." She sat back with folded arms and her resting witch face, waiting for his reaction.

Tremblay's mouth fell open. He obviously hadn't expected this rant. When he recovered, he came around the counter and stood next to her chair, resting his hand on the back of it. He leaned down, invading her space.

"I'm not a perfectionist," he said in a quiet, even tone.

His proximity unsettled her, and she leaned away from him.

"Yes, you...yes, you are," she stammered, her gaze tracking his, quickening her pulse. She glanced nervously around the office.

"No one's around. Speak your truth." He let go of her chair and straightened. "That was a good start."

"All right. Since you really want to know." His being close rattled her, but if he wanted the truth, she'd give it to him.

In spades.

"No one can live up to your standards. No one! And you constantly pick arguments," she erupted, avoiding eyes that reminded her of the Pacific Ocean.

Tremblay pointed at her. "Let's set the record straight. *You*, Miss Atwood, pick most of our arguments with *me*." He pointed a thumb at himself.

"That's not true, and you know it." She glared at him. "If we can't get along for two seconds, what makes you think we will for a whole day?"

"It would certainly make things easier for working together." He straightened. "I'm willing to try, but evidently you have a problem with that."

"I'm not the one with the problem!" Her voice rose an octave as heat flooded her. "There's no point arguing over who picks the most arguments. Can you give it a rest?"

His brows rose at her emotional outburst.

"Just for the record, you started this one." A corner of his mouth turned up. "Just saying."

"No, I didn't. Just saying." She raised her hands in exasperation. "Okay, this one's a draw. Look, I already told Angela I'd cover for her. Besides that, I have to run Kam's sled dogs."

Tremblay tilted his head in that annoying way. "How often do you run them?"

She rolled her chair away from his space invasion.

"A few times a week," she lied. She wasn't about to say she hadn't run them since she and Kira got their ganglines tangled last time.

"I ran dogs with my cousin when we worked ski patrol at Whistler." He lifted sunglasses from his pocket and put them on. "Tell you what. You admit to starting half of our arguments, and I'll help you run sled dogs. Deal?"

"What? Are you serious?" Her mom always said never kick a gift horse in the mouth, but she'd failed to mention how to swallow pride when the offer comes from the enemy.

"You know how to do everything, don't you?"

"Not everything, apparently." Tremblay gave her an edgy glance and pulled a set of keys from his pocket. He jangled them as he strolled toward the door.

She could sure use the help with Kam's sled dogs. She hadn't stuck to the exercise program Kam had set up for the summer. She threw up her arms.

"All right, I started half our arguments." Every syllable she uttered prickled her throat. "There. Happy?"

Tremblay twisted to smile at her. "Now, was that so hard? It's a deal, then." He pushed open the door.

She watched his brawny backside disappear down the porch steps, the screen door slamming behind him.

"Hi, Cohen!" a woman's voice rang out.

Raynie rocketed from her chair to peer through the screen door, curious to see who'd greeted him. Something inside her stirred, seeing Tremblay laughing with a woman she didn't know.

He's never acted that way with me. Then again, he was trying to be nice, and I gave him a cold shoulder.

But he was so argumentative and stubborn, she reminded herself...and a walking Wikipedia. Contrary to his own opinion, yes, he was a frigging perfectionist. But there was something else about him that bugged her—something she couldn't put her finger on. She sat back and thought for a minute when it hit her like a plane load of retardant.

Tremblay's mannerisms resembled Taydon's—the way he talked, the way he walked, the head tilt—especially the head tilt. Being around him chopped into her heart like a million axes. Constant reminders of the love she'd lost.

I don't like Cohen Tremblay because he reminds me of Taydon.

Now that she was fully aware of this, what was she to do with Taydon's memories? Pretend they didn't happen? Stuff them in a lockbox in the basement of her soul, so pain wouldn't jab her every time she saw Cohen Tremblay?

Taydon hadn't given her an engagement ring, so she technically wasn't his fiancée. She was in an uncategorized limbo—not a fiancée, yet more than a girlfriend. No matter how she cut it, she didn't have a playbook for this.

There were no grief playbooks for limbo dwellers.

Chapter 12

During yesterday's training, Raynie had started a heated debate about the most efficient way to saw and fell trees when building a fireline. Tupa, who was an experienced sawyer, also jumped into the argument. Then Rego and Liz tossed in their two cents, siding with Raynie. That didn't sit well with Cohen.

He'd dug in harder with his viewpoint, surprising the crew with his stubbornness. He hated wasting valuable time arguing over chainsaws brands, like Stihl and Husqvarna—their hotshot qualification clock was ticking down.

This morning he painstakingly reviewed today's agenda with Raynie before gathering the crew together. She hadn't picked apart *every* aspect of his agenda—just every other aspect—which, he supposed, was progress. At least they weren't yelling at each other like the day before, but their constant bickering ate at him day by day, souring his mood.

This afternoon it escalated when Raynie disagreed with him about how hard to push the Aurora Crew. She told him to ease up when he wanted to push them harder. He figured crew members would speak up if the going got too tough. Raynie said no, they wouldn't, because they wanted to prove themselves. The rest of the day had gone downhill from there, and Cohen's head ached.

After training ended for the day, the two of them faced off in the conference room, as they had the day before. And the day before that. Raynie picked apart what he'd said to the crew about effective leadership.

"The first rule of leadership is to treat your people like they're not idiots, and they won't act like idiots," she'd said with a stare that had drilled straight through him.

"I don't treat people like idiots! That's not what I do!" His voice rose and he struggled to reign in his self-control. He'd never lost it on the job and wasn't about to start now.

"You were talking down to the crew yesterday, like you have with me. Another rule of leadership is to treat your people like they're making a difference, and they'll make that difference." She went on to lecture him like a Super Bowl coach in a losing streak at halftime—staring with such ferocity he expected lasers to shoot from her eyes.

Cohen chewed his lip, waiting for her to finish. He was so tense he could hear himself squeak.

"Are you done?" he asked calmly. He couldn't figure out the source of her anger—whether it was him or something else.

"I'm never done when it comes to training skilled firefighters. It's up to you and me to make sure no one dies fighting fires! I don't take it lightly." Her agitation seemed to grow by the second.

Dark tendrils shook loose from her bun and hung down. He wished her hair would fall the rest of the way down.

"Thanks for the leadership wisdom," he said coolly. "I know what works in the field and what doesn't, when the safety of firefighters is at stake. And I have a good grip on the qualities of leadership."

Raynie formed a 'C' with her hand. "Know what this is? It's called compromise. Didn't they teach you that wherever you went to school? It's sort of important when working with other humans." She used the same tone as the first day he'd rankled her on the Hiland Fire.

Cohen sensed her temper percolating on a high setting, but he refused to let her bully him.

"I know all about compromise. I do it every time I talk to you. Stop playing defense, Atwood." He held his breath, hoping her cheese wouldn't slide off her cracker.

"Pot, kettle, black again, Tremblay! You're the one who's defensive! And no, you don't compromise—you believe your way is the *only* way." Raynie folded her arms. "No wonder you're single. I'll bet all your girlfriends dumped you because you suck at compromise. Am I right?" Her arms shot up in the air and her face flushed scarlet.

There goes her cheese.

"What is your *deal?*" Cohen rubbed his throbbing temples. That last grenade—no, it was an incendiary bomb—hit below the belt.

He held up his hands. "Can we please call a ceasefire? How about we put away the boxing gloves, and have a drama free, unicorn-farting-rainbows day tomorrow?" He could tell from the clenched fists at her sides that probably was not what he should have said. Too late now, it's already out there.

Oh, brother.

Raynie's eyes flashed. "You're the one who whips out the boxing gloves!" She wheeled around and stomped out of the room, leaving him oozing with regret.

"She needed to hear it," he grumbled, trying to justify what he'd said. It wasn't working—he just felt shittier.

Cohen shook his head and let out a long sigh. He switched off the light, closed the door, and ambled outside to the bunkhouse, his stomach churning at the loads of fun tomorrow would bring.

THE NEXT MORNING, WHEN Raynie walked into the conference room, she nodded politely at Cohen in front of the crew and took a seat in the back of the room. Not in her normal spot next to him at the front.

Cohen started things off. He was uneasy about delivering his next lecture but had to deliver it. He glimpsed Raynie's somber face, took a breath, and dove in.

"Here's the deal, Aurora Crew. We won't go easy on you once we're in the field. We can't. You'll sweat and cuss and sweat some more. The Alaska Fire Service didn't ask me to do your hotshot training to win a popularity contest. But I guarantee you'll be a qualified hotshot firefighter for Alaska's next fire season."

Cohen glanced back at Raynie, who was still as a stone.

"Raynie, do you have anything to add?"

She shook her head with an unreadable expression.

He continued. "This means you may have to keep fighting fire full time until you're back in Alaska next spring. Don't worry, California and other states will keep you busy until then. Colorado had one of their worst fires in the dead of winter. Conditions in The West have changed. And we must change with it. Doss will arrange for you to be dispatched to the lower forty-eight."

The room fell quiet as this sunk in. Finally, Tupa spoke up. "Most of us need the work, anyway." Heads nodded all the way around as others agreed.

Cohen's lips curved into a half-smile. "Good. As we all know, a positive attitude is vital in this game." He glanced back at Raynie, sensing she wanted to say something.

Raynie rose and moved to the front to stand next to him. He braced for the worst.

"Not only do you need a positive attitude, you also need a can-do attitude. As a hotshot crew, you'll work on the hottest, most dangerous parts of a wildfire. You'll be expected to be self-sufficient, hiking into and out of the most dangerous part of a fire. That's in addition to putting in a full day's work on the fireline."

Cohen breathed relief that she hadn't torpedoed what he said, so he continued.

"You'll be held to the highest standard as wildland firefighters. As Tara said, if hotshotting isn't for you, no one will fault you for opting out. Now I'll turn it over to my state counterpart." He shot Raynie a polite smile and took a seat in the front.

As usual, Raynie was prepared, and launched into a discussion about fire scenarios. No debates, only a healthy discussion. He had to admit, he admired her professionalism and knowledge about wildland fire. While he didn't see unicorns farting rainbows, at least she was chill today.

He hoped this was a start. They'd both said their peace and now it was time to move on. He thought a lot about it last night.

He resolved to work on compromise. And listen more instead of talking more. He'd follow her leadership advice—show Raynie he valued her work, that she was making a difference. Because deep down, he was certain she'd make a difference no matter what.

At the end of the day, Raynie waited until the room emptied. She walked up to Cohen and extended her hand.

"I'm sorry I lost my shit yesterday. It won't happen again." She looked away. "Sorry about the girlfriends dumping you comment."

"I'm sorry if I offended you as well," he said, shaking her hand. He liked the feel of it but refrained from giving it a squeeze.

"You're a good leader and I was wrong to say otherwise." She gave him a half smile and left the room.

He accepted her olive branch. They were from different camps, but their goal was the same.

Fight the damn fires.

Chapter 13

The next morning, Raynie stood in front of the twenty-person Aurora Crew, sitting cross-legged on the grass in front of the fire base building.

"Fireline performance of an Interagency Hotshot Crew is far more rigorous than what you're used to on your Type Two handline crew. Your physical ability to do the job is critical to morale, personal health, and safety." She glanced around at the nodding heads and continued. "Since you've already passed the Work Capacity Pack Test where you carried a forty-five-pound pack for three miles in forty-five minutes, you're now ready for us to brutalize you."

Tremblay pointed his thumb at her for dramatic emphasis. "She's not kidding."

Raynie gave him an odd look. He didn't correct or counter what she said. She distributed a fitness requirements list.

"We'll start your fitness requirements with you doing a one-and-a-half mile run in ten minutes or fewer, then we'll do your push-ups, sit-ups, and chin-ups. You'll be timed in one-minute increments. How many chin-ups you'll do is based on your weight." She glanced up to see what had the attention of the crew, whose necks craned toward the parking lot.

Raynie traced their gaze to Vanessa, the new dispatcher, wearing a cropped belly top and shorts so short, it looked like she waltzed around in her undies. She stood at the edge of the lawn in a Vogue model pose, waving at the crew.

Raynie rolled her eyes at the men enthusiastically waving back. She glanced at Tremblay. He didn't wave, but his gaze lingered on sassy little Vanessa.

"Not exactly appropriate dress for fire duty," commented Raynie.

"She works in an office, not in the field." He gave her a lopsided shrug. "I don't see anything wrong with it."

"Of course you don't." She put a lid on her snark. After apologizing to Tremblay yesterday, she was trying harder to get along with him. They'd each said some harsh things, and she wanted to put it behind her.

Raynie addressed the crew. "All right, everyone, let's focus. Remember: a hotshot crew's ability to perform in demanding conditions for extended periods of time depends on the fitness of individual crew members. It is physically and mentally demanding. Split into four groups of five. Choose an activity and use your phones for timers."

She waited for Tremblay to finish ogling the new dispatcher.

"Earth to Tremblay? Hello? Push-ups and sit-ups, remember? You take half of the crew and I'll take half." She waited for the pushback. No pushback. *Good.*

Instead, he inclined his head in agreement. "As you wish."

Her mouth curved into an unconscious smile. "Thanks, Westley."

Tremblay's resulting laugh filled her with a warm feeling, like a comfortable blanket. After rubbing her the wrong way for so long, this new feeling was rather pleasant.

"How do you like our unicorns farting rainbows day?" asked Raynie, looking up at him. She wished she were taller. Felt like she looked up at people most of the time.

"I like it." He moved off to work with his half of the crew, overseeing their fitness routines.

Raynie's heart swelled when she made him laugh, and she was aware that her defenses were weakening. As she watched Tupa effortlessly move through his fitness reps, Tremblay sauntered over to her.

"Now there's a guy who's fit. I'll bet Tupa can out-work anyone on this crew. I saw him in action last year."

She nodded, her heart swelling bigger—this time from his proximity. Raynie swung her focus back to Tupa, in time to catch Kenzie eyeing him, darn near salivating. Tupa gave her the side-eye with every couple of chin-ups.

Raynie suppressed a laugh and leaned toward Tremblay. "Those two appear to be into each other."

He nodded. "Kenzie's from Canberra and worked in Samoa a few years ago. She speaks Samoan. That won Tupa over. They hit it off right away last year."

"Are they...you know..." Raynie twirled her finger, liking that it was easier to talk to Tremblay now, embracing their fresh new ground of compromise. She preferred gentle sparring to combat.

She halfway expected him to screw it up.

"In a relationship? Or was your mind in the gutter?" Tremblay seemed to delight in this.

"Of course not! *Your* mind went straight to the gutter!" she volleyed back to him.

"If they do have a relationship, they're chill about it." His understanding tone spoke volumes. He leaned in and scrunched his face. "I'm sure they're just friends."

Raynie sensed he had a solid bond with the individuals on this crew, and she liked that.

Tupa glanced at Kenzie when he finished his chin-ups. "Ten more, for good measure," he said, gripping the metal bar again. When he finished, Kenzie clapped and gave Tupa a thumbs-up.

When Raynie got home from work, she reflected on the day while she fed the howling sled dogs. She and Tremblay had a peaceful day. They'd both worked hard to get along. For the first time in days, she hadn't come home with an upset stomach and a stress headache.

"Hey sled doggies, I need to exercise you," she called out to the wagging horde. "I'm too tired today, but maybe tomorrow I will. I have baking to do tonight." She talked to the huskies like she was discussing plans for the evening with a group of friends.

She petted each dog and Wacko was his usual goofy self, licking her to death. She checked Madonna's underbelly full of puppies. She wished she had the never-ending energy of a sled dog. Madonna bounced around and yipped as if she had an empty belly.

After settling the dogs for the evening, Raynie went inside and changed into shorts and a tank top with no bra. She straggled to the kitchen and pulled out the ingredients and baking pans. Best to get going on it. She would love it if her younger sister to help. She glanced at her watch.

Where the heck is Kira?

Chapter 14

Cohen liked how training went today. Overall, the crew members were strengthening their fitness abilities, which pleased him. He still had to nag them, but they did as he asked. No one complained. Not even Rego. But then he was a former U.S. Marine, which Cohen respected.

He needed shampoo and soap, so after dinner he stepped outside to walk down to the store next to the Denali Roadhouse at the other end of the main street.

Talk and laughter from a group of guys in the parking lot got his attention. A young girl sat on a tailgate, chatting with them. She looked much younger than the three guys gathered around her.

"Your name is Kira?" One of the older guys holding a bottle of beer sidled up to her.

Cohen's head snapped to attention. He remembered Raynie saying her little sister's name was Kira.

"Yes," she said, clearly enjoying the attention of the much older men.

Cohen guessed two were in their early thirties, and the third about forty, and crusty as hell. These vultures were circling, so he'd see what they had in mind, although he had a pretty good idea.

"Hello, everyone. How are things?"

The three guys eyed him suspiciously in his yellow Nomex and green fire pants. One took a pull on his beer. "Just fine. You work here?"

"Yep." Cohen casually looked over at the three men, aware he was crashing their private chat. "You guys here to apply for firefighting?"

The three exchanged *this-guy-can't-be-serious* looks.

Cohen looked Kira in the eye. "You're Raynie's sister, right?"

She seemed startled. "How'd you know that?"

He glanced at the disgruntled looks on the men's faces and turned to Kira. "Your sister asked me to give you a ride home," he lied, hoping he wouldn't go to hell.

Kira's eyes widened. "Are you that Tremblay guy my sister talks about? I've seen you at the Roadhouse."

Cohen was taken aback that Raynie had mentioned him. "I work with your sister, if that's what you mean."

"Oh." She gave a flirtatious smile to the three salivating sharks, eyeing her like a tuna.

Cohen waved her toward his pickup. "Come on, I'm giving you a ride. Your sister's worried about you."

Kira held up her phone and wiggled it. "If she were, she'd be calling."

"Told her I'd get you home." He knew what these guys had on their minds—and he'd be damned if he'd let it happen. He didn't trust these creeps as far as he could throw their sorry asses. Cohen climbed into his truck, fired up the engine, and eased it next to the truck Kira leaned on.

He reached across and pushed open the passenger door. "Let's go."

Kira shot him a disgusted look but reluctantly did as he asked.

"Bye, guys," she said in a pleasant tone, but the three men were not at all pleased. She climbed in and closed the door.

"They're too old for you." Cohen shifted and drove off toward Whispering Spruce Road.

"You don't know how old they are. They invited me to a party."

"Exactly."

She shook her head. "What's that supposed to mean?"

He didn't want to get into a thing with Raynie's sister. Staying on neutral ground was a safer choice.

"Their intentions were most likely not honorable."

"Honorable? How could you tell?" She distracted herself by scrolling on her phone, the way his sister always did whenever they'd had serious talks.

"I'm a mind reader." He recalled explaining this same thing to Shelly. Her laugh played in his mind and ached his chest. He missed her.

Cohen slowed his pickup in front of the cabin and stopped. "There you go. Your sister will be glad you're here."

"Thanks." Kira climbed out and leaned in. "Just so you know, I could have handled myself."

"I'm sure you could have." Cohen's eyes immediately went to Raynie, walking up behind her sister. His breath caught at her natural beauty. She wasn't a woman who needed makeup. In fact, he figured that would detract from her lovely face.

"Glad you're home," she said to her sister as Kira headed into the cabin.

Raynie had on cutoffs and a white tank top that clung to her form. She'd pulled her hair back into a ponytail, and she waved an oversized oven mitt in the shape of a lobster. She appeared downright domestic as she stepped over to the passenger door, opened it, and leaned her elbows on the seat.

"Thanks for giving Kira a ride home."

"No problem. Happy to do it." He loved the unfettered view of Raynie's braless cleavage, and it quickened his pulse. His heart leaped to his throat as he snapped his focus to her emerald eyes, reflecting Alaska's rosy twilight.

"You returned a human this time, instead of a dog." She smirked. "This is getting to be a routine."

"Seems that way, doesn't it?" He wouldn't mind making this a routine. He was warming to her, chipping away the ice on her shoulder, one piece at a time.

"How do you know my sister?"

He made sure Kira was inside the cabin before explaining. "Play along with my lie. I said you asked me to give her a ride home. Three guys twice her age had Kira cornered in the fire base parking lot. I didn't like the look in their eyes."

Raynie blinked. "What a chivalrous thing to do. Thanks for watching out for her." A smile played on her lips, which he appreciated.

"Happy to," he said. "Didn't intend to intervene, but I didn't trust the situation."

"I wouldn't have either."

"Those guys shouldn't be hanging out in the fire base parking lot anyway. Unless they want a fire job."

She heaved out a sigh. "I feel like a parent. Only without the giving birth thing."

He laughed. "I get that. I feel more like my sister Shelly's dad than her brother most of the time."

"Kids. What can you do?" She waved her oven mitt around and he found it comical.

He let out a breath as he got an idea. "We have tomorrow off, provided there's no fire call. Want to go on a hike?"

She lifted her chin. "Where?"

"I found another trail along the Susitna River." He could tell her wheels were spinning. "No obligation. Just figured it'd be a change of pace..."

"Sure," she cut in. "How about elevenish? I have to feed the dogs and do my baking."

"Elevenish it is. I'll bring lunch."

"I'll bring cookies." Her lips curled up as she offered an olive branch in return.

He gave her a sudden arresting smile. "You should do more of that."

"What?"

He motioned at his mouth, flashing a grin. "This. You're charming when you smile."

"Charming?" Her eyes widened at his comment. "I'd better get back to my baking. See you tomorrow, then. Training went well today, don't you think?" She didn't wait for a response. Instead, she slammed the truck door and ducked inside the cabin.

"Yes, very well," he murmured, knowing what she meant. They hadn't gone for each other's jugulars. He'd take that as progress.

Once he and Raynie got on track of fitness testing, they seemed to get along without much bickering. That's not to say they hadn't disagreed about anything. They'd talked through it calmly, without throttling each other.

Tomorrow will be better. He looked forward to it.

Chapter 15

"Hey sleepyhead, wake up. Look what I found!" Kira stood at the foot of Raynie's bed, holding a large, flat box.

Raynie's eyes fluttered open. She didn't know how long she'd been catnapping, and it took a minute to focus on her little sister looming over her with a box displaying bold black letters: *LEXO MULTI-ROTOR.*

"What's that?" She sat up straight, looking from the box to her sister, who was so excited she practically hopped in place.

"It's a drone! Come on, help me open it," said Kira, setting it down. "I'll get a knife." She headed for the kitchen.

Raynie turned the box toward her to read it. "Where did you get this?"

Kira returned with a serrated knife. "Found it in the boxes you lugged here with you."

"Oh, yeah, Taydon bought it," mumbled Raynie. "Forgot all about it."

Kira had the box open, removed the Styrofoam, and lifted out several parts of a multi-rotor drone. "It's a quadcopter. Takes four rotors to fly. These are amazing. I've watched people fly them." Kira's eyes sparkled like Christmas morning.

Raynie watched Kira unwrap the components. "This must have cost a few bucks."

"I'm sure Taydon could afford it," said Kira, offhandedly.

Raynie shot her a glance. "Why would you say that?"

Kira shrugged, avoiding her sister's gaze. "It's no secret he was dealing."

"But not in Alaska." Raynie stiffened. Surely that can't be true.

Kira gave her a reluctant look. "A girl at the Roadhouse is from Anchorage. She said she knew Taydon."

"How so?" Raynie asked, dread permeating her chest.

"Don't get mad when I tell you this." Kira fiddled with the drone parts. "He sold drugs to her boyfriend."

"That can't be right. Taydon stopped dealing after moving to Alaska. The whole point of moving here was to get him away from our hometown drug culture."

Kira gave her an apologetic look. "No, he hadn't stopped dealing. Taydon just kept it hidden from you."

"He was gone a lot but said it was for work," Raynie said faintly.

Kira hesitated. "I was afraid to bring it up—you've had such an awful time after losing him."

What a gut punch.

Poisoned hatred took root in Raynie's soul. "No doubt Taydon used drug money to buy this drone," she said bitterly.

"I'm sorry." Kira looked dejected.

Despite her anger, Raynie kept her expression neutral and her voice steady, not wanting to upset her sister.

"It wasn't your fault," she said calmly. "How long have you known?"

"A few weeks. Been trying to think of a way to tell you."

"From now on, Kira, just tell me. I'm a big girl. I can take it," admonished Raynie. "You can have the drone. I don't want anything to do with it." Taydon's lie twisted her heart from grief to revulsion.

"I can tolerate a lot, but I can't tolerate liars."

"It's mine, then." Kira tore into the plastic packaging like a million-dollar treasure lay inside, then read the instructions. "Look, it has a thermal camera."

"Once you assemble this thing and fly it, Wacko will try to jump up and eat it," joked Raynie, watching her little sister masterfully construct it.

"That's because Wacko really does think he's an eagle." Kira made a comical face, and Raynie appreciated she was trying to cheer her.

Rooby rose to her feet and stretched. She moseyed over and sniffed the drone, and Raynie petted her. "I know, Rooby. If you can't eat it, why bother?"

Kira picked up the drone. "Let's go fly her." She headed outside, barely able to contain her excitement. The sled dogs came alive when the humans and Rooby stepped outside. They stood wagging their tails.

Raynie followed her sister outside, pointing a finger at the wagging sled dogs. "No barking. We want peace and quiet for two seconds."

Wacko barked twice in response. He tilted his head, glacier-blue eyes bright with curiosity.

Kira moved past the dog yard to an empty corner of the lot. She set the drone on the ground.

Raynie eyed the nearby transmission lines. "Don't fly it near those electric wires," she cautioned. A sudden realization about Taydon dawned on her.

If Taydon was dealing and Maddox showed up to collect money when he got out of prison, that meant they'd both scored on a big drug deal. No way did Raynie want her little sister in danger—but she already was with Maddox in the picture.

"Dammit, Taydon, you rat bastard!" she erupted, angry heat flushing her face.

"I knew I shouldn't have told you," lamented Kira. "Forget Taydon, he was a loser. Mom even said so. Come on, get your mind off him. Let's fly this drone." Kira set it on the ground and stepped away from it.

Rooby sat next to Raynie as she crossed her arms to watch Kira fly the quadcopter. She tried not to think about Taydon lying to her and burdening her with this Maddox situation—but it was impossible. Her sorrow had shifted to revulsion.

Kira powered up the drone, and the four rotors whirred. She lifted it high above the spruce and birch, flying it horizontally in one direction, then another. Kira manipulated the controls, already operating it like a pro.

Raynie loved the sparkle in Kira's big brown eyes and squinted at the whirring quadcopter. "You're good at this."

"Here, you fly it," said Kira, handing her the controller.

"What if I crash it?" Raynie was tempted out of spite for Taydon. She maneuvered the drone like a helicopter, making sure not to hit the trees.

"Isn't it fun?" Kira's joy soothed Raynie's stinging heart. "We should take it somewhere where there's no trees."

"Let's do it tomorrow." Raynie remembered what else she was doing the next day. "Oh wait. After work, I'm going hiking with Cohen." Saying it out loud quickened her pulse.

Kira reclaimed the controller and landed the drone, then swiveled her head toward her sister. "Cohen? You mean that hot guy who drove me home? All the girls at work have a crush on him."

Raynie reached for her phone and scrolled with her thumb until stopping on a head-to-toe photo of Tremblay, standing next to a whiteboard. She'd taken it a few days ago on a whim. To prove this was work-related—or maybe to prove it to herself—she held out her phone.

"See, I work with him. This isn't some random guy."

Kira's eyes widened. "Oh my God! He's even hotter in this photo. Look how ripped he is."

Raynie angled her head to assess. "I guess he's not bad."

Kira shot her an incredulous look. "Not bad? He's flipping gorgeous!"

"He's one of those know-it-all types," sniffed Raynie. "We have trouble getting along."

Kira gave her a curious look. "Then why are you going hiking? If I don't get along with someone at work, I sure as heck don't hang out with them on my own time." She grinned. "I think you like him."

Raynie rushed to clarify. "No, not like-like. I mean, he's okay. He's just a coworker."

Who am I kidding? And why is the heat rushing to my face?

"So what? Go with him. It'll get your mind off Taydon." Kira picked up the drone and went inside the cabin. She had a point.

Raynie followed, with Rooby happily trotting behind. Wacko barked goodnight and the other seven huskies watched them go inside to settle in for the night.

WHILE RAYNIE DID HER baking and then cleaned the kitchen, she thought about Tremblay. She sat at the table and took out her phone. His image still displayed, and she zoomed in with thumb and forefinger until his smiling face filled the screen. She thumbed through the other photos, surprised she had more of Tremblay than Taydon.

With silent fury, she selected every photo of Taydon and deleted them from her phone. Pausing on the last, taken the day he'd asked her to marry him, she wanted to spit on it. She hated herself for loving him—for grieving him. She tapped it with so much force it hurt her finger.

"Goodbye, you lying sack of shit," she muttered.

On her way to bed, Raynie paused at a framed photo of her and Taydon on an end table in the living room. Unable to fathom how the man she'd loved had betrayed her, she picked up the photo and heaved it across the room. The frame hit the log wall and crashed to the floor.

Rooby lifted her head, startled, and Kira ran out of her room. "What the heck was that?"

Raynie forced a lighthearted tone. "Nothing. Just tired of looking at this photo. Go back to bed."

She crossed the room to gather the glass shards and sweep them into a dustpan—vowing never again to waste another precious second grieving Taydon.

Kira stood, watching. "Feel better?"

"Much." Raynie heaved out a sigh of relief after throwing away her sorrow along with the shards of glass. As for the photo?

She'd burn that later. She wanted to watch it curl up in flame and turn to ashes, just like her deceased fiancé.

After plumping her pillow just so, Raynie grabbed her phone to peek at Tremblay's sapphire eyes. She zoomed out, grudgingly admitting how hot he was. Just for fun, she zoomed in on the area below his hips. Green Nomex pants weren't the sexiest attire, but he could wear clown pants and it wouldn't matter.

Maybe Kira is right. What do I have to lose?

She fell asleep staring at Tremblay's photo. When her phone fell forward and hit her nose, she woke with a start. She turned it off, and the warmth of Rooby's fur soothed her as she drifted back to sleep.

Her last thought before dreamland was how it would go tomorrow with Tremblay.

And if she could handle the constant reminders of Taydon.

Chapter 16

The next morning, Cohen rose early to do his workout. He was pleased to see the crew doing the same thing. After running three miles and lifting weights, Cohen met Tupa and Rego as he headed to the washroom for a shower.

"Tremblay, want to take a drive to Denali?"

He slung a bath towel over his shoulder. "I'll take a raincheck on that one. Have other plans."

Rego grinned. "Let me guess. Might it be with a certain state hotshot firefighter? You turn into a Ken doll whenever she's around." Rego tapped his temple. "Wasn't born yesterday."

Cohen raised his brows dismissively, invoking a casual American accent. "It's just a hike, dude."

"Uh-huh, right. So, you can do some training coordination," deadpanned Tupa, twirling his forefinger. "Either that, or you'll wind up tearing each other to shreds."

"Right. Now, if you boys will excuse me, I have to hit the washroom."

"You mean bathroom," Rego corrected.

Cohen gave him a look of reproach. "You Americans are crass. We call it a washroom."

Tupa smirked. "In Samoa, we say it's a *faletaele.*"

"In Alaska, it's a shitter," said Rego.

The other two laughed, and Cohen shook his head. "You guys ooze class."

He enjoyed his crewmates, but after working with them all week, he could use a break. When fire season ramps up, they'll be steeped in togetherness.

"See you in the mess hall for breakfast."

"We'll save some coffee for you," said Rego, as he and Tupa headed over to eat.

When Cohen finished his shower, he spruced himself up, then headed to the mess hall to snag a cup of coffee before meeting Raynie. He noticed a new face, an eye-catching blonde seated at the long table with the Aurora Crew, talking and laughing.

"Tremblay! Have you met the new dispatcher?" Rego called to him, pointing at Vanessa.

"Angela introduced us a few days ago." Cohen didn't mention Vanessa had hit on him the first instant he met her. As he approached the table, her eyes had a radar missile-lock on him.

"How do you like working at Talkeetna Base?"

Vanessa gave him a horizontal smile so broad it stretched around Denali.

"Your crew mates are telling me what a meanie you are."

"Yes, I'm known for torturing people." He glanced at Tupa and Rego, who kept their eyes trained on the pretty new dispatcher.

Vanessa stood with her empty tray and shadowed Cohen, invading his personal space. He fought the instinct to back up and stared down into her large brown eyes.

Flirting with him for all she was worth, Vanessa reached for his hand. Gazing into his eyes, she turned his hand over to expose the maple leaf tattoo on the underside of his wrist.

"I understand you're from Canada."

He stared at her ringless hand, grasping his. "It seems that way."

"I love Canadian men. You're all so gentlemanly." Vanessa rubbed her forefinger on his wrist tat. "I transferred up here from Soldotna."

"Welcome to our fire base." He tugged away from her grip and stepped back.

"I would have applied sooner had I known how good looking you federal firefighters were up here," she purred. "Let's grab a beer sometime. I hear Susitna Brewery has terrific microbrews."

"I've heard that." Cohen had the urge to escape. "Good to see you."

"Not as good as it was for me." Vanessa sent him a flirty wave and sashayed off in her tight white pants, leaving nothing to the imagination.

When the door slammed shut behind her, Rego opened his mouth to comment.

Cohen held up his hand. "Don't say it. I know you want to. But don't." He shot a warning smile at Rego.

Rego's swoony gaze lingered on the door. "I won't state the obvious. But I will say Vanessa has the hots for you, Canada Dry. We should all be so lucky." He shot Cohen a shrewd grin. "However, we both know who's really on your mind."

Cohen maintained a neutral expression. "No one is on my mind. I'm just taking a stroll to commune with nature. Have an enjoyable day at Denali Park." He adjusted his day pack and strolled out the door.

Tupa followed him on his way out. "You're making the better choice, brah," he said in his deep baritone. "Don't forget what happened last time you hit on a woman on the Aurora Crew."

Cohen turned to Tupa. "Don't worry, I learned my lesson. And technically, Atwood isn't a member of our crew."

Tupa broke out in a gradual smile, like a cool engine warming up. "All the same, proceed with caution." He flashed Cohen a shaka sign, a Hawaiian 'hang loose' gesture with a thumb and pinky salute.

"Appreciate your concern. See you later." Cohen stepped over to the central office.

He hoped this hike would go well and he and Raynie would get along. They seemed to have hit a milestone after their intense argument the other day in the conference room.

His mother had always underscored the value of international relations, especially with Americans.

Cohen prided himself on his diplomacy.

And only time would tell.

Chapter 17

"I appreciate you covering for me yesterday," said Angela, rushing in with her arms full of what it takes to pump breast milk and chill it for miniature humans. "DOF hired a dispatcher, and just in time. Looks like thunderstorms this weekend. Y'all know what that means."

"We'll need every warm body we can get," replied Raynie as the screen door slammed.

She glanced up to see Tremblay in faded blue jeans and a plaid flannel shirt, a daypack slung over his shoulder. A camera dangled on a strap around his neck as he homed in on her.

"Good afternoon, ladies. Ready, Atwood? We're burning daylight."

"No such thing this time of year. You can't scare the daylight away." She chuckled. "You look like you just stepped off a plane from Wisconsin."

"Then I'll fit right in." He grinned.

"You could totally pass as an Alaskan in those civvies, y'all," Angela said, with a big smile.

Raynie noted Tremblay's rolled-up sleeves, revealing the red maple leaf tat on his wrist. The veins in his forearms showed a hard-working man who works out.

He looked down at himself. "Guys dress like this everywhere."

"In the backwoods of Canada and Alaska, maybe. And in logging towns," Angela said drily. "Where y'all headed?"

"Just a hike along the Susitna River. I want to get photos of Denali while she's out."

"Get them while you can. When storms move in, she won't be out for a while." Angela tossed Raynie an impish look. "Have fun. Don't do anything I wouldn't do."

Tremblay waited for Raynie to precede him out the door. When he stepped onto the porch, Vanessa stood staring at him, grinning like a toothpaste ad.

Raynie had met Vanessa when Angela had introduced them earlier. The oversexed woman lit up like a flashing neon sign whenever a man walked into the room.

"Hello, Vanessa. How are you today?" Tremblay was polite to a fault. It was laughable the way Miss Hot Pants wanted to gobble him for lunch.

"Much better, now that I've seen *you*," Vanessa tossed a disdainful glance at Raynie, then fixed her sweltering gaze back on Tremblay. "Where you off to?"

"Going on a hike to take photos of Denali."

"I'd love to come along!" gushed Vanessa enthusiastically. "I'm new to Talkeetna and haven't seen Denali this close."

Raynie coughed '*Bullshit*' into her hand.

Angela, who had followed them out upon hearing Vanessa, elbowed Raynie but saved the day. "Vanessa, glad you're here. Let's look over your schedule and go over our dispatch procedures for next week."

Vanessa flashed Tremblay a radiant smile. "We'll go for that beer sometime instead," she simpered and disappeared inside.

"Don't worry, I've got your back," Angela stage-whispered, then scooted inside after Vanessa.

Raynie lifted her brows and put on her sunglasses.

"What a friendly person."

"She is, isn't she?" responded Tremblay, with an innocence she figured was bogus. He looked at her inquisitively.

"What did Angela mean by she has your back?"

He wasn't *that* clueless about women, was he? She scrambled for neutrality.

"Nothing. Just things in general. You know, with work and all." She was curious about his opinion of Vanessa, so she prodded.

"She's really into you. What's 'that beer' you're going for?"

He positioned his shades on his nose, just so. "When I met her, she suggested it."

Of course she did. Raynie waited for more explanation.

Instead, he shifted his daypack to the other shoulder and tapped down the porch steps.

Raynie followed. Although she had no claim on him, Vanessa's blatant flirting triggered unexpected emotions she wasn't ready for.

They strolled past the Susitna Brewery and a few tourist shops. When they reached the river, Tremblay pointed to a trail on the right that wound through willow and birch.

A raven flew overhead and clicked at them as it landed on a treetop.

"Lead off to the new trail you found," she suggested.

"Sure." He walked ahead of her and led them to another trail that veered off to the left. After a mile, the trail led them to the banks of the Susitna River, where large ice chunks slowly bobbed down the river, like miniature icebergs.

As she listened to the grinding ice, she marveled at the sheer power of nature and delicate balance of life in this subarctic land. Her heart lifted, and for a few moments, all her worries flowed away with the easy flow of the river as she stood mesmerized, listening to the symphony of water and ice.

"Break-up is late this year," she called to Tremblay, scrutinizing his backside as he moved easily along the trail. She scrutinized his derriere, nicely sculpted by his jeans.

"Yeah." He nodded, pointing across the river. "Check it out."

She lifted her gaze, and her breath caught at the stunning snowy crags of Queen Denali, a towering monarch at twenty thousand feet. The mountain's blue and white majesty commanded all before her in the immense Alaska Range.

He stopped to gaze at the stunning massif.

Raynie tripped over a tree root, pitching headlong into Tremblay's side. His hand snaked around her waist to keep her from kissing the dirt.

"You okay there, partner? Glad I stopped, or you'd be a penguin perched on those ice floes about now." His Canadian accent kicked in.

Unwelcome heat crept into her cheeks as she eyed the ice chunks rolling downstream. "Thanks. I'm as sure-footed as a roadrunner on a glacier."

Tremblay burst out laughing. "That tree root had it in for you. It saw you coming."

"Good. For a minute there, I thought it was me." Once she'd discovered what made him laugh, she looked for ways to do it. It gave her a break from loathing him, though that was sometimes more fun.

He pointed to a sun-bleached log. "What do you say we cop a squat here to eat lunch?" He took the digital camera from around his neck and fiddled with it.

"It's a suitable spot to photograph Denali."

"A *suitable* spot?" She got a kick out of his unconventional word choices. Unconventional for fire, anyway.

"Would you rather I say it like you Americans?" He imitated a surfer guy from L.A. "Wow dude, like I'm totally stoked. This is like, an *awesome* spot to grab shots of Denali." He was even funnier with his deep voice.

She laughed, sinking down on the log. "You sound more Malibu Barbie than Canadian. What part of Canada are you from?"

"Salmon Arm, in British Columbia." He sank down beside her. "How long have you worked in wildland fire?"

"A few seasons in Arizona. Then my fiancé talked me into coming up here."

He gestured at her hand. "No ring? Things didn't go well?"

"He died."

"Oh, no. I'm sorry." Tremblay quieted.

She regretted her buzzkill to their conversation. "We went to high school together in Arizona. He got a construction job in Anchorage, so I came up, too. Lived together for a while, then he died in a car crash on the Parks Highway."

"That's tragic. I'm so sorry." He slid the daypack from his shoulder, letting it rest on the moss-covered ground. "When did that happen?"

"Just before Christmas. We were supposed to be married next month. I went from planning a wedding to planning a funeral."

"That's a hoser, even after five months." He blew out air. "Unfortunately, we don't get to choose when sorrow interrupts our lives. What I've found is that pain changes a person more profoundly than anything else. It changes how we perceive life. It affects everything...our goals, dreams...even our values."

She drew back and gave him a stunned look. "You're right. Grieving Taydon's loss has affected every aspect of my life." There was more to this guy than she thought.

"I take it you've experienced pain."

He didn't respond, only stared straight ahead.

They sat in a calm silence, listening to the rushing water and grinding ice, a stark contrast to Denali's blue and white quiet magnificence.

RAYNIE BROKE THE SILENCE. "What about you? Where are your folks and what do they do?"

"Vancouver, B.C. Dad owns a large construction company. Mom is an attorney."

"Where did you go to school?"

He looked away. "Princeton."

"You? Princeton?" She drew back with a surprised laugh, dropping her jaw. "How does an Ivy League grad wind up as a firefighter in Alaska? You're a walking contradiction." She wrinkled her nose. "Can you do a 'Joisy' accent?"

He grinned. "Bring me eggs, cawfee, gah-la-maaad with moot-za-rell and a Taylor ham at the dinah in Flah-rida. Then ged-owda-hee," he spewed in a nasal tone, gesturing wildly with his arms.

Raynie busted out laughing. "Hey, you nailed it! What's your degree?"

"Structural engineering."

"Let me guess. Your dad wanted you to take over the family business."

"Now *you* nailed it." He plucked a rock from the ground and inspected it. "I bought into the whole deal because my dad wanted me to. Then woke up one day realizing I wasn't living my own life. After a knock-down, drag-out with my father, I jumped into my pickup and headed to Salmon Arm."

"Why there?"

"My girlfriend had a fire job and helped me get one. Tired of our corporate motto plastered all over Canada: 'If you aren't living in a Tremblay home, you aren't living.'" He tossed the rock into the fast-moving river.

"I was the one who wasn't living."

This gave her pause, sharing a part of himself that must have been hard to confess.

"Still have a girlfriend?" She held her breath, anticipating his answer.

"Not anymore. We wanted different things, so went our separate ways. Shortly after that, I came to Alaska."

Raynie brightened at the no girlfriend reference. "At least you declared your independence. I just hope it didn't cost your relationship with your dad."

"My firefighting pissed off my parents," admitted Cohen. "But I got tired of them grumbling about me squandering my Ivy League education. They're all about money and status."

"Have you thought that maybe they didn't want to see their only son get hurt fighting fire? You should reconnect with them. You can always make money, but you can't make more family." She backtracked for a second. "Well, unless you reproduce."

He gave her an odd look. "Now that you put it *that* way..."

"I take it you weren't willing to compromise." She tried to make light of it by making air quotes. She got him to laugh again.

He suddenly looked up at her. "What music do you like? Who's your favorite of anybody, hands down?"

She looked at Denali and thought a minute. "Hands down? Van Morrison. His songs are poetry set to music. His voice is poetic all by itself. It fits the emotion in his songs, like my favorite, 'Into the Mystic.'" She turned to look at him. "How about you?"

"Funny you mentioned that song. I like the old ones, too. When you mentioned "Into the Mystic," I thought of Joe Cocker, and the way he sang it. He really got into it."

"Yeah." Raynie turned her attention back toward Denali. She noted how it glittered in the afternoon sun—a craggy white monument piercing the deep-blue Alaskan sky.

"Stay still, with Denali behind you." Tremblay squinted at his camera. "Told you before, you're quite fetching when you smile. You don't do it enough, though I understand why. Not after what you've been through." He said it casually, yet his empathy meant the world to her.

The negativity she'd harbored dripped away as she viewed him through a brand-new lens. Regret twinged her at the way she'd been treating him. She'd pick a time to tell him she was sorry, but not now. She didn't want to ruin this moment.

"Let's get a selfie." He stepped close and his arm came around her shoulder as he held the phone.

"Flash them pearly whites, little lady," he said in a cowboy manner.

She laughed at his comment. His closeness rotated her insides. She didn't know whether to bristle or be delighted with his presumptuous touch.

When he tapped the photos and withdrew his arm, she shocked herself by wishing he'd kept it there. He produced a sandwich from his daypack and offered it to her.

"Thanks." She bit into it. This guy was full of surprises.

"Despite your misfortune, are you glad you came north for adventure?" He unwrapped his sandwich and took a bite.

"My misfortune? You have quite the vocabulary." His proximity made her pulse tick up, but she kept her tone steady. "Do you want the quick summary or the long, drawn-out version?"

He shrugged. "Whatever you want to tell me. Did you fly or drive?"

"I drove my truck to Alaska."

"All that way alone?"

"Why? You think I wasn't capable of handling it?" It came out more defensive than she wanted. Her castle defenses still lingered, despite her growing attraction to him.

"I'm impressed anyone can drive long distances through remote country alone." He bumped her shoulder with his, and it tingled her.

"What did you do after you lost your fiancé?"

She sighed. "We didn't have much money. Taydon spent it as fast as he made it. I started a tiny bakery business, but we mostly relied on his construction checks. Had to move out of our Anchorage townhouse because they kept raising the rent."

"Why all the way to Talkeetna?"

"Kipp—the retardant pilot you accused me of flirting with—his brother, Kam, needed someone to watch Sleeping Lady Kennel for the spring and summer. I jumped on it. Besides…" She let out a chuckle. "A town who'd elected a cat for mayor sounds like my kind of place."

"Yeah, I heard about that. A cat named Fluffy or something."

She chewed and swallowed. "Stubbs. He was the honorary mayor of Talkeetna for twenty years until he purred his way up to kitty heaven."

His eyebrows lifted. "Didn't know cats lived that long."

"This one sure did." She wiggled her thumbs. "He was the first mayor without opposable thumbs."

He tickled her with more lighthearted laughter, then sobered, his eyes meeting hers. "You've been grieving this entire time, haven't you?" The way he said it unraveled her.

How does he do that—sense the chaos lurching around inside my brain? He makes it hard not to like him.

They sat in another agreeable silence, watching the water and ice flow downstream. Raynie basked in the sun's warmth after finishing her sandwich, then opened a can of iced tea. She held out one of her ginormous chocolate chip cookies.

"You made this?" Tremblay acted like she'd given him a gold nugget. He bit into it and closed his eyes. "Mmm, these are seriously good."

"I enjoy making them for this reason." She watched as he relished the mouthwatering treat, and it made her feel good.

He wolfed down the cookie and wiped away the crumbs. "How often do you run Kam's sled dogs?"

She let out a sigh. "Not as often as he wants me to. He showed me how to hook up the dogs, but when Kira and I do it, they inevitably get tangled."

He laughed. "I felt like that the first time I handled dogs. Requires a firm hand and getting used to handling them. And cussing helps. Once you get the hang of it, running dogs becomes second nature. Remember back to when I said I would help you run dogs if you admitted to causing half of our arguments?"

"Yes, I remember. But I didn't think you were serious."

"Well, I was serious. Still am. Let me know when to show up and I'll help you run the dogs."

"Sure. Okay." She liked the idea and couldn't think of any reason not to let him help. "Kira and I would appreciate help from someone who knows what they're doing."

"How long has your sister lived with you?"

"Just a few weeks since high school ended in Arizona."

He paused. "Despite what you feel toward me, I'm glad they assigned you to help me train the Aurora Crew."

"Well, I didn't have much choice in the matter. My boss assigned me here, so..." She let it hang there but appreciated his comment.

"Are you...have you been with anyone since your fiancé?" he asked haltingly.

"Nope. Don't have time for relationships." She stared at her lap.

"Huh." He seemed to ponder this as he finished eating. He stuffed the empty sandwich bags into his pack, along with his camera. He sat back, staring at Denali.

"Thank you for coming with me today."

"Thanks for inviting me." It impressed her they'd spent an entire hour together without exchanging barbs. He hadn't even pissed her off. Not even once.

"Can I ask you something?" he asked.

"Sure."

"Would I be correct in assuming you could use a friend?" he asked quietly.

His question caught her off guard. She turned and noted the sincerity in his clear blue eyes.

"I could always use a friend." She stared down at her lap, then flicked her eyes at him. "Are you thinking you'd like to be such a friend?"

His tender expression raised the tiny hairs on her arms, despite the warm summer day. "If you'll let me. I haven't pissed you off yet today, have I?"

She chuckled. "Not yet, but the day is still young."

He's trying to get along with me...he really is.

He leaned back, gazing at her as if he had all the time in the world.

"Did you know that sometimes I'd back out of arguments with you in order to win them?"

"Where did you learn that tactic?"

"My mother, the attorney. A typical Tremblay maneuver." He grinned.

"Stands to reason." Her breath caught at the way he was looking at her. "Why do I have this feeling you want to be more than just my friend? Though I can't understand why, since you know I'm not into you in that way."

"Let's see if I can change that."

He slid his arm around her as if it were the most natural thing in the world. Before she knew what was happening, he pressed his lips to hers.

Surprised, she flinched, then stilled. She didn't know whether to push him away or go with the moment—and kiss him back?

Should I be kissing the enemy?

It didn't take long for her to decide when he slid his gentle tongue inside of her mouth. Stunned, she took it as a green light to slip hers inside of his.

His warm, gentle kiss held her in limbo as she inhaled his freshly showered scent of musk mixed with pine. It had been forever since she'd absorbed the heat of another person. She may be a kickass firefighter, but she'd missed the security and comfort of intimacy.

Just as she relaxed into the kiss, he pulled back, clear blue eyes penetrating hers.

"I've wanted to do that ever since the Hiland Mountain Fire."

His confession astonished her. "You're the last person I would have played tonsil hockey with on that fire. Or any fire, for that matter. Now you think you can go around all hot and heavy and masculine and...and swoop in and sweep me off my feet?"

He answered by covering her mouth in another sensuous swirling of the tongues, more intense than the first time.

Her brain detonated. Silent alarms screamed in her ears.

This is a cruel attraction. What am I doing?

She squeaked out a lame protest, but he was such a good kisser, she couldn't stop. Wouldn't stop. Her body went limp.

He swirled his tongue around hers, pressing his lean, muscled body against her. She fought with herself to push him away and hated herself for losing the battle.

Weakly, she slid her hand between them and pushed on his chest, breaking the kiss.

"What is this, a power play? What are you trying to prove?"

"Absolutely nothing." His knuckle lifted her chin. "You needed a kiss, so I gave you one."

She pushed his hand away. "How do you know what I need? Also, we work together, remember?"

"What's your point?"

"You didn't ask," she grumbled. Despite her best efforts to scowl, his winning smile weakened her arsenal.

His hand brushed her cheek. "Sorry I didn't ask permission, but you called me 'hot' and 'masculine.'"

"What? I did not!" she spluttered.

"Yep, you did. You said I swooped in all hot and masculine and swept you off your feet."

"You liar, you twisted my words!" She pushed him back, her mind racing to recall what she'd said.

Did I seriously say that?

"I'm a lot of things, but a liar isn't one of them." He shouldered his pack and stood. Wordlessly, he turned and strolled back along the trail, his hiking boots tramping the duff.

"Wait—you're leaving?" She jumped to her feet. "After dropping a bomb like that?" Her voice rose an octave, laced with incredulity.

Tremblay acted like nothing had happened—like they kissed every day of the week. He stopped and turned around.

"It's time we head back. Unless you desire to be the main course for a mosquito dinner." He pointed at her. "Like you are for the one on your cheek."

She slapped herself. "You don't just kiss people and walk away, Tremblay."

"Your tongue was in my mouth. I think you can call me Cohen from now on. Come on, you like me. You just won't admit it." He gave her a close-mouthed smile and turned to resume his pace.

"What a pompous thing to say! I *don't* like you. That's the sticking point!" Raynie caught up to him. "We need to talk about what happened back there, Cohen." She said his name in an accusatory tone.

He shot her a sidelong glance, not the least bit rattled. "Chill, Atwood. You're always wound up."

"You're the one who's coiled tighter than a gnat's ass," she said, squeezing her thumb and forefinger together in front of his face. The more she pursued the subject, the more he evaded it...and the more her temper flared.

He sped up, and she matched him stride for stride, until it became a competition. But his legs were longer, covering more ground. Suddenly, he stepped off the trail and disappeared around a dense clump of alder.

"Tremblay!" she hollered, exasperated.

"It's Cohen!" he hollered back from a distance.

"What are you doing?"

"Taking a piss. Do you mind?"

She opened her mouth to retort when a cow moose and two calves stepped onto the trail in front of her. She froze, hoping the animals would move off. Instead, the cow moose laid her ears back, snorted, and put her head down and charged.

"No! Get away!" she screamed, leaping from the trail to hide behind a large spruce. The moose chased her around the tree, snorting and huffing, ears pinned back.

The calves bawled as the mother moose came around the tree to confront her. The cow reared, lifting her front legs to stomp.

Raynie braced herself for the attack.

Chapter 18

"Shoo! Get away!"

Raynie's words hit Cohen's ears, and he knew she'd encountered wildlife. He zipped up fast and hurried back to the trail. He didn't see her.

"Atwood?"

"Over here!" she hollered back, a considerable distance from the trail.

He followed the busted brush and burst out of it in time to see a cow moose at the base of a tall birch tree, her ears laid back and hump hackles raised. When Cohen saw the calves, he backed away and tucked himself behind a clump of alder.

"Where are you?"

"Up here!"

Cohen lifted his eyes to where she perched on a birch tree branch, a good twenty feet above the ground.

"How did you get up that high?" Holy hell, he couldn't have managed that.

"Shoo, moose!" Raynie yelled. "Get out of here!"

The agitated moose swung her head in Cohen's direction, but he stayed crouched behind the alder. The cow moose hesitated, then snorted at Raynie and trotted off, the young calves scampering behind her.

When he considered it safe enough to leave his hiding place, Cohen rose and picked his way through the dense brush to the birch tree. It always amused him how people dealt with moose encounters. With hands on his hips, he stood, looking up at Raynie.

"Good escape tactic, Atwood. I'm impressed. Didn't know you had climbing skills."

"I've scaled a rock face or two," she grunted, easing herself to the trunk of the tree to slide her way back down.

"At the rock gym?" he teased.

"Hardly." She slanted a scowl down at him. "Oak Creek Canyon, near Sedona."

He whistled. "So, you're an experienced rock climber but you say 'shoo' to get rid of a moose? That's a new one."

"It got the job done, didn't it?" she hurled down at him.

He watched her descend on the smooth birch bark, sliding a few inches at a time. When she was low enough to reach, he moved closer to the tree base.

"Let go, I've got you."

She peered down at him. "I can do this myself."

"Trust me. I'll catch you." He raised his arms.

"You're the last person I'd trust."

Now, that one stung. "Why do you hate me? I have my bad points, but I'm no loser."

"Never said you were." She sent an eye roll down to him. "I don't hate you. I loathe you. There's a difference."

"Because I questioned your decision on a fire?" He shifted his weight impatiently to the other foot. "I figured you still held that against me, along with all the other kerfuffles we've had. But you forgot one slight detail...we kissed."

"*You* kissed *me*. I didn't kiss *you*." Her boot slid down the bark and her knee jerked up to regain traction. "And what the heck are kerfuffles?" she grumbled.

"Sorry, but technically, you kissed me back. You didn't fight me off, either." He held his arms higher. "Are you going to cling to that tree trunk all day or what? I said I'd catch you. Let go!"

"I've got this, if you don't mind," she grunted, inching herself down like a cautious gymnast.

Cohen watched her scale back down. He liked how the muscles in her arms flexed. And he had a glorious view of her ass. He angled his head to assess it.

Not bad. Not bad at all.

When she scooted within reach, he plucked her from the tree trunk. He stumbled back, tipped, and lost his balance. Down they both went, with Raynie landing on top.

Despite the pain in his back, he grinned. "Atwood, if you want me that bad, just say so."

"Holy hell! You did this on purpose!" She disentangled herself from him and pushed herself off his chest. She stood, looking down at him. "Oh, you loved that, didn't you?" She wiped dirt and twigs from herself.

"Actually, yes. And no, I didn't trip on purpose so you'd land on top of me," he lied. Cohen grimaced, rubbing his hip and lower back. Her weight on him had caused him to hit the ground hard.

"You Canadians pride yourselves in being polite. But *you,* my friend, have a hidden agenda." Raynie bent to brush her pants. "You better get up in case the moose returns to finish us off. Are you hurt?"

"Just tweaked my back a little. A burning snag fell on me last year on a Kenai Peninsula fire, so my back reminds me every now and then." He winced, pushing himself to sit.

"Oh. In that case, let me help you up." Raynie's expression changed to concern.

At least, that's what he hoped it was. But then he never could tell with her.

She squatted next to him. "Put your arm on my shoulder and we'll lift together."

He opened his mouth to protest, but his devious male brain put on the brakes.

Let her help you, Bonehead.

"Okay," he said.

"Up we go." She grunted, helping him lift to his feet.

Given her smaller stature, her physical power astonished him. He'd think twice before tangling with her in a dark alley.

Once on his feet, he glanced around to make sure the moose and calves were nowhere in sight.

"Was that your first moose encounter?"

She chuckled. "No. I ran into a bull with a rack the size of Alaska on the coastal trail in Anchorage one time. But he wasn't aggressive. He just gave me a bored look, stepped over the railroad tracks, and munched grass."

He brushed himself off. "Lucky for you. Let's hike back, and I'll go first. If we encounter more wildlife, I'll handle it this time." He set off along the trail.

"Like I didn't handle my own moose charge?" she mumbled, stumbling after him. "Uh, Tremblay, we need to talk. Things sort of changed back there."

He turned around, walking backwards. "Nothing has changed. You still loathe me."

"Yes, I do, but…" She trailed off.

"But what?" He stopped and turned suddenly, facing her.

She smacked into him, then stumbled back with a wild-eyed look. "You know what."

"I want to hear *you* say it," he said calmly, with a neutral expression.

"See? This is what you do." She raised her arms and dropped them to her sides. "You make me say things I don't want to."

"I don't make you say anything."

"All right, we kissed. Why did you do that, anyway?" Her eyes pierced his.

"You sat next to me and smelled so good. The mountain was out, the day was perfect, and well…" Heck, it made sense to him at the time. The truth was, he wanted to taste that luscious mouth.

Her expression changed. "You want me to think you're a romantic and not a womanizer? Is that the deal?"

Cohen stuttered. "Yes! No. I mean…I like you. I know you don't like me. But you might if you would just give me a chance."

"Why would I do that?" She shook her head. "Even if I did, it would be awkward. I wouldn't want Aurora Crew thinking we were all lovey-dovey."

"Lovey-dovey? Ha!" He chortled, tilting his head. He placed his hands on her shoulders. "You can pretend, right? You can do anything. After all, you just escaped death by a pissed-off moose. What is it you're truly afraid of?"

She didn't brush away his hands. Instead, she gaped at him with her mouth open. She seemed like she wanted to say something, but nothing came out.

He wasted no time to prove his sincerity. He put a knuckle under her chin to close her mouth, then slid a hand to the back of her neck, drawing her close. He kissed her, his other hand pulling her tight against him. He was gentle and intended to show her *how* gentle. But arousal made his kiss more demanding.

She broke the kiss, her breath coming fast. "Gawd, Tremblay. If I knew you could kiss like this when I met you on the Hiland Fire, that blaze wouldn't have been contained."

"If I knew you could kiss like this, I wouldn't have let you drive away." A corner of his mouth turned up. He was as surprised as she was at having her in his arms—but not surprised with his arousal.

They stood with locked gazes and arms around each other. He was reluctant to let go. She felt good. And strong. And fierce. He liked that about her.

Raynie gasped, then swallowed. "I'm not supposed to be kissing you. I'm supposed to be loathing you."

"According to whom?" He brushed back a tendril that escaped from her ponytail.

"You seriously want to do this?" She fixed her eyes on him.

"Are you worried about what people will think?" He sure as hell wasn't.

"I have a reputation to uphold in wildland fire," she said definitively. "And I've worked hard to build it. The last thing I want my superiors to think about me is that I'm here to get a man. Some in wildland fire still think that about female firefighters."

He treaded carefully. "Trust me, that's the last thing anyone would think about you." He looked her in the eye. "Okay, we'll stay coworkers and friends."

"You've already blown past the friendship part," she pointed out.

"Guess I sped through that one. You kissed me back, so you must have feelings for me," he said in his typical matter-of-fact manner. "Unless you're just horny."

"I'm not horny!" she erupted, arms flailing. "It's just like you to say something like that. Don't you dare tell anyone. You know how fire gossip flashes around? I must have heard about you and Liz a hundred times, from fifty different people."

"That was last year. I've moved on." He growled in annoyance. "Damn. No one on fire can keep their mouth shut."

"Well, you and I will." She backpedaled. "I mean if this...if we...if you...you know what I mean." She waved her hands around.

A corner of his mouth edged up. "Is that a directive from my state counterpart?" He liked this.

"Damn straight," she said, giving him a sharp look. She only came up to his chest, and it reminded him of a mouse barking an order to a giraffe. Except this mouse could no doubt kick his ass if provoked.

"So, this..." He pointed at her, then himself. "Will remain a covert operation."

"Covert?" Her voice rose an octave. "I don't walk around kissing coworkers. I don't need complications in my life."

"No complications. Just sneaking around to protect your reputation." He gave her an impish grin. "Actually, that would be a turn-on for me." And it would. The whole clandestine affair thing would be sexy as hell.

Her jaw dropped. "You think this is funny? Women have a hard enough time working on fire, let alone people thinking we're here to land a husband."

"Hate to break it to you, but people on fire have relationships all the time. Look at Gunnar and Angela. Tara and Ryan O'Connor. One distinct advantage is not having to explain your job to each other." He sensed a tiny crack in Raynie's armor, and he intended to widen it.

"Fair enough. We'll continue sparring like wolves and bears, so no one will suspect anything about us."

"So now you've declared there's an 'us?'" She stared at him.

"After the way you just kissed me?" He grinned, noticing the late afternoon sunlight glinting her hair. "Yes. I'd say there's an 'us' now."

"Whoa, wait a minute, Hoss. Slow down. I haven't agreed to an 'us.' This is still a you and I thing. Not only that, this is warp-speed fast—I'm still back here loathing you, and it's swirling my brain."

"That means you're falling for me." If anything, he was blunt.

She gave him a mortified look. "No one said anything about falling."

He folded his arms. "Let's see. You and I started as enemies the day we met. Then worked together and fought like rabid wolverines. I offered you olive branches and you accepted them. We became frenemies. And when I kissed you, you kissed me back. So, what would you call it?" He shifted his weight to the other foot, drilling her with his gaze.

She appeared stunned, then collected herself and cleared her throat. "Frenemies with benefits?"

Tremblay took a breath before plunging head-first into gallant diplomacy.

"I'll make you a deal. I'll protect your reputation and lob as many grenades as you want in front of the Aurora Crew. If that's what it takes to win your heart, hell, I'll do it." He placed his hands on his hips. "All I ask in return is, give me a chance. Oh, and one more thing—we need to seal the deal."

He strode over to her, grabbed her shoulders, and kissed her so fiercely, she sagged against him. He ended the kiss and stepped back, his own head swirling.

"Time to head back. You coming or what?" *There.* He'd laid it out, pure and simple.

She stumbled back and gasped. "I'm not falling for you, Tremblay. I still loathe you."

"It's Cohen. Go ahead, loathe me. But you're a helluva kisser." He turned back around, smiling to himself. She'd accepted his biggest olive branch yet, and to him, that was a major accomplishment in his quest to win her over.

For now, it appeared they were frenemies...frenemies with benefits. As long as it wouldn't get in the way of their jobs.

And that suited him just fine.

Chapter 19

A ngela flew into the conference room at the speed of light. "We have a fire at Milepost Ninety-one of the Parks Highway. A Type Two Interagency Incident Management Team has been appointed, and they've dispatched the Aurora Crew."

Raynie paused in mid-scribble on the whiteboard at the front of the room, as she and Cohen reviewed methods of suppression strategies with the Aurora Crew.

"Tremblay—I mean Cohen, we have to mobilize." She stumbled over her words. It was weird addressing him by his first name. Calling him Tremblay had kept him at a safer distance before. Now, she was unsure whether she wanted that distance.

Cohen announced, "Hustle, people. Everyone, get your gear and meet at the helispot behind the fire base." He waggled a finger at Raynie. "The Incident Management Team will want to brief us."

She nodded and followed Cohen out to the dispatch desk. Vanessa and Angela were busy on the phones, pulling up info on the monitors.

Angela's fingers flew over the keyboard as she scrutinized one of four computer monitors. "Currently, this fire is at two hundred acres, eighteen miles north of Willow. The point of origin is Denali Creek, so that's the name of the fire. ADOT has closed the Parks Highway between mileposts Seventy-one and Ninety-eight," she spoke into the phone. "Aurora Crew is on their way."

Angela winked at Raynie, and she quickly added, "Yes, Raynie Atwood will be the acting crew supervisor in Tara Water's absence. Tremblay is right here. Hold on."

Angela gave the phone to Cohen. "It's Doss."

Raynie peered at the map on Angela's monitor and whispered, "Where's Tara?"

"She flew to Missoula late last night. Family emergency," Angela whispered back.

Cohen spoke into the phone. "No problem, Dave. I'm happy to incident command the Denali Creek Fire. I'll get Atwood lined out as crew boss." He nodded at Raynie.

Did I hear him correctly?

Raynie whispered to Angela, "Why is Cohen the IC on a State-run fire?"

"There're federal lands interspersed in the fire zone, so BLM Alaska Fire Service offered an experienced federal IC. Doss picked Cohen," Angela whispered back.

"Oh." Raynie's stomach flipped at this new twist. Cohen would now be her boss.

Well, this should prove interesting.

Cohen handed the phone back to Angela. "A storm is moving in with wind gusts up to forty-five, moving the fire straight into homes near Willow. Several sled dog kennels are in the path. We need to get out there fast."

He pulled out his radio. "N-74 Juliet, do you copy? This is Tremblay at Talkeetna Base."

Mel Faraday's voice came over the radio. "Copy. Whatcha got?"

"We need to transport half of the Aurora Crew to Milepost Ninety-one on the Parks. We have a State bird out of Palmer to take the rest."

"Affirmative. I'll have Juliet at the base helispot in ten."

"Thanks, Mel. Clear," said Cohen, shoving the radio into his shoulder holster. He plucked another radio from the dispatcher's desk and handed it to Raynie. "You're the Aurora Crew supervisor for this incident. After Mel drops you and the crew off, I'll stay in the state helo to do an overflight."

He gave her a fast wink. "Stay loose."

"Yeah, sure." She dashed to the gear room to get her fire pack, hardhat, and Pulaski, then hurried to the helispot behind the fire base where the Aurora Crew had gathered. All eyes were on her as she moved to the center of the crew to brief them. She competed with the whump-whump of N-74 Juliet's rotors as Mel landed his helicopter.

"Nine of you go with Mel in Juliet, and the rest go in the other helo. Our objective is to protect homes and sled dog kennels. Mat-Su is sending structural firefighters with engines from Palmer, Wasilla, and Houston to assist."

Raynie glanced around at nodding heads and noted Rego standing with folded arms, feet apart, in what she'd observed as his *let's see how you measure up* stance. Tara had shared with her that Rego was old school, a former Marine who expected every crew member to work up to speed, regardless of gender.

Raynie pointed at him. "I would appreciate you helping me get the three squad bosses lined out once we get our marching orders from the incident commander."

Rego dipped a curt nod. "Copy that."

Aurora Crew was in battle mode, adrenaline coursing through every vein. Nine crew members boarded N-74 Juliet. Raynie climbed into the front passenger seat and put on the white helmet with the hot mic and earphones. Everyone else tucked foam ear plugs into their ears as Mel amped up the engine and lifted the helicopter. She watched the yellow landing circle grow smaller as Juliet rose and headed south.

Raynie positioned the mic in front of her lips when Cohen's voice came through her helmet com.

"Incident Command to N-74 Juliet, you copy? We're staging in the parking lot of the Denali Creek Community Center. Set her down in the high school parking lot next to it." Cohen's voice was calm and smooth as silk.

Raynie wondered if his feathers ever ruffled.

Mel responded as he raised the helicopter high enough to see the billowing plumes high in the sky. "This is N-74 Juliet. Copy that."

Ten minutes later, both helos were on the ground, and everyone exited as the rotors stopped spinning. Raynie gathered the crew around her.

"Tremblay will brief us on our attack plan."

He finished talking with fire managers and strode up to the Aurora Crew.

"This is now a multi-agency project fire, with the State Department of Forestry in charge. BLM Alaska is assisting. I'm the IC for now until the state orders up their overhead team."

Rego's Bronx accent kicked in. "Tremblay, you have that shit's-about-to-hit-the-fan look."

"No, brah, you don't look happy," intoned Tupa, standing with folded arms.

"The situation is looking grim," explained Cohen. "The Alaska State Troopers have evacuated homes between mileposts Eighty-seven and Ninety-one on the Parks Highway. Winds are blowing the fire toward several sled dog kennels. No time to lose. There's your ride." He pointed at two crew transport vans.

Cohen turned to Raynie. "Have the crew lay hose and draw from the Susitna River. Take four engines with you. I'm staying to coordinate agency resources." He said it so business-like, she almost snapped out an "Aye-aye, sir!"

Instead, she positioned the yellow hardhat on her head and fastened the chin strap. "Good thing we drilled the crew on hose-lays."

Tupa spoke up. "Aurora Crew did lots of hose-lays last season down on the Kenai River. We've got this."

"Good. Let's go." She waited for the crew to walk ahead of her before turning to Cohen. "I take it this has the potential to be a clusterfuck."

He gave her a somber look. "This could develop into a critical situation with hundreds of people and multiple structures. Not to mention the two thousand sled dogs in this fire's path. The troopers have a Ready-Set-Go evac order in place for Willow and Denali Creek. They went house to house, kennel to kennel."

"We'll hold it on our end, don't worry." She patted his arm. "You'll do good. Hang in there." She wanted to give him a reassuring hug. Instead, she turned to follow the Aurora Crew.

"Atwood," Cohen called after her, as three fire bosses approached.

She pivoted to see him pointing at her. "Remember your LCES and keep me informed. And don't forget to compromise."

"Copy that."

She'd bit her tongue at his inference and couldn't believe how the tables had turned. But that was wildland fire—one minute you're someone's boss, the next minute they're yours. Now here she was, taking orders from Cohen.

She climbed into the van and settled in to study the map she'd grabbed at the fire briefing. She frowned at the multitude of red dots, showing locations of homes and dog kennels. The fire's proximity to the dot clusters made her uneasy. She took a seat and closed her eyes to regain focus before Aurora Crew reached the fireline.

She'd compartmentalized Cohen's kiss from the day before and tried unsuccessfully to dump it from her mind. Kissing him had been a rollercoaster ride—exhilarating, yet dangerous. Although he was an amazing kisser, she wouldn't let it get in the way of her job performance.

Why did I kiss him back and open Pandora's Box? I left my heart open as well.

It was because she could trust him. Contrary to what she'd first thought about Tremblay, he'd turned out to be empathetic and understanding, especially about protecting her younger sister.

People who had relationships with coworkers in wildland fire knew they'd be parting ways once the season ended. But when her temporary duty ended at the Talkeetna fire base, she'd be returning to her state hotshot crew in Palmer.

It was unlikely she'd see Cohen after that.

Before she could conjure more reasons to talk herself out of Cohen, the vans had lurched to a stop, and the crew piled out. From here, they'd take the fire engines next to the river to lay hose and pump water onto the wall of fire, which charged through the brush and thirsty white spruce.

The three squads of six people each hopped into three engines. Tupa, Rego, and Liz, the squad bosses, each took a wheel. They made their way through the smoke to the river, and each squad got busy setting up water pumps and laying hose. They took turns spraying water on the advancing flames, eating through the beetle-killed spruce.

Behind them was a string of dog kennels owned by famous Iditarod mushers. She prayed they'd evacuate in time in case the Aurora Crew couldn't hold the fire. The unsettling thought poked at her as she positioned goggles over her eyes. Raynie swung her Pulaski through ground cover to remove fuel for the fire.

"Settle those flames, people! Watch out for burning ash pits and fiery snags!" she hollered.

The snap, crackle, and roar of the fire intensified as the air temperature inched up to ninety degrees on this gusty day. Even the birch readily ignited because of the super dry conditions.

Not a good sign.

"Look out!" shouted Tupa when a burning snag fell across the streams of water.

"Flames are too intense. This isn't helping. We have to GTFO!" yelled Raynie, motioning to the crew. "Wind shifted, fire's moving away from the river. Stop operations, load up!" She had to get the crew out before the fire reached the road and burned their fire engines.

The crew rushed to gather hoses, extract the pumps from the river, and toss them all in the back of the fire vehicles. They had to get out of there. Raynie had just dragged a hose back toward the engines when flaming debris pummeled the thirsty grass all around her.

"Holy crap!" hollered Liz.

Raynie swiveled her head in time to see Liz drag a hose away from the oncoming flames. She rushed over to help, smoke choking her lungs. Raynie jumped around flames to grab more hose when her boot plunged into a deep, smoldering ash pit.

"Dammit!" Her boot caught a burning root at the bottom of the hole. She couldn't pull it out. Flames licked at her as she worked to unsnag her boot. She wrenched it out, twisting her knee, crying out in pain.

Liz saw her predicament, and so did Tupa. Together, he and Liz grabbed Raynie's armpits and dragged her away from the flames.

The pain in her knee pissed her off. "We don't need this right now! We have to get to the engines before the fire does."

Liz ran ahead with her hose, while Tupa half-carried Raynie back to the road.

Once there, Tupa helped her into the front passenger seat of an engine. Retrieving a first aid kit, Tupa pulled out an instant cold compress and snapped it to activate the cold. He pressed it to the front of her knee and taped it in place.

"That'll do till we get to town."

"Thanks, Tupa." She scolded herself for making a rookie mistake by stepping into a burning ash pit. She knew better, but she'd been so intent on retrieving the fire hose, she hadn't focused on her movement.

Her radio crackled. "Aurora Crew, this is the IC. Do you copy?"

Raynie's heart skipped at hearing Cohen's voice. She keyed her radio. "Copy that, IC."

"Status report?"

Raynie took a deep breath and keyed the mic. "Wind shifted, drove flames right into us. Had to abort the hose-lay. And..." She debated telling him she'd injured herself, then decided against it.

"We're exiting Denali Creek Road to get the engines out of here," she said into the radio.

Tupa climbed into the driver's seat and fired up the engine. Smoke created visibility problems, and they could only see ten feet in front of their vehicle. Raynie shot a side glance at Tupa. He wasn't fazed in the least.

Cohen transmitted. "Moving engines again, huh?"

"Affirmative." It took her a second to get his tongue-in-cheek reference about her moving the engines on the Hiland Fire in Eagle River. She would have chuckled, had it not been for her dumb mistake in getting injured.

"What's Aurora Crew's directive?" Raynie waited for Cohen's response, which took a few moments. She'd forgotten he had his hands full at the Incident Command Center.

"Report to the ICC. I need your help, Atwood. See you in a few." Cohen ended the radio transmission.

Did I hear correctly? Cohen needs my help?

"Wonder what he needs your help with?" Tupa glanced at her. "I'll bet he assigns us to another location."

"I'm sure he will." Raynie peered into the smoke with ash chunks pummeling the windshield. In what seemed like forever, they emerged from the smoke. Tupa turned onto the highway back to the Denali Creek Community Center.

She smiled to herself. It didn't matter what Cohen needed her help with—what mattered was, he'd asked for her help over a radio frequency God and everyone else heard to Denali and back again. It made her feel proud.

What would she say...no? She shocked herself by thinking even if Cohen had asked her to fly to the moon, she would've said yes to that, too.

Oh, God, she thought helplessly. *I'm falling.* Falling into that smoldering ash pit was nothing compared to the firestorm she was tumbling into now.

There wasn't enough retardant or a fire hose in all of Alaska powerful enough to douse *this* inferno...and she had no way to contain it even if there was. She was powerless to extinguish this new blazing passion that burned inside her heart.

Wild and uncontrolled.

Chapter 20

Cohen had a handle on what was at stake after Mel Faraday flew him over the fire in Juliet—and it scared the hell out of him. He weighed the positives and negatives: Ninety dog kennels and residences lie in the fire's path, north and south of Willow. However, most were between the Susitna River and the Parks Highway, so firefighters could use river water to hose the flames.

First, he ordered an overhead team, three village crews from the BLM Alaska Fire Service, and two state hotshot crews. His assessment was that things were at a critical point for suppression because the weather wasn't cooperating. Fierce winds gusted, and there was much at stake.

Cohen headed to the command center inside the large, rectangular Denali Community Center building and got busy on the phone. He alerted the Alaska State Troopers to prepare for an evacuation.

Six people descended on him at once, making demands and asking questions: *Are you having a town meeting? What do we tell the mushers who have to move large dog teams? How do people get through highway closures?*

Cohen held up a hand. "Hold on, everyone, I'll answer your questions. First things first." He gripped his phone in one hand and radio in the other, barking orders into both.

He needed a state liaison person until the overhead team was in place—someone familiar with state processes. It sure would help cut through all this red tape with all these agencies. He knew just the person.

He picked up his radio and keyed the mic.

COHEN STOOD IN THE parking lot, fielding questions from fire managers and the State Fire Marshall. He glanced up to see the Aurora Crew exiting engines and a large man helping a limping woman. He squinted. Tupa and...Raynie?

He walked out to meet them. "What happened?"

Raynie shook her head. "Stumbled into an ash pit. Think I sprained my knee."

Cohen squatted and examined her leg, resting his fingers on the cold compress. "Mind if I take this off?"

"Go ahead."

Tupa dragged a folding chair from a nearby utility table and settled Raynie into it.

Cohen peeled off Tupa's tape job and carefully palpated the tissue surrounding her kneecap.

"This is swollen. You'd better get it checked."

"It's just a sprain. I've done it before," she said dismissively.

"Just to be sure, I think someone should look at it," he said firmly.

Their eyes met with a challenging stare. When Raynie opened her mouth to protest, he was on the ready. "No argument. Where's the nearest medical facility?"

Raynie motioned south with her head. "Mat-Su Medical Center in Palmer."

Cohen spoke to Tupa. "Take an agency rig and drive her there." He waited for an eruption from Raynie, but she was strangely silent. She sat on the chair, obviously disgruntled. "Hey, Atwood."

She looked up, disappointment written all over her—dare he think lovely—face.

"Shit happens," he empathized. "Long as you didn't jeopardize your safety or the safety of the crew."

He recalled last year when the burning snag fell on him, putting him out of commission during another calamitous fire on the Kenai Peninsula.

Raynie let out a heavy sigh. "Right. On the radio, you said you needed my help. What's the deal?"

"If you're willing, I'd like you to lend me a hand inside the command center. I need help with the State process in this multi-agency cluster. If you agree to it, Doss will coordinate it with your boss."

Raynie had a guarded look. "And what about the Aurora Crew?"

"I'm putting Rego in charge and sending them to help build the fireline on the left flank. They'll do great with his supervision. You and I will head up the overhead team."

"Overhead team, huh? Wow," she said, with raised brows.

Cohen could tell she was considering it. He motioned at Tupa, waiting patiently in the idling truck.

"Your chauffeur is waiting. Can you walk?"

Raynie took a step and winced. "Not very well. Can't put my weight on it."

"I'll carry you." Before she could protest, Cohen had his arm around her shoulders and lifted her in a threshold carry. Although she had solid muscle, her body was surprisingly light when he lifted her.

"I could have gotten myself to the truck, you know. Stop doing things like this or I'll have to stop loathing you."

She reeked of smoke, but he liked it. Fire smoke smelled different on her. *Sweeter.*

"Think that's a possibility?" Holding her against him made it tricky to pay attention to what she was saying. He went stupid, being this close.

"Chances are slim, Maple Leaf. Loathing you is too much fun." She said it in a light enough way he figured there was hope for them to get along. For a few minutes, anyway.

"Don't worry, I won't ruin your hard-earned reputation."

He stared ahead, stepping toward the pickup, and caught Tupa's subtle thumbs-up behind the windshield. The feel of her ping-ponged his heart around like steel balls in a pinball machine.

His holding her like this roused a private, sensuous lightning storm inside him. He swallowed, staring straight ahead.

"About the overhead team," she said. "You're serious about me helping you? You can't pick arguments with me if we command this project fire together."

"Yes, I'm serious. I appreciate your skill set."

"I'm glad someone does," she quipped.

"Your leadership skills aren't lost on me," he said in a neutral tone. "As the co-commander on this fire, you'll be in charge of the state-side of the operation." He stopped next to the idling truck and set Raynie on her feet. "And you'll report directly to me as the incident commander and agree to a truce. No arguments." He grinned.

"You love the shit out of that, don't you?" Raynie grimaced. "If all you have me do is get you coffee and copy documents, then yeah, there could be an altercation."

"Come on, have some faith." He held up his hands. "All right. No coffee, no copies, no arguments."

"I'll think about it and will let you know when I get back."

"Fair enough." He opened the passenger door and helped her into the seat.

"Thanks for the lift, Commander Tremblay," she said, buckling herself in.

"Go easy on that knee." He gave her a lopsided grin, knowing how hard it was for her to thank him for anything. He closed the door and Tupa backed out and drove off.

Cohen hoped he and Raynie could set aside their differences long enough to command this fire. He lifted his radio to inform Doss when it crackled with Angela's voice.

"Tremblay, this is Talkeetna Base. Do you copy?"

He keyed his mic. "Go ahead, Angela."

"Know you have your hands full, but we have a fire close to town. Call me on my cell," she drawled.

"Copy that." He holstered his radio and fished his cell from his pants pocket. He had Angela on speed dial and tapped her photo icon.

"What's the skinny?"

"While Mel was slinging water drops this afternoon with Juliet, he reported a UAV in his airspace. He's not a happy camper and wants to know who's responsible," reported Angela.

"An unmanned aerial vehicle in Talkeetna? Not where I'd expect a drone. All right, when I get back, I'll look into it. Where's Doss?"

"Meeting with the State folks down in Anchorage."

"Where's the fire?" he asked.

"Out toward Whispering Spruce."

He lurched. "Wait, what? Whispering Spruce? That's where Raynie lives."

"And that's where Mel spotted the UAV."

Cohen let out a sigh. "Maybe Raynie has an idea who it is?"

"Possibly. Hate to rush off, darlin,' but it's chaotic here with all these lightning strikes," said Angela, her Southern drawl in overdrive.

"Thanks, Angela. Talk to you later." He ended the call.

He wondered who'd be flying drones out by Sleeping Lady Kennel on Whispering Spruce. Kira might know who it could be. He'd ask Raynie when they had some downtime.

His mind tried to recall the exact moment he fell for Raynie Atwood.

His heart screamed back...*The day I met her on the Hiland Fire.*

Chapter 21

While Raynie waited her turn to have her knee examined, all she could think about was how Cohen had said her name, like he was addressing the Canadian prime minister.

She was astonished that he'd asked her to assist him in the command center. It was a tremendous responsibility he'd be trusting her with, and now she felt worse for treating him like a dickwad these past weeks.

When the medical staff finished treating her, she hobbled from the examination room, relieved to find Tupa waiting. It was a sprain, just as she'd figured. She was thankful her knee hadn't dislocated.

"What's the story?" asked Tupa, his black man bun shiny under the fluorescent lights.

She motioned at the brace around her knee.

"Just a sprain. It'll be good as new in a few days." What she didn't say was, the doctor told her to stay off it for a week.

On the way back to the Denali Creek Community Center, she eyed the crutches positioned next to her. She couldn't supervise the Aurora Crew back on the fireline today, that was for sure.

Tupa must have read her mind. "Don't worry about the crew. Cohen put Rego in charge, with me and Liz helping. We'll keep everyone in hotshot mode."

She nodded. "I'm sorry, Tupa. I feel like I'm letting the crew down."

"Nah, you can't think that way. Stuff happens, you know?" His Polynesian accent kicked in, and she appreciated his sentiment. "You're still an *Afi* Slayer. *Afi* is Samoan for fire."

"Where are you from, exactly?" she asked.

"Born in Samoa, and my family moved to Anchorage. I fought fire in Australia and California, as well as Alaska." He pushed up the sleeve of his arm on the steering wheel, revealing the tattoos on his forearm. His black beard and matching ponytail pulled back on the prominent part of his scalp reminded her of a pirate.

"I've seen the all-Samoan fire crews working on California fires and doing the Haka chant before and after their shifts."

A hint of a smile crossed Tupa's face, and it occurred to her she'd not seen him lose his fierce demeanor.

"I taught Aurora Crew how to do the Haka. I'll teach you, too." He waved a massive paw at her knee. "When your knee heals."

"I'd like that."

Her gaze homed in on Cohen as Tupa pulled in and parked. He stood in front of the Ops center, radio in one hand, phone in the other. A horde of happy ducks flapped inside her chest upon seeing him.

"You like Tremblay, don't you?" Tupa had been studying the shit eating grin on her face. *Busted.*

"Not really. I mean, he's okay," she lied, making a clumsy attempt at indifference.

"I don't buy that. I can tell you like him." Tupa got out to help her from the passenger seat. "He kicks ass on fires. Tremblay kicked some serious ass last year on the Kenai." He handed the crutches to her.

"I heard that. Thanks, Tupa, appreciate the ride." Well, if Tupa could see her newfound affinity toward Cohen, others could too. At this point, she refused to worry about it. She tucked her crutches under her arms and hobbled to a picnic table.

The command center had grown into a sizable project fire operation: operations had the doers, logistics were the getters, planning had the thinkers, and finance were the payers. That's how Raynie had always memorized the chain of command. All reported directly to the IC, so Cohen coordinated all of it—and it gave her a sensual rush.

Cohen spotted her and strode over. "What's the verdict?"

"Nothing serious, just a knee sprain. What do you want me to do?" She could see Cohen needed help.

"Have you decided whether you're willing to work with me in the command center? I was also hoping you'd help me organize an evacuation plan for the homeowners and the musher community."

Some of the Aurora Crew seated around the picnic table stared at her as Cohen waited for her response.

She wasn't a fool and knew how to play the fire diplomacy game. No matter what her off-work relationship might be with Cohen, this was a time to step up to the plate. Thinking back to their clashes about firefighting strategies in the past, her mind raced.

Cohen must have sensed her hesitation. "You'll report to me. I'm not a dictator. We'll decide things together—lockstep, state and federal. What do you say?"

Heck, she'd already decided when he'd asked her earlier. "Of course. I'm happy to help." This was the biggest olive branch Cohen had offered yet—more like a tree—no, an entire flipping olive orchard.

"I'll make sure you have a comfortable space, so you won't agitate your knee."

Cohen extended his hand in a businesslike fashion. "Welcome aboard as the State IC."

"Thanks." She suppressed a smile, knowing Cohen did this to keep up appearances out here in front of everyone. She accepted his hand, and when he gave it a subtle squeeze, her heart tipped sideways.

No, not now. Not at work. Focus.

"Cohen Tremblay!" A female voice interrupted Raynie's reverie from across the front lawn.

She turned to see a tall blonde woman in yellow Nomex and green pants, with a large fire pack on her back, striding toward Cohen.

"Hey, Deanna! You're working this one?" Cohen smiled at the firefighter, who moved up to throw her arms around him.

The beaming woman embraced him tightly for what seemed like forever.

"The Alaska Smokejumper Base sent me down here to help. If you need a jumper, I'm your woman." She pushed back from him, giving him a once over. "Hot damn, gorgeous. You get better looking every time I see you." Deanna moved in to hug him again.

The woman's body lock on Cohen rankled Raynie, who had a sudden urge to knock the woman on her ass.

Cohen stepped back and turned toward Raynie, still seated at the picnic table.

"Deanna, I'd like you to meet a colleague. This is Raynie Atwood, the co-commander of this project fire for the State of Alaska."

Deanna angled toward her, giving her the once over. She nodded at the crutches. "Get injured on a fire?"

"Something like that." Raynie pasted on her resting professional face. Her peripheral caught Cohen glancing from her to Deanna, and back again.

An awkward pause, until Deanna said, "Nice meeting you, Raynie." She stabbed Cohen's chest with her forefinger. "I'll see you later, sweetness. We'll go have a beer. You and I have some catching up to do."

Deanna winked at him, then shot a smug smile at Raynie, before traipsing off.

Raynie watched Deanna with interest as the woman hugged and shook hands with the other firefighters. She was curious whether Deanna had dated a few, by the way some firefighters enthusiastically greeted her.

The federal firefighters all seemed to know each other, leaving Raynie with an empty fish out of water feeling. She wished she had talked to her state crews, but she couldn't, since they'd already been dispatched.

She grasped her crutches and hobbled inside the community center to begin her new role in the Incident Command section. She resolved to do her best and not screw this up.

Raynie wondered what the deal was with Cohen and the female smokejumper. She'd shocked herself with her visceral reaction. Knowing what this meant—that she cared for Cohen more than she ever thought possible—swept apprehension through her like a runaway blaze.

Her feelings for Cohen had indeed intensified—beyond intensified.

And it scared the bejesus out of her.

Chapter 22

Before Raynie knew it, it was time to stop for the day. She'd met with the department chiefs in the afternoon and gotten a running jump on coordinating an evacuation plan for homeowners and dog mushers. It had taken a tremendous amount of coordination with multiple agencies, businesses, and homeowners.

The winds had calmed for the night, allowing crews to build a containment line on the left flank. If firefighters could hold it under two thousand acres for the night, that would be ideal. If they couldn't, Raynie was prepared to tell the state troopers to activate the evac Go order for the mushing community—ninety plus mushers and a couple of thousand sled dogs.

She'd shared her plan with Cohen, and he seemed impressed. He'd asked her a ton of questions, some of which she hadn't thought of, and together they'd figured out how to resolve them.

Raynie could barely keep her eyes open, and Cohen had advised that she stop work for the day. Grateful, she'd taken him up on his offer and hobbled next door to check in at the B&B and get situated. Cohen had waited for Doss to relieve him, and he volunteered to deliver her fire pack to her room.

Raynie rested on her bed fully clothed when Cohen knocked on the door. He entered with her pack, and she motioned him to set it in a corner.

"Busy day today, huh?" He sat on her bed.

She looked up at him. "You look tired."

"I'm beat." He swung his legs up onto the bed and deposited himself next to her, letting his feet dangle over the end.

Her breath caught. She hadn't expected him to lie next to her, and his immediate nearness caused her to blank on everything except for the unseen current that passed between them. Her body twitched, and she hoped he wouldn't notice.

He threaded his fingers behind his neck. "Angela called earlier. She said Mel reported he nearly hit a drone on his way to a fire. Near Sleeping Lady Kennel." He turned his head toward her.

"Oh no, Kira." Raynie fished her phone from her pocket, seeing missed calls from her sister. She tapped Kira's number. Her sister answered right away.

"Kira? Is everything all right?"

"Hi, yeah, they almost have the fire here contained. It was twenty-five acres."

"How are the dogs?"

"Wacko got loose again, but I brought him home. I just finished feeding them all."

"Good. Thanks for holding down the fort while I'm gone. Kira, were you flying your drone today?" She glanced at Cohen, resting with his eyes closed.

"Uh, yeah, when I got off work," said Kira.

Raynie closed her eyes. "Please say you didn't fly your drone near the fire."

"I might have. Why?"

"Because you aren't supposed to operate drones in an airspace where aircraft are fighting a fire, Kira. I thought I told you that." She punched every syllable for Cohen's benefit.

He opened a wary eye and looked at her.

"Am I in trouble?" Kira asked in a faint voice.

"We'll talk about it when I get home. Take care of the dogs till I get back. Okay?"

"Sure." Kira sounded nervous, which didn't calm Raynie's fears about her flying the drone in front of Mel Faraday's bird today.

"Okay, talk to you later." Raynie ended the call and looked at Cohen.

Cohen popped his eyes open. "Not good. Mel is pissed and wants a head on a plate."

Raynie squeezed the bridge of her nose and heaved out a sigh. "Can you please not say anything until we get back to Talkeetna? She won't do it again."

"Sure," he said wearily. He looked as though he would fall asleep any second.

"Do you need help to get ready for bed?"

She shot him a wary look. "You're the one who needs help getting ready for bed. You look wasted."

His lips curved up. "I'd rather help *you* get ready for bed."

She turned her head toward him and smiled. "But all I have to do is crawl under the covers."

"In your clothes?" He looked hopeful and she chuckled.

"Maybe." She knew where this was leading, but they were both exhausted. "You better go across the hall to your own bed."

He propped himself up on his elbows. "Thank you for today. You're a good co-pilot. I'm proud of us...we didn't argue."

"No. We didn't." They hadn't done much of that lately. It felt like progress...and a little more.

Cohen yawned and rolled to his side. "I need a forklift to get me off this bed."

"Here, I'll help." She put one foot on his butt and pushed him toward the edge of the bed. "Come on, Chief, you can do it," she teased.

He dragged himself from her bed and shuffled to the door.

"Goodnight, Atwood. Take care of that knee. If you need anything, I'm across the hall." He yawned.

"Thanks. Goodnight, Maple Leaf."

Raynie watched him ease the door closed and listened to his door shut a few seconds later. She meant to ask him about the female smokejumper, who'd been insanely enthusiastic in greeting him today. She'd thought the better of it when he was too tired to stand.

She lay staring at the ceiling, well aware that her feelings for Cohen had gone far beyond anything she ever could have imagined. She couldn't believe how her nemesis had turned out to be an unlikely mentor. After she and Cohen had turned a corner in their rollercoaster relationship, she'd had little time to process it. It seemed so surreal...falling for him was the last thing she thought would happen. Funny, after fervently praying she'd never run into him again. And now?

I look forward to seeing him every day.

She undressed and brushed her teeth, wondering what Cohen was doing across the hall. The thought of him sleeping nearby sent erotic feelings to her girl parts as she slipped under the covers and drifted off to the sounds of helicopters coming and going. Everything turned hazy as she faded into dreamland. All she knew was that she had fires to fight. And she wouldn't mind at all if she fought them alongside Cohen.

Chapter 23

The next morning, Cohen awoke at five a.m., showered, and ate the breakfast provided by the generous folks at the B&B. He'd hesitated outside Raynie's door but hadn't heard any signs of activity, so he headed to the command center, which was already bustling with action.

As soon as he entered, Davc Doss flagged him down. "What time did you schedule the fire briefing? The weather forecast sucks, so we'd better plan and prepare."

Cohen glanced at his watch. "I scheduled it for seven a.m. We'll review our suppression plan for today." He glanced at his boss. "We'd better get those mushers to move their dogs. It's enough of a logistical nightmare as it is, but if we wait on the evac Go order, it'll be worse."

"Good idea. I'll talk to the Alaska State Troopers for you." Doss paused. "Sorry, I don't mean to step on your toes. I'm just used to being in charge. I'm getting too old for this game. I'm thankful you younger people are here to ride herd on things. Also, I wanted to talk to you about Raynie."

"What about her?" Cohen held his breath, hoping a bomb wouldn't drop because he had a crush on his coworker. *It's a little more than a crush,* he reckoned.

"Would you recommend her for the chief of operations job for the Talkeetna Fire Base?" Doss asked.

He stared at Doss, pleasantly surprised by his question. Taking time with his response, he knew the importance of what he was about to say.

"She has good leadership ability and knows wildland firefighting in Alaska." He left out the part about her contrary nature.

"You didn't answer my question."

Cohen said the magic words, and oddly, he meant them.

"Yes, I highly recommend her for the position."

"Good. All I needed to know. See you later; you've got the con. Holler if you need anything." Doss strode off, talking on his phone.

Cohen stared after him, happy for having done this for Raynie. He spotted Rego and Tupa walking in. "You boys are here early. Give me a briefing on how it went yesterday on the left flank."

Rego pulled up a chair, along with Tupa. Cohen poured them each a Styrofoam cup of coffee from the nearby table.

"One thing's for sure," said Rego. "When the storm hits, this sucker will blow up big time."

"We're expecting that." Cohen looked at Rego, then at Tupa. "Rego, you're the Aurora Crew supervisor until further notice." He addressed Tupa. "Please help Rego. Treat the crew like they're a qualified hotshot crew, and they'll work like it. Raynie and I gave you the foundation for what's expected. I'm assigning you to the worst part of the fire."

He eyed the two men. "Are you up to it? If not, tell me now."

"Bet your ass we are," said Rego, exchanging glances with Tupa.

Cohen had full faith in Aurora Crew's capability to handle hotshot crew assignments.

"I'm dispatching Aurora Crew now, and I'm relying on your leadership in Tara's absence. Raynie and I will coordinate homeowner evacuations with the Alaska State Troopers before this fire blows up."

"Glad you're the IC, brah," said Tupa, dipping a nod. He placed his yellow hardhat on his head, and Cohen marveled at how Tupa fit his man bun inside it.

"Thanks." Cohen appreciated that. Acceptance by the Aurora Crew mattered to him.

Tupa and Rego left to round up the crew and brief them.

An hour passed by, then Raynie appeared. She swung herself into a chair, resting her crutches on the IC table. "You're hard at it, I see."

He smiled. "You look rested. You'll need it. We have a shitty weather forecast."

"I heard that walking in."

"Right after the briefing, I've arranged for Mel to fly us around the fire perimeter. I want you to see where homes and dog kennels are in proximity to everything." He motioned at her knee. "How does it feel today?"

She put a hand on her brace. "I didn't sprain it that bad. Keeping ice on it reduced the pain and swelling."

"I'm sort of glad it happened." He smiled. "Not that I want you in pain, but I'm grateful for your help. I talked to Rego and Tupa about supervising the Aurora Crew. Gave them a pep talk about treating them like a hotshot crew. They've trained hard and it's time for them to prove up. I'm using your rules of leadership."

"I agree, it's time to prove up. Rego and Tupa will do an excellent job." His words of validation warmed her.

Cohen tilted his head. "What was that you said?"

"That Rego and Tupa would do an excellent job."

"No, the first thing." His eyes stayed on her.

"That I agree?"

"I've not heard you say those words to me. Does this mean we're compatible?"

"I wouldn't go that far," she teased. "But it's a start."

"Good. Let's get this meeting over with." He offered a hand to help her up, and she waved it away.

"Thanks, but I've got this." She rose, grabbed her crutches, and headed to the large conference room.

Cohen followed, his protective instinct watching Raynie as she maneuvered her way to the room and sat at a table in the front, with the incident command team. He congratulated himself on making progress with Raynie—and was even happier he could recommend her for the chief of operations for the Talkeetna Wildfire Base.

But he was sworn to secrecy and couldn't breathe a word.

JULIET'S ROTORS CRANKED as Raynie sat in the front passenger seat, and Cohen sat behind Mel. He wanted Raynie to have the bird's-eye view for her assessment of the situation, so she'd have the big picture perspective of the mushing community and what was involved.

When Mel lifted and swung the helicopter out over the Susitna River, a bull moose lifted its massive rack from the riverbank to watch them fly over. Birds scattered in the rotor wash, and Cohen watched their shadows float over the land.

Before long, they were over the fire. From the air, it was easy to see how the fire zigzagged around the landscape, without rhyme or reason.

Cohen spoke into the hot mic in his helmet. "See how close together some of these sled dog kennels are? Some dog yards have sixty dogs, some only a dozen." He pressed his helmet against the window to study the land and water bodies below.

Mel flew around the fire to show them the scope of the situation they faced for suppression and evacuations.

"I didn't realize the extent of mushers and sled dog teams in this area. Holy smokes," said Raynie.

Cohen enjoyed her melodic voice inside of his head. Mel pointed, and they both squinted. A musher was on a 4-wheeler with his dog team ahead of him. A truck followed behind, piled high with belongings. They were obviously evacuating.

"Are the dogs pulling that 4-wheeler?" asked Raynie, peering at the ground below.

"No, it's under power," he said. "It's just a way for the musher to exercise his team. Although his eighteen dogs could easily pull it."

Raynie twisted to look at him. "I don't like the way this fire is behaving."

"Me either," he said drily. "Turn her around, Mel. Think we've seen enough."

Mel landed behind the command post, and Cohen helped Raynie out of the bird.

He handed her the crutches. "So, what do you think?"

"I'll get the rest of this plan in place. I have a ton of phone calls to make," she replied.

"Good." They went inside, where Cohen got on the phone with the Alaska Fire Service, State of Alaska DOF, the Fire Marshal, and the state trooper's office, to coordinate information and resources to fight this fire.

Raynie's speed and agility at organizing an evacuation plan impressed him. In just two days, she had a solid plan in place. She'd set up locations for displaced dogs and mushers, after countless phone calls to make arrangements.

Together, Cohen and Raynie compiled a list of musher names and phone numbers and matched them with dots on an aerial photo map. She'd also created a Facebook page, and for those without Internet, she set up a phone hotline.

Cohen checked the latest weather forecast. The storm was moving in from the northwest. Storms brought wind, the last thing they needed. This was the calm before the storm. He smelled the electric tension that hung in the air, as everyone braced for the hell that would surely follow.

NEXT THING COHEN KNEW, it was eight p.m. After working for fourteen hours straight, he sensed the fatigue in his bones. He breathed relief to see Doss stride in to relieve him of his IC duties for the night.

"Tag, you're it," said Cohen, slapping his hand. "See you in the a.m., unless all hell breaks loose before then."

"Don't be surprised if it does. Get some sleep. You'll need it." Doss pointed at Raynie, who was having an animated discussion on her phone while she scribbled a graphic on a whiteboard. "Busy woman."

"Yep. She pulled together a plan almost overnight to get mushers and dogs situated once we give the Go order to evacuate. The tricky part will be getting everyone out in time," said Cohen.

"Glad you both have that one under control. Excellent work." Doss waved him to leave.

Raynie ended her call and gave Cohen an earnest look. "We've covered as many bases as possible, but we still need to find more evac shelters for dogs and people."

"We'll get the rest of them accommodated." He motioned at her. "Come on. We blew past dinner and must eat. And sleep. Morning could come at any minute."

"Don't have to tell me twice." Raynie grabbed her crutches and followed him.

Cohen helped Raynie upstairs to her room at the B&B and waited for her to go inside. "I ordered a pizza. When it's delivered, I'll bring it up. First, I have to shower. You know you need a shower when the soap crawls away from you. My place or yours for dinner?"

She gave a noncommittal shrug. "We can eat here. Or your place. I need a shower, too."

"Okay, your place. I'll knock when it's here."

"I'll be waiting."

He swore she had a twinkle in her eye before she closed the door.

Chapter 24

The loud knock on Raynie's door startled her awake. She'd taken a shower and had settled on her bed in the white bathrobe the B&B had graciously provided. Her deep brown tresses sprawled around her, damp and scraggly.

"Just a minute!" It took a second to remember where she was and who was knocking on her door.

Raynie bounced off the bed and scrambled to the tiny bathroom. She didn't even know where her brush was. She opened the drawers and found a small comb, but it was no help. Instead, she tamed her long tresses into a messy bun. It would have to do.

"What are you doing, splitting atoms in there?" Cohen called through the door. "Pizza's getting cold."

She flew to the door and swung it open.

Raynie hadn't seen Cohen outside of his Nomex fire shirt and pants except for the one day he had on jeans and a jean jacket. She gaped at him in all his post-shower glory, with his damp, tousled hair. He had an air of having just strolled away from a movie set. She inhaled a fresh scent of pine, fireweed, and hot pizza.

"Are you going to let me in, or what?" He grinned, lifting the pizza, looking a million in a tight T-shirt and faded jeans. His eyes roved over her and settled on her chest.

Her eyes followed his to discover her bathrobe had opened, revealing a shit ton of cleavage. She squeezed her robe together. Heat moved up her neck as she stepped back to let him in.

Cohen moved to a small round table next to a window and set the pizza box on it.

"Smells divine." She didn't know which smelled better, Cohen or the pizza. She was ravenous and pried loose a floppy slice. "I love combo pizza. How'd you know?"

"Lucky guess." His eyes met hers as he lifted a slice.

They let silence hang between them while they ate. She inhaled her first piece and reached for a second.

Cohen chomped on a third slice, then tossed his napkin on his paper plate.

"Full already."

"Me, too." She wiped her mouth, then sat back and scrutinized the way Cohen relaxed in the chair, as if on vacation.

"How do you stay so calm all the time? I watched you today. Nothing frazzles you. Not even when dozens of people milled around you like frantic Wall Street traders." She admired the red, smoky sun glinting Cohen's golden hair.

"Working with my dad had a lot to do with that, I reckon. When things went south in the construction business, getting bent out of shape solved nothing." He sat up in his seat. "Thanks for diving in today to get things organized."

She closed the pizza box. "I know it isn't our agency's responsibility, but if this fire runs, we'll be glad we set up a plan."

"How's the knee?" he asked, angling his head. His head tilt was more charming than Taydon's ever was.

She separated her robe to expose her knee. "Swelling has gone down a lot." She caught his stare and quickly closed her robe.

"What'd you do that for?" he joked.

She glanced at him in feigned surprise. "Hello? We work together."

"We're off duty right now, if you haven't noticed." Cohen's phone buzzed, and he tapped it. Raising his brows, he stashed the phone in his pants pocket.

"Command center?" she asked, her gaze lingering on his well-defined forearms, evenly covered in soft, light hair.

He shook his head dismissively. "Just a friend."

She had to know. "Was it the smokejumper you talked to today? She seemed happy to see you."

Cohen glanced out the window. "Deanna? We met on a fire down in Alberta."

"Were you two involved?"

"For a while." He glanced at her. "You know how it is during fire season. We ended it then went our separate ways."

She wanted to know more but refrained from asking.

He lifted the pizza box. "How about we stick the leftover pizza in your fridge? We can finish it tomorrow."

She rose to do it, but Cohen held up his hand in a stop motion. "I've got it. Rest your knee."

He squatted in front of the fridge, his untucked shirt lifting at the back of his waist. No plumber's crack, only lean muscle. Her breath caught at the pleasing skin display. He closed the fridge and moved to the window, peering out.

"Storms aren't here yet, but they'll arrive with a vengeance when they do." He let out a long sigh. "I'd better get ready for tomorrow."

"Isn't it weird how we live by the weather in the summer?" Raynie studied his profile in the twilight—how perfect he looked, with the soft light filtering through the window, casting a warm glow on his features. She liked this relaxed, off-duty side of him. She had to say what was on her mind. She summoned the courage.

Now or never.

"Cohen." She spoke in a sincere tone. "I know we got off to a terrible start. Thanks for trusting me with a leadership position. Any other person would have chosen someone else." She fiddled with the belt on her robe.

He moved from the window and sat on the bed beside her. "Why would you say that?"

"You know why." She hesitated. "For starters...the awful way I've treated you, and saying I loathed you."

"I could tell you had things on your mind." Cohen bumped her shoulder with his and side-eyed her. "Do you still feel that way?"

She bumped him back, her mouth lifting.

"If I truly loathed you, why would I be sitting next to you in my bathrobe?" Her pulse raced when she lifted her gaze to his blue one. "How did you know things weighed on me before I told you about Taydon?"

"There's sadness in your eyes, like you carry an invisible burden." His perceptive ability to see into her soul left her lungs without air.

"Oh." She gulped and lifted a shaky hand to her eyes.

"Grief is unbearable. Your heart physically hurts, and every breath is torture." Her voice tremored. "We were kindred spirits. When he died, a piece of me died with him." There was no point in telling Cohen about Taydon's betrayal. No point in dumping her excess baggage on him. Not when they were just getting started with the good stuff.

"When you said the man you'd planned to marry was deceased, I sensed your pain." He reached over and took her hand, rubbing the top with his thumb. "I'm so sorry that happened. But if it hadn't, we wouldn't be sitting here together."

His touch was everything, exploding her skin. Emotion pushed up as she studied his clear, understanding eyes.

"I honestly thought you hated me," she said softly.

"Hate? No. A pain in the ass? Yes."

"Then why are you so nice to me?" she asked, turning her face away.

"Because I've gotten used to it." He turned her head toward him and lowered his lips to hers. His tender, shallow kiss squished her insides, clouding her brain. It disappointed her when he drew back.

She closed her eyes, her breath glued to the inside of her throat.

"I feel terrible for all the times I was shitty to you," she choked out in a broken whisper. "Not once did I say I was sorry."

"Look at me, Raynie." Cohen's voice was firm but laced with compassion.

She lifted her lids, locking onto the cerulean windows of his soul, which she'd regrettably misjudged. Something was about to pivot in a big way, and she scrambled to prepare herself for it—for *him.*

"No apologies necessary." Cohen's lips pressed to hers, and he kissed her so deeply, her toes curled into the braided throw rug. An achy feeling pinged her down low, the same way it had the first time he kissed her next to the river.

She sensed what was coming, and she was powerless to stop it; nor did she want to. Conflicted panic fluttered her insides, and she pushed him away, breathless.

"We shouldn't do this. It's the wrong time. The wrong place. We're on a fire...I don't look good..."

She ran out of reasons as a divine revelation hit her—she was exactly where she was meant to be—with the person she was meant to be with. She gazed into his eyes, grateful for this man who'd found his way into her life. When she read what was in his eyes, she understood her life would never be the same.

"No. You don't look good." Cohen undid her messy bun, letting her hair drop. "You look absolutely beat-the-wall beautiful." He combed her hair with his fingers, then brushed his lips up the side of her neck.

"Cohen..." She gasped at the sensation he delivered to girl parts she hadn't been aware of.

He drew back. "We don't have the luxury of time. You and I both know one fire year is like eighty in firefighter years." He slid his hand under her robe and eased it off one shoulder. "All the more reason to make love with you, Fire Chick."

Goosebumps sprung up on her skin like fireweed.

"Now? What if...what if I, um, say no?" Coherent thought went on vacation, and word formation hitched along for the ride.

He brushed his thumb over her lips. "Then I won't."

"You'd give up that easily?"

"No." His definitive answer and the lip action on the side of her neck drove her insane.

"I can't think when you do that," she whispered, lust short-circuiting all logic. Her heart ricocheted somewhere in between.

"What do you want, Raynie?" he breathed in her ear.

All the doubts and fears about him that had swirled around in her mind promptly vanished, replaced by a sense of clarity and purpose. A sense of calm streamed through her.

"You."

"Good, because I can't stop."

He plunged his tongue into her mouth, and she welcomed the sweet taste of pizza and soda and Cohen. His body was solid as titanium. She'd not smoothed her hands over titanium that she could recollect—but this body *had* to be as strong. She'd always admired the ripped physiques of male firefighters, but this was the first time she'd actually *felt* one.

Her brain drove away on vacation while her heart jumped into the driver's seat.

Cohen held her face in his hands. "You're trembling."

"It's just...I'm not sure about this. Haven't done it in a while."

"Do I look worried?" He tilted her face toward his. "There's no reason to be nervous."

"I'm not," she lied, hoping to convince herself. "I'm just...you're so...and I loathed you..."

"Not anymore, I hope." Cohen kissed her while his hands sneaked inside her robe, leaving a trail of fire on her skin.

She closed her eyes. "It's too soon for this. We haven't known each other that long..." She trailed off, loving his touch, which ignited every cell in her body.

"Not too soon. Not with you. This isn't a one-night stand." His chocolate voice drifted through her, like sweet, viscous music. He lifted to peer into her eyes.

"I'll stop if you want me to. The last thing I want is to pressure you."

She was so strangled with desire, she could hardly form a sentence. Voices screamed in her brain.

Yes! No! Yes! No! Do it—you want him—you know you do. Decide, dammit!

She found her voice. "You realize this is our point-of-no-return, right?"

Cohen brushed her hair away from her face. "We're risk-takers. That's why we fight fire. If you step into this fire with me, I promise you won't regret it." The sensuous gleam in his eyes swayed her, dissolving all doubt.

"I want you so bad, Raynie."

His words propelled her to action. She lifted his shirt over his head and let it fall to the floor. Her mouth fell open as she took in his bare upper half. She glided her palms around his smooth shoulders and around his chest, loving the solid, satiny feel of the hills and valleys along his stomach.

"I take it you don't want to stop?" His baby blues darkened to cobalt, and the way he stared at her was oddly comforting.

"And suppress *this* fire? I'm having too much fun feeling you up." Her eyes followed him as he shoved himself backward on the bed until all six-foot-four of him sprawled on it.

Sudden bashfulness seized her. She pushed away to step to the window, gazing at the all-night twilight, where the sun stubbornly remained on duty. Her heart couldn't decide whether to stop, soar, or skitter.

"I love Alaskan summers, where no one says let's get there by dark," she said randomly, gently coaxing the shade down to block out the daylight.

Cohen raised himself on an elbow. "Leave it up. I want to see you."

A mix of excitement, fear, and desire caused her to stall, and she hesitated. When she pulled the shade all the way down, he protested. She put a finger to her lips.

"This is non-negotiable."

As she turned back towards the bed, and the person she was about to make love with, her breath hitched at a mostly naked Cohen lying on his side. He'd stripped down to his snug boxer briefs, and *wow*. She'd be content just to sit and stare at him all night.

She moved to the bed and settled herself beside him, pampering her knee. "It feels weird to lie prone with you, let alone naked," she confessed.

"Feels weird for me, too. But this was inevitable. I've sensed it from the beginning. Haven't you?" His eyes became hooded.

She didn't know what to say. When she'd met him for the first time, the last thing she envisioned was intimacy. She'd been too busy wanting to throttle him.

"Don't worry, we'll go easy on your knee." Cohen gripped the collar of her robe. "Lose this thing, Atwood."

"You do it," she ordered, loving the glint in his eye when she said it. She hoped they weren't being reckless, but Cohen was right; during fire season, there's never time for anything but fighting fire.

"You sure you want me to disrobe you? I know how you like control." He said it in a teasing manner, though the nuance behind his words reminded her of when they'd fought like scorch beasts in a video game.

"Disrobe me? Where do you come up with these words?" She laughed. "Even though I do prefer control, I'll let you IC this operation. But if I say stop, you'd better. Agreed?"

"Agreed. Want to shake on it?" Cohen gave her an impish grin as he pushed up to kneel on the bed.

She extended her hand, and he shook it. Then his hand dropped to tug at her belt. His movements were slow and deliberate, as if taking his time to open a much-awaited holiday gift.

She stared up at this man, this firefighter—the last human in the universe she figured she'd be having sex with right now.

He looks incredible with that tender look on his face.

A look that contrasted with his professional demeanor. She wanted him more than ever.

Five months of no sex wouldn't let her stop him, but it also made her nervous. "Hurry, before one of us chickens out."

"It sure as hell won't be me. We're in this together, Fire Chick," he joked, lifting one side of her robe and pulling it aside.

Air hit her nipple, and his eyes locked onto it. He pressed his lips to the top of her exposed breast, then slid them excruciatingly slowly to the pebbled center.

Her breaths became pants as her body instinctively arched.

Cohen opened the rest of her robe, exposing her entire body. He sat back, gazing at her, sucking in air.

"Holy smokes, Atwood."

It took a lot of guts for her to allow him this vulnerability. *No going back now.*

"I showed you mine, now you show me yours. Lose those cute little boxers." Her green light appeared to rocket-fuel him.

While Cohen shoved them down, she ditched her robe. He wasted no time trailing kisses around her chest and stomach, then kissed his way up to swirl his tongue around hers.

She loved his easy warmth, as their hands took time exploring one another. Slowing foreplay was practically impossible. Cohen's touch ignited a burning deep within her, but her aching need overpowered his gentle kisses and caresses. She sensed he was on the same frequency.

"I don't want to hurt your knee." Cohen lifted and sat back. With one hand supporting her bad knee, he placed the other under her ankle to separate one leg from the other. He rolled on protection, then maneuvered himself to lie over her, careful not to rest his full weight on hers.

"You're such a considerate lover," she whispered, easing his hair away from his forehead.

"I don't want to cause you pain—physically or otherwise," he whispered back, nuzzling her. His meticulous care with her sore knee caused a lone tear to slide from the corner of her eye and vanish into her hair.

Another tear followed when he entered her. He moved all the way inside, locked onto her gaze every bit of the way. The gentle power of his moving back and forth with his gaze fastened to hers, caused a tsunami so strong, her body shuddered wildly. Wave after wave rippled her, and she flung her arms around his neck, pressing him into her as she lost herself in him. Cohen followed with his own release.

"Ohh, Raynie..." He tensed and stilled, both of them panting.

"Stay inside," she murmured. "Please, stay inside."

Along with her orgasm came a brain-gasm...and she decided Cohen Tremblay was someone she could trust. He was tender, perceptive, and deeply internal...qualities she admired. She wished she had them.

He stayed in place, elbows propped on either side of her, to hold his weight off her. "How's your knee?"

"We just rocked each other's worlds, and you're concerned about my knee? You're scoring points by the second, Maple Leaf." She lifted her head to kiss him.

He offered her a slow, secret smile. "As the IC, it's time to demobe this operation."

"Copy that." She wished they could stay like this—physically connected for days and days, secure in each other's arms. Let everything else go on without them. Let the fires rage. Unfortunately, the world didn't agree.

Cohen rolled onto his back and stilled. The sudden emptiness left her longing for him to be back inside of her. She traced her fingers over his chest, feeling his heart beating in sync with hers. He'd won her over. Big time.

She'd come to appreciate his good points: his intelligence when it came to leading people, and the respectful way he treated everyone. His leadership was anchored in the desire to be his best. But most of all, he had a serene presence she found comforting.

I now admire Cohen Tremblay. Talk about the poles reversing.

They'd physically joined, and as far as Raynie was concerned, that meant serious commitment on her part. She had never taken physical intimacy lightly.

She wondered if Cohen felt the same.

Chapter 25

As Cohen stepped outside the next morning, a powerful gust of wind whipped his hair and rustled the papers in his hand. Ominous clouds had crept in, sending purple lightning to the ground. He eyed the thick plume of dark smoke in the distance as the storm blew up the fire.

He'd fallen asleep with Raynie after their lovemaking. He hoped he hadn't messed things up by spending the night with her. She'd been so peaceful lying there, and he didn't want to sleep in his own bed. It had been a long time since he'd shared a bed with anyone.

He flagged down Dave Doss as he stepped inside the community center.

"She's blowing up as expected."

"We're hitting it with water drops and mud drops," Doss informed him. "Tremblay, the agencies have assigned a new state overhead team to take over the command center. They've released you and Raynie, so you'll both be returning to work with the Aurora Crew. Alaska's senators and the governor are planning a site visit to this fire. The state wants their own IC and overhead team in place by the time the muckety-mucks arrive. It's political. You understand."

"Sure, I get it." Cohen wasn't surprised and knew better than to take it personally. Project fires often switched command teams. In wildland fire, things changed on a dime.

"I'll brief the incoming command staff. Then Atwood and I will rejoin the Aurora Crew."

"Maybe Raynie can get help to coordinate the evacuation plan from Talkeetna," said Doss. "But in the interim, we need both of you on the fireline."

"Sure thing," said Cohen. He spent the next hour briefing the new command staff on how many firefighters were on the fire, aviation activity, and other resources. True to the weather forecast, the winds had blasted the flames toward the rest of the mushing community.

Raynie appeared just as he finished briefing the incoming staff. Cohen pulled her aside, offered her a coffee, and explained the new situation.

"Dang it. Wish we could have worked longer in Command," said Raynie. "I was just making headway."

He grinned. "Don't worry, you still get to work with me."

Raynie shot him a look. "That isn't what I mean. I wanted to continue with the evacuation plan." She backpedaled. "Not that I don't enjoy working with you. It's just that I want to see this thing through."

"Doss wants you to keep working on what you started from Talkeetna. You can do it just as well from there."

"How can I do that and fight fire?"

"Get someone from the mushing community to help," he suggested. "You must know mushers in the area?"

Raynie thought for a minute. "Trish at Denali Roadhouse. I know she'd help. She and her husband run dogs."

"Call her," he urged. "We'll be returning to Talkeetna after work today, where you can sleep in your own bed."

"Like you did?" she quipped, the corners of her mouth edging up.

"Good one, Atwood." Cohen loved what happened last night but didn't want to presume anything. Exhausted, he'd fallen asleep and awoke that morning, wrapped around her.

"I don't have a comeback for that one."

"That's not like you, Tremblay. Did you do the walk of shame when you left my room?"

"I sure did. All the way across the hall." He gave her an impish grin. "Don't worry. No one saw me."

Raynie gave him a hesitant look. "Do you have regrets about last night?"

He leveled his gaze. "Do you?"

"I asked you first."

"It's just that I—" he started.

"Commander Tremblay!" A certain female smokejumper's voice cut in from across the busy room. Deanna strode up, her gaze fixed on him, like a wolf homing in on its prey.

"Good morning! Have you eaten? Let's grab some breakfast."

That's all I need right now. Old girlfriend barges in on new girlfriend.

He hadn't considered Raynie as his girlfriend yet, but he supposed that's what she was now. They hadn't even talked about it.

Cohen's eyes darted to Raynie, who regarded Deanna the way she used to glare at him back when she loathed him.

A young woman rushed up. "Raynie, we need your help with some evacuation locations before you leave. People have questions I can't answer."

Raynie glanced from Cohen to Deanna and back again, steadying her gaze on him.

"I'll meet you in the van when we drive back to Talkeetna."

Cohen sucked in a shaky breath as Raynie moved off to help the woman.

Deanna bumped him with her hip. "I understand you've been replaced in the command center. I wondered why they put a federal IC in charge of a fire under state jurisdiction."

"Alaska does things differently," he said absently, eyes focused on Raynie, talking on her cell.

"Come on, I'll treat you to breakfast," Deanna cajoled, linking her elbow with his to steer him down the long hallway to the community center kitchen.

"People will talk." He said it jokingly and politely unlinked her grip.

Deanna leaned into him. "That never stopped you in Alberta. From what I recall, I was your rebound after your Salmon Arm girlfriend dumped you—what was her name again?"

"Gloria." He bit back his annoyance.

"Right, Gloria. I always wonder what would have happened had you and I stayed together. Do you ever wonder that?" Deanna picked up a plate and loaded it with scrambled eggs and hash browns.

Cohen eyed her food pile, remembering smokejumpers practically consumed their own weight in a day to keep up with their rigorous schedules. He deftly sidestepped her question. "Where are you based now?" He filled his own plate and turned to find an empty table.

"I've transferred to the Alaska Smokejumpers in Fairbanks. Permanently." Deanna emphasized the last, locking her gaze on him. She swung her leg over the table bench and sat. "The Alaska Fire Service flew us down here with our Twin Otter. We're on call because we expect this fire to blow up."

"It's already ramped up with these wind gusts."

He hadn't missed her point that she was permanently based in Fairbanks. So was he.

Oh shit, that's all I need.

He glanced around nervously, hoping Raynie wouldn't walk into the mess hall.

Deanna motioned her head toward the parking lot. "When are you heading back to Talkeetna today?"

"When Aurora Crew is off fireline duty." Cohen peered out the window, glimpsing bushes and trees waving in the wind. "Depends on the weather."

"Heard you've been tasked with turning the Aurora Crew into a hotshot crew." She shoveled a forkful of eggs into her mouth.

His head bobbed, chewing his potatoes. "They're a hard-working, cohesive crew. Won't take long for them to qualify. Everyone knows their jobs, and they're good at them."

Deanna waved a fork. "Tell me about that petite brunette runway model you're always talking to. Did she get on the wrong plane from the lower forty-eight? How'd someone like her wind up fighting fire in Alaska?"

Cohen's head shot up in surprise. "I met Raynie Atwood on the Eagle River Hiland Fire. She was the state incident commander. And she's no runway model." Envisioning Raynie strutting down a runway made him chuckle. Maybe he'd fantasize about it.

"We need to talk." Deanna set her fork down, shoved her plate aside, and leaned forward with her forearms on the table.

"I was hoping I'd see you when I knew you were down here." She reached across the table and closed her hands around both of his. "I want to pick up where we left off in Canada. I've missed you so much." She squeezed his hands.

Cohen glanced up to see Raynie in the food line, gaping wide-eyed at him. Horrified, he yanked his hands from Deanna's grip. Not knowing what else to do, he motioned for Raynie to join them.

Instead, she turned her back and aimed for a seat across the room. When her stoneware plate hit the table, followed by a clatter of silverware, his stomach turned inside out. Not how he wanted this morning to go after the incredible sex last night.

"Oh, crap," he muttered, shaking his head. He stole a glance at Raynie, who stabbed her food as if it was trying to escape.

"What's the matter?" Deanna followed his glance, then sat back, nodding. "Oh, I get it. You have a thing for Miss Supermodel. I'm not a woman who gives up easily. Now that I've found you again, I'm not about to lose you like before. I want you back."

"Sorry, Deanna."

Cohen took that as his cue to leave. He shrugged with a rueful smile.

"That won't happen. We ended a long time ago, and I've moved on. You're a good person. Just not the one for me." He rose, dropping his silverware and napkin on his plate. "Be safe on fire."

Mustering courage, he moved over to where Raynie attacked her breakfast with a vengeance. He grimaced, wondering if she imagined stabbing him in the heart.

Hopefully, she wouldn't do it for real.

Chapter 26

When they reached Talkeetna, Cohen dropped Raynie off at Sleeping Lady Kennel with the Aurora Crew transport van. Without so much as a glance at him, she climbed out wordlessly, slammed the door, and hurried inside the house before losing her composure.

They hadn't said five words between them on the eighteen-mile drive. Neither wanted to discuss it in front of the crew. She'd gotten up and left the mess hall when Cohen came to her table. Later, when he talked to her, he went on and on about him and Deanna being over.

"I know what I saw!" she'd repeated each time he explained it.

They couldn't get beyond it. He stubbornly explained; she stubbornly clung to what she saw—he and Deanna holding hands. Had Cohen been playing her all this time just for a piece of ass? Or did he have a bet with the guys: *Atwood hates me, but I bet I can get her in bed with me.*

When he'd made love to her last night, she'd enthusiastically gone all in. But apparently that hadn't been the case for Cohen. Not after seeing him lovey-dovey with Deanna and holding hands with her.

Damn him! That's what I get for falling for the enemy.

Now she was back to square one, loathing him. This whole thing with Cohen had been nothing but a bittersweet chemistry.

Moving on from losing Taydon by rushing into a relationship wasn't the smartest thing she'd ever done. She'd allowed Cohen to take advantage of her vulnerability. She was doing okay on her own...wasn't she? She'd lessened her grief for Taydon and was on solid ground now. One thing she hadn't counted on was heartbreak this early in the game.

Oh well, easy come, easy go.

Rooby greeted her with whimpers and a wagging tail when she walked inside the cabin. Kira wasn't home from work yet.

Tears trickled down her cheeks as Raynie dropped her fire pack and duffle to the floor. She kneeled and buried her face in Rooby's fur, sobbing out her angst and frustration. When she closed her eyes, all she saw was Cohen holding hands with Deanna. Then he'd stumbled over himself, saying he and Deanna were long over.

What a freaking liar!

She was no dummy. The old girlfriend-wants-you-back routine was old hat. She'd done it herself with Taydon, when they broke up in Arizona after he'd moved on with someone else. She'd cornered him in a bar later on, demanding that he come back to her. He'd pulled her out to the parking lot and did her standing up against his truck in the warm desert night.

So, she understood how Deanna wanted Cohen back; but that was the hell of it.

In the van back to Talkeetna, while the Aurora Crew talked animatedly about the day's fire fight, she'd brooded, staring at the smoky landscape while Cohen drove. All the way home, she scolded herself for being stupid and getting sucked in by his charms. She should have stuck with her first impression.

After their intimacy last night, Raynie felt gut-punched this morning, seeing Cohen having breakfast with his ex—*and holding hands with her.* Nothing he said could alter what she'd seen. After last night, he'd steamrolled her heart flatter than a squished mosquito.

She sobbed her remorse into Rooby's fur for letting down her guard with Tremblay—trusting him and falling for all the things he'd said. He'd asked for another chance, and she gave it to him.

Well, guess what? No more chances.

The door slammed, and she didn't know how long she'd been on the floor with her head on Rooby's side, hugging her comfy, warm dog.

"Hey, Big Sis, good to see ya!" said Kira, setting down empty bakery trays and standing, looking down at her sister. "Looks like you had a tough day."

"Cohen Tremblay turned out to be a dickhead, just like I first thought." Raynie crawled over to the couch and climbed onto it.

Kira's eyes widened as she sat in the recliner across from her.

"You mean that super nice guy who gave me a ride home? The one you went hiking with? You said you and he worked together on the Denali Creek Fire. What happened?"

"Made the mistake of sleeping with him. Then this morning he had breakfast with his ex, holding hands. Whenever she sees him, she's all over him. He doesn't seem to mind, either." Every time Raynie thought about it, her blood boiled.

"That sucks," said Kira. "Don't you still have to work with him?"

"I'm calling Morrey tomorrow morning and telling him to reassign me back to my state crew. Cohen can train his own hotshot crew. I'm done."

"But I thought you liked him—when you weren't busy detesting him," said Kira. She petted Rooby, who'd sidled up to her chair. "Raynes, I have to tell you something."

Raynie looked up at her sister. "You already told me about the drone."

"No. Something else. Something worse." Kira's tone alarmed her, and she feared what Kira would say next.

"Avery Maddox showed up here. What's he doing here in Alaska? I thought he was in prison?" Kira stared at her sister.

Dread slammed Raynie's chest, and her blood ran cold.

"What happened?"

"One night after I fed the dogs, someone pounded on the door, yelling for you to open it." Kira's brow furrowed. "Even Mom knew he was a loser. She always kicked him out when he'd come to our house with Taydon, remember?"

Raynie froze. "Did you let him in?"

"No. I yelled through the door for him to leave. The dogs barked up a storm. I thought Wacko and Rooby would tear his flipping head off. I think he kicked Wacko because he growled like when he shakes his toys. Then Maddox screamed a bunch of 'F' words."

"Good, I hope Wacko hurt him. Kira, you should have called the state troopers. Or at least called Trish. She would have sent her husband over, even if he was off duty."

"I was scared Maddox would break down the door. He didn't, but he kicked it a few times and dented it."

Kira motioned toward the front door, then stood to get them each a bottle of water. She handed one to Raynie, who unscrewed the cap and sipped.

"Then what?"

"I peeked between the shades and saw him bending to pick up something," explained Kira. "Then the window over the kitchen sink shattered when he threw a huge rock through it. There was a note tied to the rock."

She rose to open a drawer in the end table, then handed a piece of crinkled yellow paper to Raynie. "I nailed a board on the window to cover the hole."

Raynie had been so preoccupied with her thoughts; she hadn't noticed the board over the kitchen window. She opened the note and read it silently.

I'm coming back for my money. You better have it, or you'll never see your pretty little sister again. MX.

The hair on Raynie's neck rose, and she glanced up at her sister. Horror curtained Kira's face as she clamped a hand over her nose and mouth.

"Oh honey, I'm so sorry. This must have terrified you. Why didn't you call and tell me?" She wanted to scream but had to keep it together, for Kira's sake.

"You were busy working on the fire. I didn't want to bother you." Kira spoke hesitantly. "There's someone I met at the Roadhouse. He's two years older, but he's super nice. He's training for the Junior Iditarod sled dog race."

Raynie waited expectantly, hoping for no more unwelcome news.

"His name is Jamen. I was scared and didn't want to be alone, so he spent the last few nights here." Kira gave her sister a penitent look. "Don't worry, we didn't do anything. He helped me nail the board on the window. And he helped me hook up the dogs and run them, using Kam's wheeled cart."

It took Raynie a moment to process all this. "Well, first off, I'm glad Jamen stayed with you, as long as he can be trusted. And I'm glad you ran the dogs. You're almost eighteen. You don't have to justify to me who you date—or who you have sex with. But you should have at least told Trish. Her trooper husband would have sent a car to watch the house." Guilt and anger washed over her, and she couldn't sort one from the other.

"Maddox said if we called the cops, he'd hurt us. Please don't be mad that Jamen slept on our couch. I stayed in my room, honest to God." Kira held up two fingers.

"I'm filing a police report," said Raynie, her voice shaking. "We have to get Maddox on record he threatened us. He's a felon and violated his parole. He showed up a few weeks ago. I should have told you, but I didn't want to alarm you."

"Maddox said don't tell the cops!" Kira's eyes grew big. "What if he comes back? He said he would."

"If he tries to come into this house, I'll protect us. Don't worry."

Maybe she should take the nine-millimeter and go to target practice.

"I wish you were still with that Tremblay guy. He could easily take care of Maddox. He has more muscles than God has angels."

Raynie laughed at Kira's analogy. "You're right. He does at that."

Her heart ached at the mention of Cohen, but she couldn't think about that right now. She picked up her phone and called Trish. "Are you still up? Can I come see you?"

"Sure, I'm still at the Roadhouse. Come on over."

Raynie ended the call and looked at her sister. "If you don't want to be alone, call your friend Jamen. See if he can stay with you until I get back. What's his last name?"

"Bloomington. He's from that family of famous Iditarod mushers."

"Yes, they're Iditarod royalty. Okay, see if he can come over. I'd like to meet him when I come home." She flicked her eyes at her sister. "We'll discuss the drone situation later. I'll leave Rooby here to protect you."

"Okay." Kira whistled for the golden, then picked up her phone and raced to her bedroom.

Raynie grabbed her hoodie and headed out the door. Wacko stood in the back of her pickup, as if expecting her to go outside.

"Hey, you crazy mutt. Want to ride with me into town? Come on, get in." She held open the back door, and the dog leaped out of the bed and into the cab effortlessly.

"WHY DIDN'T KIRA CALL me? She could have stayed here at the Roadhouse," bemoaned Trish after Raynie explained what happened.

"Kira didn't want to leave the dogs alone. She was afraid Maddox would do something to them after he kicked Wacko." Raynie motioned out the window at her truck, where Wacko sat contentedly in the passenger seat. One ear flopped forward as usual. This goofball dog had grown on her.

Raynie told Trish the entire Maddox saga, starting with Arizona and ending with his threats.

"I don't know what money he thinks I have. Obviously, he and Taydon had done some kind of drug deal. Kira told me Taydon had been dealing in Alaska when he said he was clean." She shook her head. "He lied to me."

Trish handed her a tissue before the first tear fell. Raynie couldn't hold it in anymore. Her earlier tears were over Cohen, but the fresh pain of Taydon's lies had sliced her like a sword.

"Oh, God, Trish. Everything just hurts so bad. I'm so angry, I want to punch something. I can't even tell Taydon how much it hurts that he lied to me. Like I didn't matter to him." Her sobs racked her shoulders.

Trish lifted Raynie from her chair and hugged her, while Raynie cried on Trish's shoulder.

"Put Taydon to rest along with his betrayal. The two of you weren't meant to be, that's all. I'm sorry he lied to you. If you hadn't found out the truth, you'd be grieving for a man who was someone else with you. Maybe it was supposed to happen this way. Anger can make grief worse, or it can end it."

Trish drew back and handed her a tissue. "You'll have to choose."

Raynie nodded, knowing Trish was right. She took a few shaky breaths to compose herself. "I'm no longer going to grieve someone who was a fake and a liar. I guess I'll let anger end it, even if it's not the right choice."

"There is no right choice. Just the one that's good for you." Trish smiled and handed her another tissue. "I know it's hard. I'm not saying it isn't. And if you want to punch something, I have some straw bales out back we use for our doghouses. Go to it any time you like."

Raynie laughed through her tears. "I might take you up on that. Thanks, Trish. You're a good friend."

Trish lifted Raynie's chin. "If this Maddox creep even burps in your direction, call the troopers. Kira says you have a firefighter boyfriend. Maybe he can stay at your place for a while? I don't like the idea of you two staying alone with this felon on the loose."

"No, not a boyfriend—I mean, we weren't—aren't technically together. It's a long story." Raynie shook her head. "I'm thinking of calling my boss in the morning to reassign me back to my state hotshot crew."

"It's not like you to walk away when things get tough." Trish's mouth turned up. "Unless you've fallen head over heels."

Raynie swallowed. "If I were head over heels, I'd want to stay."

"That's exactly why you should stay." Trish smiled. "Sleep on it first. Don't make rash decisions when you're emotional. Why not try to work it out with...?"

"Cohen Tremblay, from Canada. We've worked together these past several weeks, training his hotshot crew, and he's the one who had me help him in the command center for the Denali Fire."

Trish raised her brows. "I saw you walking with him a few days ago. You talked and laughed like old friends." She brightened. "Hey, I hear you organized an evacuation for the mushers."

"Yes, I was hoping you could help," said Raynie, thankful to change the subject. "I got a good start at the Denali Creek Community Center." A lonely pain pierced her, remembering how she and Cohen had worked on it together.

"We created a Facebook page and a phone tree. I arranged with Denali Equine Supply for people to park RVs and set up tents in their parking lot for the large dog teams."

"Sure, just let me know what you need help with. The troopers said the evacuation is going okay so far, even though several have lost homes and dog kennels," said Trish.

"Since you talked me into staying, I'll be back working with the Aurora Crew." She thought of Cohen, and her stomach ached. "We're heading to the Denali Creek Fire early tomorrow morning."

"E-mail me what you've organized so far," said Trish.

"We still need accommodation for up to two thousand dogs," explained Raynie. "I'll email you my Excel spreadsheets and I'll drop my binder off in the morning on my way to work." She let out a long sigh.

"The people who've lost homes and kennels need help to get back on their feet."

Trish's face lit. "I have an idea. Why don't we have a firefighter auction? Like the annual bachelor auction we do here every winter that I help to organize. I can do this one and plenty of people will help."

"That's a fantastic idea!" Raynie caught her excitement. "We can also do a firefighter calendar with male and female firefighters. I can get enough people to do it."

Trish gave her a sly look. "Will the guys take their shirts off?"

Raynie stared up at the ceiling. "I bet I could talk a few into it. The women won't, though. I'll have the ladies wear tank tops with their Nomex pants and a Pulaski in their hand. But not too sexy. They still need to look like wildland firefighters."

Trish beamed. "This sounds fun! But how can we schedule it when firefighters are out fighting fire?"

"It'll have to be when fire activity calms down." Raynie's heart leaped at the idea of raising money for the displaced homeowners, mushers, and their dogs.

"I'll get Aurora Crew started on the calendar, and we'll all help with the auction." Raynie glanced at her watch. "I told Kira to have her new friend come over. I don't want her being alone with all this craziness going on."

"Her new friend, as in Jamen Bloomington? The whole town is whispering about those two. He shows up with those puppy dog eyes whenever Kira is working. It's so cute." Trish sighed. "I remember those days."

"I'm glad Kira found someone like him. He sounds like a good person." Raynie turned to Trish. "Thank you for your shoulder to cry on...and giving me something to look forward to with this firefighter auction. I appreciate your help with the evacuation."

Trish patted her shoulder. "That's what friends are for. I don't know why you and Cohen parted ways. Most times, we need to step back and breathe, and think about the reasons to end a relationship. It may surprise you to find it isn't what you thought. Give Cohen another chance."

"Already gave him a chance." Raynie let out a loud long sigh.

"So, give him another." Trish gestured toward the display case. "By the way, while you were gone, Kira did a fabulous job keeping the Roadhouse supplied with muffins and rolls. Tell her I appreciated her doing that."

"I will. Goodnight." Raynie stepped outside into the night air, the smell of smoke reminding her she had to get ready for morning.

She opened the driver's side door. "Hey Wacko, let's go home." She rubbed his ears, and the husky wagged enthusiastically, and licked her hand. A twinge twisted her chest as she climbed into the pickup.

Give Cohen another chance? Isn't that what I did before? But I miss him.

A stark realization hit. She was so busy being stubborn, she'd refused to listen to Cohen. Her mother used to complain about her stubbornness.

She had to face Cohen in the morning, whether she liked it or not. She'd cooled enough to have an adult discussion. What made her nervous was that Deanna would have regular access to Cohen when the Aurora Crew returned to Fairbanks. Raynie couldn't compete with that—unless she moved to Fairbanks. That was out of the question.

As she drove home, the smoke turned the sun into a traitorous red ball, reminding her of the guy she'd planned to marry who was gone forever.

And the one she'd mistakenly let into her heart.

Chapter 27

When Cohen walked into the Talkeetna Wildfire Base early the next morning, Angela immediately flagged him down as he stepped up to the dispatch desk.

"Doss put you in charge of the base," she said. "He had to go up to Fairbanks. Instead of going back to the Denali Creek project fire, you and the Aurora Crew will stay here to respond. Fires are popping up like someone poured gas on everything."

"Don't say that. The last thing we need is arson." Cohen shifted the fire pack on his back.

"Put your gear in Doss's office. He said you and Raynie could use it while he's gone." Angela pointed as she answered the dispatch phone.

At the mention of Raynie, Cohen's gut twisted. He nodded thanks and headed down the hall to the conference room. He stopped at the closed door with "Doss" scribbled in a black marker on a paper taped to the door. When he opened it, he stopped in his tracks.

Raynie sat at Doss's desk, tapping on her laptop.

"Good morning," she said in a neutral tone, continuing to type.

"Morning." Cohen hadn't slept well last night, after yesterday's fiasco. When he woke up this morning, he resolved to settle things with Raynie. He'd worked hard to penetrate her steel walls of defense, and he wasn't about to give up on her now.

We were intimate—doesn't that count for something?

No time like the present to plunge into the core of the matter. He pushed the door closed, but it unintentionally slammed.

Raynie jumped. She stopped typing and gaped at him as if he'd slammed it deliberately. He used it to his advantage.

Cohen dragged a chair to the side of the desk. "You and I are discussing what happened yesterday. And the night before. Right now."

Raynie continued typing, and he sensed a battle of wills lining up on both sides.

He closed her laptop. "Right. Now."

She twisted in her chair, with daggers in her emerald eyes. She folded her arms in a defensive posture, the way she used to do back when she loathed him.

Here we go again, sighed Cohen.

"What?" she flipped at him in a frosty tone.

He steeled himself. "Tell me the real reason you're pissed. And no bullshit. Be straight with me." He was careful to keep his tone firm, but not overbearing.

Mother taught me well.

Raynie chewed her lip. "Where do I even start?"

"Try back at the Hiland Fire when we first met."

"Why? We've already hashed that one out. My issue is with what I saw yesterday."

"What you saw, or what you think you saw?" He blew out a stream of air. "On the Hiland Fire, you were angry with me for questioning a strategy decision. You don't like your authority being questioned, do you? And be honest."

He steadied his gaze on her, noting the silver necklace around her neck. A flame was etched on the silver heart. He wondered about the significance.

Probably from her former fiancé.

She lifted her eyes to meet his. "No, I don't. But not because you questioned me. Because of the condescending way you did it in front of the crews."

"We've already discussed this, and I apologized. Again, sorry I came across that way. It was never my intent. I didn't know you. I had no clue about your experience or your capability, so I questioned your decision. You act like I assassinated your character."

"You practically did."

"You judged me. And you judged me again yesterday when you saw Deanna and me at breakfast." He scowled. "You're blowing all of this out of proportion."

Raynie gave him a death stare. "I know what I saw."

He spoke in a quiet but resolute tone. "I said this to you yesterday, but you wouldn't listen. You were too busy being stubborn, so I'll say it again. Deanna and I were together a few years ago during fires in Canada, then we went our separate ways. I promised no commitment. She pressured me, but I don't feel right with her. She's too alpha for me."

"How quaint. You're both alphas, so you cancel each other out." Raynie's mouth cut a straight line. "You weren't exactly fighting her off yesterday, from what I could tell."

"She wanted to get back together. I said no." He threw up his arms in exasperation. "Why won't you believe me?"

Raynie stood and walked to the window, staring out at the parking lot.

"Do you know what my sister told me? She said Taydon was dealing drugs right under my nose. And I didn't know it. He told me he went to his job site every day, but he was dealing." She pivoted to face him.

"Taydon lied to me and betrayed my trust."

He raised his brows. "What does that have to do with us?"

"It has everything to do with us." She leaned back on the windowsill. "After you and I made love for the first time, when I had finally talked myself into you, you shattered my heart the morning after. You said all the right things while making love to me. Then after that, you acted like nothing happened—like *we* never happened."

Oh no, tears were about to fall. He didn't want her to cry, but she'd just gutted him.

"How can you say that?"

Raynie swiped her cheek. "I felt betrayed again. You not being honest—like you were playing me until someone better came along." Her voice tremored, and she swiped her cheek.

Her wild assumption rattled him, but worse, it shocked the hell out of him.

"Betrayal? How could you think that after...after..." He shook his head, bewildered. This wasn't a discussion that should have taken place at work. But dammit, he had to know what was on her mind.

"What else was I to think? Flip it around: what if you walked in and saw me holding hands with...with...Rego, or someone?" Her voice rose, and she quieted, glancing at the closed door.

Her Rego reference caused Cohen to bark out a laugh. Visualizing Raynie and Rego—fifteen years her senior—created a comical image in his head. "Sorry, but I can't picture that. It's just...wrong."

"You know what I mean." Her mouth twitched, despite attempts to keep a serious face.

Raynie burst out laughing, and he laughed with her until happier tears ran down their cheeks.

Cohen stood and moved to her. "You need to know something. Betrayal isn't part of my repertoire. Please don't fault me for what other dickheads have done to you." He cocked a brow. "Besides, I can count on one hand how many times I've slept with a woman."

"Repertoire? You and your big words!" She swung her long braid behind her shoulder. "Give me a break. I wasn't born yesterday. Someone with your looks has to fight them off with a Pulaski. Try counting with *both* hands."

He regrouped. "All right, maybe a hand and a half. I don't know the exact number. Anyway, that's not important." He rested his palms on her shoulders. "What *is* important—I haven't felt about anyone the way I feel about you."

And he damn well meant it.

"Honestly? Do you really mean it? If you demand honesty from me, then you must do the same." Her eyes steadied on him. "For starters, will you be seeing Deanna when you're both back in Fairbanks? She seems determined to have you."

A fair question. "Told you before, I have no interest in her. So no, I won't be seeing her."

All he knew was that he wanted Raynie Atwood—and more than just a friend. Whenever he looked at her, whenever she came near him, she drove him wild.

But he had to work with her.

Her mouth twitched. "In the future, should you question any decision I make on a fire, I won't tear your head off. I'll quietly strangle you instead."

His heart ticked up at penetrating Raynie's defensive armor. He wanted to blast the damn thing off her once and for all. He grabbed her hand, pulled her away from the window, and pulled her into him. When he kissed her, she made that little whimper that always amped him.

Raynie reached up and grasped the collar of his yellow Nomex shirt to pull him closer. She slid her hand up to run her fingers through his hair.

He loved swirling tongues with her—she was good at it. Along with a host of other things he'd discovered she was good at. He broke the kiss to make another point.

"Just for the record, I've played no one, least of all you." He sealed his statement with another kiss.

Raynie palmed his chest. "You said you wanted to discuss what happened the night before last. Which parts do you wish to discuss?" She gave him a provocative look that made Little Cohen stand up and salute.

No, not now! No hard-ons in Doss's office!

"The last thing I want you thinking is that our making love didn't matter to me," he said earnestly, lifting her chin. "It meant everything to me."

He feverishly settled Little Cohen down as the fire base sprang to life. He let go of Raynie and stepped back.

"Does this mean you don't loathe me now?"

Raynie laughed. "I'm done with all that. It's no fun being mad at you anymore."

They stood gazing at each other with such excruciating sexual tension, if they didn't do something about it in the next nanosecond, naughty things would be going down in Doss's office.

A sharp knock on the door caused both to jump. Raynie scurried to her seat, while Cohen adjusted his shirt collar and smoothed his hair. He rolled his shoulders back and straightened.

"Come in!"

Rego poked his head in and eyed Raynie, then Cohen. "Angela said I'd find you both here. We have a fire call. Grab your gear. Aurora Crew is responding."

"Thanks, Rego. We're on our way." Raynie feigned innocence, as if she hadn't been making out with Cohen like their helicopter was going down.

Rego gave them each a quizzical look, then backed out, seemingly unsure as to whether or not to close the door. When he finally did, Cohen caught Raynie's eye, and both of them burst out laughing.

"You and Rego—yeah, that's a good one," he choked out, lifting his fire pack.

Raynie plucked her fire pack from the corner. "Next time, I'll use Tupa for my example. He's better looking."

"A logical choice. Good to see you back in greased grooves, Atwood," he teased, smiling broadly. "Let's go kickass on a fire."

As he grasped the doorknob, Raynie tapped his shoulder. When he turned around, she grabbed his collar and pulled him to her for one last kiss.

"That should last you for a while. Now open that door before I do you in the boss's office."

"Just don't call out Rego's name." Cohen swung the door open.

They laughed all the way down the hall and out to the main office.

Relief swept through him. Now that he and Raynie were back on track, he was ready to smack down fire with his crewmates. But most of all, with *her*.

Life had reclaimed its sweetness once again.

Chapter 28

Raynie's adrenaline kicked into overdrive upon seeing the tall flames. As they drove to the fire in the transport van, she was relieved that she and Cohen had patched things up. She believed him that his past involvement with Deanna was over. Though, what still jangled her nerves was Deanna's determination to get him back. She'd known smokejumpers with the ability to rule small countries, and Raynie figured she'd have some competition on her hands.

She hadn't competed for a guy before, but she was no shrinking violet. She had no problem going head-to-head with Deanna. In fact, she looked forward to it.

Well, bring it!

The fire burned on both sides of the road about eight miles from Sleeping Lady Kennel. She wasn't concerned about the fire heading toward Kam's cabin, as long as the prevailing winds blew toward the Parks Highway. Unfortunately, there were homes, small subdivisions, and several sled dog kennels in that direction.

Tara Waters was still in the lower forty-eight, which meant Cohen was the crew supervisor for this fire. So far, the Aurora Crew was the only resource committed to this one since the size was still only twenty acres. They had faced worse fires and contained them in one day. Raynie figured this would be no different.

Everyone got to work laying hose from Salmon Lake to reach the flames on the east side of Birch Spur Road. Cohen had instructed the crew to keep the flames from reaching an alpaca ranch on a nearby homestead, which was square in the fire's path, along with a couple of lodges and river guide businesses.

Raynie set the water pump next to the running stream and Liz appeared next to her.

"I'll help you connect the hoses. Haven't had a chance to talk to you. How was your stint at the incident command center?"

"It was fun. We got things organized in a short amount of time."

Liz worked fast, screwing on a nozzle. "So cool that you and Cohen were the show runners. I heard you kicked some serious ass in organizing an evacuation plan."

Raynie laughed as she wrestled with a hose clamp. "It was just a couple of days, but Cohen and I got it wrangled. What do you think about a firefighter auction to help people who've lost homes and dog kennels?"

"That's a terrific idea. When were you thinking of doing it?"

"We'll have to wait and see. Trish at the Roadhouse is helping me organize it. They do an annual bachelor auction, and she's willing to organize one for firefighters. We'll auction off men *and* women for date nights." Raynie was so excited, her words toppled over each other. "And we can make a firefighter's calendar to sell before the auction, so people can see who they're bidding on."

"I love that," said Liz. "How do you plan to do the photographs?"

"I was hoping you would do it. When I mentioned it to Angela this morning, she said you've taken sexy photos of exotic dancers down in Vegas."

Liz laughed. "She said that? Can't keep a secret around here. Knowing Aurora Crew, I'm sure they'll do it. I can get the guys into some cool masculine poses. But sexy isn't what we want women to portray in wildland fire. I'll have them do wholesome girl-next-door poses."

"Fantastic," said Raynie. "They'll sell like hotcakes."

Cohen shouted from downriver, "Hey, you two got that pump running yet?"

Raynie had been working on it as she talked. She could do it with her eyes closed. She gave a thumbs-up to the tall blond who made her heart beat fast just by looking at him.

"We have flow!"

Cohen returned a thumbs-up, and Raynie caught herself from blowing him a kiss. Not here. Not in front of the crew.

"Control yourself," she muttered under her breath.

Liz grabbed the hose, stretching it along the ground toward the flames. "We'll talk later. I'm super excited about this. Mind if I tell everyone?"

"Please do," said Raynie. "After we demobe from this fire, I'll announce it to the crew." Talking about the auction fundraiser got her all keyed up to start on it.

Trish would no doubt have already spread the word around town, through her gossip pipeline at the Roadhouse.

Raynie tightened the chin strap of her hardhat and lowered goggles over her eyes. The flames crackled and snapped as they climbed the ladder of fuels from the ground to the bushes, where they jumped into the low spruce branches.

She grabbed another hose to lay it, then yanked on the nozzle to spray the flames. It kicked back a bit when the water surged, so she spread her boots apart to stabilize herself. Her knee niggled her a little, forcing her to shift weight to her good leg.

Raynie's radio crackled with Rego's voice. "Wind is picking up on our end. How is it on yours?"

She'd been preoccupied and hadn't paid close attention to the weather. She now observed fast-moving clouds, birch leaves fluttering, and treetops waving.

She keyed her mic. "Breezy. Wind is blowing south. Don't like the looks of those dark clouds."

As the words left her lips, a fierce gust of wind whipped the spruce, creating a dancing wall of flame. Trees were dense in this boreal forest, and the birch weren't slowing flames as they usually did. The drought had dried everything.

She lifted her nozzle to squirt the flames when she heard shouting. Her radio sprang to life with sounds of chainsaws and Tupa's voice.

"The fire is running on our end. Hoses aren't working. Flame lengths are too high."

"She's coming at us too fast. Pull the hoses and move back to the road," ordered Cohen.

Rego cut in with another transmission. "Winds made her jump the fuel-free barrier, and now she's burning on both sides of Birch Spur Road...heading toward structures."

Smoke filled the air, and Raynie coughed as she stumbled back with her hose to get away from the running blaze. Dammit! Why couldn't the weather cooperate until they could get a containment line around this thing?

She keyed her radio. "We need to call ADOT and the troopers to close the road. Don't want traffic in this area."

"Good call. I'll take care of it," panted Cohen into his mic.

Raynie listened to radio traffic as she jogged with her hose. Cohen ordered mud drops and water dumps to protect the two businesses. He contacted Talkeetna Base and requested Angela to notify the business owners to prepare for evacuation. His authoritative voice exuded confidence, like he could conquer any fire situation.

She snapped herself to attention and rushed to the river's edge, arriving at the same time as Liz and Kenzie. The women disconnected the hoses and pump and wrestled the equipment across the grassy tundra into the fire engine. As dark smoke surrounded them, Raynie pulled her neck bandana up over her nose and mouth.

"This is nasty, mate," said Kenzie, her Australian inflection kicking in.

The radio crackled. A hoarse voice grunted out words. Alarm spread through Raynie's chest to hear Cohen.

"I'm trapped in the lake!"

"What do you mean *in* a lake?" Raynie keyed her mic.

"Flames pushed me in." He coughed. "Too much smoke. Can't see. Plus, I can't swim."

"What do you mean you can't swim? Seriously?" She broke into a run until her knee nagged her to slow down. "All right, hold tight. I'm on my way!"

"You won't get through the flame wall." Cohen coughed so hard, she was afraid he'd swallowed water.

"I'll find a way." Her voice shook as she ran. "Keep your mouth and nose near the water's surface, less smoke there. When you get tired, flip onto your back. Stay on the radio with me," she instructed.

Dammit, where's the mother flipping lake?

The next transmission garbled. She remembered Cohen had attached his radio to his shoulder holster so he could key it without holding it. But if his radio became saturated, he'd lose communication.

She keyed hers. "Tremblay, do you copy? What's your status?"

No response. A pause, then Rego's voice on the radio.

"Atwood, we lost track of Tremblay in the smoke. Do you see the lake?"

"Not yet. Stand by."

She peered through her goggles at the wall of surging flames, like a living, raging monster, hellbent on killing her. Smoke from burning pine needles and tar choked her breathable air, ravaging her nostrils and suffocating her lungs.

She retrieved her phone and prayed for cell service. She crossed her fingers. One. Two. Three bars! She tapped her maps app and typed in Birch Spur Road. The lake came into view, and she zoomed in on it. Next, she turned on her GPS, and it showed her she was only a few hundred yards away. At least she was headed in the right direction.

Raynie keyed her radio. "Tremblay, this is Atwood. Do you copy?" She waited, but he didn't key his mic.

Scorching debris and sparks rained down all around her and she dodged them as best she could. She knew it was hazardous stepping through the burned black. She eyed glowing pockets of flame still hungry for tree roots.

Raynie prayed the soles of her boots wouldn't melt.

Up ahead, she saw a dark thing. Was it a bear or a moose? With so much smoke, it was difficult to stay oriented. She held her breath, moving toward the dark thing. If it was wildlife, it wouldn't be alive. Suddenly, her feet splashed and she stumbled into water.

The lake!

"Cohen? Cohen! Answer me! Where are you?" She listened, but it was hard with the wind rustling the scorched treetops and fire eating its way around the small lake. The water was an eerie orange, reflecting the flames.

She half ran, half stumbled, making her way through the smoky gray along the shoreline. She peered through her goggles at the orange-tinted water, dark and foreboding in the thick smoke. Her foot caught on a rock, and she tripped, falling face first into the water.

Oh shit, my radio!

She flailed wildly to push back onto her feet and tossed her radio and daypack onto the blackened shore. Wiping the water from her face, she waded out to her thighs.

"Cohen! Answer me! Where the hell are you?"

No response. Her heart thudded her rib cage as she fought to stay positive.

"Cohen! Dammit, answer me!" She dove into the water, swimming further from shore. It was hard to kick with her heavy boots. She twisted herself, peering into the smoke.

There! Something in the water! Something yellow.

She dug at the water with her arms, swimming freestyle as fast as she could, her clothes dragging her like a dead weight. As she approached, Cohen was face down in the water.

Oh God!

Raynie sprang into autopilot with her lifeguard training from forever ago. He couldn't have had his face in the water for more than a couple of minutes. Her mind raced—how long since his last radio transmission? Ten minutes? Five? She treaded water, spitting it out as her head bobbed. She rolled him over and his mouth hung open, eyes closed.

"Cohen! Can you hear me? Cohen!" She slapped his cheeks. No response.

Kicking hard to stay afloat, she flung an arm over his bulk in a cross-chest carry and pulled them both through the water with her stronger arm. After an eternity, her boots touched the sandy bottom. She immediately felt Cohen's neck for his pulse. Faint, but it was there.

She checked his breathing. No breath.

"Shit, Cohen!" she cried out.

Raynie dragged him onshore and rolled Cohen to his side. Time was critical. No way could she lift him to do a Heimlich maneuver. Instead, she pounded a sharp blow between his shoulder blades with the underside of her fist. She pounded harder, and water spurted out, draining out the side of his mouth.

She rolled him onto his back, tilted his head back, and blew air into his lungs.

"Cohen, breathe, dammit!" she shouted between breaths.

She blew more air into him, and he spluttered and coughed. She rolled him to his side so he could aspirate water.

"Oh, thank God!"

Tears of relief mingled with droplets of lake water on her cheeks. She retrieved her soggy radio and keyed it. Nothing. Her phone was just as useless. At least the fire had moved on, but snags above them still burned. She had to get them away from the burning trees, but Cohen couldn't move.

He drew his knees into a fetal position, coughing more. Coughing was good; it meant less water and more air in his lungs.

"You're okay, Tremblay." She rubbed his back, eyeing the burning snags around them. "But I have to get you out of here."

She waited until his coughing subsided, then helped him sit.

"What happened?" he choked out. He blinked, then stared. "Why are you all wet?"

"I just pulled you from the lake."

He coughed like an old smoker.

"Why was I...oh, yeah...fire pushed me in." He coughed more. "Where's my fire pack? I dumped it before I went in the water." He glanced around, his body convulsing from coughing.

"It's ashes by now. Why'd you wade into deep water if you couldn't swim?"

"Wind blew the flames over the shallow water. The bottom dropped off. Had no choice." He cleared his throat.

"You can do everything—ski, mush dogs, incident command fires—but you don't know how to freaking swim?" She was incredulous. "Don't they have swimming pools in Canada?"

Cohen swiped his hand over his face. "Stayed afloat as long as I could. But these damn things—" He slapped his boot. "Kept dragging me down."

"Come on, we have to get out of here." She tugged his arm around her shoulder, helping him to his feet.

"How did you find me in this hellacious smoke?" He was unsteady and leaned on her.

"Your yellow shirt. Thank God someone made these yellow. When I got you to shore, you weren't breathing, so I blew air into you. You scared the crap out of me, Tremblay."

She urged him forward just as a burning snag whumped to the ground in front of them. They stumbled backward.

"Terrific. Can't go this way." She spotted what she hoped was another safe pathway through the blackened forest. "This way. Watch your step."

They picked their way along the smoking black ground, with Cohen's weight bearing down on her. She had to get them out into the open, away from the charred and unstable trees. After slogging for a few hundred yards, they finally reached what was once a grassy clearing...now an eerie moonscape.

"I can manage." Cohen stopped to remove his arm from her shoulder. He shook his head. "I'd be dead if you hadn't..." His voice caught in his throat, and he took her in his arms. "You're one hell of a firefighter." He squeezed her so tight she never wanted him to let go.

"This is the wettest hug I've ever had," she joked.

Voices in the distance drew closer, and Raynie spotted the Aurora Crew's yellow shirts in the shadows of the devastation. She didn't care that she and Cohen were dripping wet. She didn't care that her knee hurt like hell. And she no longer cared that the rest of the Aurora Crew saw them with their arms around each other.

Had she lost Cohen, he would have been the second man she'd loved and lost. But he was alive.

And that's all that mattered.

Chapter 29

Cohen had to rest his lungs before jumping back into the fray. Doctor's orders. Raynie had gone back out to fight the Salmon Lake Fire with the Aurora Crew. He'd tried convincing her to rest her knee but lost the argument. She claimed she had to supervise the crew since he had to rest his lungs.

Talk about walking wounded.

So, here he was, two days later, sitting at Doss's desk, typing up an after-action report about his lake incident and why he wound up face down in the water. Not one of his better decisions but retreating into the lake had seemed like the only viable choice.

Someone tapped on the door, and Mel Faraday stuck his head in.

"Got a minute?"

"Sure," said Cohen. "Take a seat."

Mel flopped into a chair across from him. "Did Angela inform you about the drone incident when I was slinging water with Juliet?"

"She did, and I've been meaning to talk to you about it. This Salmon Lake Fire delayed things a bit." Cohen took his fingers off the keyboard and sat back.

"Heard about Salmon Lake. Glad you got out of that all right."

"We lost containment, and the fire ran," Cohen said dismissively. He was embarrassed about the incident and reluctant to recount the gory details. "Tell me about the drone."

"It came out of nowhere, and almost collided with Juliet's windshield," said Mel. "We need to find out who's flying drones near these fires and put a stop to it. It's a serious offense."

"Give me the details." Cohen's chest clenched at what he already suspected.

Mel filled him in on the day, time, and the GPS coordinates.

"I'm not the only pilot who had a near miss with a drone. Other aircraft spotted it, too. You need to spread the word: no drones are allowed near wildfires." Mel adjusted his baseball cap and stroked his silver mustache.

"We'll get a public service announcement out. I'll look into your incident. Thanks, Mel."

Mel rose, rolling his toothpick to the other side of his mouth. "Thanks, Tremblay. Appreciate it." He tapped the desk and left the office.

Cohen typed Mel's GPS coordinates into his laptop, knowing full well what would pop up. Sure enough—Whispering Spruce Drive. He knew what he had to do.

He strolled out of Doss's office and told Angela he was heading to Denali Roadhouse for lunch. His lungs were still sore, so he drove, rather than walked. When he entered the Roadhouse, a woman's voice commanded his attention.

"You're Cohen Tremblay. I've seen you here before. I'm Trish, the owner."

"Pleased to meet you." He swiveled his head toward Trish's toothy smile. "I want to talk to one of your employees. Kira Atwood."

"What's this regarding?" She posed it as a question, but it was a demand.

"A matter concerning a fire Kira may know about," he said as casually as he could. "I know Kira's older sister, Raynie."

Trish gave him a knowing look. "Yes, I know. Raynie has talked about you."

He chuckled. "I hope it was good."

"Not all of it. But mostly." Trish winked, and Cohen wondered what Raynie had said about him.

Trish waved Kira over. "Come here a minute. This young man wants to talk to you." She turned to him. "Nice meeting you. Don't be a stranger." She moved off to ring up a customer.

Kira finished pouring coffee at a table and walked over.

"Hi, Cohen. Raynie said you had a close call on a fire."

His brows raised. "Yes. Your sister helped me out of a run-in with a lake. Can I talk to you for a second? Won't take long. Just need to ask you about something."

"Sure. Let's go outside, where it's quieter." Kira motioned him toward the door, and they stepped out to the parking lot.

"Raynie thought I should talk to you." A little white lie, but he hoped Raynie wouldn't mind. "Were you flying—"

Kira held up her hand. "I know what you're going to say. Yes, it was me. My sister already talked to me about flying my drone near wildfires. I stopped doing it. Now I fly it elsewhere."

"One of our helicopter pilots was upset you nearly crashed your drone into his windshield."

Kira rolled her eyes. "My drone wasn't anywhere near that helicopter. When I saw it coming, I steered the drone away from it."

Cohen took a breath. "I didn't come here to debate what happened, but when a helo pilot who's focused on fighting fire points out a near miss with a drone, I have to address it. You need to know this." He handed her a brochure.

"Flying drones next to a wildland fire is a federal crime punishable by up to twelve months in prison and a twenty thousand dollar fine. The law sees it as interference with firefighting efforts."

"Oh my gosh, I didn't know that." Kira's eyes grew wide as dinner plates.

He wanted to make sure she understood. "Temporary flight restrictions are implemented around wildfires to protect aircraft involved in a firefighting operation. All drones are prohibited from flying in these restricted areas." He sounded like a walking rulebook, his voice firm to hammer his point home.

Kira's face contorted in horror, and she shrieked, "Am I going to prison?"

He raised his hands to calm her and stifled a chuckle at her overreaction.

"We can't prove it was your drone our helo pilot saw that day. I wanted you to know the seriousness of this, so you don't do it again. Okay?" He studied her, hoping she wouldn't come unglued and get him in trouble with her older sister.

Instead, she leaned forward with a solemn expression. "I have to tell you something."

He braced himself. *Now what?* "Okay, shoot."

"My friend—his name is Jamen—he and I flew our drones in that field out by where you guys store your fire equipment." She quickly added, "Don't worry, it was nowhere near the helicopter landing area in back of the fire base."

"Oh, good." He gulped. Now he was curious. "Go on."

"We took a break and were sitting on the grass to look at what the drone recorded. Jamen is teaching me how to take aerial photos with it."

"Uh-huh," said Cohen, waiting expectantly.

"We were flying the drone back-and-forth in that big grassy field next to the building. When we played the recording, we noticed a guy get out of a dark blue car parked in front of the door," explained Kira.

"Are you talking about the fire cache warehouse?"

Kira brushed the hair away from her face. "Yes, the building with the Fire Cache sign."

"What kind of car?"

"An SUV," said Kira. "Didn't have an agency thing on the side, like your fire trucks have. The guy went to the door and had something long in his hand, like a screwdriver or something. He opened the door with it."

Cohen straightened at this information. "Then what?"

"We saw the guy walk out with boxes that he put in his car. He got in and drove off. We just figured it was one of the fire base guys."

"Can I see this footage?"

"Jamen has it," said Kira. "He's on his way here for lunch. I'll call and tell him to bring it."

"Thanks. I'd appreciate it." Cohen made a mental note to check who had keys to the fire cache.

Kira stepped away to make her phone call, then came back. "Jamen has it with him. He'll be here soon."

Not a minute later, a large red pickup pulled into the parking lot with a tall dog box on the truck bed, *Bloomington Kennel* on the side in large, elaborate letters. Alaskan huskies poked their heads through the round holes in the individual boxes. A younger man, who Cohen guessed to be twenty, climbed out. He was tall, like Cohen, but better looking.

He strode toward them with a camera in his left hand, extending his right to Cohen. "Jamen Bloomington. Pleased to meet you."

"Cohen Tremblay. Thanks for bringing this over. Do you mind showing me what you and Kira recorded? And the date of the recording?" he asked Jamen.

Jamen glanced at Kira, who gave him a flirtatious nod. Cohen could see she was smitten by this guy.

"The same day that jerk came to Sleeping Lady Kennel, trying to get into the house," said Jamen.

"Jerk?" Cohen gave Kira a quizzical look.

"Avery Maddox. He was in prison in Arizona, but now he's out." Kira's voice shook, and Jamen put his arm around her. "Jamen came to stay with me after Maddox showed up at the cabin. Raynie was gone fighting fires."

This revelation shocked Cohen.

Why hadn't Raynie mentioned anything about this?

She hadn't shared much with him about her personal life.

"Let's see the footage."

The three of them grouped in a huddle next to Jamen's sled dog truck to peer at the playback. Kira gasped and her hands flew to cover her mouth.

"Oh my God, play that back again!"

Jamen backed it up. When the man was in full view, heading back to his vehicle, Kira said, "Stop and zoom in."

When Jamen did, Kira shrieked. "That's him! Avery Maddox!"

"Let's see that." Cohen held out his hand.

Jamen handed him the camera. The man in the footage had long, dark hair that parted in the middle. He looked like someone who wanted to avoid detection.

"He broke in and stole fire equipment? What would he want with that?" mused Cohen. He had trouble fitting the puzzle pieces together. He glanced up.

"Why was he at your house?"

Kira's lips trembled. "Raynie will kill me for telling you this. Maddox threatened her, and he also threatened me. He says my sister owes him money."

"Threatened to do what?" Cohen blew out air and squeezed the bridge of his nose. "Kira, tell me everything. I don't care if Raynie told you not to say anything. This is serious stuff."

Kira poured out the whole Maddox saga, starting with Arizona. She explained that Maddox had sexually assaulted Raynie's best friend and how Raynie had testified against him. She also explained that Taydon had continued dealing in Alaska when he'd supposedly cleaned up his act.

"I only told Raynie this past week. She didn't know."

"Why did you wait so long to tell her?" Cohen couldn't believe Kira had kept this from her older sister.

"I knew it would break her to know. She took Taydon's death so hard. I just couldn't." A tear rolled down Kira's cheek, which she quickly wiped away.

"A while back, Maddox showed up at our house when Raynie was home alone. He demanded his money and threatened to do to my sister what he did to her best friend back in Arizona—and then do the same to me."

Jamen pulled Kira in close, and she sobbed into his chest.

"I'll kill the bastard!" vowed Jamen.

Cohen didn't doubt for a second that he meant it. He held up his hand to Jamen.

"You and me both. But law enforcement must handle this." His head spun with questions. Did Angela or anyone at the base notice a break-in or that anything had gone missing? Why hadn't Raynie told him about Maddox?

"Raynie will be mad I told you all this." Kira swiped at her cheeks. "I wanted her to tell you so you could protect her."

Trish suddenly appeared around the corner of the Roadhouse.

"Excuse me, but the lunch rush has started. I need you inside, Kira."

Jamen handed Kira a hankie, and she wiped her eyes. She squeezed his hand, and Cohen caught an affectionate glance pass between them.

Kira lifted tear-stained eyes. "Cohen, my sister hasn't come right out and said this, but I know she's in love with you. Just want you to know that."

Jamen bent to give her a peck on the cheek before Kira hurried back inside the Roadhouse.

While her words had warmed Cohen, his greater concern was for both women's safety. What did this Maddox creep want with fire equipment? Unless he wanted to sell it.

Trish narrowed her eyes. "What did you say to Kira that upset her?" she demanded.

Cohen didn't want to go up against this formidable woman. *When in doubt, truth always works best,* according to his mom, the attorney.

"I asked her questions about flying her drone near a wildfire. She showed me a video of someone breaking into our equipment cache at the fire base. Has Raynie mentioned anything about a Maddox person?"

Trish stepped close, drilling him with her stare. "Can you be trusted? I need to know if I can trust you."

He took a long breath. "I'm in love with Raynie Atwood." *There.* He said it out loud for the first time. "Does that answer your question?"

"Well. Okay, then." Trish gave Jamen an authoritative look. "Thanks, Jamen. Go eat your lunch now."

"Oh. Oh, yeah." The young man turned to go.

"Jamen, wait," Cohen called after him. "Can you make me a copy of that recording?"

Trish answered instead. "Of course he can. He's a Gen-Z. They can't function without a computer." She winked at Jamen.

Jamen grinned. "I'll make sure you get a copy."

"Thanks." Cohen patted his shoulder. "Bring it to the Talkeetna Wildfire Base and give it to Angela if I'm not around. Got it?"

"Yes, sir." Jamen about-faced and strolled inside for his lunch.

Cohen chuckled at the young man's "sir" reference, making him feel older than dirt.

Trish stepped closer. "Talk to Raynie about filing a police report. My husband will help her with it." She started back to the restaurant, then stopped and turned around, hands on her hips.

"If you break Raynie's heart, I swear I'll sic every sled dog in the Mat-Su Valley on your ass. Are we clear?"

"Yes, ma'am. Crystal."

This woman sent chills down his spine. If Trish was this fearsome, what was her cop husband like? And with that, she spun around and headed into her restaurant, no doubt to strike terror into the soul of anyone dumb enough to screw with her world.

Cohen hopped inside his pickup to drive back to the fire base. But first he took a detour to the fire cache to do some investigating on his own. He fished his phone from his pocket and tapped the icon for the office landline. When Angela answered, he asked if anyone had noticed whether anything had gone missing from the fire cache.

"No one has said anything," she replied.

He stepped on the gas, bounced across the railroad tracks, and skidded to a stop in front of the building, scanning his brain for a way to tell Raynie he knew all about her unsettling situation.

He wondered how fast his "I love Raynie Atwood" would get back to her. He kicked himself—maybe he should have told Raynie first? His timing sucked, but at least he'd told the truth. He couldn't think what else to say when Trish cornered him about being trusted.

His protective nature had kicked in, and Cohen planned to track down this Maddox scum. If the prison system hadn't fixed him, Cohen sure as hell would. His mind buzzed at how he'd find the guy and confront him.

No way would he let anything happen to the Atwood sisters.

Chapter 30

The Aurora Crew finally wrangled a containment line around the Salmon Lake Fire, with the help of a dozer. It took a few days to do it, but they succeeded. As Rego drove the transport van back to the fire base, Tupa sank down next to Raynie.

"How's that knee holding up, Boss?" Tupa called all fire supervisors "Boss," and the fact that he addressed her that way warmed her heart.

It meant acceptance.

"It's tweaky, but I'll get ice on it when I get home," she said. "You all performed like a hotshot crew out there today, and I'm proud of you." She meant it, too. She'd not worked with a wildland fire crew with this much cohesion, integrity, and sheer determination to get the job done.

"Wanted to tell you something," said Tupa. "When Rego and I went to the fire cache to get chainsaws, we noticed most were gone, except for the two we got."

"How many were in there before?"

"Angela had us do an inventory when we first got here after the state stocked it with equipment. There were at least ten chainsaws. We figured another crew borrowed them, or we would have said something."

"Okay, thanks Tupa. I'll talk to Angela."

"Tell her the door lock needs replacing. It's loose." Tupa leaned back and closed his eyes for a quick nap. "Oh, by the way. I want to be Mister December," he murmured.

Liz had informed everyone about the firefighter auction, but they'd seemed more excited about the calendar. The crew exchanged raucous jokes as they debated who should be the centerfold. Liz had informed them there were no centerfolds on calendars.

Rego suggested they start a firefighter magazine and have a centerfold contest.

RAYNIE PUSHED OPEN the door to the log cabin, leaving her fire pack leaning against the cabin outside, so she wouldn't stink up the house with smoke. She'd breathed enough of it the past several days and wanted to breathe fresh air.

As she opened the door, a tail-wagging Wacko greeted her with energetic barks, while Rooby greeted her with a massive yawn after waking up.

"Kira?" she hollered. She stepped outside and scanned the dog yard. No sign of Kira. She pulled out her phone. *Check in, please*, she texted.

Her phone pinged Kira's response: *I'm at Jamen's. Staying for dinner. Talk later.*

Raynie went back into the house and headed for the bedroom. She left her smoky yellow fire shirt, green pants, boots, and socks in the mudroom. Her knee had swelled, and she planned to ice it after a hot shower. Her phone pinged a message. She tapped it, happy to see it was from Cohen.

Have you eaten? I want to cook you for dinner. Can I come over?

"Huh?" She scowled at the phone, furiously tapping her thumbs.

Cook ME for dinner??

The three dots danced right away.

*F*cking phone! I want to cook you SOME dinner. Not FOR dinner!*

She laughed out loud and texted back.

Sure! I'll be in the shower. Come on in.

She stopped short of tapping a heart emoji. She wasn't the heart emoji type.

Cohen beat her to it with a smile emoji. Now she wished she'd texted a heart.

"Give it time, we've just started this—whatever it is," she murmured.

She undressed and stepped into the shower. She tugged out her hair tie and tipped her head back. Something crashed in the kitchen—sounded like a pan fell to the floor. Her head shot straight up like a chicken.

Did I remember to lock the door? No, I didn't.

She turned off the shower and tiptoed naked to the living room to lock the front door. She'd unlock it when Cohen showed up.

The refrigerator door slammed, and her head jerked up. She squealed.

Cohen's head shot up and he froze. A head of lettuce plunked to the floor. "You're naked! And you're wet!" His astonished expression was hilarious, and if Raynie wasn't so mortified, she would have laughed.

"I didn't expect you this soon." She glanced wildly around for something to cover herself. She snatched a dish towel from the oven door handle, while Rooby stood wagging her tail. She tried unsuccessfully to cover her private parts with the too-small towel.

"I've seen you naked. Don't be embarrassed," joked Cohen, bending to rescue the lettuce.

"I know, but...this is so out of context." Her entire body blushed pink with the awkward situation. Their intimacy was too new for her to feel at ease toddling around him in her birthday suit.

"Ha, out of context?" He laughed. "Sorry I startled you. I was driving here when I called. I need to talk to you about something." His serious tone had her concerned.

"What is it? Did something happen at the fire base?" She tried not to sound alarmed.

"Finish showering, then we'll talk." He moved to the sink to wash the lettuce.

"Should I be worried? Wait a minute, I can't stand the suspense."

She delighted in Cohen's domestic display, but his serious expression made her uneasy. She darted to the bathroom to dry off, then covered herself with a huge bath towel and returned to the kitchen. She pulled a chair from the kitchen table and sat.

"What's on your mind?"

Cohen sank into the one next to her with two bottles of water. He opened them and slid one to her.

"I talked to Kira earlier today about flying drones near fires. Mel stopped by the office and asked me to look into it. The

GPS coordinates he gave me were near your place on Whispering Spruce."

"Is Kira in trouble for flying her drone?" Her pulse picked up.

"No. But that isn't what concerns me. Kira told me about Maddox." He frowned, fixing his gaze on her. "Why didn't you tell me?"

"I didn't want to involve you," she said defensively. "We were busy with fires, and I had zero time to focus on personal stuff." She looked up at him. "I would have told you, eventually."

"When?" His tone was sharp. "When it was too late?"

"I plan to file a police report." She shrugged, trying to mask her fear.

"Good. Because it appears he also broke into the fire cache," he said matter-of-factly. "Kira and Jamen showed me their drone footage. I called the troopers to report it. They have a BOLO out for Avery Maddox."

"A Be-on-the-Lookout?" Raynie's brows shot up. "That explains why Tupa told me chainsaws were missing from the cache. He thought someone had borrowed them."

"Maddox is dangerous. I don't want you anywhere near him. You don't know what he's capable of, and I do. Trust me, you don't want to mess with him."

"All the more reason I want to protect you and Kira. You shouldn't be alone," Cohen said definitively. "I want to stay here until they catch him. Starting tonight."

"I'd love for you to stay here, but please don't feel you have to." What she really wanted was to fall into his arms and live there, to feel secure.

"Sorry I didn't tell you about Maddox. I wanted to handle it on my own."

"I don't mean to tell you what to do. But as a friend and coworker, please take my advice. Don't deal with Maddox on your own. He sounds dangerous. What's this about him saying you owe him money?" His sincerity tugged at her heartstrings.

She picked at the label on her water bottle. "I don't know what money he's talking about. All I can figure is that Taydon owed it to him, and now he's convinced that I have it. But I don't." She lifted her eyes to his, finding deep concern.

"Report him to the state troopers," he suggested. "He's a felon and they need to know he's violating his parole."

"I know. I will." Her voice wavered, appreciating his calm, reassuring presence. "I'm so glad you're here."

"Me, too." His gaze dropped to the cleavage peeking over her towel, and seeing his eyes widen, she melted.

She rose from the table. "I'm going to finish my shower. You can shower, too, if you like. You know, whatever." She spoke quickly, surprised by the inference of her words. "We'll have dinner afterwards."

"Talked me into it." Cohen's face lit up like an airport runway.

His agreeable nature shot straight to her lady parts, and it occurred to her that somewhere along the way, he'd stopped picking arguments. Despite the ongoing tension between them, she'd become oddly comfortable with their continuous bickering.

Was this the new and improved Cohen?

"Okay, then," she said awkwardly. "Come in when you're ready." She stood and walked back to the shower, turning it on.

She stepped in, excitement galloping her heart. Would he take her up on her subtle invitation? She ached for him to hold her.

She didn't have to wait long. Her eyes popped when Cohen's hands came around her waist. She closed them and leaned back on him. When he rested his chin on her shoulder, she twisted and opened her eyes to behold him, all raw and naked, gazing down at her, water streaming down his sculpted chest and stomach, glistening his skin.

Dizzy and off-balance, the shower stall seemed to sway. She was relieved he held her in his arms because she nearly fainted.

"This is our first shower together," he murmured into her ear. "And I plan to make it a memorable one."

Raynie gasped as his words supercharged her. She slid her arms around him.

"How do you plan to do that?"

"This, for starters." He cradled her face and lowered his lips to hers, water droplets running down their faces.

Her heart squished, and she envisioned it all goopy, dripping down and swirling the drain. Dizzy with arousal, his touch made her ache in places she didn't know existed.

He lifted his mouth from hers. "I haven't properly thanked you for saving my life. I want to show you how grateful I am." He kissed her cheek, then trailed kisses down her neck.

She gently lifted his head to look into his gorgeous blue eyes. "You would have done the same. That's what crew members do for each other, remember?" She was acutely aware of him moving her heart necklace aside to nuzzle her breasts.

"You're more than a crew member. If not for you, I wouldn't be standing here." He slid his hands up to her neck, fingering her necklace.

"Why do you wear this?" Cohen held her silver heart from Taydon.

She reached up and unclasped the necklace and rested it on the soap tray. When the heart landed face down, she took that as kismet.

"The reason no longer exists." In that exact second, Raynie made a monumental decision.

His slow smile told her he knew the reason.

This isn't rocket science. Cohen is an intelligent guy.

"Turn around. I give a kickass shoulder massage." He soaped his hands and sensuously moved his fingertips and thumbs in expert circles, in a deep tissue massage. "You're tense, you have knots. Relax, Fire Chick..." His voice was an elixir, stimulating every part of her body along with his magic fingers.

Her groans sounded lusty, but it was because his fingers worked miracles on her sore muscles.

"Ooh, right there. Don't ever let anything happen to those fingers," she breathed, her body sinking into comfortable bliss. She was putty in his hands. When he finished, he turned her toward him.

"How's your throat and lungs?" she asked, peering through the shower spray.

"Better. How's your knee?"

"Good, now that you're here."

"Stand still." Cohen squirted shower gel onto his palm, then rubbed his hands and smoothed it on her skin. He glided his palms around her breasts and massaged those, too, then worked his way down to her waist, massaging each individual muscle and tendon. He played them like a guitarist.

"Oh gawd, that feels good," she moaned. "Add sexy masseuse to your never-ending list of skills. You're like a James Bond."

"Spread 'em, Atwood," he drawled in a lazy, seductive tone. If he ordered her to stand on her hands, she would—she'd do anything for him right now.

What a far cry from before.

She fastened her gaze to his. "Tremblay, I'm trusting you right now—with everything I am—everything I have to give. Please promise you'll never give me a reason not to trust you." It didn't matter that her emotion surfaced because the shower spray washed away her tears.

"I promise. You can trust me." He kissed her forehead. The way his lips lingered there convinced her he meant what he said.

She slid her foot sideways to give him whatever access he wanted. She no longer noticed water spraying her skin, as Cohen became the center of her undivided attention. Her breathing shallowed, and she dug her fingertips into his biceps, keeping her eyes on his.

Cohen moved his hand down to her center and massaged it for a while before easing a finger inside her. Her sensitivity meter was ready to detonate as he continued massaging her, all the while kissing her on the lips. His kiss became more demanding as her little moans excited him. Her heart thrashed around when her eyes drifted to his erection. She slid a palm down to touch him, loving his smooth skin as she took him in her hand. He brushed her hand away and turned off the shower.

"We're moving this operation to dry land." His mercurial look sent vibrations up and down her spine.

"Copy that," she said, following him from the shower. He had a bath towel ready for her and dried her off. When he kissed where he'd dried her skin, she found it incredibly erotic. "You have a magic touch, you know that?" she purred.

"We could have been doing this sooner." His eyes stayed on her as he attempted to hang a towel on the towel bar. He missed. When it hit the floor, a corner of his mouth lifted.

"See what you do to me? I go stupid. Can't even hang up a towel."

"Don't let this go to your head, but when I look at you, I wonder how your parents made such an amazing human being." Joy and certainty flooded her senses, leaving her euphoric.

"Aw, you say that to all the guys." Cohen wrapped a towel around his waist, then draped a large bath towel around her shoulders. He grasped her hand.

"Come with me, Fire Chick." He led her to the bedroom and closed the door. "When's Kira coming home?"

"Not for a while. She's at Jamen's house."

"Good." Cohen bent to pull back her bed quilt. "I'll tuck you in. Then I'll tuck myself in with you." A glint of humor crossed his face.

"I like your idea of a sleepover. Will you read me a story?" she teased, reaching down to tug off his towel, letting it fall to the floor.

"No, but I'll tell you one as I make love to you." He moved to the window and pulled down the thick, white shade to block out the ever-present Alaskan twilight.

She marveled at his round, muscled derriere, and she had an urge to squeeze it. Not wanting to miss a single move he made on his foray to the bed, she steadied her gaze on him as she slipped between the sheets. A rush of excitement somersaulted her stomach when he crawled in beside her and took her in his arms.

He trailed kisses over her, spending considerable time making love to each of her breasts. Her back arched, and he slid his hand down to pick up where he left off in the shower.

She couldn't believe how ready he was for her, but she wanted control. She lowered herself down onto him until he was seated deep inside of her. Pain shot through her knee, reminding her she'd have to be creative with this maneuver.

"Straighten your legs," he breathed, slipping his hand under her knee to support it. His awareness of her tender knee only elevated his standing with her.

Cohen did all the moving, and she held onto his waist until she cried out. "Oh God, Cohen!"

He moved faster until she peaked. An overwhelming body rush blasted through her, sending ecstasy to every cell.

"I love you—inside of me," she added quickly. She didn't want to be the first to say the "L" word.

She wasn't ready to say it, despite Cohen's stranglehold on her heart.

The negative thoughts and feelings she'd had about Cohen in the beginning faded to a distant memory. She was ablaze with passion for a man she never pictured herself with, let alone someone she'd fallen in love with...a well-educated, smoking hot firefighter from Salmon Arm, Canada.

The monumental decision she'd made...was to love him.

Chapter 31

Cohen's original idea was to talk to Raynie about what Kira had said, then make her dinner. He'd had solid intentions, but when Raynie had bounded out naked and dripping wet, all logical thought evaporated like icicles in an inferno.

Raynie's shower invitation had knocked him back with shock, and all he could figure was that he was *falling*.

Hard and fast. Not caring where he landed. This was an epic fall—as if he floated like a vermillion cloud of retardant, lingering in the air before descending to the earth to protect it from the ravages of fire. That was the best way he could describe falling for Raynie Atwood.

He told Trish he was in love with her, but why couldn't he say it to *her*? Why was he hesitating?

Holy hell. He knew why.

If I say that I love her—what if she doesn't love me back? What then?

Cohen pondered all this after Raynie drifted off to sleep. His stomach growled, and he remembered he'd promised her dinner. He lifted the arm he had wrapped around her and rolled over to get up.

"What time is it?" asked Raynie, suddenly awake.

"A little after nine p.m."

She rubbed her eyes and sat up. "Where's Kira?"

"At Jamen's, remember?" said Cohen. "I bet you're hungry. I'll go finish making dinner."

"Wait, I'll help." Raynie threw back the covers, treating him to the graceful, angled lines of her back as she rose from the bed. She lifted the sheet to cover herself.

He chuckled, pulling on his jeans. "It's a little late for that, don't you think?"

"I'm still shy. You're still my coworker, for crying out loud."

"You've never been naked with a coworker?" Humor crossed his face as he tugged on his Henley.

"Hmm, let me think. Can't remember the last time I tore off my clothes and hooked up with a dude on the fireline."

He laughed. "Now there's something I haven't yet seen on a fire."

"Given time, I'm sure you will." She dropped the sheet and placed her hands on her hips. "All right, take a good look at my body after test driving it. But don't you dare tell anyone you've seen me naked."

"I'll just say we've had mind-blowing, knock-your-socks-off sex." He delighted in seeing her naked backside while she rummaged through hangers, settling for a white T-shirt.

Turning, she caught him watching her, before she stooped to pick up her jeans.

"While you're ogling, please open my top drawer and toss me some undies." She pointed.

"When was the last time your coworker fondled your intimates?" He opened the drawer and peeked inside, staring at the plethora of colorful choices.

This is pure unmitigated heaven and sexy as hell.

Raynie laughed. "My intimates? You sound like an underwear ad."

"Do you wear these under your Nomex? Hell, now these images will live in my head next time we fight fire." He stared into the drawer, mesmerized. "What color?"

"Doesn't matter. Hurry before the universe expands or my sister shows up." She shot him an urgent look.

He reached inside the drawer and lifted a purple bra and red undies.

"How about a party vibe?" He dangled one from each hand.

"This is just plain weird," she said with a bemused expression. "The man I despised is now messing around in my underwear drawer."

He grinned at his good fortune and tossed them to her.

Raynie caught them and clutched them to her chest. "Tremblay, how about you go make dinner? I'd like to dress in private."

"Sure thing." He finished dressing and sauntered out to the living room. Something caught his eye, and he glanced out the window.

A dark blue, beat-up SUV sat idling behind Cohen's pickup in front of the house. Squinting, he recognized the same vehicle in Kira's drone recording. His pulse quickened.

"Well, well, it's the dickwad." Cohen eased to the front door and peeked out the narrow window beside it.

Cohen fished out his phone and tapped the speed dial to the state troopers.

"The man who broke into the state fire warehouse is here at Sleeping Lady Kennel. Whispering Spruce Road. He's threatened the caretakers, the Atwood sisters." He ended the call and shoved his phone into his pocket. He didn't have time to field endless questions.

He scanned his brain to think of a way to detain this motherfucker. He opened the door and stepped outside, quiet as a ninja. Maddox had exited his vehicle, but Cohen couldn't tell where he'd gone.

Alarmed, Cohen rounded the corner of the house, scanning the dog yard with all eight huskies, barking stranger danger. Wacko gave away the intruder's position by pointing his snout toward the back door. The husky strained at his drop chain, growling.

Cohen raced to the back of the cabin to see Maddox jiggling the door.

"Hold on there, buddy! What the hell are you doing?" He stormed toward Maddox, who wasn't the least bit fazed as he spun around to face him.

"I'm checking the gas meter," he said casually, his eyes sizing Cohen up.

Cohen eyed Maddox's hand inside the pocket of his gray hoodie.

"Come on, you can do better than that." He motioned his head toward the loser's truck. "Gas people don't open doors and they drive company rigs. You're the dickwad who broke into the fire warehouse, and you also threatened the Atwood sisters."

Cohen was confident he could take down the douche before finding out what kind of party favor, he gripped inside his pocket.

Maddox shrugged. "Don't know what you're talking about."

"Of course you don't. People who lie so easily must have spent time in prison." Cohen took a step forward. "Like in Winslow, Arizona."

At the mention of his former residence, Maddox's head snapped up.

"Who the fuck are you?"

"Why are you trying to break into this cabin?" Cohen took another step forward. "Seems to me that's a parole violation."

Maddox straightened to his full height and glowered. "I asked you a question. Who are you?"

Just then, Rooby raced around the corner, answering Wacko's barking with her own growling and snarling. When Cohen saw the golden, he knew Raynie wasn't far behind.

"Atwood, stay there!"

Instead, she rounded the corner to see Maddox and Cohen facing off. Cohen turned his head to the side, eyes trained on Maddox.

"Get back inside. I'm handling this."

"Cohen, no! He's dangerous!" she yelled back.

"So am I!" Cohen spat out, his eyes glued to the scumbag in front of him.

"Okay, tough guy, let's see what you got." Maddox's hand yanked out of his pocket, snapping open a lethal switchblade that glinted in the eerie red twilight.

"Two can play this game." Cohen reached inside his pocket for his low-tech fire knife and pushed the four-and-one-half-inch blade open with his thumb. Not as formidable as Maddox's miniature machete, but better than nothing.

"You threaten these women again and I'll twist this into your heart, rip it out, and toss it to the dogs," threatened Cohen.

Maddox lunged forward, swiping his blade across Cohen's stomach. Cohen jumped back, evading contact. Wacko and the rest of the sled dogs jumped around with frenetic barking.

"Maddox, stop it!" screamed Raynie. "You hurt him, and I'll kill you! I swear it!"

"Ha, so this is your new lover," sneered Maddox, snaking toward Cohen. "Taydon hasn't been dead half a year, and you're already whoring around. Give me my money and I'll go," he snarled at Raynie, his dark eyes on Cohen.

"I told you. I don't have your money!"

The terror in Raynie's voice electrified Cohen. No way would he allow this loser to harm her or Kira.

"Cohen, stop! Please," pleaded Raynie, her eyes swimming with fear.

"Stay back!" Cohen responded, never taking his eyes off his opponent.

A police siren sounded in the distance. Maddox also heard it, leaped back, and sprinted to his vehicle.

"Won't do any good to run, asswipe! You know they'll catch you," hollered Cohen, chasing after him.

Maddox leaped into the driver's seat and fired up the engine. He spun out, spraying gravel and dirt behind him, just as a state trooper's cruiser turned onto Whispering Spruce. Cohen pointed to where Maddox had gone, and the cruiser sped off in pursuit. Another cruiser pulled up and rolled to a stop in front of Sleeping Lady Kennel.

The trooper climbed out, while Cohen hurried to Raynie to put an arm around her shoulder.

"You and I are going to have words, Tremblay," she said, gritting her teeth.

Trish leaped out of the passenger seat and raced to Raynie, hugging her.

"Are you all right? I see your protector is here."

Raynie shook her finger at Cohen. "Don't ever confront Maddox again. He's ruthless."

"Better me than you," said Cohen. And he meant it.

"Raynie, can I have a word? Trish tells me you might want to file a report," said Trooper Mason. He motioned to his vehicle. "Step over to my cruiser."

Raynie gave Cohen a somber look. "We'll talk when I'm done." She strode over and got into the vehicle.

Trish turned to Cohen. "You confronted Maddox?"

"He tried to break in. I had to stop him."

"Never confront a known felon. You're just asking for it," admonished Trish. "But you did right by calling it in."

Cohen stared at Raynie, sitting in the cruiser. "Thanks for coming so quickly, Trish. Do you always go with your husband on calls?"

"Not usually, but since this involved Kira and Raynie, I jumped in the car. We can get away with these things in a small town." She paused, then steadied a look of concern on him. "Raynie has been through a lot. She needs stability in her life."

He opened his mouth to respond when Raynie climbed out of the cruiser and stepped over, giving him her stink-eye.

Trooper Mason called out to his wife. "Let's go."

"You two, take care. Don't do anything stupid." Trish returned to her husband's vehicle and ducked inside, leaving Cohen and Raynie standing in the front yard.

"YOU COULD HAVE BEEN seriously hurt," chided Raynie, heading inside the cabin to the kitchen.

"But I wasn't," said Cohen, following her. He moved to the cutting board and salad bowl he'd set out before deciding to join Raynie for a shower.

"But you could have been," she insisted. "I can handle this. I don't need you to protect me. I don't want you to be involved."

"Too late for that now, isn't it?" He picked up a vegetable cleaver and chopped lettuce to calm himself. Adrenaline was one thing when fighting fire, but a whole other thing when someone tried slicing him with a nine-inch switchblade.

Raynie took a seat at the kitchen table, nursing a bottle of water.

"Tell me how you wound up in a knife-o-rama with Maddox."

Cohen explained walking out and seeing his truck, then tracked Wacko's giveaway to seeing Maddox at the back door.

"If he saw my truck parked out front, I can't figure out why he'd still try to break in."

"He's fearless and hurts anyone who stands in his way. That's why I didn't want you taking him on." Raynie looked up at him.

"You're built like a brick shit house, but something tells me you aren't the fighting type. Or were you one of those campus toughs at Princeton, calling yourselves the Ivy League gang?" She made a gangbanger gesture, flashing him thumb-and-pinky hand signs.

"Hey, I've been in a kerfuffle or two. I can hold my own with a handful of rat bastards." And he could. He could easily have taken Maddox down without the blades.

"I'll bet you can, Bad Boy," she said in a seductive tone. She stood and wrapped her arm around his waist, her other hand on his bicep.

"Keep talking like that, and this dinner won't get made." He leaned down and kissed her just as the door slammed.

Kira bounced into the kitchen. "Caught you two!" she said happily, tossing her keys and purse onto the kitchen table.

She had that moosey-eyed look Cohen always referred to when someone was smitten. When Kira saw her sister's serious expression, she stopped short.

"Did something happen?" She looked at Cohen, then Raynie.

Raynie explained what happened with Maddox. "The troopers are searching for him, so only a matter of time before he's caught. Please don't worry."

"I don't want him coming back here," said Kira, fearfully.

Cohen let Raynie do all the talking to reassure her younger sister. He'd step in if necessary but didn't want to step on Raynie's toes. Lord knows he'd done enough of that early on when they worked together. He tossed moose burger patties into a fry pan and turned on the heat.

"Drug addicts will do anything to get money," said Raynie. "Taydon may have owed him money, but I have no clue where it is."

"Do you think the cops will catch him?" asked Kira.

"Yes. They're looking for him." Cohen flipped the patties over, put a lid on the pan, and stepped back with folded arms. "I know you don't want my protection, but I can stay here until he's caught. Just thought I'd throw that out there."

"You don't have to..." Raynie countered.

Kira cut in. "Yes, he does! I feel safer with Cohen here."

Her eyes had an urgency that shot straight to Cohen's heart. He thought of his little sister.

Raynie stared at Kira, then leveled her gaze at him. "We'd love for you to stay here. You can protect us with your four-inch Leatherman tool." She smirked at him.

"Hey, my trusty Leatherman stabbed a bear in the nose one time when he tried coming inside my tent."

When Raynie burst out laughing, he pretended to be offended.

"What's so funny?" asked Kira.

"You should have seen Cohen." Raynie acted out the scene for her sister. "Picture Maddox, a hardened criminal, pointing a scary-long switchblade at Cohen. Then badass Cohen, acting all tough with his puny little fire knife." Raynie had a tough time getting the words out between peals of laughter.

Kira laughed along with her while Cohen tried not to feel affronted. "My fire knife is the only weapon I carry. I just hadn't test-driven it on a felon."

"Show him *your* weapon." Kira nodded toward the living room.

Raynie rose from the kitchen table and returned with the nine-millimeter in her hand, muzzle pointed at the floor. She worked the slide like an expert, and opened the action to show him it was unloaded.

"What are you doing with that?" Cohen's eyes rounded with unease.

"Taydon got it for bear protection."

"That's why they make bear spray." He gestured for her to give it to him to make sure it was unloaded. "Know how to use this?"

"If you want to practice, I'll help you."

Raynie tilted her head. "You're a handgun expert too? The list keeps growing." She motioned at his smoking fry pan. "You're also an expert at burning moose burgers."

"Whoops!"

He handed back the weapon, grabbed the pan, and shoved it under the faucet. Water sizzled into steam, and he waved his hand back and forth. He returned the pan to the stove and turned off the burner.

"Have you fired that gun?"

"Yep. Taydon took me to the Birchwood range in Chugiak. I'm an excellent shot, actually."

"Don't use it unless you have to. With me here, you won't have to. But if I were you, I'd keep it in your nightstand." He pointed at Kira. "Don't touch it if you haven't handled one."

"Okay." Raynie exchanged looks with Kira.

"Dinner is served, ladies." Cohen plated the burgers and salad for the three of them.

"Love a man who can cook," said Raynie, seating herself at the kitchen table.

He warmed at her love-a-man comment and handed Raynie the salad bowl. He spoofed an Italian mom's accent. "Eat, eat, you're skin and bones."

Raynie laughed. "You're too much, Tremblay."

When they'd finished eating and cleaning up, Kira said goodnight and went to her room.

Raynie rose from her chair and moved to him. "Thank you so much for cooking us dinner. And thanks for stopping Maddox. I wouldn't have wanted to use that gun."

"I'll try to leave you alone tonight. We both need sleep." He took her in his arms.

"Most of all, thank you for that lovely shower, Mr. Magic Hands." Raynie slid her palms down his chest. "You don't have to leave me *completely* alone."

Cohen's other brain sprang to life in his jeans. He faked a yawn and stretched.

"I suddenly feel tired."

"Me, too." Raynie grinned, led him to her bedroom, and closed the door. Rooby scratched to come in, and Raynie opened it to let her retriever pad to her dog bed in the clothes closet.

"I secured all the windows and doors. I locked everything to within an inch of its life. Plus you have me here with my trusty Leatherman." Cohen grinned, lifting his T-shirt over his head.

Raynie undressed and crawled into bed. Lying on her side, she threw back the covers. "Hurry and slide on in here. Make yourself at home."

His gaze hitched on her cleavage. He had the rest of his clothes off in an Anchorage minute. He slid in beside her.

"You were my hero protector at Salmon Lake. Now I'll be yours."

Before she could protest, he put a finger to her lips. "I know you can protect yourself. But it wouldn't hurt to have both of us doing a BOLO." He followed up with a kiss.

Something told him neither one of them would get much sleep.

Chapter 32

The next morning, Raynie's phone pulsed with the tune of "Fever." Bleary-eyed, she rolled over and tapped it.

"Hello?"

"Plan on coming in today?" chirped Angela.

"Oh no, what time is it?" Raynie sat up and twisted to look at Cohen, who was dead asleep.

"Forty-five minutes past starting time." Angela paused. "You wouldn't know where Cohen is, would you? No one has seen him since yesterday."

Raynie sat up straight, her brain whirling to grab the right words.

"Cohen? Uh, geez, not sure where he is," she lied, trying to sound convincing. "Sorry, I slept like a slug in the dirt. Be there in fifteen."

"Sounds good, y'all," said Angela, ending the call.

Raynie stretched her arm to feel Cohen's solid body under the covers.

"Tremblay, duty calls. We have to get it in gear."

"Mmm," he moaned. "Got to finish my dream. Give me five minutes."

"This isn't like you. You're like a donut maker. Up and chipper before the crack of all-night twilight." She slid her palm around his bicep and whispered in his ear. "This better be an amazing dream. You're making us later than we already are."

Cohen rolled over, blinking his gorgeous blue eyes. "What do you mean?"

"We're forty-five minutes late, Mr. Chief of Operations. Bad form for the person in charge."

"Oh, man." His eyes bulged as he stared at the ceiling. "I'm still spent, and I wasn't even on a fire yesterday."

"You're getting old. Either that or you used a shit ton of adrenaline threatening Maddox with your Leatherman," she teased.

"I'll never hear the end of that, will I?" He pulled her down for a kiss, but she resisted.

"Nope. Morning breath. Come on, we have to book." She pressed her lips to his cheek, liking the sexy morning stubble she'd not seen before.

Both sprang from the bed and hurried to dress. They rounded up what they needed for the day.

"Fire pack, fire pack," she muttered, fluttering around to find her Nomex shirt and pants. They dashed around, trying not to crash into each other.

Kira burst through the back door. "Madonna had her puppies! Come see them!"

Raynie glanced at Cohen. "Have I mentioned one of Kam's sled dogs was pregnant?"

"No, you've not mentioned that little detail."

"Kam said he'd bred her before he left. So much has been going on, I forgot to tell you. We're late anyway, so a few more minutes won't matter. Come on, let's go see." Raynie dashed out the back door after Kira.

The dogs yipped and barked when the three of them arrived in the dog yard. Madonna's wooden doghouse was the closest to the cabin, where the sisters could keep a close eye on her.

"I checked on Madonna last night, and she didn't seem to be in labor or anything," said Kira, stooping to peek inside the doghouse. "I put this old blanket on top of her straw bed a few days ago." Kira stood and moved back. "Look how cute they are."

Raynie and Cohen squatted, and Madonna eyed them as she nursed her five puppies.

"Good, there's plenty of milk to go around," said Raynie.

"Mind if I check them?" asked Cohen.

"If Madonna will let you."

Cohen talked to the Alaskan husky in a soothing tone. "Can I check your babies, Mom?" He offered his hand for her to sniff.

Madonna eyed him warily, but to Raynie's relief, the husky licked his hand in an *okay, you have my permission* move.

"Just want to be sure their little umbilical nubs are okay. I helped my cousin whelp his bitch's pups." Cohen lifted a squirming male.

Kira frowned. "That's not nice."

He laughed. "No, that's the accepted term in canine breeding. I know it sounds derogatory, but that's the vernacular." He glanced at Raynie, then inspected the rest of the litter. "All look healthy. Three males and two females. Kam has thirteen sled dogs if he keeps the litter."

Raynie picked up a male and held him to her cheek. "They're so silky soft."

Cohen stood and looked at the large metal enclosed kennel with a concrete pad that stood empty.

"Time to move Madonna and the pups in there. You don't want a wolf or a bear having access to them in the dog yard." He stooped to see if the doghouse was attached to the ground. He easily lifted a corner. *Good.* "Ladies, we need to get Madonna and the puppies out so we can move the doghouse inside the kennel."

Kira and Raynie eased Madonna out, and they pulled out the blanket where the pups snuggled into each other. Cohen grabbed hold of the doghouse and dragged it inside the enclosed kennel.

"There. Set the puppies inside."

The women each took a side of the blanket and carried the pups back to the doghouse. When they had the pups situated inside, Madonna leaped in and settled herself next to them for nursing.

"Thanks, Cohen. We'd better get going," said Raynie. "Kira, please feed the dogs, and don't forget the muffins for Trish. Tell her I'll call later about the auction."

"I'll take care of the dogs," Kira called back from her room. "Jamen will drive me back during lunch to check on them."

"Fantastic." Raynie fished her truck keys from her pocket.

"Leave your rig. I'll drive us," said Cohen, moving up behind her.

Raynie preferred to err on the side of caution. "Let's drive our own. We don't want to pull up in the same truck," she pointed out, breathless from all the rushing around.

Cohen moved to her and brushed his lips across hers. He drew back to look at her.

"This is fun. It almost feels like we're..." He stopped.

"Like we're what?" she asked in a laughing voice, her gaze fastened to his.

He clearly struggled for words. "Like we're...not coworkers. Like we're, you know, special friends."

"Special friends with benefits. And no longer frenemies?" She sensed what he was trying to say, but she wouldn't put more words into his mouth.

"Yes, that's what I meant." He lurched toward his truck. This was the first time she'd sensed an awkwardness in him. Usually, he oozed with confidence. "See you at the salt mine."

"Sorry you ran into Maddox. I'm thankful you were here." Raynie paused.

"Cohen?"

He twisted to look at her. "Don't worry, I won't."

"How do you know what I was going to say? You won't what?"

"I won't tell anyone I spent the night here."

She stared at him, amazed. "Add clairvoyance to your multitude of talents. Thanks, Tremblay." She smiled at his concern, and climbed into the driver's seat, her heart bouncing all the way to the fire base.

RAYNIE ASSEMBLED WITH everyone else in the conference room for the daily fire briefing. Cohen ran the meeting and announced the final tally of losses from the Denali Creek Fire: Twenty-eight primary residences, six commercial structures, and thirty-four outbuildings had been destroyed. Zero fatalities of people and canines.

"Thanks to Raynie Atwood, the evacuation plan went seamlessly with the mushers getting their teams out," said

Cohen, at the front of the room. "Raynie had set up temporary shelters, and people are now allowed to return to their homes."

Cohen was in full on boss mode, and she loved his easy ability to morph into professionalism on the job. No one in the room would ever suspect they'd spent the night having amazing, beat-the-wall sex. It would remain their dirty little secret.

Angela elbowed her and leaned sideways. "I'm onto you, Atwood. I can read you like a book," she drawled in a whisper.

Raynie drew back in surprise. "Don't know what you mean."

Kenzie sat on the other side of Angela and leaned forward, waggling her brows at Raynie. "Can't bullshit a bullshitter," she whispered, winking. "You're moosey-eyed."

"You're imagining things." Raynie grimaced for good measure, to convince them.

"Raynie will brief you on some ideas she's come up with for a fundraiser," said Cohen, motioning to her.

She jerked upright at hearing her name. "I will?"

"The auction and calendar, y'all," said Angela out the side of her mouth.

"Oh, right." Raynie shook herself from her dream-like stupor and strode to the front, carefully keeping her distance from Cohen, who stood to the side with a neutral expression.

"Everyone on the Aurora Crew knows we're planning a firefighter auction and a calendar. The town of Talkeetna has promised to help. Trish, from the Roadhouse, will organize the auction." Raynie glanced around the room. "It's time to do sign-ups so we know who'll be taking part."

"What if we're married?" Rego piped up.

"Did you get married, brah?" asked Tupa. "Hey, thanks for inviting me to the wedding."

Everyone in the room chuckled.

"Just asking," said Rego. "Married firefighters won't be auctioned, will they?"

Raynie laughed. "No. This is for singles. The person who wins the highest bid will go on a date with the firefighter—lunch, dinner, whatever."

"Ooh, I like the whatever," said a male crew member from the back of the room, eliciting more laughter.

"Angela has the signup sheet at her desk," explained Raynie. "Don't feel pressured if you don't want to take part. I've talked to my state hotshot crew, and they agreed to do the auction. Trish hopes to have twenty men and twenty women."

She continued. "I have faith you'll all help pull this off. Trish will get volunteers to set up chairs, concessions, and everything else. All we have to do is supply willing firefighters. And a couple of emcees." She glanced around the room. "If anyone has questions, you know where to find me."

"When's the auction?" asked Tupa. "I, for one, would like to take part." He said it formally, eliciting teases and catcalls from around the room.

"We can't wait until after the fire season. We're hoping to do it during a lull after the Denali Creek and Salmon Lake Fires are mopped up. Hopefully, next weekend, if the weather holds. If we're called out on fire, then we'll postpone it."

"We'll pull it off. Right, people?" Rego looked around for approval and got it with plenty of nods and clapping.

"We're also making a firefighter calendar. All we need are twelve volunteers, half men, half women. If we get more, we'll do group shots. Angela will have the signup sheet for the calendar, too."

"But I don't want to get naked!" yelled a whiny random voice that caused peals of laughter.

"Don't worry, you'll keep your clothes on. No bare man chests," said Raynie in a laughing voice.

Rego raised his brows. "We'd sell more calendars with our clothes off."

More whistles and catcalls as Rego shot up from his chair and unbuttoned his fire shirt. Someone sang a strip tease melody. More joined in as Rego put his hand on the back of his neck in a model pose, making kissing noises at Tupa.

Tupa spread his arms. "Who's gonna do our hair and makeup?"

Kenzie pinched his man bun. "What are you talking about, mate? Your makeup is already tattooed." She pointed at the dark designs on either side of his thick neck.

"I'm taking the photos, so get with me after you sign up," Liz called out.

People started talking all at once, and it warmed Raynie's heart the Aurora Crew was willing to help raise money for those who'd been burned out of their homes.

Vanessa stepped into the room with a Bluetooth attached to her ear.

"Fire call! The Denali Creek Fire needs mop-up help. Aurora Crew is being dispatched."

Everyone groaned. Mop-up was gritty, dirty work, but an important part of suppression.

"I'm giddy with excitement to feel soil and ashes with my bare hands," said Rego, hustling out the door with the crew.

"Aurora Crew, get your gear and meet in the lot," announced Cohen. "We'll drive both transport vans to the Denali Creek Community Center to report in, then drive to the site. Let's go!"

The room emptied, and Raynie hung back, watching Cohen gather papers and maps from a table.

"Thanks for the warning about calling me up to talk."

He glanced up. "Figured you'd want to remind the crew about the fundraisers and what the town is planning. If we get fires, we'll have to postpone."

"I know. I'll keep my fingers crossed." She offered him a suggestive smile. "Time to get dirty, Tremblay."

He returned an irresistibly devastating smile. "Thought we did that last night?"

"Ooh. You're right." Raynie bumped him with her hip and aimed for the door. "Had I known you were this witty, I wouldn't have wasted time loathing you."

"Don't worry, I plan to make up for lost time," he murmured, following her out.

"Then I better up my workouts," she said over her shoulder. It took every ounce of her willpower not to turn around and climb him like a stripper pole. She'd never felt this way about anyone.

Ever.

Chapter 33

Two Weeks Later

"And so, without further ado, Talkeetna, we're going to bring these firefighters out here. Ladies, escort them up to the stage, please!" announced Liz into the cordless mic she held in her hand. She looked like a Las Vegas show girl in her clinging glitter-gold evening gown, sporting just enough cleavage to make her elegant.

The jam-packed audience's enthusiasm was electric, and Raynie loved how Liz and Kenzie fed on it as the auction emcees. Tara had volunteered to help Raynie backstage.

"Is everybody ready?" Raynie stage-whispered behind the gargantuan black curtain stretched across the stage. "Women in the front line and guys in the back. Just do what Liz says," she instructed. "And if you get stage fright, just roll with it."

Easy for me to say. I'm not up for auction.

Raynie had volunteered to be Stage Mother, as Liz had christened her. Her job was to keep the firefighters organized and calm backstage. Calm being the operative word, as several firefighters fidgeted, paralyzed with stage fright.

Everyone except Rego, who took everything in stride. He could face a wall of flame and strut along a runway of screaming women with the utmost of confidence.

It amused the Aurora Crew women that some of these hulking firefighters could charge into a burning building yet were terrified to get onstage and strut their stuff for the hordes of bidders eager to win a date.

"Okay, ladies first!" Raynie called to the group milling around like a hive of honeybees.

Vanessa had wormed her way into the female lineup, though she wasn't a firefighter. Raynie had let her sign up, figuring the sexy dispatcher would fetch a high bid. After all, this was for the homeowners. It still irritated her how Vanessa flirted with Cohen. The downside to hooking up with a beautiful man was that other women repeatedly drooled over him.

"Ladies and gentlemen, we have forty firefighters from state and federal hotshot crews, plus firefighters who were gracious enough to join us from the Anchorage and Eagle River City Fire Departments. Please give them a warm Talkeetna welcome!" announced Liz, to whistles and applause.

A local band played lively stripper music as the curtain opened, revealing the forty firefighters. The audience cheered, whooped, and hollered. The people onstage stayed in place, moving to the beat, twirling, and dancing. This was unrehearsed, and Trish said not to worry, to let people be themselves and have fun.

Raynie loved how the retired DeHavilland Beaver hung suspended from the towering ceiling. The workhorse of float planes only enhanced the hot firefighter vibe the auction organizers were hoping for.

After fighting the Denali Creek and Salmon Lake fires, Raynie delighted in seeing the firefighters having a fun time. A weak low-pressure system had sprinkled rain on the thirsty Mat-Su Valley, and residents were grateful for the fire reprieve.

But as with all things, residents knew it wouldn't last. Summer was far from over.

Raynie had decided Cohen was the superlative choice for selling calendars, since he was the best looking guy on the Aurora Crew. She'd positioned him at the entrance to lure people inside.

"Now it's time to begin the auction," announced Kenzie into her mic. "Our firefighters will go backstage, and each will come out and strut their stuff. Let the bidding begin!"

Raynie admired Kenzie in her form fitting gown. The sexy dress and her Aussie accent delighted the men in the audience. Tupa almost fell off the stage when he saw her.

Liz, of course, was another knockout in her Vegas glitzy gown. Liz and Kenzie bantered seamlessly back and forth like old, experienced emcees at a beauty pageant.

The firefighters milled around backstage, and like a good stage mother, Raynie had set up tables with water and cookies along a back wall. Liz announced the first firefighter to auction. They'd each pulled numbers from a hardhat, so they'd know their order.

Rego stepped up to Raynie as Firefighter Number One.

"How do I look, Stage Mother?" She noted he'd tucked his bright yellow shirt all the way inside his pants. Most of the time, his sooty shirt stayed untucked, with one pant leg inside his boot. It was his fashion signature.

"Not too shabby," she said, straightening his collar. "Now get out there and strut your stuff. Make 'em scream for you, so they bid lots and lots."

Rego gave her a thumbs-up. "Copy that, Stage Mother."

"Here's our first firefighter of the evening," announced Liz. "Mr. Nick Rego, from the Aurora Crew. Nick is a strapping lad from the BLM Alaska Fire Service. He enjoys long walks on the beach, sweltering summer nights, and sipping piña coladas in the moonlight. Check this out, ladies!"

Rego stepped in front of the curtain. Liz covered her mic, while Kenzie muttered, "What a load of donkey dung. Rego is all about hunting moose!" They laughed uproariously, causing Raynie to peek through the curtain.

Raynie barked out a laugh as Rego pranced down the runway like a sexy supermodel. The audience loved it, erupting with cheers and catcalls. She ducked back behind the curtain.

"Tara!" she stage-whispered. "You gotta see this!"

Tara rushed over to join Raynie peeking through the curtain. Women were on their feet, clapping and hollering. One offered Rego a long-stemmed rose, which he accepted and stuck between his teeth as he strutted. The noise was deafening as women showed their appreciation.

"Wow! Look at him rockin' it!" Tara cracked up laughing.

Rego played it to the hilt, shaking his booty at the ladies on his return trip back to the stage. He held out his hands to slap palms for extra effect. When he returned to the stage, Liz patted his shoulder.

"And now let's hear from Mister Nick!" She handed him the mic.

"Good evening, ladies," he said in his deep, thick Bronx accent, winking at a doe-eyed woman in the front row. "Let's get this party started!"

Screams ensued, and the audience went nuts. Everyone laughed when Rego formed prayer hands and batted his eyelashes.

Kenzie led off. "Let's start the bidding at one hundred dollars. What do you say?"

Raynie held her breath, hoping some of the older ladies in the crowd would bid on middle-aged, balding Rego. A white paper plate shot up with the bidder's number.

"Woohoo!" shouted Liz, pointing at the bidder. "We have one hundred! Looking for one-fifty?"

A plate shot up.

"Yes!" exclaimed Liz. "How about two-fifty?"

Another plate shot up.

The bidding kept going until it slowed, and Kenzie yelled, "Sold at eight hundred!"

The audience cheered, and Rego pointed at the winning bidder, a middle-aged woman with long silver hair, wearing multi-colored tie-dye, jumping up and down, clapping.

"Fantastic!" Raynie clapped until her palms reddened.

"Now it's time for Firefighter Number Two!" announced Liz, her smooth voice flowing out of the speakers. Raynie admired Liz and Kenzie's emcee skills.

Raynie made sure each firefighter made it onstage when their number was called. Firefighter Number Twelve had gone missing when Liz announced him to appear. Stage Mom Raynie found him in a backroom, hitting on glitter-gowned Vanessa with her heaving bosom.

"Get your butt out there!" She showed no mercy toward the guy. He scooted out onstage to uproarious laughter.

Finally, it was intermission. Twenty firefighters had been auctioned, and the tally was closing in on twenty-five thousand dollars. Liz, Kenzie, and Tara moved backstage, and Raynie couldn't stop gushing about what a wonderful job they were doing.

"Oh, I almost forgot! I'm supposed to be out during intermission to help Cohen sell calendars!" Raynie skittered off and hurried through the hangar, to the front of the building.

Trish had set up a few long tables with the calendars in neat, organized piles. She glanced up as Raynie approached.

"Glad you're here. These things are flying off the table. We can hardly keep up." She motioned at Kira and Jamen sitting behind their table, busy counting change for a customer.

She glanced around. "Where's Cohen?"

"He took a restroom break," said Trish, smiling at two women who stepped up to buy calendars. "He sold all the calendars, and we had to open another box."

Raynie inserted herself behind a table. "Kira, if you need a break, go ahead. I'll be here through intermission."

"Okay, thanks." Kira grabbed Jamen's hand and led him off down the busy street.

Talkeetna had a festival atmosphere with everyone in town for the auction. Not a room vacancy could be found, and the fire base offered the field for pitching tents and parking RVs. Several people gathered in clusters discussing the fires, wishing they'd settle for the summer. But firefighters knew better.

Something caught the corner of Raynie's eye. It was Cohen, walking back from a nearby restaurant, holding a soda. She lifted her hand to get his attention when a woman with long blonde hair suddenly flounced up to Cohen. She threw her arms around his neck, then cradled his face and planted a kiss on his lips.

Who the heck is this?

Raynie recognized Deanna's laugh. What about 'No' did Cohen's ex not understand?

Deanna had spun him around with his back to Raynie, so she couldn't see his face. She noted the short white skirt, showing tanned, muscular legs, and a tight tank top, revealing a bulbous chest.

She debated marching over and interrupting the little soiree, but multiple customers had accosted Trish with calendar purchases, and needed Raynie's help. In between customers, she kept an eye on Cohen and Deanna.

The next time she glanced up, Deanna still had her arms around Cohen, kissing him on the lips—and not just a friendly peck either—she had him in a lengthy lip lock.

Raynie's first instinct was to run up, pry them apart, and toss Deanna into next week. Instead, she gaped, open-mouthed, watching her guy's ex move in on him. Was this always going to happen every time this woman saw Cohen? Because so far, she'd had her hands all over him like she was the current girlfriend.

Over my dead body.

Her mind raced with what to do. Just as Raynie rose to walk over, Kira rushed up.

"Stage Mother, they need you inside. It's time for the second half of the auction. Liz and Kenzie are looking for you."

"Yeah, okay." When Raynie looked up to find Deanna and Cohen, they were gone.

Chapter 34

Cohen couldn't find Raynie and needed to talk to her. He'd had an epiphany after meeting Deanna, and he wanted desperately to talk to Raynie, to let her know how he felt. She must be backstage, herding the rest of the firefighters through the auction.

He hurried through the crowd, then up the stairs to backstage. He moved through the firefighters waiting to meet and greet the boisterous audience who'd imbibed during their rowdy intermission.

Raynie suddenly appeared next to him in a knockout form-fitting glitter gown, with a slit up one leg, complete with stilettos. She'd piled her hair on top of her head, long earrings dangled, and her lips were a hellacious pink. She resembled a Miss Alaska pageant contestant.

"Liz!" she stage-whispered through the curtain. "Come backstage!"

When Liz ducked behind the curtain, Raynie handed her a piece of paper.

"I'm Firefighter Number Forty-One. Here's my bio," she declared primly, with a killer side glance at Cohen.

He figured the universe would implode before he'd ever see Raynie Atwood in a pair of high heels and a low-cut gown with her boobs hanging out.

"Wow, Atwood. You look...incredible!" His lust meter hit the roof and bounced back again.

She swiveled her head toward him. If lasers could shoot from her eyeballs, he'd incinerate.

"Raynie, what's wrong? Why are you dressed like that?"

"Fuck you, Tremblay!" She about-faced and marched off, stilettos clicking on the wooden floor. She tripped and Cohen grimaced, expecting her to take a header.

He had an instinct to rush in and catch her, but Tupa's gorilla hand snapped out and snagged Raynie's arm, preventing her from crashing to the floor.

"Thanks, Tupa." Raynie continued to the snacks and beverages table.

She must have known Cohen would follow because she abruptly whirled on him. "You have some nerve!" She riveted her accusing gaze on him.

"Tell me what's going on," he said in a low, level voice.

"No. *You* tell *me* what's going on!" Her voice was glacier-fed—no chance of *this* ice melting anytime soon. "For starters, explain why you were making out with your ex on a public street?"

He stiffened as though she'd struck him. A wave of apprehension swept through him as the light bulb turned on.

She saw me with Deanna.

"Raynie, are you going to believe what you think you saw, or what actually happened?"

"Oh, I get it." Raynie flashed him a fake smile. Her tone was clipped and pissed-off. "We're playing the what-you-saw-isn't-what-you-think-you-saw game again." She clasped her hands and squealed in pretend delight. "Oh, I love this game!"

"Deanna was so drunk she could barely stand." Cohen tamped down his frustration at Raynie's determination not to listen.

"Oh, the poor, unfortunate thing. You must have had to kiss her so she wouldn't fall." Her voice dripped with sarcasm as she feigned a sad face and unscrewed the lid of her water bottle. For a split second, Cohen thought she'd toss water at him.

"Deanna told me she's engaged to be married and was out celebrating with friends."

"I didn't see any friends," Raynie shot back. "All I saw was her hanging all over you, as usual. And you not fighting her off." Her mouth became a straight line.

He hesitated. "She said she wanted one last goodbye kiss. Before I knew it, she grabbed hold and wouldn't let go." He felt like he was sinking in quicksand the more he tried to explain.

"Oh, you poor baby. She's so strong you couldn't push her away." Raynie had daggers in her eyes. "You're so full of shit, Tremblay it comes out your eyeballs. You said you were done with her." She said it with such venom he felt the strike.

"I am," he insisted. "She's marrying a smokejumper."

Raynie scoffed. "Oh, really? Wait'll he finds out his bride-to-be pines away for *you*." She placed her hands on her hips. "If she's marrying a smokejumper, why was she lip-locking another man?"

"I don't know—she was drunk out of her mind and wanted one last goodbye kiss."

"Ohh!" howled Raynie. "Give me a flipping break! Whenever she sees you, this stuff happens. She sticks to you like a virus!"

He blew out air in exasperation. This was heading downhill fast.

"She was inebriated. I hung onto her so she wouldn't splat on the ground." He knew it sounded lame, but it was the God's honest truth.

How can I convince her?

"The poor, defenseless smokejumper. How chivalrous of you!" Raynie mocked sympathy for his plight. "I forget you're a shining knight—savior of women. There's no greater devotion than a loyal, devoted protector, a champion of love. Always on the ready to rescue damsels in distress." She waved her open bottle, splashing water everywhere.

By now a crowd had gathered—the Aurora Crew, Raynie's state hotshot crew, the Anchorage firefighters—all milled around, watching their secret affair explode into the open and unravel like a faulty parachute.

Cohen stood speechless, taking her jibes rather than lashing back at her.

She continued her rant. "Whenever Deanna is around, she's all over you. I hate this—hate that you're turning me into an insanely jealous wild woman!" She glanced around at the curious faces. "And I don't give a flying flip who hears this, either! You're a—"

"I came here to tell you something," interjected Cohen. He thought about reaching for her hand but stopped himself.

"Oh, really? What could you possibly want to tell me after making out in public with your old girlfriend?" She pointed at herself, then at him. "Doesn't this—us—matter?"

"Of course it does. Why would you think otherwise?" He shook his head. "And I wasn't making out with her!"

"Firefighter Forty-One!" hollered Tara, running back to them. "Get your hiney out on stage, Atwood. Liz just announced you, so you have to get out there," she said breathlessly, glancing at Raynie and Cohen, who stood glaring at each other.

"Are you two duking it out again? Figured you both would at least have a peace accord by now."

"Yeah, right, like that would happen," said Raynie through clenched teeth. She slammed her water bottle into his belly and let go. Before he could grab it, the bottle plunged onto his athletic shoes, water splashing everywhere.

Without another word, Raynie spun on her stilettos and clicked her way through the gauntlet of firefighters who parted to let her through as she hurried to the stage.

"What the heck did you do, Tremblay?" grilled Tara. "I've never seen Raynie this hosed."

"I...it's...there's..." He stared after her, his heart ripping apart. Why didn't he tell Raynie he loved her?

Instead, I told Trish. What a loser.

The heaviness of every thought he hadn't expressed weighed on him like an anchor.

He turned to look at Tara. "Long story."

She gave him an empathetic smile. "They usually are."

COHEN SPRINTED ALL the way out to the ticket table where Trish stood talking to Kira.

"I need one of those paper plate things." He pointed, breathing hard from his run.

Trish looked confused. "You want to bid?" She sounded like he'd declared he was scaling Mount Denali.

"Yes. Hurry, I need one of those." He snapped his fingers, and Kira handed him a paper plate with "450" scrawled on it with a black marker.

Kira's mouth fell open. "Why? I thought you liked Raynie."

"Your sister is auctioning herself."

Kira gulped. "She's what? No way! Why would she want to date someone else when she has you?"

"I pissed her off." He let out an exasperated sigh. "She saw me with an old girlfriend."

Trish gave him a direct look. "And what were you doing with said girlfriend?"

He let out another sigh and ran a palm over his face. "See, that's the problem. Kissing her." He shook his head helplessly.

"Only, I didn't kiss *her*. She kissed *me*."

"You told me you loved Raynie." Trish leveled her gaze. "Have you gotten around to telling her? It's not rocket science—just three little words, the most powerful ones on earth. Wars are fought and won over them. People move mountains and cross oceans because of them. Do you get what I'm saying, or do I have to pound it into your brain?" Her words slapped him like a tsunami.

"No. I...I..." He supposed he deserved Trish's wrath as well as Raynie's. "I've been meaning to tell her—"

"Gah, men! You guys are clueless when it comes to women!" Trish slapped the paper plate into his hand. "Raynie Atwood is special and requires a special effort. You'll have to earn her. It takes guts to love someone. So, man up and get your fanny in there, Mr. Hotshot Firefighter. You may not get another chance."

They locked stares, then Cohen sprinted inside, hoping he wasn't too late.

"I've never had to try this hard with any woman," he muttered as he ran, wondering how the hell he intended to pull this off.

Or maybe he wouldn't.

It was a crap shoot, but he'd never forgive himself if he didn't at least try to show Raynie he meant everything he said. While he knew he was a charmer, he didn't lie when it came to expressing his feelings.

By the time Cohen reached the hangar, the bidding was over a thousand. Raynie stood on the stage between Liz and Kenzie. She looked so flipping gorgeous, he wouldn't have believed it was her had he not seen her beforehand. She wore her defiant F.U. look that he knew all too well back when she loathed him.

And apparently, she still did.

"Do I hear eleven hundred for Raynie Atwood?" Liz's voice came over the speakers. She scanned the room, making a wide sweeping motion with an outstretched arm. "Going once! Going twice!"

Cohen's hand shot up from the back of the room, waving his paper plate.

"Eleven hundred!"

Liz squinted, the stage lights in her eyes. "Someone in the back bids eleven hundred!"

Several men rose from their chairs, twisting to see who'd intruded into their bidding war for the firefighter beauty onstage. A plate shot up.

"Thirteen hundred!"

"Whoa!" someone yelled, and the audience laughed and cheered.

Cohen's heart thundered as he calculated his bank account at warp speed.

Screw it, I'm going all in.

Liz spoke into the mic. "Do I hear—"

"Two thousand!" Cohen cut in and hopped up onto the runway. He stood still in his yellow Nomex shirt and green pants, paper plate held high, like the Statue of Liberty. He waved it at the three women onstage.

A collective gasp reverberated around the hangar, then electric silence as necks craned to see who'd put up the bid.

Liz was the first to recover. "Do I hear two thousand five hundred?" She pointed at a bidder seated near the front.

"How about you, sir? You bid thirteen hundred."

He shook his head. "Too rich for my blood!" he called out.

Liz paused for dramatics. "Two thousand going once—going twice—sold! To the gentleman in the back."

Kenzie waggled a finger at Cohen. "Come claim your prize, mate."

The women in the audience cheered as Cohen strode along the runway toward the stage. The men clapped with incredulity, leaning into one another, whispering indiscernible comments. Cohen wished he could hear what was being said.

A woman yelled, "Hey, he's one of the firefighters!"

Even louder cheers erupted as the audience realized what was happening.

"The firefighters are bidding on each other?" someone yelled.

"How romantic!" another woman shouted, followed by applause.

"What in the moose-dropping, belly blue bear blazes are you doing?" Angela howled incredulously from the front row as he passed her.

Without breaking stride, Cohen responded with a broad toothy smile as he moved to Liz, Kenzie, and Raynie. He looked directly into the love-of-his-life's eyes as he took the mic from Liz's hand and turned to face the crowd.

"I bid two thousand for Miss Raynie Atwood, the bravest, sexiest wildland firefighter I know!" he announced into the mic, then handed it to Liz.

He stepped toward Raynie and took her in his arms. He planted a kiss on her he figured would melt every pair of panties in the audience. He teased her lips with a sensuous tongue but kept his kiss shallow.

Cohen lifted off, noting Raynie was too astounded to speak. He stepped back, winked at her, then sauntered back the way he came. Taking his sweet time to high-five the bevy of hands reaching for his, he felt like a rock star.

One woman leaped to her feet, tugging his pant leg. "I'll pay a hundred bucks if you kiss *me* like that!"

"Can we bid on *you*, please?" another woman yelled from across the room, eliciting laughter. Others echoed her sentiment, and sexy whistles sounded. He turned to see his three astonished crewmates onstage, still as statues, gaping after him.

Liz stood speechless. Kenzie glanced at her, then raised her mic to her lips.

"It appears this firefighter has taken a shine to our lovely Raynie."

"Good on ya, mate." Kenzie grinned and pointed her mic at him.

Cohen beamed back at her. He pointed to Raynie, then himself in a *you're mine* gesture—and dropped his pretend air mic. He no longer cared to conceal his attraction to her. Flashing his broadest smile, he jumped off the end of the runway and ambled out of the hangar. Cheers, hollers, and applause followed him all the way to the door.

Pride swelled his chest after showing the woman he loved how much she meant to him.

Our fire is out of containment. And the entire universe knows it.

Raynie's reputation concerns were a moot point as far as Cohen was concerned.

Let the sparks fall where they may.

Chapter 35

When Liz and Kenzie finished the auction, Dave Doss stepped onstage to explain how the funds would be used. He thanked the audience for showing up for a worthy cause and held up some calendars.

"Hurry and buy a firefighter calendar on your way out, before they're all gone!" he encouraged as people stood to go.

Raynie's crewmates converged on her all at once, as if she'd won the Miss Alaska title. Kenzie was the first to gush. "I was right. You and Canada Boy are a thing."

Raynie's brain was still in a state of shock at Cohen's bid of two grand.

Two thousand bucks? Who does that?

"I knew it all along," Angela joined in. "I picked up on both your vibes a long time ago."

"That was—well yeah—that was..." Embarrassment blossomed on Raynie's face, and she didn't know what to think. Her brain had dissolved into mush and her heart melted into goo.

"You're the only firefighter who brought in two grand," said Liz. "I couldn't believe it when I saw Cohen lift that number and jump up to that runway. Boy, when Cohen falls, he falls hard," said Liz, patting Raynie's bare arm. "You're a lucky woman."

"Thanks. I know." Raynie's brain muddled with confusion, and she needed time to think.

"I have to find Cohen. Talk to you all later?" She wondered where he was and hurried off to change into jeans and a T-shirt, then returned the borrowed gown to Trish and thanked her. Her thoughts jumbled as she walked toward her truck at the fire base.

It seems I've misjudged Cohen yet again.

"Hey, Atwood!" a woman's voice called out behind her. "Raynie!"

She whirled around to see Deanna striding toward her. She wasn't sure whether to turn around or throw a punch. Neither choice would be ideal, so she stood her ground, watching Deanna approach with a cup of steaming coffee in her hand.

"I saw Cohen bid two grand for you at the auction. Why did you put yourself up for auction? You're no longer interested in Cohen?" Deanna's hair was in a messy bun, but she seemed to have sobered.

"What business is it of yours?" Raynie said coolly, looking her square in the eye.

Deanna held up her hand with a huge rock on her ring finger.

"I'm engaged to be married. I thought I wanted Cohen back, but after I saw he was totally into you, I knew I had no chance. But I have someone just as wonderful now." Deanna gave her a lop-sided grin. "Besides. It's easier to marry a smokejumper than a hotshot. You and Cohen are both hotshots—you belong together."

"Uh-huh. Now I have the permission of the ex-girlfriend?" Raynie lifted her chin in a haughty tilt at the taller woman. "Just one minor fucking detail—why the hell were you kissing Cohen if you're engaged to be married?" She waited while Deanna stared off, sipping her coffee.

"My smokejumper crew threw me an engagement party here after we demobe'd from the Denali Creek Fire. I wanted to kiss Cohen goodbye, since I got engaged. I didn't mean anything by it." She looked at Raynie. "You know how mother effing alphalicious he is."

"You're lucky I didn't toss you into the river," said Raynie, in a controlled tone that took quite some doing.

Deanna made an up and down assessment and grinned. "I'm sure you could, too."

"Tell me something." Raynie folded her arms and shifted her weight. "Do you feel entitled just because you're a smokejumper? Like you can have any guy you want, even if he's someone else's?"

"Well, sure. Ya gotta work the angles." Deanna stared into her coffee cup. "Hey, I'm sorry. You have a right to be outraged. It won't happen again."

"Apology accepted." Raynie's mouth formed a straight line. "Make sure it doesn't happen again. You've been officially warned."

"Understood." Deanna tossed down the rest of her coffee. "I like you, Atwood. I hated like hell losing Cohen to you, but I like you. You're willing to fight for him, and that's admirable."

When did I turn the corner, wanting to fight for Cohen?

Somewhere along the way, she had—because he was worth it. How quickly things had changed.

Deanna glanced behind Raynie at the Aurora Crew women walking up. "Be safe on fire. Go easy on Tremblay. He never once made a move on me, no matter how much I threw myself at him. I've never seen him into anyone like he is with you."

"Two thousand bucks. Holy crap." Deanna whistled and ambled off, then hollered back over her shoulder. "You're both invited to my wedding!"

Yeah, that'll happen.

"Oh, hey, congratulations." Raynie wished she meant it, but only said it out of polite obligation.

Angela, Liz, Kenzie, and Tara ambled up to join Raynie as she continued to the parking lot. "Wished I could have heard that conversation just now, y'all," said Angela with a sly grin. "But first, now that you and Cohen are out of the closet, fill us in."

"Yep, we want the deets," said Kenzie, shaking a cupful of ice. "Don't know anyone who spends two grand for a date with their girlfriend. That's a new one."

"You know we won't leave you alone until you do. Cohen won't tell us anything," said Liz.

Raynie laughed. She reached her vehicle and stopped while the women gathered around her. "Remember the Hiland Mountain fire in Eagle River?"

"Yes," said Tara. "Back when I was sick and couldn't go with the crew."

"What I remember is how you and Cohen argued like you hated each other," said Liz.

"We did," said Raynie. "Well, at least I did."

"I've never known Cohen to even hate a mosquito," said Tara, laughing. "What did he do? Let me guess, he questioned your authority."

"How did you know? Did he say something?" Raynie wondered if he'd bragged about it.

"Only that the state IC was a little testy about where to move vehicles." Tara laughed. "Cohen's way of describing it."

"You guys bickered over everything," said Liz. "If he said go, you said stop. If you said move the trucks, he said leave the trucks. We took bets on who'd win the argument. I won most of them by saying it was a draw."

Raynie's mouth opened in surprise. "Really? I had no idea."

Angela linked her elbow. "When did the pitty-pat thing happen?"

Raynie hesitated. After keeping their relationship under wraps, it seemed surreal to talk about it. "Well, we went on a hike one day along the Susitna River..."

"I knew it!" exclaimed Angela. "I noticed a difference between both of you after that. I have a sixth sense about such things. Just one thing, y'all. If you had the hots for Cohen, why did you put yourself up for auction? Or did you two have that planned?"

Raynie debated whether to share the whole sordid saga about Deanna. No point in doing that. "We had a disagreement. I got pissed and entered the auction to spite him." It was partly true. "I'm so happy the auction was a rocking success."

"Thanks to you and Trish for organizing the event," said Tara. "We sold out of the calendars. We could make it an annual thing, don't you think?"

"I can't wait for Doss to cut the check for distribution to the homeowners." Raynie opened her vehicle door. "Thanks for everyone's help."

A smile spread across Tara's face. "Copy that. I'm so happy for you and Cohen. And I mean that with all my heart."

"Thanks. Tonight was fun. See you all tomorrow." Raynie closed the door and started the truck. As she drove and turned left onto Whispering Spruce Drive, she noted it was after midnight.

I hope Cohen is waiting for me.

She tapped his number for the millionth time. Finally, her phone pinged a text:

Figured you needed space, so I'm sleeping in my bunkhouse at the fire base. I've asked the state troopers to patrol your place tonight. Looking forward to my two-thousand-dollar date. C.

Exhaustion consumed her, but her brain churned like a frappe setting on a blender. Lying in bed, she closed her eyes. Up popped the image of determination on Cohen's face when he'd marched onstage, announcing his bid for her.

And it had melted her heart.

She wondered if Cohen had that kind of money. But what really blew her mind was that he'd done it in front of everyone.

Actions speak louder than words.

RAYNIE JERKED AWAKE to a loud scream from inside the house, followed by angry barking. What was Rooby barking at?

Oh my God, Kira!

Raynie leaped out of bed in her T-shirt, snatching her jeans and putting them on. Almost as an afterthought, she retrieved the nine-millimeter from the drawer and grabbed the magazine lying next to it. Jamming it into the weapon, she flung open the door, dread strangling her chest at what she'd find.

It didn't take long to discover Kira sitting in a kitchen chair in her T-shirt and undies. Rooby stood growling and snapping on one side, ears back and hairs raised at Maddox, standing on the other side. Tears streamed down Kira's cheeks.

"How the hell did you get in here?" demanded Raynie, trying to control the tremor in her voice. She glanced out the window.

Where are the troopers Cohen said that would patrol the house?

"Your boyfriend's not here to save you." Maddox's comment prickled her spine.

Dammit! I left my phone on my nightstand.

Maddox yanked Kira to her feet, with the blade tip to her neck. Rooby charged at him, and he kicked her. She yelped and backed away, snapping and growling. Raynie had never seen her golden act this way.

"Don't touch my dog again!" Her eyes darted to Rooby, then focused on Maddox.

"You get to watch while I help myself to your little sister," he snarled. "Each time I ask you for my money and you don't tell me, I'll do her again. And again. And again. And that's after I slice her." He dragged the knife tip up and down Kira's arm. "And then I'll do the same to you. Or maybe I'll kill all your dogs, starting with that one." He jerked his head toward Rooby, growling on the floor.

"No!" Kira choked out, crying so hard it enraged Raynie.

"The hell you will!" Raynie raised the pistol and leveled it at Maddox, holding it with both hands just as Taydon had taught her. She tried to keep her hands from shaking.

Rooby let out several sharp alarm barks.

"Control that dog, or I will," threatened Maddox.

"Rooby, lie down!" ordered Raynie, eyes on her gunsight aimed at Maddox.

Rooby lowered herself with a low, long growl.

"Aw, lookee there. It's a firefighter with a gun. Give it to the grown-up. You don't know how to use it," taunted Maddox.

"You hurt Kira or my dog—I'll kill you!" gritted Raynie, training the nine-millimeter on Maddox, hoping like hell she remembered how to fire it. Her hands shook so much she had a tough time steadying her weapon.

"You won't shoot me, Atwood—you don't have the guts. You're too scared. You can't even hold the gun." He shot her a smile that would've looked good on anyone but this degenerative asswipe.

"Let her go, or I swear to God, I'll end you," snarled Raynie, shocked at herself for uttering such words.

"Tough talk for a firefighter. Hey, aren't you a big hero protector?" He smirked. "I think not. Or I wouldn't be here with a knife to your sister's throat."

"You pathetic loser!" She had to keep him talking while her mind raced. Her primary concern was Kira, and all she could focus on was the tip of the knife to her sister's throat.

"Ladies and gentlemen, here comes the first demand," Maddox announced in his game show voice. He pointed the knife at Raynie. "Put down the gun. Better yet, take off your clothes so I can enjoy this." He ran a suggestive, disgusting tongue along his bottom lip.

"No, Raynie, don't!" Kira shook her head, tears filling her eyes.

"Shut up!" Maddox backhanded Kira so hard, his blow knocked her to the floor.

"Kira!" screamed Raynie, her heart in her throat as she placed her forefinger on the trigger. "You'll pay for that, Maddox." Her hands shook even harder. She could barely steady the gun.

"Uh-uh-uh!" taunted Maddox, waving his knife at her in a clown-like fashion.

"Lose the gun or your sister's dead."

"Not before you are." She summoned every ounce of calm to stop the gun from jiggling.

"I'll have your sister's throat slit and this knife in your heart before you touch the trigger." Maddox flaunted the knife, turning it back and forth.

Raynie's peripheral vision caught movement on the floor. She didn't dare drop her gaze to Kira, who'd bent her knee and was drawing her leg up ever so slowly, poised to kick. Raynie held her breath and braced for whatever Kira was about to do.

Kira's foot shot out, kicking Maddox's knee sideways, and knocking him off balance. He screamed in pain, and Raynie hoped Kira had broken his knee.

Raynie screamed at her golden. "Rooby, get him!"

Rooby lunged at Maddox and sunk her teeth into his leg, violently shaking it.

As Maddox went down, Raynie's eye caught the glint of metal hurtling toward her, and she pulled the trigger. As the gun went off, she glanced down to see blood seeping through her T-shirt.

The last thing Raynie remembered was Rooby barking.

And Kira's screams.

Chapter 36

Overnight, the state had blown up with fire starts. Lightning had moved in, starting one hundred thirty-eight fires overnight. The scorching sun was back, all traces of rain evaporated. The elevated temperatures had returned.

Cohen left a trail of dust behind him as he drove down Birch Spur Road. Thick smoke hovered over the tundra like an unwanted guest, creating zero visibility for aircraft. Heavy smoke had settled throughout the entire Matanuska-Susitna Valley, posing challenges for aerial firefighting.

Doss had asked him to do a ground recon on several road accessible fires, so they'd know where to direct air tankers and helicopters to the hot spots when visibility improved. So far, Cohen had spotted twenty-two fires burning. Lightning had ignited most of them, and humans had caused the rest. He'd called in the coordinates to Angela.

Raynie hadn't shown up or called in. He'd tried contacting her all morning. She hadn't answered or responded to his texts, which concerned him. He tried calling again as he drove.

Dammit, Raynie, answer your phone.

His heart stumbled with guilt for not spending last night at Sleeping Lady Kennel. Raynie had been so upset, he'd figured they both needed space, even after his heroic dramatics of bidding for her. He'd done it to prove a point—that he loved her.

He just had a helluva time trying to say it out loud, for fear she wouldn't say it back.

Lightning had ignited a fire on the other side of Salmon Lake, and it raced toward Talkeetna. The dense beetle-killed spruce fueled the fire and sped it so fast, the aircraft couldn't slow it, let alone stop it. Talkeetna Base had dispatched the Aurora Crew to this one, with Tara as the crew supervisor. He didn't go with them, as Doss needed his help at the base.

The ramped-up fire activity jammed radio traffic, and Cohen had a tough time keeping track of the new starts. His phone sounded in the seat next to him, and he picked it up, peering out his windshield at distant flames.

"Cohen, this is Angela. Thought you should know this." Her tone alarmed him. It was out of character for her to sound distressed.

"What is it?"

"Last night, there was a break-in at Sleeping Lady Kennel. That same guy who broke into the fire cache—Maddox—he got inside and pulled a knife on Kira and Raynie."

Cohen skidded to a stop. Spruce trees on both sides of the road rushed in and rushed out again. His heart slammed his chest.

"Are they all right?"

"Yes. Raynie has a cut on her shoulder, and Kira has a welt and a laceration on her face, but they're okay. Kira called nine-one-one, and the troopers responded. They were taken to the local clinic, where they each got a few stitches."

"What about Maddox?"

"Raynie shot him."

"She what?" he spluttered. "Is he dead?"

"No. He's in an Anchorage hospital, under police guard. He won't be going anywhere unless there's bars on the windows, y'all," replied Angela.

"Where's Raynie?"

"Doss told her to take the day off, but she insisted on coming here. She and Kira spent the rest of the night at the clinic and all morning at the Alaska State Troopers office, giving their statements."

"I should have been there," he lamented. "Guess everyone knows we're involved by now."

"Oh, you think?" chirped Angela, laughing. "Everyone and their cat knows after last night's outstanding performance at the auction. That was so Hollywood romcom, Cohen. You deserve an Oscar." She chuckled.

"I messed things up last night. Or rather, Deanna did." Recalling the hurt on Raynie's face made him wince. He was a dickwad for letting her down and it'd cost him two thousand dollars, but he'd wanted to make it up to her.

"Vanessa called in sick with the porcelain flu after spending the night with her winning bidder, a smokin' hot Anchorage city firefighter. So, Raynie offered to help with dispatch because it's crazy town over here."

"Glad Kira and Raynie are okay. Tell her to call me."

"I'll do that," said Angela. "Hey, I'm super thrilled for both of you."

"Thanks." He spotted a new smoke plume up ahead. "Found another start. I'll text the coordinates."

"Copy that. Visibility has improved, so Mel is headed your way to drop off Ryan and Gunnar to aid a village crew."

"Good. I'll watch for Juliet." Cohen studied the topo map he kept on the dash. "The closest landmark to this new fire is Hellbrook Lake, so call it the Hellbrook Fire."

"I got it," said Angela. "The whole town is talking about Raynie saving her younger sister's life. And how she saved yours on the Salmon Lake Fire."

"She's an incredibly brave woman," he said, wishing he was back at the base to tell her himself.

"Yep. You're a lucky man, Tremblay."

"I know. You don't need to say it." He nodded at the windshield, glimpsing a helicopter circling a distant smoke plume. "Tell Raynie ..." He stopped.

"That you love her?" Angela said quietly. "It's time you told her yourself. You told Trish, and everyone else knows—except Raynie. You're falling down on the job, Tremblay."

"Trust me, those will be the first words out of my mouth when I see her." Cohen flagellated himself again.

"Good man. Be safe out there."

"Thanks, Angela." He ended the call and slid the cell into his pocket. He grabbed his day pack, attached the radio to his shoulder holster, and put on his red hardhat.

The *whump-whump* of rotor blades hit his ears as he exited the truck and leaned on it. He lowered goggles over his eyes and peered through intermittent smoke at Juliet.

He keyed his radio. "N-74 Juliet, this is Tremblay on Birch Spur Road. Have you in sight. Heading in to get a read on the fire at Hellbrook Lake. Is that where you'll draft?"

Mel's voice came back. "Copy that. But first, I'll drop off Ryan and Gunnar to help a village crew a few miles from here.

On my way back, I'll sling some drafts from the lake. Then I'll go back to pick up Ryan and Gunnar."

"Copy that. I'll be heading back to base shortly."

"Sounds good. Clear," said Mel.

Cohen heard excited voices in the background he figured were the smokejumpers onboard. He stepped off the road and hiked three quarters of a mile across the thirsty tundra. Twenty minutes later, Juliet's engine sounded in the distance. He shoved his goggles up onto his hardhat to get a glimpse of Mel's bird descending rapidly.

Something didn't sound right. Juliet's engine had a knocking sound. Then, silence. Juliet must have lost power. *Not good.*

Cohen eyed the descending helicopter as Mel maneuvered it through the auto-rotation process, using the momentum of the rotor's upward flow to keep it turning and avoid a hard impact. Cohen tried to gauge where Juliet would land, but the tall spruce hindered his view.

Sounds of chopper blades ripping through tree branches reverberated Cohen's chest. Heart thudding, he broke into a run, crashing through the brush. Dead tree branches snapped and poked him as he tore through them. He lowered his goggles to avoid losing an eye. Finally, he emerged from the dense trees surrounding a small lake.

Juliet floated upside down in the water a few hundred feet from shore.

"Holy hell!" Cohen dumped his pack and waded into the lake, taking care not to go too deep after his last lake escapade. The tail rotor still twirled as Mel's head broke the surface, his shiny white helmet easy to spot. He slowly swam toward Cohen.

"Are you the only one on board?" yelled Cohen as Mel came within shouting distance.

Mel nodded. At least he'd dropped off the men first. Mel rolled onto his back and sculled the rest of the way in, his boots dragging his legs under.

When Mel floated close enough, Cohen grabbed hold of his flight suit and tugged him onshore. He undid Mel's chin strap and eased off his helmet.

"Are you hurt, buddy? Anything broken?"

Mel panted. "Don't think so."

"I'll notify the base. They'll send a chinook to lift Juliet. Can you walk to my rig about three quarters of a mile, or do you want an airlift? Could be awhile. Every available helo is working fires." Cohen helped him to a sitting position.

"I can make it." Mel eyed Juliet's tail rotor sticking out of the water. "First time my bird has gone swimming. Took me a second to realize I was upside down in the water, she flipped over so fast."

"Juliet's officially baptized. Glad you're okay, buddy." Cohen slapped Mel's shoulder and helped him to his feet.

The two men hiked to Cohen's truck, with Mel stopping every so often to rub his knee.

COHEN TUCKED MEL SAFELY into the passenger seat of his agency rig. He then radioed Talkeetna Base to notify them Juliet was down, and to dispatch another helicopter to retrieve the smokejumpers. When he finished, he glanced at Mel, his dejected look and wet mullet resembling a dazed hippie.

"Are you sure you're okay, buddy?" Cohen returned his gaze to the road, hoping not to collide with vehicles speeding toward him. A fire engine zoomed past with headlights on, and Cohen made sure his were on as well. "Another helo is on the way to pick up Ryan and Gunnar."

"Hope it can land in this heavy smoke," said Mel, as a shadowy shape flew over them. "Holy hell, that fixed wing is going down!" he suddenly shouted, pointing to the left.

Cohen slammed the brakes and slid his window down in time to see a Cessna hit the middle of the beetle kill, nose first. The sound was horrific—crunching trees and metal, followed by abrupt silence.

"Holy shit, not another one down!" Mel was out the door, limping toward the crash.

Cohen snatched his first aid kit from the back seat and bolted after Mel. When the men arrived, fire had erupted, burning one side of the crumpled plane. He prayed the flames weren't close to the gas tank.

"We need to get those people out before the gas tank explodes!" yelled Cohen over the crackling flames igniting thirsty spruce.

The two men wrestled the back door open, where a man and a woman sat dazed in the back seat. The man struggled to unclasp his seat belt, panic in his eyes. The woman was barely conscious.

"Hold on, we'll get you out," assured Cohen, working fast to unbuckle them. He yelled over his shoulder. "Mel, get the pilot out!"

He addressed the conscious passenger. "Anyone else on board?"

"No," said the older man.

The plane had landed at an angle, so gravity was on his side as Cohen extricated the passengers. "Put your arm around my shoulder," he instructed the portly man, lifting him out.

"Help my wife first. Leave me here," the man grunted as Cohen eased him to the ground.

"I have to get you away from this aircraft," Cohen said calmly to the woman. She was barely conscious as he pulled her from the wreckage. From what he could tell, her neck and back weren't broken. He carried her, running as fast as he could to put distance between her and the plane. He set her gently on the grassy ground.

"I'll be right back," he assured her, unsure whether she heard him.

Cohen sprinted back to the plane, and Mel met him as he approached. "The pilot is dead. I'll help you carry the man."

The two men grasped each other's elbows to create a seat to carry the large gentleman. They set him next to his wife just as the gas tank exploded.

Cohen instinctively hunched over the woman to protect her from flying debris. Fortunately, none of it hit them, though Cohen felt the blast of intense heat.

"That was a close one. Don't need another fire, though." Mel pointed.

Cohen glanced up to see the wind had taken the fire from the plane and blown it through the thirsty spruce. Now two fires burned toward Talkeetna.

"Shit," muttered Cohen. "Wish we could have gotten the pilot out."

Mel blew out air. "Yeah. The woman has a broken arm, and she's wheezing. Maybe a punctured lung. She needs medical attention. The man got away with cuts and bruises and a twisted ankle. They're lucky."

"Let's load them inside the rig and I'll drive them to Alpine Clinic. This woman may have to be airlifted to Anchorage," said Cohen. Mel helped him load the injured plane passengers into the back seat.

The man cradled his wife's head in his lap and tears squeezed from his eyes. "I persuaded her into taking this flight. She said it was too smoky and we shouldn't go. We were going to the glacier near Denali, then suddenly we hit. Should have listened to her." He shook his head, clearly distressed.

"What's your name, sir?" Cohen recognized shock.

"Mike," the man breathed out.

"Mike, I need you to keep talking. Understand?" Cohen handed the radio mic to Mel. "Inform Talkeetna Base about the fixed wing crash and relay our status."

Mel alerted the fire base and medical clinic they had crash victims to transport. He twisted toward the man in the back. "Mike, keep your wife talking. Tell her she'll be okay."

Cohen's cell sounded, and he answered. "Tremblay."

"It's Angela. We haven't heard from Ryan and Gunnar. We've lost radio contact." She sounded anxious.

His brow furrowed. "I thought you dispatched a helicopter to retrieve them."

"Yes, but aviation is on hold until the smoke clears enough to fly. Plus, we heard the fire ran, and everyone had to scramble to a safety zone. We've lost contact with Ryan and Gunnar—no radio and no cell phones."

"Don't worry, Angela, they'll be all right. What's the status on Aurora Crew's fire?"

"They had to retreat. The winds were gusting, and they couldn't get a line established. The fire has already burned homes and sled dog kennels."

"Where's the leading edge of the fire?" Dread knotted Cohen's stomach.

"Just a minute. A million people are talking to me. Hold on..." Angela came back. "The head of the fire is burning toward Sleeping Lady Kennel, less than a mile away. Raynie and Kira must evacuate along with everyone else in that area."

Cohen's entire body numbed, and the phone fell from his hand.

Chapter 37

Raynie bolted from the state trooper's office near Denali Roadhouse and jumped into her truck, speeding toward Sleeping Lady Kennel. Jamen had given Kira a ride home from the trooper's office. Angela had called to report the fire was advancing toward Kam's place, and she'd dispatched the Aurora Crew to hold off the flames.

Heart pounding, Raynie strapped herself in, flinching when the seat belt touched her wound caused by Maddox's knife. By some miracle, she'd instinctively ducked when she'd pulled the trigger. All of it was a horrific blur.

As she turned onto Birch Spur Road, her handheld radio crackled with Cohen's voice. She reached for it on the passenger seat and cranked up the volume.

"Talkeetna Base, this is Tremblay. Do you copy?"

Angela's voice came back. "Copy. What do you have?"

"A fixed wing crashed a few miles down Birch Spur Road and I'm responding. Also, Mel ditched N-74 Juliet in Salmon Lake. I'm close by, so responding to that too. I'll keep you posted. Clear."

Raynie scrambled for her radio. "Tremblay, do you copy? This is Atwood."

Radio silence.

She repeated her transmission. "Tremblay, do you copy?"

No response.

Her cell phone sounded, and she fumbled it from her pocket. With one hand on the steering wheel, she peered at the Caller ID. Talkeetna Base.

She tapped her phone to answer. "Angela, Cohen's not responding."

"He's probably off the radio helping Mel and the other people," said Angela.

"I can't believe Juliet went down. I thought she was invincible. I hope the plane passengers are okay." Raynie stared ahead in disbelief. "I want to help Cohen, but I have to get to Sleeping Lady Kennel."

"Don't worry, you know Cohen can handle it." Angela sounded like she was about to cry. "There's something else, too. I can't raise Ryan or Gunnar on the radio."

"When was the last transmission?" Alarm seized Raynie's gut. She hated it when things happened in threes.

"Two hours ago, after Mel transported them to help a crew in trouble. Do you think they were onboard when Mel ditched his helo?" Fear was evident in Angela's voice.

"He probably dropped them off first. Cohen will let you know when he gets to Mel. Try not to worry."

"Working on it." Angela paused. "You'll probably pass him on the way to your place."

"Dammit, I need a clone. Hang tight. I'll keep you posted." Frustration racked her. She desperately wanted to help Cohen but had her own situation.

"Aurora Crew is on their way," said Angela. "Keep in touch." She ended the call.

Raynie peered ahead at the ominous smoke plumes as she turned onto Whispering Spruce Road. She skidded to a stop, kicking up clouds of dust, and sprinted from the truck toward the cabin. Winds were already blowing ash and debris onto Kam's property.

Kira ran out to meet her, terror on her face. "The flames are almost here! What do we do first?"

"Get the dogs out." Raynie dashed to the dog yard, where the sled dogs were staked on their drop chains. Their combined barking was so loud she couldn't hear anything else.

"Kira, back the truck up so we can load them into the boxes!"

Smoke blew over the top of the house, and fire debris and ash blew in with it.

Raynie sprinted over to the dog yard, guilt flooding her that she hadn't gotten here earlier. Not only were the dogs hungry, they'd also been exposed to this smoke. She had to get them out, and fast.

Kira backed up the truck, and the sisters opened the eight dog boxes. One by one, they unhooked the hyperactive barking dogs and loaded them into individual boxes. Their heads popped out of the round air holes.

Only then did Raynie hear Rooby barking up a storm inside the house.

"Oh my God, Rooby!" She eyed the advancing sea of flames as she sprinted toward the cabin to let out her precious golden.

"Kira! Get inside, grab only what you need, and toss it all in the back seat!" she hollered at her sister, who was loading the last sled dog.

The sisters dashed inside the cabin, each racing to their rooms. Raynie yanked the dresser open, snatched clothes, and stuffed them into her duffle. She didn't have much. She reached behind the nightstand to yank out her phone charger cord when she paused at another framed photo of her and Taydon.

She didn't take it. Instead, she grabbed the folded paper plate with Cohen's auction number Angela had given her and shoved it inside the front of her yellow fire shirt. She raced to the bathroom to grab toiletries only to spot the silver heart necklace hanging from the shower soap dish.

Everything about Taydon is in the past. Leave it.

Raynie choked back a sob, knowing this was closure. She ran to the living room and spun in a circle. Nothing out here was hers.

"My baking equipment!" she remembered, rushing to the kitchen. She flung open the cupboards and grabbed her stack of cookie sheets, the mixer, and the rest. Stuffing what she could into her large duffle, she slung it over her shoulder and bolted outside. She flung the duffle into the backseat and tossed her baking sheets to the floor.

Kira followed, tossing in her backpack, duffle, and laptop.

Raynie sprinted outside to the dog yard shed and dragged a sack of dog food to her pickup. Wincing at her shoulder pain, she hefted the sack and heaved it inside the back of the truck.

Another truck barreled down Whispering Spruce Drive and braked to a hard stop. Cohen got out and strode toward her.

Raynie ran toward him and threw her arms around him. "Oh God, Cohen! The fire is taking Sleeping Lady Kennel." She choked out a sob.

"Thank God, you're all right!" He squeezed her hard, and she was thankful for his hold on her. "I'm so sorry I didn't stay here last night."

Raynie squeezed him. "It's over with now. Is Mel all right? What about the plane crash victims?"

"They're in my truck." Cohen let go of her. "I had the ambulance meet me here since I'm staying to help the Aurora Crew."

Two fire engines pulled up in front of the trucks, and the Aurora Crew hopped out and began stretching out hose-lays. Tupa strode up to them.

"We'll hose down the house to hold off the flames."

Raynie swallowed hard. "Thanks so much, Tupa. I'll help!"

"Wait!" Cohen held up a hand. "You and Kira get the dogs out first. Take them to one of the evacuation sites."

"But I must fight this fire!" She was desperate to do her part to defend this kennel. She feared Kam returning home to a pile of ashes.

Cohen cradled her face. "Listen to me, and don't be stubborn. You were hurt last night. Don't overexert yourself. The Aurora Crew is here now."

"But Cohen, I have to help! This is my job!" She was frantic. *I can't just drive away!*

"First, get Kam's sled dog team out of here. Then come back and help." The wind gusts whipped Cohen's hair around his face as he bent to give her a quick kiss.

He lifted away and cradled her face, peering into her eyes. "I want you to know that I..."

"No-o-o!" Kira cut him off, screaming and rushing toward them. "Raynie, help!"

"What is it?" Raynie twisted from Cohen's grasp and turned to her sister. The panic in Kira's eyes terrified her.

"I can't find Rooby and Wacko! And Madonna and the puppies are missing!"

"What do you mean you can't find them?" Fresh panic ripped through Raynie. "Aren't they in the truck? Didn't you load Wacko in his dog box? And Madonna? Oh my God—the puppies!"

"I can't find Wacko. And Madonna and her puppies are gone. I've searched everywhere." Kira stared at her, wild-eyed.

"Dammit!" Raynie raced inside the house.

"Rooby? Rooby, come! Rooby!" she yelled, dashing through each room. She ran out the back door and circled the cabin, then checked each doghouse in the dog yard. No Rooby. No Wacko or Madonna's pups. In all the excitement, she'd let Rooby out of the cabin, but figured she'd stay close like she always did.

"Oh God, no!" Tears sprang to her eyes.

Cohen appeared next to them. "What's wrong?"

"Rooby, Wacko, and Madonna are all missing. So are Madonna's five puppies," Kira sobbed.

"How the hell did Madonna and the pups get out of that kennel enclosure?" Cohen grimaced. "I'll look for the dogs and the puppies. Don't worry, they can't be far. You need to get the other dogs to the fire base. Now!"

A chunk of burning wood landed next to them as the wind gusted airborne debris ahead of the fire. Water streamed on them as the Aurora Crew sprayed over the rooftop of the cabin.

An ambulance pulled up, and Cohen glanced at the couple in his truck. "I have to help load Mel and the crash victims into the ambulance."

"Promise you'll find my dogs!" The roar of the incoming blaze sucked up Raynie's words as it ate through the field next to Kam's property.

"I promise! I'm sure they fled north, into the woods. I'll head in that direction. Go!" yelled Cohen. He headed to the ambulance, where paramedics were loading the plane crash victims. Cohen helped Mel into the vehicle and slammed the door closed.

As Raynie and Kira leaped into the pickup to get Kam's dog team out of harm's way, she noted Cohen putting on his hardhat and goggles, then strapping on his fire shelter. A heavy dread shot through her and she reassured herself Cohen knew what he was doing.

Raynie changed her mind and handed Kira the truck keys. "Drive the dogs to the field behind the fire base. I'll call Trish and tell her to get you and the dogs situated. I'm staying here with Aurora Crew to protect the kennel."

"You need to come with me!" Kira cringed as her frantic eyes darted nervously toward the oncoming wall of fire. "Will you be okay?"

"You know I will." Raynie gave her sister a quick hug. "Go! You'll be fine. Just go slow through the smoke and keep your lights on. Keep your phone charged, and if you have problems, call me, okay?" Raynie hoped her urgency didn't scare her younger sister. "You can do this."

"Okay," nodded Kira, squaring her shoulders. Taking a deep breath, she climbed into the driver's seat.

Raynie waited until Kira pulled out onto Birch Spur Road before retrieving her phone and tapping Trish's number. "Kira is evacuating the dogs. She's in Kam's truck with the dog boxes. Can you square her away on the fire base field site?"

"Yes, I'm here now. I brought food from the Roadhouse and could use Kira's help getting food and beverages to evacuees who are already here."

Raynie let out a shaky breath. "It's funny what you think is important. All I could think of was to save my bakeware. You'll see it piled in the truck. Please tell Kira to feed and water the dogs, okay?"

"I'm on it," Trish assured her. "Go fight fire. Kira and the dogs will be okay."

"Two dogs are missing. And a litter of puppies," Raynie's voice broke. "And my Rooby is gone, too. Cohen went to look for them."

Raynie scanned the chaotic scene but didn't see him—only the fire engines and Aurora Crew, steadily spraying water around Kam's spacious cabin.

"Don't worry, he'll find them. Just don't do anything stupid. Stay safe. Promise?" Trish invoked a motherly tone.

"Yes," Raynie choked out, trying with all her might to hold herself together. A gust of hot wind blew ash at her. "Have to go. Talk later."

Raynie shoved the phone into her pocket, then rummaged the inside of her truck for her fire pack, making sure her fire shelter was attached. She grabbed her Pulaski and strapped on the pack when her cell sounded.

"Cohen?" she asked anxiously, staring in the direction he'd gone. It was useless to see anything with the heavy smoke.

Angela responded. "They still can't find Ryan and Gunnar and the village crew. I'm sick with worry."

Raynie's pulse quickened. "They know how to take care of themselves. This is what smokejumpers train for, remember? Hold it together, okay?" She glanced furtively at the advancing wall of flame. "I have to go. I'm helping the Aurora Crew."

She ended the call and hurried to Rego and Tara, overseeing the hose operations. She lowered her goggles over her eyes.

"Has Cohen come back?"

"Not yet!" yelled Tara, her voice diminished in the roar of flames, crackling wood, and popping rocks. She kept her hose trained on the house, trying to keep it saturated. Others on the crew were hosing down nearby fuels and vegetation to slow the flames.

Raynie knew thirsty dead spruce, even saturated, couldn't resist flame. This did nothing to calm her nerves. Worrying about the dogs, Cohen, Ryan, and Gunnar struck her with a force so strong it numbed her.

The main part of the fire tossed flaming debris ahead of it, causing spot fires. A burning piece of spruce landed on Wacko's doghouse. Raynie unspooled another hose, made sure the water pressured it, then hurried to the dog yard. Holding fast to the nozzle, she squirted the top of Wacko's doghouse.

God, Wacko, where are you? And the puppies?

A tear fell out, thinking of Rooby in this chaos. The dogs didn't stand a chance in this conflagration.

A sudden wind gust swept flames onto Kam's property, gobbling the spruce that bordered his land, destroying the understory. Flames swept the raspberry and blueberry bushes, devouring fireweed—annihilating everything and sparing nothing.

Aurora Crew had every available hose spray trained on the cabin. The wind was too strong and powered flames up and over the rooftop. Tara shouted at the crew to be careful if the fire jumped over the cabin and other structures. She barked orders into her radio and requested retardant drops.

Raynie's radio jammed with voices and somewhere in there she thought she heard Cohen but wasn't sure. An eternity passed before the drone of a spotter plane sounded overhead. Tears of relief pooled Raynie's eyes.

"Retardant ship's coming!" she yelled joyously.

"Aurora Crew, retreat to your vehicles!" ordered Tara. "Max is here with Jaws and he's dropping a load!"

Raynie, Tara, Rego, and Tupa bolted for one engine and clambered inside. The rest of the crew piled inside the other two engines. The unmistakable rumble in their chests indicated the jet was approaching for a drop. Raynie tearfully prayed as she watched the doghouses burn. The entire dog yard was ablaze, and flames licked the back side of Kam's cabin.

Everything in the truck vibrated as the retardant pilot opened the jet's gates and cascaded its load over the kennel. The truck bounced, as a glop of Phos-chek hit it, turning the windshield a bright red.

"I hope that quells the flames." Raynie switched on the wipers, peering through the orange red streaks as the rubber smeared the glass.

Rego slid a window down. "We'd better get these vehicles out of here." His expression was grim. It was now up to the aerial firefighters to save Sleeping Lady Kennel.

"We can't leave Cohen here!" Raynie's heart thundered a zillion miles a minute.

"We'll come back for him, don't worry," said Tara. "Come on, we have to go!"

Raynie understood the logic. After all, she'd made a similar call when she commanded the Hiland Fire. Only this time, Cohen's life was at stake.

She gave Tara a frantic look. "I have to move Cohen's truck."

"You have your own vehicle to move. Someone else will get Cohen's," countered Tara. "Do you have his keys?"

"Dammit! Cohen has them." Raynie's stomach flipped as she glanced helplessly at his truck.

"We're out of time," urged Tara. "Get in your own rig." Tara pulled out, leading the fire vehicle procession.

Raynie spotted the last fire engine, with Rego and Tupa in the front seats. She jumped out of her rig and ran up to the driver's side. Rego slid the window down.

"I need help to get Cohen's vehicle out of here. Do either of you know how to hotwire a truck? Come on, Rego, you're from the Bronx," she coaxed, urgency in her voice.

Rego pointed. "In case you haven't noticed, there's a fire bearing down on our asses."

"If it were your truck, you'd want someone to do the same," Raynie pointed out.

The men exchanged insane looks and Tupa groaned in exasperation.

"The things I do for love!" He pushed open the passenger door and ran with her to Cohen's shiny pickup. "This rig better be unlocked to release the hood, or we're out of luck."

Raynie prayed Cohen hadn't locked his truck. Squeezing her eyes closed, she gripped the searing door handle, intense heat penetrating her leather gloves. A surge of relief flashed through her as she flung the door open. Smoke and fire retardant in the air tasted metallic, leeching the moisture from her lips. She fumbled for the hood latch on the driver's side floor. Finding it, she gave it a yank, releasing the hood.

"There you go, Tupa!"

Tupa lifted it and leaned into the engine. He moved to the driver's side and kneeled on the dirt road, reaching up behind the steering wheel.

"I need some light on this," he grunted.

"Okay, hang on." Raynie pawed through her pack for her headlamp. She flipped it on and shined it on Tupa's busy hands. The engine roared to life.

Tupa straightened. "Now I suppose you want me to drive it out."

"Would you mind?" She scanned the woods. "Cohen is in there somewhere and we have to get him out!"

"He can take care of himself. Come on!" shouted Tupa.

A thunderous boom shuddered Raynie. She snapped a horrified gaze toward the flames gobbling Kam's cabin. While the retardant drop had slowed the onslaught, it hadn't stopped it. This fire had a savage force of will, ripping through tinder dry spruce, each tree a torch. Towering flames spread with the speed of a runaway train, faster than anyone could run.

"Oh God, no! Tupa, oh my God!" Hysteria seized her. She choked up and froze, eyes wide at the catastrophe playing out before her. A helpless tear leaked out and rolled down her cheek.

"Look at me, Atwood!" Tupa's hands gripped her shoulders. He lifted a hand, pointing to his eyes, then hers. "Don't lose your shit! You said this is what we train for. Your words." He was right, and she knew it.

She nodded, fighting to compose herself.

Tupa patted her shoulder and waved Rego to go on ahead. He climbed into Cohen's truck, waving Raynie to hers. "Let's get the fuck out now. Don't worry, we'll find Tremblay."

Raynie raced to her vehicle, swiping at her cheeks. She cranked the engine and followed Tupa, eyes fixed on Cohen's brake lights, wishing he was at the wheel. She fixated on the *Beautiful British Columbia* license plate, praying that someday Cohen would take her to see Canada—if she saw him again. She scolded herself.

Don't think like that!

She must find Cohen. As soon as she can safely walk into the black, she must find him.

Alive.

Chapter 38

Cohen wasn't crazy about the idea of walking into the unburned green to look for Raynie's dogs. He knew Rooby was dear to her, as was Wacko in his goofy, crazy way. But Madonna and her puppies gave him cause for concern.

It baffled him how the gate latch had been opened in the kennel, enabling Madonna and her puppies to escape. He figured they couldn't have gone far, because the puppies were too small to run any distance. The dogs had turned to their instincts for survival and scampered off when the predatory fire roared at them.

He kept a careful eye on fire behavior, thanking his instructors for all the training and fire situations where he'd calculated fire behavior, and guessing where fires would be heading next. No time for guessing now. He'd lost count of how many of the ten standard firefighting orders he was violating, and there would be hell to pay later on. He would deal with the consequences later. In the meantime, he had to rely on his skills and instincts.

Raynie counted on him to find the dogs and he didn't want to let her down. Cohen picked his way through the tundra, whistling and calling for Rooby and Wacko. He hoped Madonna would be close by.

"Rooby! Come!" he repeatedly hollered, smoke twirling in front of him with every step. He had GPS on his phone, but with spotty cell service in remote areas like this, he also carried a compass and a topographic map for backup.

Animals fled from fire, so Cohen gambled on the fact that the dogs would've headed north of Sleeping Lady Kennel. He'd made sure Raynie knew the direction he intended to go. He just had to hope the fire wouldn't catch up to him before he found her dogs.

"Rooby! Wacko? Where the hell are you guys?" he yelled at the top of his lungs. He whistled repeatedly, but no canines came bounding with wagging tails.

By now, the Aurora Crew would have hosed down Kam's cabin and the grounds surrounding Sleeping Lady Kennel. He prayed the sled dog musher wouldn't return to a smoking ruin.

A gust of wind thrust a snap, crackle, and roar straight into him from the runaway head of the fire. Smoke preceded it so thick that Cohen had to don his goggles and cover his nose and mouth with his bandana. He had to lower it when he hollered for the dogs.

He peered left and right as he hiked, to see if there was any place the dogs could have taken refuge. Sled dogs had a strong denning instinct, so he inspected old bear holes to see if Madonna had sought safety with her puppies.

A sharp bark snapped his head up to attention. He listened, but the roaring fire made it impossible to hear anything clearly. There it was again—another bark. This time to his left. He dashed toward the sound, hollering and whistling.

He stopped and removed his glove to insert fingers into his mouth, whistling as loud as he could. With a yip and a crash through the dried foliage, out bounded Rooby, eagerly searching for Cohen, tail waving from side to side like a golden feathery flag.

"Here girl, come here," He waved the retriever to him.

Rooby scurried up to him, madly wagging her butt from side to side, then curved her head toward her rear in a submissive stance, whimpering.

Cohen squatted to pet her. "Where's Madonna and the puppies, Rooby? Where's Wacko?"

Rooby barked, and Wacko appeared from the dense stand of trees. He barked and yipped, his one ear flopped over in his usual goofy look.

"Take me to the puppies. Where are they?"

Cohen cajoled the dogs as if they understood his questions. He wished he had treats. He walked in the direction where they'd bounded out of the woods. Rooby ran ahead to a small, grassy clearing that surrounded a pile of rotted wood.

As he approached, it wasn't a woodpile, but an old Alaskan cache house—the kind hunters and trappers built to store food supplies up off the ground. This one was still intact, although it had fallen over and rested on the ground at a slight angle.

Cohen's boots crunched sticks and brush, as he neared the old cache. Madonna emerged from inside of it, and pulled her lips back in a low growl, and the hair on her back bristled.

"Hey Madonna, hey girl," said Cohen in a soft voice. "Let's get you and your pups to safety, okay?" He willed her to understand, hoping the protective sled dog wouldn't attack. He had to win her over if he was to get them out before the fire burned through.

Smoke had gathered in the clearing and the roar of advancing flames grew louder. Rooby and Wacko stood staring at him, their tongues hanging out. They were thirsty.

Cohen unsnapped the canvas strap of his canteen holder and unscrewed the lid on his water bottle. Pouring water into his cupped palm, he offered it first to Rooby, then Wacko. The dogs lapped greedily, wanting more, licking their lips to get every drop.

He reached out to Madonna, sheltering in the dilapidated cache house. Pouring water into his cupped palm, he coaxed her.

"Come on, Madonna, drink." All the while, he cautiously gauged the smoky tendrils twisting their way into the little clearing.

The sled dog perked her ears, tilting her head at hearing her name. Sniffing his hand, she licked her lips. Cohen eased it under her snout, and Madonna licked his palm clean. He offered more, and she lapped the water from his hand. Her pups seemed to be all right, snuggled together, asleep.

Rooby and Wacko wagged tails and sat, waiting for another handful of water. Cohen gave them each one, then stood and took a long pull from the bottle and snapped it back into place. He removed his fire pack and rummaged through it to pull out a burlap bag used to beat out flames when spruce boughs weren't handy. He'd have to carry the pups.

Shaking out the bag, Cohen stared inside at the rough material, the pungent burlap smell wrinkling his nose. He'd have to line the bag before putting the puppies inside. Quickly shucking his yellow Nomex fire shirt, he then stripped off his T-shirt to wrap around the tiny pups.

Rooby stared at him, her tongue hanging out.

"Don't get any ideas," he muttered jokingly, as she wagged at him.

He slipped back into his yellow shirt and shouldered his fire pack just as Madonna left her shelter to sniff around and tinkle. He seized the opportunity to nestle the five pups inside his T-shirt, then set them inside the burlap sack. The husky hurried back to see what he was doing. He showed her the puppies, then he gently positioned the bag over his shoulder, the litter of pups resting on his back. Madonna barked, then she stood back and growled.

"Madonna, your pups are fine. Come on, let's go."

He and the dogs had to get the hell out of the unburned green—the most dangerous place to be next to a runaway blaze.

Cohen lifted his cell. No bars. *Dammit!*

Checking his compass, he figured going west would be the quickest way to cut across the path of the fire. Eventually, he'd hit Birch Spur Road and catch a ride back to town. Turning west, he called the dogs to follow.

"Rooby! Wacko, come!" The golden and the goofy sled dog happily followed, but Madonna retreated to the cache house and squatted next to it.

Cohen turned around, disappointed she hadn't followed. "Madonna, come!"

The dog didn't budge.

Sighing in frustration, he rested the burlap sack on the ground, peeking to make sure the pups were okay. Two squirmed while the others slept, but mostly they seemed fine.

Digging through his pack again, he found a coil of nylon rope used to tie down rain-fly tarps when spike-camping on fires.

Reshouldering the pack, he uncoiled the rope, and tied it to Madonna's collar.

With one hand holding the puppies in place over the pack, he used the other to stretch the rope straight behind her like a musher. He yelled a command to the sled dog.

"Madonna, hike!"

As if on autopilot, Madonna stood at full attention, then took off trotting, with the end of the line wrapped around Cohen's fist. When she'd pulled it taut, she kept going, nearly yanking Cohen off his feet.

"Haw!" Cohen commanded, and the husky veered to the left, pointing west, the direction he needed her to go. Simulating a sled pull was a gamble, but at least it got the husky up and moving. He wasn't sure he could also carry her out with his full load of pack and puppies.

Once Madonna took off, Cohen had to run fast to keep up. Rooby and Wacko trotted along on either side, hopping deftly over downed timber or rocks that Cohen tripped on every now and then with his clunky fire boots.

A strong wind gusted thick, choking smoke straight into them, followed by the jet engine roar of a raging fire storm, and the crack of exploding wood. The fizzing and popping from superheated timber sounded like a firearm on auto-fire.

He scanned the area for an optimal place to deploy his fire shelter. Nothing optimal in this dense timber, thicker than dog hair; dogs and human would surely die. Flaming debris rained down on him. Rooby yelped when a burning chunk bounced off her back.

Dammit, we have to find somewhere away from these trees!

He couldn't live with himself if he were to survive, and the dogs didn't. He'd never be able to face Raynie. He wished she were there, firing snarky comments at him, helping him figure out a solution. But she wasn't there; he was on his own.

God, I've never needed anyone the way I need Raynie right now.

A spray of sparks flew ahead of the main fire, smoldering in the treetops ahead of Cohen. A spot fire ignited to his right, spooking the dogs. Wacko leaped to his left to walk with Rooby. The puppies whimpered, and Madonna lifted on her hind legs to sniff the burlap sack.

Cohen made an exasperated noise. The dogs looked up at him.

"Shit damn, now which way do I go?" he asked them, perplexed.

Cohen fumbled the topo map from his pocket that he had pre-folded to his location. No bodies of water nearby, but he saw symbols showing wetlands. This area was famous for being boggy, and he had to find a bog and fast. He jammed the map back into his pocket.

"Hike! Hike!" Madonna sprinted forward, and Cohen ran as fast as he could holding onto the rope attached to her collar.

Smoke choked him. Flames rapidly advanced, and he only had nanoseconds to decide.

Out of nowhere, a cow moose and her calf bolted out in front of Madonna on a dead run. Madonna gave chase, and Cohen hoped the moose wouldn't veer in a different direction.

He ran as fast as he could, trying not to trip on rocks and tree roots. The husky seemed intent on catching the moose, running so fast Cohen's lungs hurt. The cow moose suddenly kicked up water, and she and the calf splashed through it. They'd entered the wetlands, as Cohen had hoped. The moose disappeared into the spruce.

"Whoa!" yelled Cohen, to halt Madonna. Stopping in the shallows, the parched dogs eagerly lapped water.

"Hike!" he yelled, and Madonna led them to a bigger clearing with deeper water.

Cohen could have kissed the moose for leading them there. To his delight, he stood knee deep in the water. Still not the safest place, but better than nothing. The wildlife had long gone.

"Whoa!" he hollered to Madonna. "Good dog!"

The husky stopped and circled back to check on her puppies. Rooby and Wacko were in water up past their legs, but they didn't seem to mind. The water was a temporary relief in this conflagration now surrounding them. The dogs continued lapping water as if it would vanish.

This would be a tricky maneuver, but Cohen had no time to lose. Ash and embers singed his tongue as if the devil licked it. Stifling air pressed down. No saliva. He couldn't swallow. Time to deploy his fire shelter.

How the hell will I fit three adult dogs, me, and a sack load of puppies inside this shelter?

Cohen stuck the neck of the burlap sack between his teeth and clamped them together, as he couldn't set the puppies down in the water. He reached behind and retrieved his fire shelter. He tugged it from the case, yanked the cords, and shook it out.

"Rooby! Wacko! Come here!" he commanded, spitting around the burlap clenched in his teeth. The terrified dogs sidled in next to him, and he crouched down, spreading the fire shelter over them.

He tied the end of Madonna's rope around the neck of the sack and draped it around his neck, so the sack hung on his left side. As long as Madonna sat in front of him and wouldn't bolt, this might work. He wrapped a corner of the shelter around Rooby and another around Wacko and held the corners with each hand.

This has to work.

He had no other choice. They couldn't outrun the blaze. He tasted ash, a bitter mixture of wood and dirt. The fire bellowed like a savage dragon, hellbent on destroying in the blink of an eye what took decades to grow and mature.

Don't panic. Keep my shit together. If I panic, the dogs will, and we'll all turn into ash.

Cohen held the shelter down over the dogs and himself as best he could, pressing the dogs close to him. Flames swept the clearing from all directions, obliterating all sound except their tornadic roar. Crouching low in the water, he did his best to keep the puppies above the boggy surface—and prayed the dogs wouldn't panic and run—or they'd all die.

A dog barked; Cohen didn't know who. Another yipped and cried. Madonna howled and Cohen felt her tense and brace, as if ready to run.

"Whoa, Madonna, whoa Madonna..."

He didn't know how many times he repeated the husky's name as the raging fire whipped around them. The natural water barrier certainly helped, but the winds tore at his shelter. He gripped it so tight, he worried his hands would cramp and lose their hold. Despite his layers of protective Nomex, heat encased his fire shelter and pierced him as if he was the delicacy cooking on a closed outdoor grill.

The hot destructive flames licked at the very edges of his shelter. He prayed it wouldn't melt and collapse on him. A burning tree crashed into the bog in front of them. Madonna yelped and yanked herself away from their huddle.

Cohen watched helplessly as the sled dog bolted, jerking the burlap sack from around his neck and dragging the bundle of puppies through the water—straight toward the destructive flames.

Chapter 39

The Aurora Crew's procession of three fire engines and two crew-cab pickups pulled into a scenic overlook, a perfect vantage point to watch the air attack operation in the valley below. They were on hold for the time being, waiting for the green light to resume their fire fight.

Raynie swung her truck into a parking spot in front of a large, flat rock. She climbed out and perched on it, binoculars trained toward Sleeping Lady Kennel. Thick black smoke rose in billowing mushroom-shaped clouds, rising higher and higher, causing a tightness in her chest. The retardant ships picked their way around the smoke for clear views of their drop zones.

She was grief stricken at the overall destruction. Not only was Sleeping Lady Kennel a total loss, other homes and kennels were too. She observed the smoking ruins and sucked in a breath.

I'm a complete and utter failure. Here I am, a firefighter, and couldn't save Kam's kennel.

At least she'd gotten the dogs out. An overwhelming surge of guilt made her want to run screaming down the road.

"There goes Max for another drop!" Tara joined Raynie on the rock and they each trained their binoculars on the DeHavilland Canada Dash 8-400AT air tanker, dropping slurry down below.

Raynie watched the red gel float gracefully down to its mark, remembering when Cohen said it was performance art in the sky. She longed to hold him. Laugh with him. Argue with him.

Please let Cohen and the dogs be okay.

"Tara, I know I shouldn't be scared, but I am. Cohen is down there in the green, and we lost Kam's sled dog kennel..." she choked up.

"I'm sure he's fine. Though I daresay his decision to hike into the green wasn't the best. But try not to worry. He's either walked out with the dogs or he's hunkered in a safety zone." Tara put her arm around Raynie's shoulder and squeezed it.

"I'm sorry. I've been consumed with my worries and forgot what you must be going through, not hearing from Ryan and Gunnar." More guilt ripped through Raynie. She ran a palm over her face.

Tara smiled. "Ryan, Gunnar, and Cohen are the Delta Force of fire. They know what they're doing."

"I know." Raynie felt helpless as a bystander. "I just want to get back down there and fight that damn fire."

"Not yet." Tara lifted her chin. "Raynie, I'm going to tell you something that you may or may not know. But now seems a good time to tell you. Were you aware that Cohen recommended you for the chief of operations position at Talkeetna Wildfire Base?"

Raynie numbed for a moment. "He what?"

"Cohen told Doss to hire you in the chief position because you're an outstanding leader. Doss told your state boss. Angela saw the paperwork and told me. You aren't supposed to know, so zip it." Tara gave her a broad smile.

"Wait a minute, so Cohen did that?" Raynie stumbled back. "Are you messing with me? Because if it's true, that's like winning the wildland fire lottery for me."

"It's true. I wouldn't fib about something like that." Tara flashed a wider smile. "But that's not the cool part."

"What could be cooler than that?" Raynie was enamored with the first part.

"Cohen had recommended you to Doss in the beginning when you two didn't get along. He had confidence in you from the start."

"He did?" Raynie turned her head away, recalling the awful way she'd treated him at first. She bit her lip to mask the intense emotions bubbling up inside her, but her voice still wavered. "Well, that's just like a firefighter, isn't it? Pisses you off one minute, then trips over himself doing something nice in the next."

When Tara saw the well of emotion, she hugged Raynie. "One thing I know about Cohen. He feels things intensely, and when you win his loyalty, it's forever. And you've won it." She let go and stepped back. "And it doesn't hurt that he's so dang smart."

Raynie smiled. "I mean, like, yeah...Princeton."

Tara nodded. "I know, right? Doss and I saw that on his resume when he applied last year. Cohen asked us to keep it confidential, so I've never said anything. I'm surprised he told you."

"Well, I was surprised he chose firefighting over structural engineering." Raynie gazed into the distance. "Took me a while to realize his good points. Like when I saw his protective side when Maddox showed up at my house."

"And Cohen saw *your* protective side when you helped him at Salmon Lake," said Tara. "He looked at you with such adoration that day I saw fireworks explode between you two. I don't know anyone who'd pay two thousand bucks to date their own girlfriend."

I don't need exploding fireworks. I only want Cohen.

"Aurora Crew, do you copy?" Tara's radio crackled with Doss's voice. "Air attack gave the green light for crews to go back in. The Hellbrook Fire has slowed, and I want a hotshot crew to douse hotspots."

Tara responded. "Copy that. We're on our way."

"Also, Ryan O'Connor and Gunnar Alexanderson are on their way back," said Doss. "We sent a helo to retrieve them."

Tara's hand flew to her forehead in relief. "Thanks for that info. Aurora Crew is on the way back to the Hellsbrook Fire."

"Copy that. Clear," said Doss.

Tara holstered her radio, looking sheepish. "I didn't tell Doss that Cohen hiked into the green to find the dogs, since he violated firefighting regs. Doss doesn't need to know."

"Cohen will appreciate that. But his honesty will get the better of him, so I'm sure he'll come clean in his after-action report." Raynie let out a shaky breath. "I still can't raise him on his cell or on the radio. Excuse me, I have to visit the restroom."

Raynie stepped briskly into the woods and stepped between birch and spruce to put some distance between herself and the others. She stopped and leaned against the white bark of a birch. Her trembling hands covered her face as she uncorked the firestorm of emotion, she'd bottled to keep a brave front.

Out poured all the fear, guilt, love. Fear, apprehension, love. Fear, gratitude, love. Always the fear.

But mostly, always the love.

THE FIRE VEHICLES ROLLED to a gradual stop at what used to be Sleeping Lady Kennel. Raynie sobered as she scanned the blackened destruction. Small fires burned close to the ground on parts of the cabin. She couldn't tell where the rooms had been.

The only identifiable remains were the charred fridge and stone fireplace.

Members of the Aurora Crew climbed out of their vehicles. No one said a word as they picked their way along the road and stood in a crooked line, surveying the smoking devastation.

Raynie strode up to Tara. "Cohen headed north last I saw him. We should drive along Birch Spur Road to search for him there. He would have walked either east or west, to get away from the running head. I'm thinking west, toward the road."

"That makes sense. The dogs couldn't walk through the black without burning their feet," reasoned Tara.

"Not to be a Dora downer, but it'll be short of a miracle if he rescues all eight dogs from that flipping mess," said Raynie. "Let's leave some of the crew here in case he shows, and the rest of us drive up the road."

"Everyone hear that?" Tara called out. "Half stay here, half go with Raynie." Tara deferred to her, and Raynie appreciated it.

Raynie leaped into her truck and punched the accelerator. Crossing fingers that she wouldn't crash into anything, she sped through a layer of yellow smoke so thick she could grab it with her hands. The sun's red ball poked through, and she viewed it as a beacon of hope.

As she guesstimated how far Cohen may have hiked in this direction, she peered into the charred sticks that used to be black spruce trees. The fire left tufts at the treetops, looking like spiky aliens scattered over the landscape. After the fire swept through the boreal forest, all that remained was a barren, soundless void.

No bugs. No birds.

Nothing.

The deafening silence after a destructive fire had always torn her heart into a million pieces. Regret sliced through her like a scythe.

What if Cohen died in the fire? Oh God, I can't lose another love again. Why didn't I tell Cohen how I felt about him?

She was so preoccupied with her thoughts, she'd parked, climbed out, and had stepped into the smoking black without remembering how she got there. Her entire body numbed.

Liz, Tara, and Kenzie followed. "We'll walk in a grid, like we do in mop-up. Spread out fifteen feet apart. I'll track it on my topo map." Tara waved her map, worn out and folded, with dirty corners.

Liz lifted her phone. "I have a few bars, so I'll track our position with the GPS." She hesitated, darting her eyes at Raynie. "We thought it best to have us three here for moral support, in case...well, in case..." She trailed off.

Raynie finished for her. "In case we don't find Cohen alive. Thanks, I appreciate it."

Fires still burned in the valley, and the breeze brought the smoke in. The women cinched bandanas over their noses and mouths as they worked their way through the pungent reek of the freshly blackened forest.

"Alright, let's check out this hellscape," said Raynie, stepping toward it, fearing what they'd find.

"Watch out for squirrel caches," cautioned Tara. "And smoldering tree pits."

"And falling snags," intoned Liz.

Raynie's chest grew heavier with each step she took. Not knowing what they would find was excruciating. Her head pounded with smoke and stress. Her insides hollowed like an empty tomb, each time she thought of Cohen.

She also worried about Kam, but by now he had probably heard the unwelcome news about Sleeping Lady Kennel from other mushers in town. She took out her cell and tapped Cohen's number for the zillionth time.

Nothing.

Tara keyed her radio every so often. "Tremblay, do you copy?"

Silence. Although Tara hadn't told Doss about Cohen's quest to find the dogs, Doss probably knew by now with radio silence on Cohen's end.

Raynie played back all the moments she'd spent with Cohen, from the moment they'd met that first day on the Eagle River Hiland Fire. She chuckled to herself at the way they'd irritated each other.

Cohen had been the persistent one, the patient one. He'd burst through the barricades she'd thrown up to him whenever he tried for a piece of her heart. And now? He'd won all of it. She tried to pinpoint when, exactly. For sure, when he'd jumped onto that stage waving his auction number with the winning bid.

Or was it before that, when they'd worked together commanding the Denali Creek fire, or maybe it was that first kiss next to the river?

Cohen touched her in a way Taydon never did. She wanted to climb inside Cohen's soul, so she could live there forever with his honesty, bravery, and kindness. He could question her decisions all he wanted, if he'd only walk out of this alive.

She let out a sob, then steeled herself. She stepped onto the wet, spongy ground and surveyed the area.

"We hit a bog!"

Liz hollered back. "I stepped in it, too."

In the water up ahead, Raynie spotted something red. She splashed toward it, then stopped and stared. Bending over, she lifted a large red T-shirt. She shook it out and gasped. *Salmon Arm Wildland Firefighters* displayed on one side of the dripping shirt.

"Oh, God!" she shrieked. "I found Cohen's T-shirt!" She pressed it to her chest as if it were a long-lost treasure.

The others hurried over, scrutinizing the shirt. "He obviously came through here. But why did he take off his T-shirt?" Raynie whirled in a circle, trying to find out which direction Cohen might have headed.

"Let's get back out to the road." Raynie's heart sped up.

Tara's eyes widened. "He might be there by now!"

"Come on!" Raynie sprinted back the way they'd come, unconcerned whether the others kept up. She hoped beyond hope Cohen would be there, waiting for them. It took her a good thirty minutes to reach Birch Spur Road. She hadn't realized they'd walked so far.

Finding her way through the smoking black, she finally reached the road. She scanned the vehicles, but no sign of Cohen or the dogs. Soon the other women appeared from the charred landscape and opened the doors to the vehicles to munch granola bars and sip water from water bottles.

Tara tried Cohen on the radio again. Nothing.

Raynie glanced up at more smoke billowing in their direction and gave up, wondering which fire it was from since much of the Mat Su Valley was in flames. She took off her hardhat and shook out her damp, sweaty hair, then removed her goggles.

A movement caught her eye in the billowing smoke a few hundred yards away. A golden retriever and an Alaskan husky plodded out of the smoke and stopped, their heads craned back toward something. Her breath caught.

And there he was.

Cohen appeared from the billowing smoke, almost in slow motion like a scene from a disaster movie, striding across the black with Madonna at his side. In one arm, he held two puppies. His other hand gripped a bag slung over his shoulder.

"Cohen! Here Rooby, here Wacko!" Raynie shouted at the top of her lungs. Her water bottle slipped from her hand, and she sprinted across the charred earth. She laughed, cried, she didn't know what, turning her face to the sky.

"Thank God!"

"Go get Raynie," Cohen commanded the dogs in a raspy voice. Rooby barked and ran toward her favorite human.

"Rooby-Doo! Come here, oh Rooby!" She ran toward the golden and fell to the ground, hugging her, kissing her, letting

Rooby lick her face. The dog wagged and whimpered, and Wacko nosed in for his share. He, too, licked her face.

Raynie scratched his ears, gazing at the man she loved as he moved toward her like a heavenly apparition. She sprang to her feet.

"Cohen! Thank God, you're all right!"

"Why wouldn't I be?" He flashed the biggest, most beautiful smile she'd ever seen on his gorgeous face. "Took me a while, but I found the dogs."

Cohen's yellow shirt was unbuttoned, revealing his bare chest, covered in ash and soot. Not a trace of hair on that lovely chest—apparently it had burned off.

"Someone, take these pups, please." His voice dripped with exhaustion.

"We'll get the pups. You get Cohen," whispered Tara, elbowing Raynie. She turned to Liz and Kenzie. "Come on, ladies, grab a puppy! Good to see you, Tremblay," said Tara, striding toward him.

Raynie knew Tara had been just as worried. She also knew Tara wouldn't go easy on Cohen for hiking into the green next to an uncontrolled blaze. After all, if Raynie had been his supervisor, she would have read him the riot act for violating several of the watchout orders.

He was safe now. That was the important thing.

Liz and Kenzie hurried to take the two puppies and welcome Cohen. They relieved him of the burlap bundle with the rest of the whimpering pups inside and rushed to get all the canines some water to drink.

Tara spoke on her radio. "Aurora Crew, Tremblay is here."

Rego radioed they were on their way.

Raynie couldn't take her eyes off Cohen. She knew he was beyond fatigued, but to her, he was a vision that reduced her to tears.

"Get over here, Atwood," said Cohen in a husky voice, with outstretched arms. "No need for tears."

She rushed to him, laughing. And laughed some more.

Cohen lifted her, and she wrapped her legs around his waist. She clung to him with such intensity, he grunted and coughed. "Atwood, I can't breathe."

"Why didn't you answer us on the radio? We called and called."

"Drowned my radio in the swamp." Cohen walked slowly, nuzzling her ear. "I never want to lose you. Ever. That's all I could think about."

"I don't know what I would have done if you hadn't come back." Her voice shook. "You shouldn't have risked your life for the dogs."

"Didn't do it for them—I did it for you." His emotion was apparent in the powerful way he held her. "You know I love you, right?"

"Been wanting to hear you say that since forever." Raynie hugged him tight, hearing the words she now wished she'd said first. She cradled his face to kiss him. He tasted like smoke. She removed his hard hat and tossed it to the ground.

"You're no longer a blond," she teased, fingering his sooty, shorter hair. She peered closer. "The fire gave you a haircut, and your eyebrows are gone."

He reached up to feel them. "At least my skin didn't broil. It sure felt like it did, though."

"Don't worry, you're still pretty." She kissed where each eyebrow had been.

"No matter what happens from now on, I won't worry you that way again." The way he said it made her breath catch.

Cohen set her back on the ground, and she picked up his hardhat. "Let's get you back to the base. You must have swallowed barrels of smoke," she said, leading him to her truck.

"You could say that," he said, his voice raspy.

Tara and the others had the tailgate down and had lifted Madonna onto the truck bed, so she could nurse her pups. Kenzie poured water into several cups and let all three dogs drink as much as they wanted. She had to keep refilling the cups.

"Glad to see you, Cohen," said Tara, clasping his hand and shaking it. "Got a little tense there for a while. I didn't want to report a missing firefighter."

"For the official record, I wasn't missing—just out of radio contact and a tad delayed on a rescue," he said, wiping a singed brow.

Tara chuckled, shaking her head. "Although you violated God knows how many of the ten standard firefighting orders."

"Don't worry, I'll fill out an after-action incident report."

Raynie glanced at Tara with a wide grin. "See? I told you."

Liz moved up and squeezed his arm. "Your lady love was beside herself. You worried the frigging daylights out of her...and the rest of us."

Raynie's eyes darted to Cohen's empty belt. "So, you deployed your fire shelter?"

"Yep." Cohen explained how he'd found Rooby and Wacko, and how they led him to Madonna and the puppies in the old cache house. And how he couldn't get Madonna to follow unless he went into mushing mode. His dramatic description of deploying the fire shelter to cover him, three adult dogs, and a sack of puppies, was short of miraculous. He had everyone laughing by the end with his funny depictions of dog behavior.

"A burning tree fell next to us and scared Madonna. She bolted, and I had the sack of puppies attached to the same rope I had her on. Luckily, I grabbed the burlap sack just as she dragged it away from the shelter. I yanked the rope she was tied to and got her back under the shelter. By that time, the main push of the fire had blown through, but I still had to keep all of us under that damn shelter."

Cohen paused, wiping his forehead. "I babbled like an idiot to keep those dogs still. I said the Pledge of Allegiance and prayed a Hail Mary—then wound up singing Christmas carols—couldn't remember the words to anything else." He chuckled, shaking his head.

Raynie knew it hadn't been a laughing matter. "I can't imagine the horror you experienced when the fire blew through that bog."

"I can," said Tara. "Burnovers suck when you're trapped in a fire shelter."

"Wacko burned his paws. I think that's why he's limping." Cohen bent to scratch the husky's flopped ear.

Kenzie lifted Wacko up to the truck bed and inspected his paws. She did the same for Rooby and Madonna. "Their pads are raw, but mostly okay. You should probably have the vet examine them."

"Thanks, Kenzie, I'll do that." Raynie turned her attention to Cohen and moved close to him. As long as she lived, she'd forever remember the way he'd materialized from the billowing smoke in slow motion, like a hot firefighter beer commercial.

The rest of Aurora Crew pulled up, and everyone bailed out.

"Welcome back from the bowels of hell, Tremblay!" shouted Rego, as he strode toward Cohen and man-slapped his back. Cohen coughed, stirring Raynie's protective instincts.

"Go easy on this guy. He's a smoke-eater." She was concerned about his lungs, especially after she pulled him from Salmon Lake on the last fire. She patted his arm. "You need medical attention, my friend."

"I'm fine," said Cohen, coughing up a lung.

"You made me get my knee checked, so I'm making you get a lung check," she said firmly. "This isn't up for debate, Mr. Dog Saver."

Tupa shook Cohen's hand and deadpanned, "You know better than to argue with this woman, brah. She'll take your head off."

"Tell me about it." Cohen raised what was left of his brows, and everyone laughed.

"Raynie and I saved your rig from torching." Tupa pointed at Cohen's truck parked on the side of the road. "Sorry, brah, we had to hotwire it since you had the keys."

Cohen's eyes widened as his hand flew to his pants pocket. He lifted out his truck keys and jiggled them. He glanced at Raynie's nodding head, then back to Tupa. "Thanks, I owe you both one." He winked at Raynie, flipping her heart over.

She was thankful to hear everyone's lighthearted voices after the day's tragic events. Cohen was truly the man of the hour, evident by the expressions on everyone's faces. Raynie's jaw dropped, listening to him recount the earlier part of his day;

helping Mel after ditching N-74 Juliet and extricating the victims from the plane crash.

Raynie had come full circle with her judgement of Cohen Tremblay: she now had profound admiration and respect for him.

What an incredibly stark contrast to my first impression.

A twinge of guilt poked at Raynie for having misjudged him. She stepped away to make the dreaded call to Kam. As she'd suspected, he'd already heard Sleeping Lady Kennel was a total loss and he was in the process of boarding a plane to Anchorage.

When Raynie ended the call, Cohen had finished briefing the crew. As everyone prepared to go, he trained his gaze on her.

"And now for the next order of business. It seems I have a two-thousand-dollar date owed to me."

Raynie suddenly remembered. She reached inside her fire shirt and pulled out the now crumpled paper plate, holding it high.

"And here's the winning bid!"

Cohen grinned, walking slowly toward her. "I'm going to kiss you now. Right here, in front of everybody. You got a problem with that?"

"We sure don't!" yelled Rego, followed by laughter. "This I gotta see."

Raynie placed her hands on her hips. "Tremblay, don't *say* you're going to kiss me. It ruins the moment. Just do it, already!"

"My mother taught me to always ask permission." Despite his bone-deep exhaustion, he still had a swagger.

"That never stopped you before." She gave him a curious look. "Who was your mother anyway, the attorney general?"

"She's the Minister of Justice for Canada." Cohen came to a halt and stretched his arms wide, summer-sky eyes sparkling on his sooty face. Snatching the wrinkled paper plate, he swooped in and swooned Raynie, plundering her mouth in an over-the-top display.

She tasted smoke.

"Whoo-ee!" erupted Tupa and several others, causing Raynie to laugh into Cohen's mouth.

When he finished kissing her, he set her on her feet. "Don't worry, you'll meet my mother, eh," he said in his exaggerated Canadian accent that made her want to climb him like Denali Mountain.

"So, you'll be reconnecting with your mom and dad?" Raynie put her hands together. "That makes me happy. I want to meet Shelly."

"You will." The way he said it had her thinking their new relationship would last long after the fire season ended.

"Let's give them more to cheer about," joked Cohen, then deepened his kiss. He seemed to enjoy the hoopla, and he played it up big time.

"Hold that pose for next year's calendar!" Liz cried out, whipping out her phone.

Cohen's luscious kiss left Raynie's head spinning, and she jokingly lifted her foot up behind her for Liz's photo. The entire Aurora Crew looked on, whooping and hollering. When he ended the kissing marathon, he straightened and held the paper plate high, turning in a circle.

This elicited more whoops and hollers from his crewmates.

Aurora Crew's profound support of their relationship filled Raynie with gratitude and touched her deeply. She heard it in their voices, and it meant the world to her. Her universe had expanded, and her heart along with it. She felt bonded to these people she now considered her friends.

Never had smoke tasted so good.

Chapter 40

E*nd of Fire Season*
Alaska's wait-a-second weather had ushered in a low-pressure system that finally delivered rain instead of lightning. For the past several weeks, Aurora Crew had worked extended shifts, running from one wildfire to the next. With the help of bulldozers, they built containment lines by removing surface fuels down to mineral soil to stop the fires from spreading.

They'd been successful in containing most of the blazes. Between Tara's supervision of Aurora Crew, and Cohen and Raynie's training expectations, their overall proficiency level as a highly skilled hotshot crew had become clear. Dave Doss had driven to the road accessible fires to observe the Aurora Crew in action and came away pleased with what he'd seen.

Raynie, Cohen, and the rest of the crew gathered in the fire base conference room for a final fire briefing.

"The State of Alaska has completed the hiring for the Talkeetna Wildfire Base," announced Doss. He motioned at Raynie's boss, Morrey, who stood and moved to the front of the room.

"I'm pleased to announce that Raynie Atwood has accepted the position of chief of operations for the Talkeetna Wildfire Base. Come up here, Raynie. Hearty congratulations!"

Everyone gasped in joyous surprise and applause broke out, with fist pumps and outbursts of, "Yeah!" from Tupa, Rego, and the rest of Aurora Crew.

Raynie rose to stand next to her boss, shaking his hand. "This is because of you wonderful people, whom I had the pleasure of working with this past month—which sometimes felt like a lifetime." She gave the crew a teasing grin. "When we work with new people in wildland fire, we should be mindful of our judgments and first impressions." Her gaze darted to Cohen, leaning against a wall.

He blew her a subtle kiss, and several in the room chuckled at her reference, remembering the never-ending battles she and Cohen had in the beginning.

"I'm honored to be chosen for this job." Raynie looked at Doss. "This is the best fire crew I've had the honor and privilege of working with—even though you're federal," she teased, scanning their faces. "But I won't hold it against you."

Doss smiled as everyone erupted in laughter.

"Good job, Stage Mom!" Rego flashed a smile at her from the back of the room. "You not only saved the day rescuing Tremblay's sorry ass from a lake, but you also helped get a few thousand sled dogs and their mushers to safety. Not to mention the auction and calendar fundraisers. I'd say those are quite the accomplishments by any standard."

Raynie flashed him a wide smile. "Thanks, Rego."

Everyone applauded and Tupa called out, "Time for a celebratory Haka!"

The crew sprang to their feet and lined up to do a ceremonial Haka dance, with Tupa leading. Ever since he'd introduced the Haka to them a few fire seasons ago, the crew had adopted it as their celebratory tradition. Grunting, and thrusting out his tongue, Tupa bulged his eyes, then squatted. He beat his fists on his chest and stomped his feet, punctuated by more tongue thrusts and eye bulges. The rest of the crew followed along, including Cohen, Kenzie, Liz, and Angela.

Raynie looked on, amazed. When they finished, she clapped and cheered.

"I feel honored, thank you!" She'd not seen Cohen dance, let alone do a ceremonial one. Naughty thoughts wiggled into her brain. She made a mental note to ask him for a lap dance later.

"Tupa, you better teach me how to do that," she said, laughing. She immediately sobered. "There's no doubt in my mind that the Aurora Crew will qualify for hotshot status by next fire season."

Wild cheers and shouts reverberated throughout the room, filled with smokejumpers and other firefighters. The biggest shocker was that Deanna was present.

"That's it for now, folks," said Doss. "Gather your gear for the drive back up to Alaska Fire Service in Fairbanks."

When the room cleared, Cohen waited for Raynie. He looked especially hot in his clean yellow shirt and green pants that hugged his perfect form. All she wanted was to be alone with him and show him how she felt.

"I plan to hang around Talkeetna for a while. I told Kam I'd help him rebuild his cabin when I'm officially released for the season," said Cohen. "Glad you moved into the barracks until you got situated." He reached out to squeeze her shoulder.

"Kira enjoys staying at the Roadhouse. She doesn't have to commute to work, and Trish gave her a good deal on room and board. Jamen likes it too. He especially likes that Kira turned eighteen last week."

Cohen laughed. "I'll bet he does. Have you had a birds and bees talk with Kira yet?"

"That was the first thing I launched into after she blew out her candles at the Roadhouse birthday party. She rolled her eyes and laughed at me," replied Raynie.

"Told you when fire season wrapped up, I'd collect on my two-thousand-dollar date. I'm thinking a twenty-four-hour marathon, to get my money's worth." He gave her an impish look. "Starting tonight."

She wanted to know about his plans after the next twenty-four hours. "What are you thinking of doing after Talkeetna?"

"Been meaning to talk to you about that. If I have to cross over to work for the state so I can be near you, I will."

His declaration spun her heart. "You would do that?"

Cohen shrugged. "Why not? I can work on a hotshot crew for the state just as well as anywhere else. I don't have to stay with the feds, as you Americans call them."

"What about the Aurora Crew?"

"I'll stay long enough with AFS to make sure they qualify for hotshot status. When that's done, I'll apply to the state. They have openings for next season on your Palmer hotshot crew."

"Oh, Cohen, I don't know what to say." She grasped his hands and squeezed them. "Tara told me you'd recommended me for the chief of ops job for Talkeetna Base. She said you did it back in the beginning...back when we didn't get along."

He smiled down at her. "I realized your potential before you did. I knew you were capable of remarkable things. Wildland fire needs good leadership. And you're an outstanding leader." His sincerity and the way he said it took her breath away.

"Thanks so much, Cohen. No one has ever said anything like that. It means the world to me...*you* mean the world to me." She gazed up at him with so much love she had a tough time containing herself. But they were still technically on work time.

Cohen drew her into him, and she hugged him hard. "There's something I want to show you," he whispered, then took her hand and led her along the hallway to Doss's empty office. He closed the door and retrieved a rusty metal box from his duffel.

"Guess what this is?"

She shook her head. "Haven't a clue."

Cohen opened the blackened, fireproof box, revealing a stack of hundred-dollar bills. "There's fifty grand here. Kam found this in the ashes and said it wasn't his. So, it must be yours."

Her eyes widened at the heavy metal box she'd tossed in with Taydon's stuff when she'd left their Anchorage duplex. She'd not been able to unlock it and forgot about it when she'd shoved everything into the bedroom closet in Kam's cabin. Her jaw dropped.

"This must be the money Maddox was after."

"Don't forget Officer Mason asked us to testify when his court date arrives," Cohen reminded.

"Oh, that's right. But I can't accept this cash. It's drug money." She looked up at Cohen. "I'll give it to Kam. He needs it more than I do."

Cohen gave her a look she'd never forget as long as she lived—one of love and admiration.

Someone knocked on Doss's office door. "Ahem! I know you two are in there!"

Raynie opened the door to see Deanna and a man she didn't know. She and Cohen exchanged startled glances. Before they could respond, Deanna interjected.

"Sorry to interrupt. I just wanted to say how happy I am that you two found each other." Deanna gave her a warmhearted smile.

Raynie couldn't help wondering what was behind it. She sensed Cohen tense and stiffen.

"Hey, don't look at me like that!" said Deanna in a lively tone, looking at their slacked jaws. "I mean it. I'd like you to meet my fiancé, Samuel Zuckert, from the Missoula Smokejumper Base. I'm officially inviting you two to our wedding this fall in Montana."

Raynie went into territorial mode and instinctively moved closer to Cohen. She slid her arm around his waist, tucking him into her side. Cohen's mouth twitched when she did it, and he pinched her waist.

"Congratulations," he said politely to his ex, and nodded at Samuel.

Raynie echoed his sentiment and idle chat was exchanged before Deanna and her fiancé said goodbye and disappeared out the door.

Cohen murmured out the side of his mouth, "Hopefully now she'll leave me alone."

"I told her if she goes after you again, I'd toss her into the river with the ice chunks." Raynie gave him a lopsided grin.

He gave her a knowing smile. "Always said I wouldn't want to meet you in a dark alley. But what a rush it would be watching a hotshotter tangling with a smokejumper. I'd pay money and buy popcorn."

Angela stuck her head in. "Hey, you two, Ryan O'Connor wants everyone out in the main office. He has an announcement. I'm pretty sure I know what it is." She displayed her cat-ate-the-canary look and ducked out again.

Curious, Raynie and Cohen wandered out to the main office, where people crowded around.

Ryan O'Connor stepped to the center. "Tara, please come join me." He waggled his finger at her as she stood behind the dispatch desk, talking to Vanessa about who was mopping up which fires.

"What are you up to, O'Connor?" Tara narrowed her eyes and rounded the counter to stand next to him.

The entire room collectively gasped when Ryan suddenly took a knee.

"Holy shit, it's about mother flipping time!" Rego exclaimed, and everyone burst into laughter.

"I thought about this the entire time I was stuck out on that fire with the village crew. Gunnar and I had a long chat after we high-tailed it to safety and waited for air transport. There's no time like the present," said Ryan, eyeing his buddy.

Gunnar nodded back, his arm around his wife, prompting a grin from Angela.

"We all know how insane our jobs are. That's why we do this, right?" Ryan glanced around at the cheerful faces. "You all know how hard wildland fire is on relationships, doing what we do." He reached into his pocket, produced a small box, and flipped it open.

"Without wasting another second—Tara Waters—Fire Woman—will you marry me?"

Tara, who Raynie had never seen cry—nodded a tearful, enthusiastic "Yes" to more cheering and applause.

"About damn time, O'Connor!" yelled Rego.

Raynie hugged Tara. "Congratulations. I'm so glad I got to know you and work with you," she gushed. "Looking forward to working with you in the future."

"Same here." Tara hugged her and spoke into her ear. "Hang onto Cohen. He's a treasure worth fighting for." She drew back and winked, then she and Ryan left the office.

"I hope you know how lucky you are," sniffed Vanessa, flicking her eyes in Cohen's direction. She said it with disdain, but Raynie still appreciated the sentiment.

"I do." She glanced at Cohen, who grasped her hand.

"Now, about that date..." he teased, tugging her out the door.

COHEN HELPED RAYNIE hook the sled dogs up to the exercise cart. He'd made good on his promise to help her run the dogs, since Kam was busy rebuilding Sleeping Lady Kennel. Trish had offered to keep his dogs until Kam rebuilt his dog yard.

Trish had rounded up volunteers to build doghouses, and Kira and Jamen had enlisted their friends to paint them in bright colors and letter the dog names above the openings. People had donated dog food, and Raynie was happy to see thousands had contributed to the PleaseFundUs page she'd set up a month ago.

Cohen had been mysterious about their two-thousand-dollar date, but she wasn't surprised that it involved running the dogs. He wasn't the restaurant date type; he preferred the outdoors. He'd patiently instructed her on the mushing commands of hike, gee, and haw, to guide the sled dog team.

They stood side-by-side, riding inside the wheeled exercise cart the dogs pulled. Jamen had recommended that they take the dogs on a smooth, back trail that ended upriver on the Susitna.

When the team reached the river, Cohen yelled, "Whoa!" and the dogs halted.

"Step off your chariot, Fire Chick." He offered her his hand.

Cohen looked glorious in his dark green Henley and blue jeans, with his outgrown golden hair, the back of it brushing his collar. She could have jumped his bones right then and there.

"This is perfect," she said, taking in the unimpeded view of Denali Mountain, in its bold glory, flanked by Mount Foraker and Mount Hunter, outfitted in blue and white on this beautiful, sunny day.

"This is where I first fell for you."

Cohen grinned while pouring water into dog bowls and handing them to her to distribute to the huskies. Rooby sat, waiting patiently, and Wacko and Madonna barked at the front of the team. Wacko licked Madonna's face, and she snarled back. Dogs will be dogs.

"You didn't fall for me when we met? Because I knew that very second, I wanted you."

"Oh, come on. I was a total jerk to you." She rolled her eyes.

"Yes, you were. And it turned me on."

"That's just...twisted." She feigned a look of disgust, but joy bubbled up inside of her.

When Cohen finished with the dogs, he moved to her and took her in his arms.

"I reserved a lakeside room at the Grayling Resort for tonight, compliments of Trish and Mason." He took his time kissing her, then lifted his lips from hers.

"Rego said that almost-died sex is better than make-up sex."

She smiled. "But we had make-up sex after you saved the dogs."

"Yes, but after thinking about what could have happened, we've progressed to 'almost-died' sex."

She laughed. "In that case, we'll have to have almost-died sex every time we demobe from a fire."

"Exactly," said Cohen. "This is why we get along now. Great minds think alike."

Raynie lit up. "I have an idea. Let's go to the wildlife rescue center to check on the coyote pups we rescued from the Hiland Mountain Fire. I want to see how they're doing."

"Great idea. Let's drive to Palmer tomorrow." Cohen leaned in for a kiss while the dogs barked and wagged their tails, eager to run again.

Raynie ignored the barking, never wanting this kiss to end. She looked forward to their "almost-died" sex later, at Grayling Lodge. Finally, she and Cohen would have time to enjoy each other, and get to know each other—without their jobs. Without fire. Without interruption.

Cohen lifted his lips from hers. "This means we're no longer frenemies, right? On a professional level, you realize this doesn't change anything. I'll still question your decisions."

"And I'll still defend them. You've seen me at my worst, so it's all downhill from here." She grinned, knowing the challenges that lie ahead, yet confident they would face them together.

"And I've seen you at your best." Cohen was charming and he knew it, but she didn't care.

She suddenly remembered his license plate, with *Beautiful British Columbia* across the top.

"I can't wait to see Vancouver and meet your family." She looked up at him with a mischievous grin. "If someone would have told me a month ago that I'd be kissing you, do you know what I would have said?"

"No, what?"

"That I'd rather kiss a sled dog."

She grasped Wacko's head and kissed him on the side of his snout. When the husky licked her face, she backed up, laughing.

She gave Cohen a cat-eyed look.

"On second thought, I'd rather kiss *you*."

THANKS SO MUCH FOR reading Alaska Blaze! If you enjoyed it, please tell your friends and family about this series...and please take a moment to post a review on Goodreads and Amazon. Reviews make an enormous difference for my success as a writer, and they help readers discover the story! Also, listen to the Alaska Blaze Playlist on Spotify. Log into your account and search for Alaska Blaze.

Author's Note

Alaskan huskies are a breed born to run. Running and racing sled dogs is not cruel or inhuman. On the contrary, these dogs love to run. They thrive in our arctic and subarctic conditions and environment. Having lived in Alaska for forty years, I can attest that those who own and run sled dogs have an unparalleled love for these animals. While cases of mistreatment and cruelty to dogs are present in all breeds worldwide, sled dogs are not prone to such occurrences more than any other breed.

Bonus Content!

Want to know what Liz and Jon do after Alaska's fire season ends?

Download the <u>Alaska Blaze Bonus Story!</u>[1]

---

1. https://dl.bookfunnel.com/1zfhi8mf86

Also By LoLo Paige

Next in the series is <u>Alaska Firestorm</u>[1]

Check out the rest of the Blazing Hearts Wildfire Series. Each is a standalone and doesn't have to be read in order!

Alaska Spark
Alaska Inferno
Alaska Blaze
Alaska Firestorm
Alaska Flame

---

1. https://www.amazon.com/Alaska-Firestorm-Opposites-Workplace-Wildfire-ebook/dp/B0D86RXQKJ

2

If you read Alaska Spark, find out why Ryan became a smokejumper and what led him and Tara to Alaska for a second chance at love. Download Alaska Dawn, the FREE prequel to the series by joining my VIP Readers List at *LoLoPaige.com*[3]

---

2. https://www.amazon.com/Blazing-Hearts-Wildfire-Complete-Trilogy-ebook/dp/ B0CBK61S91

3. *https://www.lolopaige.com/*

Want to read lighter fare? Check Out LoLo's Romantic Comedies!

Everybody Loves Polar Bears
Flights, Fights, and Christmas Lights
Cupid's Kerfuffle
Hello Spain, Goodbye Heart
Irish Thunder

Acknowledgements

Ahuge thank you to former logger, commercial fisherman, educator, and Montana wildland firefighter, Marc Simenson, who helped me plot this story. You're a fantastic business manager and all-around good guy. I think I'll keep you.

Kudos and thanks to S. R. Cyres, for his insightful poem at the beginning of the book, and for his help as a beta reader and an insightful editor. Thank you for keeping me on track with my story. And a huge thank you to my beta readers, Ray Braun and Judy Winslow, for their thoughtful editorial comments.

A special thank you to Marianne Schoppmeyer, for her stories about what really happened when the Sockeye and McKinley fires ravaged the musher community back in 2018 and 2019. She had me in laughter and tears at the plight that all the dog mushers faced back then to evacuate sled dogs and people before those fires overtook several of their homes and dog kennels.

Another special thank you to the late Henri Bisson, former Director of the U.S. Bureau of Land Management, Alaska State Office, for helping me with plot points and wildland fire scenarios. Rest in peace, Henri. You are sorely missed. Grateful to my former employers at the U.S. Bureau of Land Management, Alaska Fire Service in Fairbanks, AK, the National Interagency Fire Center in Boise, Idaho, and the U.S.

Forest Service. I'm proud to have worked for the agencies who employ wildland firefighters.

And finally, many thanks to the technical fire experts on the Authors Fire/Rescue Facebook page: Ken Shoemaker, Tom Squires, and others who patiently answered my questions about resources and equipment used in city/structural firefighting.

Grateful for my furry besties, the Mandy Lorian and Rooby Doo, my superstar goldens, who promised not to toss their balls onto my keyboard while I wrote this novel (as long as I bribed them with treats).

About the Author

LoLo Paige is an award-winning author in both romantic comedy and romantic suspense. Her action-adventure, romantic suspense books about wildland firefighting have topped the Amazon Bestseller Lists in the U.S., Canada, and Australia. The Blazing Hearts Wildfire series books have received several indie awards for best romance. Publishers Weekly has featured her books, and as a former wildland firefighter, LoLo's true story about escaping a runaway wildfire in Alaska's dangerous Interior won a 2016 Alaska Press Club award.

Follow me on Amazon, Facebook, and Instagram! Want to learn more about my books? Join my VIP Reader's List on my website and download *Alaska Dawn*, the FREE prequel to the Blazing Hearts Wildfire series at LoloPaige.com.